THE ANTAGONISTS

A NOVEL

Dear reader
Happy reading!
Tina x

TINA BISWAS

FiNGERPRINT!

Published by
FiNGERPRINT!
An imprint of Prakash Books India Pvt. Ltd.

113/A, Darya Ganj, New Delhi-110 002,
Tel: (011) 2324 7062 – 65, Fax: (011) 2324 6975
Email: info@prakashbooks.com/sales@prakashbooks.com

facebook www.facebook.com/fingerprintpublishing
twitter www.twitter.com/FingerprintP
www.fingerprintpublishing.com

ISBN: 978 93 8836 993 0

Processed & printed in India

For my wonderful family, and especially my girls Vivian and Maggie Bear

People who have achieved the trappings of power
for no reason they can see are afraid of losing those
trappings. They are insecure because
they see too many like themselves.

The Mimic Men, V S Naipaul

The candor stopped just where it should have begun.

American Pastoral, Philip Roth

THE UNITED TIMES OF INDIA

Devi claims fire at Lohia Hospital no accident

Updated: 12 Jan 2013, 09:10 IST

KOLKATA: "Terrorists are terrorists and murderers are murderers."

This is Paramita Guha Roy's response to the devastating fire at The Lohia Hospital in South Kolkata, in which one hundred and twelve patients perished just before dawn break this morning.

Visiting the burnt-out site in the immediate aftermath of the blaze, West Bengal Chief Minister Roy stood before a crowd of the patients' angry relatives and told them that the fire had been due to disgraceful negligence and shameful absence of value for human life. She further assured them that those culpable for the fire would be promptly dealt with.

When asked how she had been able to establish so quickly that the fire was due to negligence, she replied, "There are no accidents!" Pressed to clarify this comment, she elaborated that it had been shown time and again that there were certain elements of the business community in Kolkata who put profit above all else, at all times. “It is very clear that some rich businessmen in our midst are not knowing what morality is—they are knowing only money.”

The hospital’s owner, billionaire businessman Sachin Lohia, will be visiting the hospital to make a statement of his own.

Read 7 comments:

Arjun (Kolkata), 13 January 2013, 09:12 a.m.

1. Fact: Marwaris have always been about money at any cost. 2. Nobody wants to work for them except those who have no other choice. 3. Having said that, you have to acknowledge their business acumen and ability to make money. 4. Although Gujus and Parsis are fairer employers. 5. Modern Marwaris are changing as they know you won’t get the best employees if you continue to behave like haramjada. 6. But I support Paramita on this—that building was not safe. 7. And if they leave WB, so what? Someone else will take their place.

Krishnan (Mumbai), 13 January 2013, 09:19 a.m.

Common sense and decency should prevail in Kolkata. I will put Paramita’s unwarranted comments down to a lapse in judgement and a cack-handed attempt to show anger on behalf of the grieving families, especially considering how far behind WB lags economically and how much investment it needs. And who’s going to invest? The Marwaris. So if she knows what’s good for her political career, she has to promote a harmonious atmosphere for investment amongst the business class (Marwaris) who have resided in WB for centuries.

Prince (Pune) replied to Krishnan, 13 January 2013, 10:10 a.m.

Business class? Thief class would be more accurate.

Abhishek (Chennai) replied to Prince, 13 January 2013, 10:17 a.m.

Yeah, because anyone who dares to make money is a thief. If it weren't for the Marwaris, all those Bengali intellectuals would be sitting around in a shanty.

XYZ (XYZ), 13 January 2013, 09:40 a.m.

The Marwaris aren't being persecuted. They're getting what they deserve, and have deserved for a long time.

Vishnu (Delhi), 13 January 2013, 10.20 a.m.

I think what we're forgetting here is that we have laws and this case should be decided by those laws. What's the point of all this aggro?

Arjun (Kolkata) replies to Vishnu, 13 January 2013, 10:40 a.m.

The point of all this aggro is that PEOPLE HAVE DIED.

I

The first that Sachin Lohia, industrialist, philanthropist, egotist, knew of the fire at the hospital was when a reporter from *The United Times of India* had stood on his marble doorstep on Belvedere Road in South Kolkata, demanding that he comment on it.

Obviously, he hadn't opened the door himself, there was a butler to do that, but the message had quickly been conveyed from butler to front-of-house maid to chambermaid to valet.

"Sir, there has been a fire at your hospital. Fatalities have occurred."

Fatalities have occurred; the benefit of insisting on an English-speaking valet.

Your hospital; the drawback of insisting on naming the place after himself.

The reporter, a Miss Tapati Ghatak, had been welcomed in, lest turning her away implied that Sachin had something to hide or, even worse, did not think the matter required his personal attention. Sitting on the Louis XV Serpentine sofa in his study, Miss Ghatak had sprayed him with spitty little questions about responsibility, guilt, and greed. And then Anil Thakur had marched in and told her to get out. Our priority is not to speak to journalists, he told her, it's to speak to the people affected by this tragedy.

Anil was Sachin's youngest but most trusted adviser. He was not of the old guard—the duckers and divers, the brawlers and trawlers. Anil had an illustrious schooling from St. Xavier's, a PPE degree from Oxford, and an MBA from Harvard. He had worked for one of the top three strategy consulting firms in the world. He was unimpeachably professional. So if Anil had told the journalist to get out, then that was the right thing to do.

Along with Anil and his other advisers, Sachin watched the large plasma TV, housed in an intricately carved mahogany armoire. Devi, chief minister of West Bengal, was holding a press conference right outside the fire-wrecked hospital, accusatory plumes of smoke billowing into the damp, grey sky. In front of the hospital, on its steps, a cartoonish podium had been set up. Behind it: Devi. Under her nose: a proliferation of microphones, attached roughly by gaffer tape. Behind her: a gaggle of followers, their faces various shades of brown, some excited, others indifferent, yet others serious and intent. There was no distance between Devi and these people; their bodies were actually touching hers. Indeed, the only sign that marked out Devi was that she was a woman and the rest were men. The followers looked at the cameras, proudly waiting to be captured for posterity. The spectre of those who had burned to death did not seem to dampen their eagerness to be a part of the proceedings. Anil shook his head at their indelicacy.

"Terrorists are terrorists and murderers are murderers!"

That damn woman, *Devi*, in her ludicrous white sari, he

thought. So supercilious, so sanctimonious, so furiously without irony.

Suggestions ricocheted around the room. There were eleven directors of the hospital, of which Sachin was only one. Four of them had already resigned and abdicated responsibility, why shouldn't Sachin do the same? Go on the offensive: threaten to pull all of your businesses out of this godforsaken place, and leave them to scrabble around in the dirt. Play the victim: you're being unfairly blamed for an accident because you're a Marwari—label Devi as prejudiced and unjust. Blame the fire service: it took too long for them to arrive! The fire service took too long because of the intractable traffic and the pot-holed roads, which is the fault of the State Transport Department!

But whilst Sachin's other advisers were striking wildly, trying for fours and sixes, Anil presented a dead bat.

He bit on his lower lip and wiggled his jaw from side to side.

If Devi was playing the long game, he thought, play the longer game.

If Devi was acting like the big person, act like the bigger person.

A journalist asked Devi whether the directors were criminally responsible and whether they would go to jail.

The room fell silent.

Closed-toe shoes were appropriate for the occasion, Sachin thought. Open-toed chappals, though utilitarian and commonplace, might indicate some amount of negligence or at least a lack of gravitas. What was required was a statesmanlike presence tempered with humility and a sense of noblesse oblige. This was also why it was imperative to not give his press conference in front of his lavish mansion but in front of the hospital, the scene of a terrible and tragic *accident*.

Preened and primed, Sachin took a deep breath and climbed into the back seat of his chauffeured S-Class Mercedes with tinted windows. Anil followed. The chauffeur was playing perky Hindi pop songs. Sachin told him to turn off the music.

Grim facts had started to emerge. What should have been an uneventful fire in the hospital kitchen had quickly spread into the internal power room. From there, to the central storage facility containing oxygen tanks. From there, to everywhere.

One hundred and twelve patients had perished. None of the staff though—all of them had escaped in time. No heroes in this tragedy, then. No valour, no knights. Instead, a bunch of poltroons who would rather leave the ill and vulnerable to their miserable fate than even *try* and summon the fortitude to face the odds. Bengalis, Sachin thought abjectly: all moral courage and physical cowardice. And if the latter trumped the former, so be it!

The car was at a standstill. Again. Anil fiddled around with his phone. Again. The traffic was no thicker or louder than usual but in his current mood, Anil was less horn-please and more horn-shut-the-fuck-up.

Sachin looked through his darkened window and thought: people have died. Please god, don't let me be responsible. I can take many things but not that.

The car started. Again. Sachin took a deep, stoic breath. Anil glanced at him with admiration. In Sachin, he saw not so much strength as the absence of weakness. The eyes that didn't show fear, the lips that never trembled, the nostrils that never flared. In another time and place, Anil speculated, Sachin would have made a great leader: grace under duress, a sense of higher purpose, an admirable indefatigability. A man who would take all-comers.

Anil looked at his emails again and updated Sachin.

Claims were being made that the hospital did not have sufficient fire-fighting equipment. That one woman had called her husband to tell him she was suffocating from inhaling smoke. That the recommendations from a previous fire inspection had been roundly ignored. That the families of the bereaved had already vandalised what was left of the hospital reception, angry at not being given more information about what had happened.

"How can I tell them what happened, when I don't yet know myself?" Sachin asked.

"Tell them you will be thoroughly investigating all claims," Anil replied.

"Will that be enough?"

"That's all there *is*. At least for now."

Anil once again looked at his phone. Now a claim was being made that this was a case of mass murder. He rolled his eyes and, exasperated, turned the phone off.

As they turned the corner, the wreck of the hospital came into view. Sachin remembered when it was first being built . . . the steel beams, the tangles of electric wires, the bare concrete columns. Now it looked as if it had regressed back to those early days, but instead of filling him with anticipation, as it had then, it filled him with melancholy. To his mind came the image of a baby and an old man: hairless, toothless, fragile, yet one full of hope and the other hopeless.

Anil, on the other hand, looked unfazed while surveying the destruction. The jagged edges, the blackened walls, the mangled cables. To him it was an alien landscape, distancing, isolating. He simply couldn't imagine what had happened in this place only hours ago, and he didn't really want to imagine it either. He just wanted to make sure that it never happened again.

The car came to a stop. Time.

The assembled relatives were surprisingly restrained; their

earlier cacophonous ire had dissipated to a low hum. By now, the living patients had been moved to another local hospital, the dead to the mortuary.

The tired and grimy firemen who had tackled the blaze had gone home. Some of them, who had never before dealt with such an extensive blaze, had been disturbed by what they had seen: a coughing old man crawling around on the floor like a sick dog; a bed-bound pregnant woman heaving for air, her head then lolling to one side, one hand still on her swollen stomach; a young man with a broken leg trying to break a window with his crutches, only to start convulsing wildly then collapsing against the broken glass; an elderly woman sitting upright in her bed, in her clasped hands a picture of the holy man Ramakrishna, splattered with her blood-flecked vomit. The sick, the frail—this was their swan song.

A few uniformed policemen—for crowd control when Devi had imperiously insisted on visiting the hospital even as the firemen were still trying to clear up—remained, but now that she had left, they seemed less bothered about being seen to do their job. Instead they were making phone calls to mothers and wives to update them. And in some cases, elevating their role—in bringing the situation under control—from ruthless to gallant, and from cold to compassionate. For even if the city's inhabitants were not prone to violence, the police liked to make sure that no one was tempted to take matters one step further, even if that involved them using disproportionate force themselves. Sachin spotted them and felt a degree of relief. Despite having several experiences of the police being corruptible and unscrupulous, he also wagered that in such circumstances, they would earn their keep and protect him from any physical violence which might erupt. After all, there were numerous journalists milling around. Even in the oppressive heat of Devi's regime, words and their close allies, images, were still to be respected.

The journalists themselves fell into two camps: older and younger. The former were slower, more considered, surreptitiously listening to conversations that weren't theirs to listen to, subtly sniffing around both the emotional and physical debris, making notes in their extensive mental notepads. The latter were hastier, eager to make their mark, to be given a gold star for their efforts. With scant regard for punctuation or even meaning, their thumbs worked frantically to bombard their editors with snippy emails written in text-speak, as if they were teenagers arranging a night out.

Sachin eyed them up suspiciously. He believed journalists to be a mercurial lot, sometimes obsequious and flattering, sometimes hostile and inimical. The only constant was that they always wanted something. Figuring out what it was they wanted was the key to dealing with them. He caught sight of Tapati Ghatak with her cell phone clamped to her ear, her lips moving animatedly. He had a feeling that he hadn't seen the last of her.

Meanwhile, Anil was having the podium, on which Devi had stood earlier, removed. He wanted no reminder of that woman present whilst Sachin addressed the crowd. If she had stood there, like a judge at her raised bench, her pointing finger full of self-righteous castigation, then Sachin would stand right in the well and speak with the members of the gallery, not at them.

Voices became less muffled, more clear, and insistent. People were becoming impatient. Better to speak before impatience became insurrection.

Sachin took a deep breath and remembered what Anil had advised him: he had to absorb the people's anger, make it his own. The mistake would be to put up his defences and let their anger bounce off him. Keep your head held high but don't puff out your chest. Keep your tone even without being monotonous. Keep eye contact but avoid staring. Don't scratch your bollocks. Despite Sachin being an old hand, Anil couldn't risk any slip-ups.

"First, my genuine and heartfelt condolences to all of you, who have lost a loved one here today. I stand before you deeply pained and profoundly sad that this tragedy has occurred in a place which was, above all, a place of hope."

Anil scanned the crowd. The first few bars of the song, although sombre and in a minor key, had caught their attention. Sachin frowned, sighed, and continued, "There are questions to be answered, that I know. And you *deserve* answers to those questions. But you deserve honest and truthful answers—and those are the kind of answers that need time to be found. *Anyone* can point the finger of blame; *anyone* can hurl groundless accusations; *anyone* can spew out invective and insults; the most calculating can even try and make political capital out of calamity; but I will not allow the truth to be held hostage and for expeditious explanations to take the place of in-depth inquiry."

The lessons in elocution and rhetoric, provided cheerfully by a gap-year student who had read Classics and English at Magdalen College, had just justified their cost, Anil thought. He glanced at the journalists. A few seemed bemused, a few looked cynical, but all of them were at least listening, and intently. Good. They weren't the only ones who could ply and mould sentiment. Sachin now looked up towards the sky as if he was beseeching an even higher power.

"So, as angry—and rightly angry—as you are, I beg that you give me the time and the opportunity to establish exactly what happened and why."

"Or are you just going to run and hide like the others?" a male voice suddenly shouted out.

Sachin nodded with empathy.

"I promise you, Sir, that I will not run from this situation because I have nothing to hide."

Anil looked at the man who had called out. He could tell from the man's expression—a tensing in the jaw, a brief flare of the nostrils, a darkening of his irises—that he was not satisfied with Sachin's answer, yet he could not find the gumption to answer back.

"In the meantime, I have set up a ten lakh fund to assist those who have been affected by this tragedy, details of which will be available from my office."

The crowd looked surprised; was this some sort of trick or was Sachin Lohia really putting his money where his mouth was?

"And not only will I be carrying out a full and thorough investigation of how this tragedy came about, I will also participate in all respects with the police enquiry."

Now the crowd looked disconcerted. Men like Sachin Lohia rarely felt any sense of obligation towards anything but their own conceit.

"Is it true you bribed the fire inspector to pass the safety inspection?" A different man this time, phlegmatic, more aloof, perhaps even a sneer in the raised eyebrow. He was a government plant, of that Anil was sure. Why else would the question of a bribe be brought up, unless the seemingly incorruptible Devi—who had won the election partially on an anti-bribery ticket—had directed it? Especially as no one had been bribed. Well, not yet, anyway.

"As I said, Sir, I will participate in all respects with the police enquiry," Sachin repeated earnestly.

"Does participate mean lie?" the man replied. "After all, that's your business, isn't it—lying and stealing and cheating?"

"Sir, I am a businessman, not a liar, nor a thief, nor a cheat. And as a businessman, I have done all I can to serve my community, the community which I now stand in front of."

"Your community! Isn't your community a load of money-grabbing Marwaris!"

Anil bristled but Sachin allowed himself a gentle, avuncular smile.

"That may be your opinion, Sir, but it is not one I share."

Back in the car, Sachin looked at Anil, exhausted, and raised his palms with a shrug. Anil chewed on his lip.

"The blame game is just that—a game. So we'll play it."

Sharmila, Sachin's wife, had finally risen from bed; her saggy cheek still sported creases from the pillowcase. She tilted her chin up at him. She can't even be bothered to move her mouth anymore, thought Sachin, glumly. For years he had taken Sharmila to various doctors, but none of them could diagnose anything actually pathologically wrong with her. So then came the homeopaths, the herbalists, the healers with magic hands, the registered practitioners of unregulated practices, the specialists in universal energy. *They* offered numerous diagnoses and remedies, but these made no difference to her torpor, and Sachin realised that she was what she was.

It hadn't always been that way. In the beginning of boy meets girl, she had been a quick-witted scrapper. She had had to be; that's what happens when your own parents don't look after you—you learn to look after yourself. Not that she had ever thought to blame them: they had been poor, elderly, already depleted from a lifetime of hardship, and she had been not so much their late-life miracle as their eleventh hour misfortune. But if she hadn't been raised with any of the usual advantages—love, nurture, education, discipline—she had been gifted with a trait which could not be easily learned. The instinct to survive at all costs.

Sachin had first bumped into her at their hometown's Durga Puja, taking *prasad* to distribute to those too elderly or infirm to attend themselves. How charitable, he had thought. But then she had told him a few days later, with a sly smile, and sporting a new sari, that the recipients had all insisted on pressing a few notes into her hand and it would have been disrespectful not to accept. How canny, he had thought!

So there she had been: synapses crackling, a little rough, always ready, brimming with withering put-downs, self-sufficiency, and coquettish cockiness. Compared to her, Sachin had been a model of reserve and reticence. For despite his ambition, his savvy, his readiness to bust his chops, Sharmila was the one willing to drop her shoulder and give people a little shove, to find crafty ways of being persuasive. Indeed, Sachin was absolutely certain that if it weren't for her, he would not have come so far. He had learned much from her. The drive to outdo, to win, to prevail, that *she* had drilled into him. Or maybe it had always been within him, but if so, it was she who had drawn it out and then tempered it like steel. Steel. Another one of his businesses. As the industries Sachin worked in became heavier, so had Sharmila. Slower, too, a weariness in her step, an audible thickness in her breath. The once bright eyes became darker and appeared to sink into her face. The smile, impish, knowing, which once played on her thick brown lips, gradually faded. The youngster who he had first met, not classically beautiful, but imbued with a solid, workaday attractiveness, now stood in front of him as a plain, stolid, middle-aged woman.

What upset Sachin even more was not that his wife's appearance had diminished, but that her personality had diminished alongside. This attenuation had progressed as his business deals became less under-the-table, more above-board. By then, Sachin was making the kind of lakh lakh *taka* which necessitated a formal relationship with a proper and above-board bank. There was no room under the mattress for that kind of stash, and there was a limit to how much money you could turn into gold jewellery. And this degree of wealth also meant that Sachin found himself in a position where he could explore and indulge his every appetite. For a man who had once lived in something akin to a hollow concrete cube, this unfolding of panoramas and aspects to the world, thrilled and impressed him. Eagerly he entreated Sharmila to join him on this new adventure. So came trips to classical music programmes, to the theatre, to auction houses, to art galleries, to book readings. Yet whilst these experiences kindled Sachin, they seemed to extinguish Sharmila's flame. Why do you always have your nose in a book, she had asked him, where is reading about made-up stuff going to get you? Too late he came to the realisation that Sharmila had thrived on a state of perpetual war and turmoil. She was a soldier who belonged on the battlefield. For her, peacetime and its genteel appurtenances meant only a life full of dreariness.

Now, Sachin suddenly wondered whether this incident might actually arouse Sharmila from her withdrawn state. In the past, this would have been exactly the kind of circumstance that would have brought out the beast in her. Having explained the situation, he looked at her hoping he might have provoked a flicker of interest. She sipped a cup of tea; he could tell from its syrupy consistency that she was still taking three teaspoons of sugar in it even though he had told her that the proper way to appreciate its flavour was without. Then she put down the cup and shrugged.

Taking slow steps, he padded to his study and sat down in his antique throne chair, with carved lion heads on the ends of the padded armrests, at his leather-topped desk. Carefully, he opened the book he was reading, *Life Lessons from Hindu Mythology*.

> What makes a true king? To answer this question, I refer to Rama, the ruler of the kingdom of Ayodhya, and the perfect king in Hindu mythology. Think of his seat: a golden throne. Think of the ornate canopy above his head. Think of his splendid spear, his magnificent bow and arrow, his fearsome trident. Think of Hanuman, his loyal monkey-

general, bowing at his feet. Think of Sita, his wondrously beautiful wife! These are the accoutrements of majesty, are they not? These are the chattels of a supreme leader. Yet Rama is willing to relinquish all of this for Ayodhya, because a true king knows that his actions must always be in the best interests of his people, not of himself. He even abandons his pregnant wife, herself a model of perfect womanhood, when one of his subjects casts doubt over her chastity. Compare his actions to those of the demon-king Ravan, who abducts Sita and takes her back to his kingdom of Lanka, imprisoning her in the Ashok Vatika. Instead of returning Sita to her husband and avoiding a war, he, thinking only of himself and his desire, clings on to her, thereby inviting upon his people a fierce and destructive war in which his kingdom is destroyed and his subjects killed. You see, reader, Ravan sees his kingdom's inhabitants merely as minions to do his bidding and to perpetuate his status. He deprives them of their power and uses them as if they belong to him. Rama, on the other hand, understands that he belongs to his people, not the other way around. He empowers them; they, in turn, listen to Rama and pledge their loyalty to him. So, in the end, it is Rama, who has the humility to accept that he is lucky to be in a position to serve his kingdom, not Ravan who believes in his own supremacy, who is the true king.

II

Dr. Anima Acharya stood on her lawn, a luscious green quilt, admiring the borders which were heavy with fragrant flowers. The garden was in an old zamindar residence in North Kolkata (the zamindar in question being Anima's great-grandfather). Gravid guava trees laboured under the strain of carrying their bulbous fruit, their spindly branches at the point of snapping. Lady Finger banana trees squatted nearby. From Carambolas hung multitudes of bright yellow star fruit, which appeared as decorative Chinese lanterns. On the ground were fallen custard apples, like broken hearts. A few parakeets twittered around an elaborate marble birdbath. In the dusky light, lulled by gin, Anima almost expected a talking monkey in a bellboy uniform to jump out of the trees.

She was smoking a cigarette, the first time she had done so since her student days at Presidency. As she inhaled deeply, she thought, *They say you never forget how to ride a bike; you definitely never forget how to smoke a cigarette.* The cigarette itself she had filched from her driver. When he had inadvertently caught her rifling through the car's glove compartment, he had pretended not to notice, but she hadn't shown any embarrassment. "I was just after a cigarette. I hope you don't mind." Although he was quite shocked—the lady of the house smoking, a lady smoking full stop—he was pleased that he had been of some sort of service. Besides, he had pilfered enough from her in the past. He did wonder though what had happened which necessitated the succour and comfort that only a cigarette could bring. What he didn't know was that fifteen minutes ago, Anima had heard a little beep. Her husband, Professor Pranab Shastry, was in the shower; the beep had come from his jacket, which was slung over the valet stand. No doubt one of the guests was running extra late or perhaps even saying they couldn't make it for some reason or other; her phone was broken and at the repair shop, the guests had been asked to contact The Professor if the need arose. So, she dug out his mobile phone. And on the phone was a text message from 'P'. No first name or surname. Not one of the guests.

Missing you. Can't wait to see you again . . . P xxx

A sharp intake of breath. Anima froze for a few seconds.

Recovering from her shock, she carried out a textual analysis. As Pranab was a professor of English Literature at The University of Kolkata, she hoped he would appreciate that. The gerund really pissed her off. For some reason, missing was so much worse than miss. It was the grammatical equivalent of a sigh. It was pathetic. And the longing implied by the ellipsis—so sentimental and twee. It was clearly a younger woman. She racked her brain to think who 'P' might be. Ah yes, Polly, the PhD student. Researching something to do with postcolonial Indian literature. He had mentioned her a good few times. She had even been to the house to sip tea and talk about Bijay Kumar Das. So clean-cut. So sweet.

But of course therein lay the peril, the bitter pill hidden in a mouthful of sugar. Acting highbrow, then getting down and dirty. She wasn't even pretty! Young enough, though, to flatter an old man's shrivelling ego.

Oh darling, Anima thought, apparently you're not *that* clever.

And what had Professor Shastry, that model of scholarly chasteness, what had *he* told Polly? That his wife no longer understood him, did not appreciate him, could not provide what he needed? Men and their needs. The biggest swindle in the history of conjugal relationships, bigger even than the men-simple-women-complicated model. Anima's puffs became less frantic, more measured. Her fury—the immediate, leaden fury of a betrayed wife—had already started to lighten, to be replaced by a more reflective sensibility. The mistake would be to act on an impulse, to say whatever came to the tip of her tongue. He was better with words too, would be able to take hers and make them mean something else. Then suddenly she was angry with herself: I knew I should have just bought a new phone, she thought. And now this! I would rather not have known. But now I know and I can't unknow—brains are not designed to unknow! When people talk about forgiving and forgetting, they fundamentally misunderstand what we're capable of. And yes, I can forgive, but whatever it is I do, the point is that I now have to do something, even if that thing is to pretend I never saw the text and do nothing!

She dropped the end of her cigarette to the ground and patted it with her sandalled foot. Then she heard tentative footsteps approach her from behind. More than thirty years and still he was slightly timid in her presence.

"Ah, here you are!"

Anima turned around to face her husband. She wanted to imagine that there was guilt written on his face but what she saw instead was a face as solicitous as always.

A moment from their early years in London came to her: her most favourite flower was tuberose—it reminded her of India—but despite having scoured florists across the city, she could not find one who stocked them and had had to be satisfied with gardenias. Then one late summer evening, The Professor had taken her to his office and on a windowsill in the corner of his room, was a cluster of tuberose growing in a pot. He had grown them himself—and Anima knew that in the English climate, they would have needed an enormous amount of attention and care. And love. She had been lucky once. For thirty-two years, in fact. But luck never lasted.

And what did he see? She didn't know, except she was sure it wasn't the woman who had closed her eyes in bliss as she had inhaled the fragrance from the delicate bevy of tuberose, sitting in a pot on a sunny windowsill in London.

"The guests will be here soon . . ." he smiled.

Ah yes, the guests. The guests for whom Anima had sent out her cook to buy black tiger prawns, red spinach, Ilish fish, pointed gourd. She was in no mood for either the guests or the food now. Although another gin and tonic, heavy on the G, light on the T, might hit the spot.

"Is the food ready?" she checked.

The Professor tilted his head.

They heard the doorbell.

"Shall we?" the Professor asked with a small smile, putting his hand out. Without answering and looking down at the ground, Anima started to walk back towards the house. The Professor put his hand in the small of her back as if to guide her. His touch left her cold, although she did her best not to shrug him off. She didn't want to make a scene just as the guests arrived.

There were five of them. Manik Majumdar, now retired, but who had once been employed in the Indian Administrative Service and who had also once been noted as 'a man of supercilious integrity' in a book on corruption and bureaucracy in Indian politics; his wife had been taken ill, so was unable to attend. Purnima Mitra, a friend of Anima's from their schooldays at La Martiniere, and her husband Saradindu Mitra, a belligerent barrister who specialised in land use and labour law. (The joke was sometimes made that La Martiniere's motto, *Labore et Constantia*—by toil and perseverance—had prepared Purnima well for married life with Saradindu!). Tapan Ghosh, an environmental engineer who ran his own consultancy, and whose personal resources seemed to become healthier in inverse proportion to the natural resources which he was asked to appraise. And last and least, Tapan's wife, the physiognomically-named Dimple, about whom there was not much to know.

These were the people who, through geography, history, and sociology, now counted as The Professor and Anima's close friends, the recipients of dinner invitations, desultory phone calls, inconsequential emails, and if Anima could remember, puja gifts. Yet although The Professor seemed to have wholeheartedly engaged with them, for Anima these friendships, even with her old pal Purnima, had not really solidified. They seemed like the skin on a pan of boiled milk, clingy but easily broken.

The guests were led through into the library for preprandial drinks. The library! The others could have square footage and air conditioning and security guards, but they didn't have history. History which reminded them that whilst Anima's forefathers were dressed in silk and jewels, hosting classical music evenings in the columned courtyard with its Italianate fountain, their predecessors were, at worst, working their fingers to the bone weaving jute or cotton. Of course, everyone pretended that they never thought about such an indelicate matter, but it was always there in the background as precisely that: the background. For, despite the pervasive and progressive mood of egalitarianism, its insistence on the essential sameness of all people and its requirement of viewing a person as only an individual and not as part of a greater procession, they could not, as if at the sound of a hypnotist's clap, disavow centuries of reliance on caste and categorisation and simply knowing one's place. And now, in the age of equal opportunities and instant millionaires, these old-timers clung to this way of classification as a way of determining who was truly of the elite and who was simply jumped-up. Anima herself was ambivalent about her status. How could anyone ever be truly proud of their family history when it simply had nothing to do with them? Was it not just a fallacy to believe that some people were innately superior? This understanding was in her head. Yet her heart had a different understanding: that she was superior because people treated her as superior, not only because of her own achievements but because of her breeding.

She sipped on her gin and tonic. She wondered what sort of background her husband's new paramour came from. Nothing too distinguished, that was for certain. After Anima and the surety which her old money and cultivation bestowed upon her, and he, from only a 'good family' with nothing but one generation of school leaving certificates to show for itself, no doubt he would wish to step down to less rarefied air where he could breathe easily again. Whilst, at the same time, partaking in the luxuries and revelling in the cachet which being married to Anima allowed. He might have been a professor but hard cash could reach the parts which academia couldn't. But yes, someone, then, that he could indulge, foster, take under his wing. She imagined how much he would enjoy being invited for dinner at this girl's house—the humbled parents, the cheap gas stove with two burners working overtime, the bucket and jug in the bathroom hidden away, the meretricious painting of some Indian subject (a woman carrying a brass pot on her head or a man playing the sitar) on the wall—pretending not to notice a thing whilst noticing it all.

A servant came and whispered to Anima. Dinner was ready. Anima became conscious that she had not said a word to her guests. She hoped they hadn't realised that something was the matter.

Generous albeit standard compliments about the food were issued and then the guests got down to business.

"Did you hear about the fire at Lohia's hospital?" Manik asked eagerly.

Of course, everyone had heard. But who was going to be the first person to say what all the guests wanted to say?

"Yes, a very sad business," nodded The Professor.

"Exactly—everything's a *business* to them," Saradindu replied firmly, "even people's lives."

"They've taken over," nodded Purnima; this for the benefit of The Professor and Anima, who were considered semi-visitors—after all, they still couldn't drink the local water without falling ill.

"*Who*'s taken over *what*?" The Professor asked, pretending not to know what Purnima had meant.

"The Marwaris!" exclaimed Tapan with some amount of disgust. "Who else! They run everything in this city now—if you can make money from it, they're involved. And you know what they're like—if you shake hands with one of them, you have to count how many fingers you get back!"

"I didn't realise you found making money so repellent," The Professor replied pleasantly. Too pleasantly. Tapan understood the insult. Everyone understood. There was a brief silence before Purnima said, unable to stop her eyes from shining, "It was in an English newspaper, you know—*The Guardian*—about a week ago!"

She had tried very hard to not sound impressed, Anima knew. For all the years when Anima had been living in London and Purnima in Kolkata, in all their conversations, Anima had fastidiously tried to avoid any implication that she had been the one to 'do better' by dint of moving away. Indeed, she had made a point of talking about how much she missed Kolkata in order to give Purnima the impression that it was *she* who had made the right decision to stay. That Purnima had never had any other option was overlooked. Anima's intuition that Purnima needed to feel that she had in some small way surpassed her had become clear the first time Purnima, as a student, had seen Anima's family home. Within Purnima's mind there had been a range of possibilities as to where Anima might live. With Anima's bearing, the way she spoke, her mannerisms, Purnima had speculated that it would be the upper end of her imaginings, perhaps a separate dining and living room, maybe even a room for a servant. She hadn't seen the library and the billiards room and the courtyard and the salon coming. Not only that, but Anima was taller, slimmer, better looking and brighter, and there was a kernel of envy and pride in Purnima which meant that she would not allow herself to be bested in every single category. Yet, despite all of this, she still couldn't help but be pleased when the place she had been born in, grown up in, and lived in, was mentioned by an English newspaper.

"Really?" asked The Professor, though no doubt he knew. "Well, if there's a tragedy, it might as well as be of the scale to receive a mention in the World News page of *The Guardian*!"

The guests could not tell if he was joking or not. Maybe it was that English sarcasm—an affliction he had picked up in his time away and was yet to be cured of.

"I saw the article," said Manik, glumly. "It was, of course, all about the terrible state of affairs here. Corruption, laziness, no value for life, and so on. We don't need some foreigner coming in lecturing us and giving us pitying glances. I saw three BMWs on the A J C Bose road today. Why don't they write about that!"

This countermove invigorated the guests; even Purnima was quick in changing her expression from one of being impressed to one of being offended.

"Yes, well it's not like we're all drowning in excrement!" —Tapan.

"Affluence and effluence—only one letter apart!" —Saradindu.

The guests chuckled. The Professor turned his lips out and frowned; he liked the wordplay if not the sentiment.

"Well, if we want them to keep their white noses out, perhaps we should stop taking aid money from them?"

Manik looked down at his plate, split a chilli between thumb and forefinger, and muttered, "After what they did here, we deserve some sort of reparation . . . Made to be second-class citizens in our own country . . ."

The ultimate fallback: the second-class citizen argument. Only one step away from slavery or the Holocaust, and blisteringly hot coals for anyone to even try and tiptoe over. But The Professor, brave or maybe foolhardy or perhaps just with heat-resistant feet, wasn't deterred.

"If you want to be treated as an equal, you have to be an equal. No point in continuing to play the victim, however convincing the testimony."

Even Anima herself, usually quite unflustered by her husband's analytical expeditions, stopped eating for a moment, if only to gauge the reaction. But they were strangely quiet, allowing The Professor to expand.

"Maybe their real point is that our increasing wealth seems to be in inverse proportion to our compassion. Once upon a time we would have at least pretended to care—we had dear old Jyoti Babu to thank for that—but now we just say, what are you looking at that slum for, look at my S-Class."

Anima stared at her husband, expressionless. Sometimes he

was an insensitive prick. The guests looked down at their plates, some of them rocked their head from side to side as if his point was worth consideration if not assent. The Professor now looked at Anima. Mistaking her blankness for agreement, he smiled, adding, "Yes, the big shame about India is that our poverty doesn't make us more humane, it makes us less so. We've seen it for so long, it means nothing to us anymore. In fact, our lives are lived according to an increasingly selfish agenda—and we are only concerned with what we have, not with what others don't have . . ."

The guests did not like being told this. They were all quite certain that, in their own way, they did what they could for those less fortunate than themselves, even if they could not articulate exactly what that was. Anima wondered who would even the score and how. Any minute now, someone was going to quote Tagore, she was sure of it. Instead, it was Saradindu who said, "Well, they're all coming back now—those English-Indians and those American-Indians, now they want to be Indian-Indians!"

"But they're not coming back *here*," Tapan frowned. "They're coming to Mumbai, Delhi, Chennai, Bangalore, even Hyderabad. No one's coming to Kolkata."

"Mumbai, Chennai, *Kolkata*. What happened to Bombay, Madras, *Calcutta*? Or are you applying for your certificate in postcolonial endonyms?" The Professor prodded.

None of the guests knew what an endonym was but they all understood The Professor's jibe. For a man who had lived away from home for more than thirty years, it was, they thought, somewhat presumptuous. Anima, who would have once been impressed by this instinct in him, which she had considered one to search and examine, was now of the opinion that it stemmed from something far less honourable: the instinct to denigrate and belittle. She felt like picking up his plate and tipping the contents over his head—an appropriate response, if there even was one, to the dinner-time use of the word 'endonym'—but the restrictions of polite society kept her in her seat.

"Well, *wherever* they're coming to," Manik retorted, "it's not here. Even those bedraggled, unwashed tourists you see all over India—the ones wearing the big bags on their backs—even *they* don't come here."

"Good! I don't want those sort of idiots to come here, drinking *bhang* lassis and speaking a lot of nonsense," huffed Saradindu. "I once had the misfortune of sitting near a couple of them on a train from Cochin to *Bombay*. Of course they were in sleeper class for the experience of noise, dirt, and overcrowding, and the opportunity to, quote, *interact with Indians from all walks of life*. I was there because it was a last-minute trip and all the AC tickets were sold out! Of course, I could tell from the way they were speaking so nicely that back home they were from a very singular walk of life!"

This raised a chuckle from everyone, but before the wave broke against the shore to disappear forever, Tapan leant forward, shaking his head.

"We're never going to be the next China at this rate," he said, sighing.

"Why would we want to be the next China?" replied The Professor, genuinely interested.

"Yes, why should we always be the follower not the leader!" Dimple's first contribution to the evening. That had not been The Professor's point but before he had a chance to explain, Dimple continued, chin raised, "You know they eat everything. Even insects." Dimple's distrust of a whole country was based on only the dietary habits of its people. She didn't know much else about the place, in any case. Mao, The Great Wall, chicken chow mein: that was the entirety of her knowledge. For the first time, Anima was interested enough to involve herself.

"So?" she asked, gently, but with enough torque to insist that Dimple answer.

"Well, you don't think it's a bit too much? I mean, they even eat dogs—you had a dog, didn't you, back in England?" There was concern in Dimple's eyes.

"Yes, I did. A golden retriever. I assure you that the Chinese did not eat him." Anima realised that she had said 'I did' not 'We did'. Already my subconscious is looking back and rewriting history, she thought, the thirty-two-year-old *we* fragmenting into you and I.

Dimple glanced at her husband, uncertain. Had Anima made a joke or was she expecting some further evidence of the omnivorous nature of the Chinese? He wasn't sure either, so responded, "And how's your work?"

Anima was the owner of a private surgery which, by dint of its location, had ended up specialising in the ailments of the wealthy: diabetes, obesity, heart disease, high blood pressure, gallstones, gout. Indeed, there were a couple of guests around the dining table who had visited her surgery recently.

What she wanted to say was: tedious, unsatisfying, mundane if lucrative. When she had retired from her practice at the National Hospital for Neurology and Neurosurgery in London, Anima had not intended to work on returning to Kolkata. She had imagined for herself an exciting and carefree retirement, with The Professor by her side, travelling to new places, learning a new language, picking up a new hobby, all from the base of her beautiful family home. Unoriginal, she would concur, but no less appealing for it. But after the initial six months of settling into a different and more self-indulgent routine, she was very surprised to find that she longed to return to the demands and exigencies of a daily job. After years of physical and mental pressure, her neural pathways could not seem to adjust to her new, slower pace. Her clock did not say tick-tock-tick-tock, it said tick-tick-tick-TICK. So, she had approached the local hospitals to see if they might make use of her. But as enthusiastic and knowledgeable as the doctors there were, they were lacking in resources and did not have access to the kind of medical machinery and technology that Anima was used to working with. It would have been like working in a good neighbourhood restaurant after working at a Michelin starred one. But could she face going back to London again after the big goodbyes and the grand intentions? There was something peculiarly shaming about the act of leaving ceremoniously only to return diffidently. So it was The Professor who suggested she set up her own private practice. Something to keep her busy, a chance to reacquaint herself with general medicine. Suddenly, the notion that The Professor did really care for her—he had never been anything other than supportive of her career—flitted through her head but she quickly dismissed this as self-interest: he just wanted to keep her earning so his lifestyle didn't suffer!

The mandatory license was applied for, and in under a year, Anima had set herself up in a large, purpose-built clinic in one of the most salubrious neighbourhoods, simply because that was where it was easiest to set up. At first, she had been revived by the different set-up: the different nurses, the different way of working, the different patients, their different problems. But after a while, these differences dissipated, and all she was left with were the moans of the middle class who seemed to view consulting a doctor as part of their routine, much like going to the dry-cleaner or the street-side shoeshine boy. Soon, she was down to writing prescriptions (she was quickly forced to put to one side her concern about the rise in antibiotic-resistant bacteria: the common cold, an upset stomach, a broken arm—patients with these ailments all demanded antibiotics), and in particularly intractable cases, writing referral letters. She felt reduced. A whole life's work for *this*. She thought of giving up but she had nothing to give it up *for.* A strange trap. A fine fog of apathy settled around her. She had very little to say; moaning about other people's moaning had a galling pettiness about it. She thought again of The Professor's new woman . . . girl . . . *interest.* Ah, of course, *that* was the attraction. The undimmed righteousness of youth, the vigour, the passion. The simple belief that there *was* a point to it all. Not yet trammelled by the disappointments and distrust of the autumn years.

It took Anima seconds to run through all of this. After a moment, she replied, "Fine, thank you."

III

They were keeping her waiting on purpose, of that Devi was sure. But why? Because they were scared of her or because they weren't? Either way, she knew what was coming. She took a deep breath and reminded herself that what marked out a leader was not necessarily skill or even talent but the will to keep going, to not give in, to stay in power! Don't stop to question yourself. A still target is easier for others to hit. Let other people wonder why you're in power but never wonder that yourself. Self-doubt is the beginning of your end. These days, Devi spent a lot of time thinking in aphorisms.

There was a knock at her door. For a moment, she slid down in her seat and let her pockmarked cheek rest against the cool mahogany of the desk, the only piece of furniture she had kept from the room's last incarnation. She was half-tempted to just let them knock until they finally went away. The long days of campaigning, the hours spent canvassing and cajoling, the nights spent hustling and haranguing, even *then* she had never felt quite so spent. For preparing to be in power, no matter how much you tried to visualise it, imagine it, conjure it, in no way prepared you to *be* in power. The dilemmas, the disagreements, the never-ending disputes—and that was just with people on your side. Figure in the enemy—a single deadly individual, a forceful group, a clear and present danger, an amorphous threat—but in whichever form, very definitely all around, and what you were facing was an atomic level headache. And wrinkles. Good job she had a permanent scowl to disguise them. Not that Devi cared about losing her looks. Indeed, not only did she not care for her own appearance—the frizzy hair and straggly eyebrows attested to that—but she frowned upon other women who did. To Devi, even the act of applying lipstick was pornographic. What she hadn't figured out was that her overt display of self-abnegation would itself encourage more prurient questions than if she had gone a little easier on the all-white chasteness, thrown in a jazzy printed sari or maybe a slick of nail varnish every now and then. For what everyone was interested in was what was going on underneath the un-starched sari, or rather, if anything had ever gone on. Coyly, "Do you think she has ever had a boyfriend?"—this from the modest lower classes, the servants and the household staff, afraid to speak too openly about someone who was to be respected. Politely, "Do you think she's a virgin?"—the salaried classes, the clerks, and the teachers. Brazenly, "What do you think she'd do if she saw an erect cock?" "Have it arrested."—the chattering classes.

Another knock, more insistent.

"Come," she said, managing to lift her head and summon some steam.

The director of the rural livelihood, self-employment, and self-improvement opportunities project entered, followed by Manish

Ray, the minister for backward classes. The director looked glum, the dark circles around his eyes even blacker than usual. Devi intuited that he had been losing sleep not because he had failed but because he had done himself out of a job. Manish Ray, meanwhile, looked more circumspect. Devi wondered whether he was hoping he *had* done himself out of his current position. Either way, her immediate instinct was to look down on them both, albeit for different reasons.

"Do be sitting," she said, not so much a request as an order.

They did as they were told, taking the chairs set out in front of her desk. Manish cleared his throat a little theatrically.

"I'm sorry to say the funding has been pulled."

Devi looked at his cool expression. He didn't seem sorry at all.

"How much?" she asked, although she knew that it was the amount of money that mostly came from institutions with 'World' or 'International' in their title.

"Fifty crore," the director mumbled. His share of that, both over and under the table, was now gone, too.

The funds had been retracted because they had not been used. 'Milestones have simply not been met' as the bank official had put it. This was not because the director was unaware of the milestones. Indeed, he himself was incentivised to meet them by receiving payment for each step completed, for each box ticked. Yet he had neither the ingenuity nor the gumption to organise and motivate disparate groups of employees to work together and put the interests of the state and its people above their own sense of self-importance. No, not people. *Bengalis.* Two other states taking part in the project had managed, no problem. One other state had also failed to use the funds—and suffered the same consequences—but that was because it was stuffed full of illiterates, who were probably still using their thumbprints as their signatures. West Bengal had failed, however, because its people were *too* literate. Too many ideas, too many opinions, too many cavils and quibbles all around. The curse of the intellectual: all words, no action. Indeed, no action *because* of the sheer volume of words, which bore down on anything that even looked like alacrity.

"Why is this happening?" Devi snarled.

"Milestones weren't—" the director began.

"I am knowing that," Devi cut him off, "I am meaning *why* were milestones not being met? That was your responsibility, wasn't it?"

The director started to pule and grouse, blaming his subordinates, blaming the bank, blaming the rural villagers, blaming bureaucracy, blaming the weather. If he could have, he would have blamed his own mother for giving birth to him and landing him in this mess.

Devi's dry, rubbery lips turned downwards. There was something singularly unattractive about a grown man dithering and making excuses for himself. No wonder she despised most of the men in her commission. All big big talk and ripe behinds, but underneath the swagger, beggarly little shits. If only she could get rid of them and replace them with clones of herself.

"I have been listening," Devi sighed, putting up her palm and closing her eyes for a moment. The director knew he was done. Manish cleared his voice theatrically again. Devi imagined strangling him with his own vocal cords, then opened her eyes.

"What?" Devi said, staring at him. There was not even an attempt at civility now.

"Would you like me to commission a report?" Manish asked.

Devi's eyes darkened.

"I am already knowing what incompetent idiots you all are," she snorted, "I am not needing it in writing."

Manish was expressionless. He was used to *this* Devi, the short-fused harridan, always ready to scold and belittle, not the beatific, bounteous goddess which the moniker implied. The director, however, was surprised to be on the receiving end of Devi's coarseness—he thought that this demeanour was reserved for agitators and political enemies—and glanced towards Manish. Manish responded by looking at the floor as if he had spotted something of great interest near the corner of Devi's desk. It was time for the director to leave. Eyes stinging with shame, he rose to his feet, and managed to work his way to the door.

"This thing . . . Is it being caused by those *goondas*?" Devi questioned.

The thugs to whom she was referring were The Communists and their supporters. Ever since she had ousted them from power after an unprecedented thirty-four years, she had become convinced that they were trying to unseat her not using the tools of democracy, as she defined them, but through underhand and unfair tactics, as defined by her, too. Hence, any time something did not go her way, an opinion poll, a debate, a plan, a traffic light, she would blame them.

It would have been much easier for Manish to concur and indeed, would take some of the heat off him, but out of some perverse sense of integrity or maybe just rebellion, he shrugged.

"I doubt it."

Devi's nostrils flared. What did he know? Well, he had actually been one of them before he had seen sense and joined her. Perhaps a dreg of misguided loyalty remained, she surmised.

"Hmmm," Devi managed, picking at a sliver of dry skin near her thumb and nodding mainly to herself.

"What should I say to the Press Office department then? For the papers," sighed Manish, already enervated by the meeting and more than ready for a stiff drink or ten.

Again, without warning, Devi boiled over.

"What am I caring what those jackals are writing about me!"

Instinctively, the Oxford-educated Manish mentally corrected her phrase—'write' not 'are writing'; Devi was terribly attached to her present participles. His favourite instance was when she had told a cheeky reporter, "You are crossing the line!"—a rather forceless rebuke compared to the definitive "You've crossed the line!" which she had intended. Suddenly, Manish had a mental cartoon of the reporter casually ambling across a white painted line whilst Devi, with a scowl, watched him do so. A smirk came to his lips but he managed to swallow it. Then he looked back at her and realised that she wanted some sort of response or at least acknowledgement. He was quite tempted to answer that if she didn't care what the press thought of her ("If you don't care what the press writes" or, maybe, for her benefit, "If you are not caring what the press is writing"), then why did she have a folder of all her favourable clippings in a folder in the top drawer of her desk? But he knew this would be like teasing a caged bear. And there had been incidents where other people, either more imprudent or daring than himself, had been dragged through the bars, mauled, and left for dead.

"You have to care what's written about you because your people pay attention to what's written . . ." he said carefully. In these situations, the possessive pronoun 'your' always seemed to lower her temperature.

Devi twitched. Yes, *her* people. The people who she so assiduously served, whose well-being informed her every decision, whose health, prosperity, and uprightness she sought to advance at every chance, even if, *at times*—she bristled momentarily—they were ungrateful and critical. Whilst other politicians were wining and fine dining, and jetting off on holiday aboard the luxury yachts of billionaire industrialists, Devi was unswervingly and unfailingly committed to the betterment of others, not herself.

"That's right, is it not?" Manish followed up, gently.

"I am supposing so," Devi conceded, po-faced.

"So, what shall I tell them?"

Devi brought together the thumb and little finger of her right hand and alternately flicked each nail.

"We must not be lying," she said firmly.

"Yes, but there are ways of telling the truth," Manish said encouragingly, raising his eyebrows. Trying to familiarise Devi with *spin* was like trying to explain the concept of colour to a blind person.

Devi looked at him suspiciously, although Manish noted that she didn't outright object.

"We have to be helping those people one way or another. By hook or by crook!" Devi demanded.

The English phrase caught Manish slightly off guard and he instinctively pulled his torso back in his chair and raised an eyebrow. Did she realise that it meant by whatever means necessary, fair or foul? Or was she just misguidedly using it to stress her point that something needed to be done?

"When you say by hook or crook . . .?" he asked delicately.

"I am meaning by hook or by crook!" Devi raged, her brow furrowed.

"I see . . ." nodded Manish, although he didn't see. "Well, what about some sort of private-public partnership in the area? Promoting education, employment, technological advancement, investment in human capital, and endogenous growth?" Then noting Devi's sceptical expression, he added, "Helping people to help themselves!"

Devi mulled this over.

"What you are suggesting, precisely?" she asked, cocking her head to one side.

Manish turned out his lips. There was nothing *precise* about what he had said. It was intended as a starting point. A holding statement whilst they figured out what they were actually going to do. But Devi seemed to like it.

"Well, obviously I don't have details," he began, but seeing that Devi's eyes were narrowing again, he added brightly, "*but* . . . I think we should go for something ambitious, something substantial, something that shows everyone 'Bengal means business'! No more of these silly little NGO-type projects, installing biogas digesters in every villager's backyard, and running Arsenic mitigation programmes!" He leant forward, his eyes shining, surprised at how passionate he felt all of a sudden, as if the act of saying these words had imbued them with significance and authenticity.

"Bengal means business," Devi repeated, licking her lower lip, "*Bengal means business!*" She nodded slowly and thoughtfully.

Manish, seeing his chance, leant forward even further, and added in a low voice, "And this time, *you*'ll be in charge."

Devi stopped nodding. She now arched her neck to the side, paused, and lifted it up again—a small but distinct motion meaning *yes*. She was fed up of being at the mercy of patronising, chino-wearing foreigners, all *long term sustainability* and *supporting local development*, turning up acting like god and making her jump through hoops!

"That is being agreed, then," she granted, adopting a more conciliatory tone for the first time in the meeting. "We will be discussing this . . ." she pursed her lips whilst she thought of the right word, "*enterprise*, at the next cabinet meeting. I will be looking forward to your further briefing at that time."

Manish dipped his head in assent. Realising that he had just created a surfeit of work for himself, he wasn't feeling quite as ardent as he had been just minutes ago. The concomitant realisation that he had handed himself a chance to fuck up—and fuck up on an ambitious, substantial scale—gave him a further chill. Devi, meanwhile, was now warming up nicely.

"We are always being distracted by petty matters," she frowned. "It's the enemy's diversion tactic, you know—making us waste our energy pettifogging instead of concentrating on the real issues of the day . . ."

"Yes, we must concentrate on the real issues," Manish replied, trying to pass off his glumness as seriousness. "I'll brief the press office."

He rose from his chair before Devi had the chance to ruminate any further. Suddenly, he preferred the ursine version to the bovine one.

Devi watched him go. As soon as the door was closed behind him, however, her growing fortitude rapidly dwindled and she was once again left feeling hollow and devitalised.

What a day! What a month! First, the fire at the hospital—that murderous Marwari's hospital! Then, the *hartal* by workers protesting against the increase in the price of, well, everything. That had brought the city to a standstill and cost the economy millions. Now this. But whom to turn to for succour? No one understood. All Devi had to find refuge in were her principles, her dogma, and her incorruptibility. That, and her clippings folder. Carefully, she opened her top drawer and pulled out the manila file. Then she put on her sturdy reading glasses. With a deeply-lined finger, she turned a plastic sleeve and settled on an article from an American magazine, which she interpreted as celebrating her rise to power and her influence. Feisty: yes! Determined: yes! Scrappy: she'd had to look up that one in the dictionary, but probably! Divisive? Only because people disagreed with her! And they had finished on a positive prediction: that her power would only grow. Her spirit somewhat revived, she reminded herself that she was admired, especially by the Americans. They had even awarded her accolades for her influence! She smiled a little as she read another American piece on her street-fighting spirit. That's right, I am a street-fighter, she thought, and street-fighters don't fight to win the admiration of the judges and to score points, they fight to win, however ugly it gets. She put away the folder still smiling.

And then she opened up her bottom drawer and carefully took out her dolls, tucked right at the back. An Indian Barbie (she had not been able to find one dressed in a white sari—perhaps Mattel had thought it a little creepy to introduce Widow Barbie—so had picked the least showy one, dressed in navy blue) and a good number of Indian Kens (they came dressed only in gaudy sherwanis). She seated the Barbie on the desk with two Kens lying prostrate before her. She tried to position Barbie's arms into a crossed gesture as best as she could. She smiled. And then she made Barbie stand up and kick one of the Kens right off the table. Fortuitously, the Ken fell into the wastepaper basket, which tickled her.

There was a knock on her door. She put away the dolls with haste and after readjusting herself to seem more composed, called, "Come."

Priyanka, a slightly nervy young woman from the Press Office entered. She was skinny, all gangly arms and legs, and holding a sheet of paper as if it might be a stick of dynamite.

"Where shall I put this?" she asked diffidently.

"Bring it here," Devi said. Priyanka approached cautiously, placed the piece of paper on the edge of the desk, and then stood for a moment, considering whether to ask Devi if there was anything else that she needed. But then, expediency trumped professional courtesy and she reversed at speed, hoping she wouldn't be called back.

Devi waited for a few seconds to make sure that Priyanka would not be returning with a question or a clarification, then, picked up the piece of paper and read it carefully. They had done a reasonable job: facts tempered by the correct interpretation to give a picture that, whilst painted in mainly subdued colours, had a final sense of quiet and contained optimism. The pulled funding was not a failure then, but merely an adjustment in circumstances. Indeed, an opportunity to do something bigger and better.

Devi sighed and leant back in her chair. Then, in a fraction of a second, she bounced back up, grabbed the piece of paper and looked at her watch. It had taken only ten minutes for the Press Office to come up with this. Devi shook her head, her nostrils flaring: like an obituary of a VIP, this piece had been written in advance, with only a few tweaks made to bring it up to date. Because they had guessed, from the start, that the project would be a failure.

IV

Will *the minister of mines be pleased to state*, blah, blah, *the quantum and value*, blah, *the total expenditure incurred on investigations*, blah, *the measures to be taken by in order to adopt latest extraction technique*, blah, blah—Anil's eyes finally slowed down—*the progress made in regard to commercial exploitation of such minerals and their allocation to private companies.*

Anil smiled and looked up at Dr. Debolina Majumdar, of the West Bengal Directorate of Mines and Minerals, who was delicately sipping on a glass of white wine in the French restaurant located in The Grand, one of the most venerated and luxurious hotels in Kolkata.

The first time Anil had visited what was, at that point, the grandest hotel in town, had been as a child. He was eleven or twelve, just on the cusp of observing the world beyond his own immediate interests and concerns. His parents, Rudra and Annapurna, had decided to take out their extended family for Christmas dinner. They had suddenly decided that it was smart to celebrate Christmas in a more elaborate fashion; their wealth, accumulated from their proprietorship of a daily Bengali newspaper, allowed them such extravagances.

Anil, an only child who wasn't used to such familial liveliness, had withdrawn from the noisy table. He had instead chosen to gaze through the restaurant window into the central courtyard, surrounded by palm trees and housing a gloriously turquoise swimming pool. At one end of the pool, a table had been set up, covered in a thick, white tablecloth and glowing tea-lights. Around it, a couple of airline pilots and a bevy of glamorous airhostesses. Anil had made his way to the party dining by the pool, mesmerised by their style and their glitter. There, he had asked a particularly ravishing airhostess whether they were celebrating her birthday. She had laughed and told him, no, they were celebrating the launch of a new direct flight from London to Calcutta.

Now, looking out at that same swimming pool, Anil speculated that the likelihood of a reputable airline celebrating the launch of a direct flight from London to Kolkata was negligible, even if a new international airport had already been built (which ran well under full capacity). But no point in being critical, he thought. The majority of the city's residents had a BA (Hons) in Bitching and Moaning, and look where it had got them. No, I'm a doer not a complainer, he told himself. The problem with most people, he believed, was that they mistook emotion for morality. Cry about this, beat your chest about that, but actually do nothing to improve the situation. He, on the other hand, was loathe to emote in order to signal his virtue; there was something so childish, so self-centred, so *incontinent*, about doing so.

An elderly waiter, with a watchful gaze that only years of service could bring, smiled at Anil. Anil indicated that he and his guest should be given a few more minutes, and the waiter smiled and moved on, gracefully. Anil watched him go and remembered an incident from his St. Xavier days.

He couldn't remember exactly when, maybe when he was in seventh grade, but a boy called Rishi Reddy had joined at the start of the year. He was the son of a filthy rich Mumbai textiles merchant and a loud, boastful, entitled little fuck. The Jesuits didn't have a chance with him. This was especially clear when a group of boys, including Anil and Rishi, would visit the local ice cream parlour after school. All the other boys were polite and courteous to the waiting staff but Rishi took it upon himself to regularly humiliate and degrade, just because he could, a particular elderly waiter who had worked in the parlour for years. The other boys, despite feeling deeply uncomfortable, said nothing; it was apparent that if they pulled up Rishi on his behaviour, they would become his next target. All except Anil. He wasn't scared of Rishi mocking him. But neither did he want to give Rishi a lecture; what he wanted to do was *teach Rishi a lesson.*

Who was it that had come to inform him of the call? Ah yes, good old Bilal, the housekeeper, with his bright orange hennaed beard. Babu, babu, telephone, telephone! Tell whoever it is that I shall call them later—I'm doing my homework now. But person is very mad, babu, you must come now!

"What have you said, Anil?"

"Who's this?"

"It's Rishi! What have you said?"

"What are you talking about?"

"I'm talking about you saying I beat up that old Muslim guy from the ice cream parlour!"

"He has a name—it's Nasirul Malik."

"Whatever, he's been beaten up and the police came to tell my dad and they even showed him a photo of the guy with a black eye and a broken nose, and then they said the guy said that *I* did that to him, and then they said that *you* said so, too! What's going on, Anil?"

Anil still remembered Rishi's voice—the incomprehension and sheer panic.

"Well, you *did* do it. I saw you."

"What, what are you talking about, Anil, what—"

"Yes, I would have helped Mr. Malik but you scared me, you had this crazy look in your eye . . ."

"Anil, what's going on, is this some weird game or have you gone mad?"

"Me, mad? I think it's quite clear who the mad one is. Anyway, I'm sure your father will get you out of trouble, he always does."

Nasirul Malik didn't even have a bank account; the whole amount had to be handed to him in cash. And looking at the stacks of notes filling the suitcase, the stacks of notes which meant that he would never have to work again, he certainly agreed with what that worldly-wise young man Anil had told him: that both the pain and the lie were for the greater good.

As for Rishi himself, he had been promptly dispatched to Bishop Cotton School in Shimla where the motto was 'Overcome Evil With Good'. For the greater good, indeed.

Anil thought about this with a smile, then thumbed through the appendices, table after table of numbers, and grinned at Dr. Majumdar again. She was a neat and trim old woman, made more with an eye for efficiency than artistry, but with her starched sari, boy's cut, and compact features, she looked quite handsome and not at all out of place. In her company, Anil, with his rolled-up sleeves, expensive loafers, and ready smile, seemed relaxed, perhaps even solicitous. If anyone had bothered to look at the two of them, they would assume that a successful young man was taking out his mother for a treat. That suited him fine. What he didn't need was some big mouth indecorously gobbling up lunch whilst grandstanding for all and sundry. No, he needed someone quiet and reckonable, and someone who would be satisfied with what he had to offer, which, in this case, was more than a comfortable retirement.

First, he thought, some general but germane chit-chat; I should ease her in whilst she chews on her Chicken Boudin.

"It seems hard to believe, doesn't it," Anil mused, "that in the 1950s, we were India's powerhouse—I mean we held more than a quarter of its industrial stock."

"It doesn't seem hard to believe sitting in *here*, does it. . .?" Dr. Majumdar replied lightly.

Anil smiled.

"Well, no," he concurred, "in fact, at the start of the 1960s, we were still one of the three richest states in India—the place to really live the good life!"

"You seem like the kind of man who is well acquainted with living the good life . . ." Dr. Majumdar smiled.

Anil shrugged.

"So, where do you think it all went wrong?" he asked. "I mean, I think what people fail to grasp is the enormity of the decline. It's quite possible that in the modern world, no other city has ever faced such an economic catastrophe!"

Am I laying it on too thick? he thought. But I need to impress upon her that this is bigger than two people in a fancy restaurant!

Dr. Majumdar stopped eating, put down her fork, and looked seriously at Anil.

"I think it's we Bengalis, with our taste for philosophical abstraction and political idealism. We started to question the basis and integrity of our success—not for us to just sit back and enjoy! So came the era of industrial action. And businesses pulled out left, right, and centre."

"And the government didn't help . . ." Anil added.

"When does a government ever help? All politicians are shameless."

"Well, especially The Communists, yes? Political violence. Desperate underinvestment. Structural decay. It's almost like they *wanted* to destroy West Bengal!"

"The people elected them," Dr. Majumdar replied neutrally, "seven times."

"And now they've elected Devi," Anil said, just as neutrally. "Perhaps Bengalis are as keen on extravagant rhetoric and hare-brained schemes as they are on philosophical abstraction and political idealism?"

"Perhaps."

So, she won't reveal her political colours, Anil thought. That's okay. It's not necessary. In fact, perhaps it's for the better. Though he couldn't help but finish with a joke.

"I read this the other day and I found it quite amusing. Question: When is a road not a road?"

Dr. Majumdar smiled, frowned, thought, and then shook her head.

"It's when the road has faced fierce heat, high humidity, and monsoon rain for over thirty years and no one has bothered to repair it. And what the Left is meant to be famous for is public work programmes!"

Dr. Majumdar allowed herself a smile.

"Very good . . ." she said, dabbing at her mouth with the linen napkin.

A waiter approached their table and tried to discreetly work out whether they were finished.

"Dessert?" he asked politely.

Anil, with a hand gesture, deferred to Dr. Majumdar.

"Why not!" she replied with some enthusiasm.

"Of course, Ma'am, I'll bring you the menu," the waiter nodded and then turned to Anil, who put his hand up and shook his head. He glanced at Dr. Majumdar. By the look of her trim figure, she did not seem like a person who overindulged. If she was ordering dessert, it was because she felt that she deserved a reward for her efforts. That was a propitious sign. But he knew what he wanted to hear and he wished to avoid swaying her answer by asking her leading questions. Instead, as the waiter brought her the menu, he again picked up the bound minutes from the meeting and started perusing the appendices. Now and then, he furrowed his brow as if some piece of information might not be quite to his liking, but still he stayed quiet, until finally he spoke.

"About this . . .?" Anil wafted his hand in the air. He didn't want to be too direct. She was elderly after all, she deserved respect. Indeed, she was an elderly *lady*—respect doubled. Indeed, an elderly *Indian* lady—respect squared!

"What needed to be done was done and what needed to be said was said," Dr. Majumdar said calmly, with a sideward tilt of her head.

Anil smiled and nodded in response. The woman had survived for a long time despite the exigencies of living in a city disproportionately blessed by the gods of bureaucracy, mismanagement, and neglect. A most unholy trinity: each of them dangerous enough individually, but lethal when working together. So, if anyone knew what needed to be done and what needed to be said—and to *whom* it needed to be said—it was she. If you can't beat them, join them? You bet. An instinct to somehow make something of yourself despite the odds? Nothing to be looked down on there. In fact, something to be looked up to.

"The GSI have identified the area you're interested in as having OGP," Dr. Majumdar said soothingly. "Clean and extensive block with high grade coal, a nice geological area, perfect for longwall mining."

"Are you trying to dazzle me with technicalities or just drown me in them?" Anil smiled.

"Geological Survey of India," she explained, "Obvious Geological Potential."

Anil allowed himself a little laugh that sounded apologetic but was anything but.

"But of course, Doctor. We wouldn't be interested otherwise, would we?"

The Royal *We*? The Editorial *We*? The Patronising *We*? Whichever one it was, it made Dr. Majumdar switch her attention from the dessert menu, however enticing, to Anil.

"And of course I stressed the importance of *realising* that potential," she added.

"Of course," Anil replied, one eye still on the document.

". . . And realising it in an efficient and timely fashion."

"Indeed."

". . . For the benefit and uplift of the state and its people."

"Naturally."

". . . In order to achieve national goals as pertains to economic and financial parameters, also."

"Certainly."

Anil put down the document, smoothed the cover page with his hands, and then bit down on his lip, whilst trying to work out how best to extract the truth of the situation from her. Suddenly, he realised how dependent he—and the whole enterprise—was on a shrewd old-timer who was looking for a way out, not a way in. Now the reasons for which he had chosen her seemed to be exactly the same reasons for why he shouldn't have. Of course, she wouldn't get paid in full until the mining lease was granted but he still needed to know how well she had performed before any more time and money was spent on pursuing the opportunity.

"Might we move onto the details of the conversation?" he asked, politely. "Just so I can get a real sense of where we stand."

What had happened was this, Dr. Majumdar said, reassuringly matter-of-fact.

After a high level meeting in Delhi, the federal government had reviewed the GSI's nationwide findings, and allocated the coal blocks to each of the states. The usual big players that were permanently plugged into the grid of governmental gossip had already carved out their portions of the pie. The big projects in Maharashtra—the wealthiest state, the state that welcomed industry and business, that was *built* on industry and business—had been snapped up immediately. Sweeteners had been sent, lips had been licked, hands had been shaken. Soon after, the projects in reliable, conservative Rajasthan, the ostensible home of mining and quarrying, had been taken. Then followed the ones in forward thinking, ambitious, Odisha, the location of one of the federal government's Special Economic Regions, and an all-round good egg. Next was solid, dependable Karnataka, manufacturing hub and home to 'India's Silicon Valley'. Then investor-friendly, cheery Chhattisgarh, the ground underneath it full up with extractable goodies, the ground above it peopled by those who knew how to extract them—and more importantly, *wanted* to.

"Are you telling me," Anil asked, not entirely surprised but still somewhat disappointed, "that no one else is interested in West Bengal?"

"You know how it is in our hometown," she said, raising an eyebrow. "Big businessmen being asked to literally sing for their supper. Not everyone can sing in tune. Not everyone *wants* to."

Anil smirked at Dr. Majumdar's reference: at a recent summit about investment in West Bengal, Devi had *inexplicably* asked a Captain of Industry to sing her a song at the end of a meeting, as if she was a nursery teacher dealing with her playgroup. Improbable.

Embarrassing. True. Neither Anil nor anyone else from The Lohia Group had attended—or been invited—but the general consensus from those who had witnessed the scene was that it was one of complete bafflement followed swiftly by utter consternation. How on earth was such an action meant to foster confidence in prospective investors? What next? Dance-offs? Apparently, the business bigwigs in Mumbai were making the joke that if they wanted to find favour in Devi's investment regime, they'd have to take singing lessons first. West Bengal: the brunt of the joke. Again. Anil's smirk turned into a frown.

The waiter returned to take Dr. Majumdar's order: a frivolous chocolatey concoction. Anil waited until he was out of earshot, and then leaned in.

"But *surely* there are companies other than ours that are interested in the block?"

"Of course," Dr. Majumdar shrugged, "but the two other big players weren't able to secure the necessary permits for the last blocks they were allocated, so they're out of the running. And the other contenders, well, perhaps they're not such reputable companies . . ."

"Reputable?" Anil raised an eyebrow; he now wondered whether Dr. Majumdar herself had been destroying reputations as part of her remit. She seemed quite capable of it.

"It's all relative, yes?" Dr. Majumdar shrugged again. "And we wouldn't be here, would we, if the whole system was infallible?"

"Are you saying we're the best of a bad bunch?" he jested.

Dr. Majumdar smiled, a smile that gave off a feeling of almost carnal knowledge.

"If I thought you weren't capable of delivering what you say you will, I would not have been open to *discussion*. Besides, I am not so unscrupulous as to put my private interests above the public's general good. I have read J S Mill, too, you know."

So, she had done her research, too—and knew about his PPE degree. Good for her.

The waiter came and put down Dr. Majumdar's dessert; the way that she and Anil had immediately stopped talking in his presence made him scurry away. Dr. Majumdar watched him go, lifted a forkful to her mouth, and added, "And, in my experience, considering how long-term a mining project is, how resource-intensive it is, how demanding it is, well, you can't have some greengrocer giving it a go and then pulling out when the going gets tough."

She put the fork in her mouth and made an appreciative noise.

"Well, from what I hear, greengrocers have been looking to diversify ever since the onion crisis," Anil quipped, taking a sip of wine.

Dr. Majumdar threw her head back and laughed loudly.

"Indeed!"

There was little more for Dr. Majumdar to impart. Put simply, she had made the case to those even higher than she and cleared the way for The Lohia Group to be granted the mining lease for the coal reserves that had been discovered in Balachuria, should Anil choose to throw his hat into the ring. Of course, it being an auction, The Lohia Group would have to pay the highest price, but as it was very unlikely that any of the other pre-qualified bidders could match what The Lohia Group could pay, it was pretty much a done deal.

Finally, they finished off on a little bit of personal chit-chat. She had been married for coming up to fifty years. Her husband was now retired but had worked in administration. Half of the people working in this city are administrators, yet what is there to administrate over apart from the administration! Her joke. A case of too many chiefs, not enough Indians. His joke. She asked him about his family. No, no wife. No, no girlfriend. No, no *special* friend. No brother, no sister. But I have parents! he had cheerfully said, and some visiting cockroaches. You should put down poison. For my parents? They're not that bad! They both laughed at that.

Anil saw Dr. Majumdar to a taxi in the hotel's forecourt and bid her farewell. She seemed slightly giddy; whether it was the wine or the conversation or the thought of her swelling bank balance, he wasn't sure. He, though satisfied with the proceedings, was a little more circumspect. The whole thing was laden with risk, and not the sort that could be calculated simply using the fixed cost structure and the contribution margin ratio. However, he was once again pleased with his choice of Dr. Majumdar. She had enough experience and influence to be heard, but was not so prominent that she would easily fall under any suspicion of improper conduct. Besides, as far as he was concerned, it wasn't so much a matter of corruption as one of efficiency, a proper allocation of resources. Plus, she was seemingly level-headed and sensible; in the past, he had had to extract himself from some rather hairy situations when dealing with businessmen who had turned out to be egomaniacs or imposters or outright swindlers. But, he had learned on the job and now he knew who was likely to be a liability and who was likely to deliver the goods. In any case, Anil thought, not only was she serving herself and his company, she was actually serving the public in the best way she could. All of this in a manner that displayed none of the posturing and self-congratulatory puff which Anil had come to expect during the course of this kind of exchange. If only for that, he was relieved.

Yes, he had negotiated well with her. And knowing how to negotiate—wasn't that, above all, the key to business? Wasn't that, above all, the key to life!

On his way from Chowringhee to Sector One for another meeting, he realised that he was being driven through Tiljala, home to one of the city's largest slums. Anil asked his driver to turn off the air conditioning and then rolled down his window. He was not invigorated by the clamorous street noise, the view of life being lived to the full on every path and alleyway, the sense of humanity not only prevailing but thriving despite the hardships it faced. He was utterly exasperated. Just the other day he had read an article about the rising number of multimillionaires in Kolkata. Great, he had thought, at least the super-rich are stocking up on Lamborghinis. But what about the poor bastards on twenty-seven rupees a day?

Anil, always keen to resolve rather than lament, had less than a year ago proposed an innovative scheme to Sachin, because whereas others saw slum-dwellers, he saw a ready and willing workforce with a very particular skill: reclamation. Paper, iron, tin cans, glass and plastic bottles, polythene carry bags, these ragpickers gathered up what others discarded, and made their living from it. But they were inefficient and not as productive as they could be. Listen, Anil had said, let's make this a part-philanthropic, part-business venture. First of all, we invest in the slum itself: improve conditions and sanitation, so that our workers are healthy. Then we organise them, give each team a certain area of the city to work in and provide them with the tools they need to do their job properly, everything from face-masks and overalls and litter-pickers to local collection sites where they can deposit their bags, so they're not limited to what they can carry and they're not wasting valuable time lugging bags back home. Then we provide another team with a facility where the material can be separated, weighed, and packaged efficiently. And then they sell the material to us to be recycled; we'll be the sole buyer. They get ahead and so do we.

From here had followed elaborate plans for food waste collection, a waste-to-energy site, and a state-of-the-art landfill. I'm telling you, Anil explained to Sachin, integrated waste management is very important and very lucrative. And this is a nice in.

Sachin had been impressed with Anil's vision and canniness but not immediately bought over. The whole project would require a sizeable investment. And on the philanthropy front, he had been very keen on a temple as his next venture, not a slum.

We don't need another flashy temple, Anil told him. Do something useful with your cash. Besides, spending money on a temple isn't good economics; you never know what return you're getting! Well, he's right about that, Sachin thought.

So came numerous meetings with various organisations from the municipal authorities to NGOs doing aid work to the corporations who would provide running water and electricity to the slum. So many moving parts, and Anil trying to piece them all together. Slowly. Methodically. It was exhaustive and exhausting work. Then, just as he thought he was getting somewhere, along came Devi with her beautification programme. Her urge to clean up the city meant that the open vats from where the ragpickers picked their wares were suddenly replaced by giant compactor machines, leaving them nothing to pick. The poorest people in the city were suddenly without a livelihood. Anil was beyond irate, he was appalled. Once again, the woman had shown a total lack of judgement and anticipation. Did she ever, *ever* actually think things through to their logical conclusion? If you were really a woman of the people, he had thought, you'd do something for those people who don't even have a vote!

The car came to a stop at the traffic lights. Rabindra *sangeet* started to blare from the speakers fixed to them; another one of Devi's ideas. Yes, put an Elastoplast—one of those Mickey Mouse and Friends ones that distract a little child from what lies underneath—over a gangrenous wound.

He rubbed at his temple. For an unusually unflappable person, thinking about Devi and her various idiocies still managed to make his blood boil. He needed to calm down before his meeting. He rolled up the window.

"Put the air conditioning on high!" he told his driver.

After his meeting, Anil went back to his flat on VIP Road. Despite the driver being on a monthly salary, Anil was generous in tipping him and told him to spend it. Get that money moving around the local economy—the sweet shop, the grog shop, the brothel for all Anil cared—instead of squirrelling it away in some stainless steel cooking pot or fusty hidey hole. As he was fond of quoting: money is like manure. If you don't do anything with it, it's just a pile of shit. But if you spread it around, it helps things grow.

Of course, he could have lived with his parents in their hyper-luxurious house in Alipore but after spending a good many years living on his own and taking care of himself, he couldn't be doing with all the staff milling around and the conundrum of at once having too much room and too little personal space (the maid neatly arranging his boxes of condoms in his bedside drawer—though he never had sex at home, only in hotels). Besides, his parents were barely ever there, spending most of their time jet-setting around the world. What was the point in living in the family home if there was no family there?

He opened the triple-locked door to his flat and surveyed the scene—the tiled floor, the highly shined carved wooden furniture, the bamboo-framed glass-topped coffee table. The flat had been rented furnished; nothing was to his taste. But a very minor hardship; he didn't spend much time in the flat anyway. Indeed, he barely needed a quarter of the two thousand square feet because, for most of the time, he lived in his head.

At his desk, Anil went through all of the research documents for the umpteenth time. Even though his own team—a semi-autonomous organisation existing within The Lohia Group, handpicked by himself, and going under the department title of Corporate Exploration and Expeditions—had carried out the due diligence and he implicitly trusted their judgement, at the end of the day, Sachin listened to *him* not his team. Legal conditions, institutional frameworks, productivity norms, processing efficiency, manpower development, health and safety, infrastructural facilities, displaced person rehabilitation, technology transfers, environmental protection, foreign exports—he needed to check this chicken from every angle, giblets and all. Mining was old school and hard-core. It was what the men did whilst the boys played with their computers. But was he man enough to take it on?

Sachin hadn't realised that he might enjoy prison quite so much. At first, there was shock. She won't—she can't—do that to *me*! But a month after the fire, there he was, being led to his cell. Of course under Devi's rule, it was becoming quite apparent that she could and would do anything to anyone. Only the other day, an academic, the holiest of holy persons in a place that worshipped knowledge, had been thrown into jail for making a joke at her expense. Surely not having a sense of humour is a greater crime, Sachin thought, she'd receive a life sentence for that! But once the consternation had worn off, he had come to realise that there were some fringe benefits of, as he liked to think of it, *some time alone*, whilst he awaited trial.

First of all, there was the complete lack of connectivity. No mobile phone, no computer, no tablet, no real-time connection with anyone he couldn't physically see. Instead, he had unreal-time, where his personal experience of the passing hours became elastic and erratic. Apart from the set punctuations of wake up, lights out, and mealtimes, at points he felt that it was taking hours for a single hour to pass, and at other points, only minutes. For the first few days, this absence of rhythm caused him to lose balance, as if what had been holding him up were the regular bleeps and buzzes of technology. Romantically, and somewhat unfeasibly, he had also expected that he might receive a letter or two, but they had not come.

He was worried, too, about what was happening in the world outside, the fear being that his business would start to disintegrate without him at its helm. Panic, from mild to severe, filled him as he thought of various disastrous—and unlikely—scenarios. But who knew what was unlikely anymore! He was in jail on some trumped up manslaughter charge; how likely was *that*!

At the start, when his mental machinations became too much to bear, he would seek out conversation with the guards or other inmates who were also awaiting trial for crimes which they did not elaborate on—and it seemed that it was not correct jail etiquette to ask. In the days before going in, he had imagined that the supervisors would be cruel and the inmates hard. Accordingly, he had geared himself up to be cold and unfeeling. Yet he had found that they were generally cordial and respectful and not at all interested in making his life hell. Of course, money helped, when did it not? Sweets, cigarettes, newspapers (his journey from front page to oblivion, he noted, was swift), antiperspirant, Nivea moisturiser, were procured for him. An extra pillow and another blanket were found for his dingy bed. Occasionally, a guard would sneak in some Chinese food. He could even receive visitors outside of visiting hours, although, with the exception of Anil, he wasn't particularly interested in seeing them. Sharmila made no contact at all. His reputation as a man of huge power and influence also cushioned his landing; both jailers and jailees wanted to talk to him about job opportunities or business ideas or simply ask for advice on matters that he had no idea about—although he always managed to find something palliative to say.

Soon though, his body and mind became used to the extended, idling silences, and instead of casting about for another human to engage with, he started to enjoy the sound of his inner thoughts. Mostly, he thought of his childhood and his history, or at least a well-fabricated past.

He had been told that his family, along with many other Marwari families, had come from Bikaner to Kolkata and set up shop at the same time as the railways were being built. Whilst in Bikaner, his people had provided provisions for local Rajput armies, but once they had travelled east, they branched out into the wholesale distribution of jute and cotton. Brothers, cousins, nephews, everyone became involved.

The local British firms, impressed by the Marwari efficiency and work ethic, welcomed them on board, keen to take advantage not only of their network but also their access to finance. Because although the Brits might have thought them to be generally inferior, no one handled money better. Not that they were trusted—with their complicated trading structures and financial dexterity, they were viewed as slippery (that oily skin) and crafty (those large noses—good for sniffing out filthy lucre).

So whilst the Brahmin Bengalis didn't deign to do anything so crude as make a living, it was left to the Marwaris to dedicate themselves fully and shamelessly to the pursuit of profit.

Which is what Sachin's family had done. Until The Downfall. Details were sketchy but apparently one of his ancestors, affectionately known as The Sisterfucker, and as much a cocksman as a businessman, had taken a liking to the wife of a prominent British businessman. But despite his sobriquet, it wasn't his sister he wanted to fuck—and considering how events unfurled, that would have been the preferable option. As far as psychological reasoning went, it was postulated that his material success and subsequent status had caused him to become jaded with the local girls on offer. Money itself was a high that caused him to pursue higher highs. So, he had started to crave the delights of what he considered to be more exotic fruit. His relations had done their utmost to first distract him and then dissuade him. But his heart wanted what it wanted—and his organ situated lower down was even more insistent.

Of course he was caught.

The Sisterfucker had neither denied what he had done nor apologised for it—the only two appropriate actions for a man in his position, his family thought. Instead, he seemed to be under the impression that as he had been in no way coercive, underhand, or devious, and in fact had made his intentions blatantly clear to the woman, the most he could be charged with was being indiscreet. To his aghast family, this laconic response, devoid of contrition, and seemingly without any concern for how his misdeed reflected on them, indicated only one thing: he was insane. And if there was one thing for which there was no room in his family, it was insanity—the fiendishly recalcitrant cousin of stupidity. They disowned him immediately. Then, their prestige well and truly punctured, they begged the businessman for forgiveness, and tried to make amends by denouncing The Sisterfucker as the scourge of the family, the blackest of black sheep. They even offered him favourable terms of trade and special arrangements.

The businessman was having none of it. Soon after shipping his wife back to England, he cut off all ties with Sachin's forefathers. Not only that, but through a well-targeted and efficacious smear campaign, which focused on the hostility and downright *vulgarity* of The Sisterfucker whilst neatly sidestepping the issue of his own wife's complicity, he made sure that not one upstanding gent, who cared one jot about protecting his family from unscrupulous and ungrateful animals, would do business with them either.

Soon, Sachin's family started to disintegrate due to the incessant recriminations and bickering, as well as the fact that the bottom had fallen out of their business and despite their best efforts, nothing could provide the boost it needed. Some blamed karma, believing it was their success which had invited such punishment. Others blamed the ascendancy of material achievement and its corollary, the degeneration of virtue. Yet others blamed the foolishness of becoming involved with foreign people in what was ostensibly a foreign land. The Sisterfucker was not the cause, then, just a nasty symptom.

Eventually, the family split three-way. The go-getting majority left Bengal and made their way back to Rajasthan to start afresh in the place they considered their spiritual home. Another more adventurous group sailed to Kenya, where they began a new life in Mombasa as textile merchants. It was only the minority of defeatists, pessimists, and brooders who stayed put; through his father, that was Sachin's branch.

So, from rich and successful favourites of The Raj, they turned into poor and forlorn outsiders. By the time Sachin came along, his father was eking out a living as the proprietor of a small dry goods shop in a town forty miles west of Kolkata. His father did not have dreams of expansion or advancement or enterprise. He did not have dreams at all. Aged only thirty-five, he died from an indeterminate and undiagnosed illness. Only mother and son were left. The few distant relations left in the area had their own problems and having another two mouths to feed was not a commitment they wished to take on. It was then that his mother Asha decided to become a servant at the house of the local Bengali

Brahmin priest, superficially full of all those virtues—piety, charity, probity—that his caste were apparently blessed with. But in his eyes could be seen a hint of something less savoury; a compulsion to feel superior and the attendant need to belittle. Sachin, with his child's intuition, had him pegged from the start. Asha, with her judgement impaired by despair, by weariness, by the need for everything to be all right for once in her life, did not.

The priest himself was so impressed with Asha's dedication that he thought her and her son worthy of betterment. So he started to impart to them knowledge of philosophical, religious, and classical texts, emphasising the spiritual, the transcendental, the metaphysical. Both Asha and Sachin enjoyed these sessions, although Sachin had wondered, even then, whether giving his mother a pay rise might have been more of a boon. And despite Asha's gratitude that this man had deigned to elevate her, Sachin was always wary of the priest's manner: not warm and teacherly but conceited and overbearing. His real lesson seemed to be that he knew more than them and always would. But still, in a world that had so far proven to be quite heartless, this little display of benevolence, whatever the underlying instinct, was something that Sachin welcomed.

In fact, soon Sachin began to overtake his mother in the learning stakes. She was delighted. The priest seemed more circumspect. He started to test Sachin about what he had learned, asking questions which a scholar would find difficult let alone a young boy. If the priest wasn't willing him to fail, then he certainly wasn't willing him to succeed. But there was nothing Sachin liked more than a challenge. Determined and resourceful, he systematically set about keeping step with the priest. Yet the priest always seemed to stay ahead; and Sachin started to become disgruntled by his condescending laughs and dismissive head ruffles. Asha told Sachin not be so silly. How could he expect to know more than a priest? A priest! What she failed to understand was that it was the priest's attitude which Sachin objected to. As Asha had it, if the priest behaved like he was better than everyone else, it was because he *was* better than everyone else! But Sachin wasn't buying that. His mind raced trying to work out how he could outfox the man. Then, one day, it occurred to Sachin that this wasn't just a game of knowledge, it was a matter of tactics, too. If the priest was *so* knowledgeable, then he wouldn't mind answering a few questions himself.

Asha's face had been a picture when Sachin had stood in front of the priest one afternoon and suggested just this, her tongue out in shame, her eyebrows raised in shock, her eyes bright with excitement. My son is such a rascal! Sachin, say sorry! But the priest himself said that he would be happy to answer the boy's questions and Asha said no more, a hint of pleasure at her son's boldness pressed into her lips. Why don't we play for money, Sachin said. I give you ten rupees if you answer all the questions correctly, you give me ten if you don't. The priest shook with laughter. This boy is a hoot, but fine, ten rupees it is.

Sachin began, asking questions of such simplicity that the priest barely had to think before answering. The priest laughed a lot and shook his head at the boy's foolishness. It was only when the priest seemed to have almost lost interest that Sachin asked him, with no change of tone or pace: In which text had Kali first been written about in the way she is now understood? Easy, the Atharvaveda. Sachin, looking a little uncertain himself: Are you sure? Of course I'm sure! Sachin shook his head, a smirk on his face. Well, I don't think you're right. Of course, I am—Kali was first mentioned in the Atharvaveda. The Atharvaveda—that's your final answer, yes? Yes! Then I'm afraid you've made a mistake. The priest's eyes narrowed and his lips pursed. This one was a cheeky little bastard. Sachin didn't back down: In the way she is *now* understood—that is her present form as the warrior goddess of the battlefield who defeated the demons and drank their blood—that's in the Mahabharata.

The priest's nostrils flared: Well, I misunderstood your question, you should have put it better. Sachin shrugged lightly: If you weren't sure what I meant, why didn't you ask me? The priest, now on the verge of apoplexy, managed to rise: I have proper work to do now, I can't spend all day messing around. He turned around to walk back into the house.

What about my ten rupees, Sachin called out at a respectful level of sound, not shouting, but still with force. The priest turned on his heel. *What?* My ten rupees. The priest, a look of disgust on his face, flicked his hand, as if he was shooing away a mangy stray dog.

But you did agree to ten rupees, Sir. This was Asha, her head slightly bowed but her voice firm. The priest looked at her and shook his head with utter dismay. Then the vitriol came spewing out. You lot are all the same; always money, money, money. Money first, then everything else. So greedy that you don't have any respect even in a priest's house. You should be apologising for your son's behaviour, instead you're condoning it. I tried my best to educate you, to culture you, but your greed is in your blood. I've had my fill of your sort; don't bother coming back.

So there it was: *your sort.* After that, Sachin had limited his relationships with Bengalis. He was as wary of them as they were prejudiced about him. Of course, as his empire had grown he had employed them, but he had never allowed them into his inner circle—those positions were reserved for *his sort.* That was until Anil.

Sachin remembered quite clearly the first time he had met Anil and the first question he had asked, after noticing Anil's surname—Thakur—on his resume: So . . . you're a Bengali Brahmin? And

Anil's reaction: a furrowing of his brow and a slightly mystified laugh. Well, yes, I suppose I am but does anyone care about that kind of rubbish anymore? And immediately, Sachin had liked him.

How long ago was that? Five years ago? Almost six? It was only a few months after their initial meeting, Sachin remembered, that his and Anil's relationship had cemented.

Anil had invited him to a screening of a short film by Syan Gain, an old St. Xavier's classmate who had made quite a name for himself as a poet, musician, filmmaker, and general purpose *artiste*. Anil had told Sachin that he thought that Syan had turned into a bit of a pretentious dick who tended to strain for profundity, as if he had been constipated by all the accolades that he had been fed; Sachin had laughed uproariously at this. But, Anil had continued, he wanted to be supportive since Syan was not only a classmate but also an old family friend.

After the film—twenty minutes of a crow picking at various bits of litter in close-up followed by a single line of dialogue "We are all scavengers"—there had been a reception at which Anil had introduced him to Syan. Sachin had not really understood the meaning of the film—that is, if the film actually *had* any meaning—but, taking his cue from the other guests, he congratulated Syan on his philosophical musings about our place in the world. Yet, instead of simply accepting the compliment, Syan had eyed up Sachin, giving him a look of derision.

"I thought you were more about finance than philosophy, yah," he drawled. "What's the difference between a Mero and a crow? Meros have bigger beaks."

And despite his stature and wealth and success, Sachin had stood in that room of beautifully turned out, philosophical Bengalis and felt like an uneducated beggar. He said nothing because he didn't know what to say. It was Anil who replied, "Syan, I had the *suspicion* that you had turned into a *gudh* but you've just confirmed it. Who the hell do you think you are? You, a person who has been handed everything on a plate, talking down to a man who is nothing if not self-made. And what really bothers me is that you have no idea how superior this man is to you. So, fuck you. Fuck your superiority. And fuck your crow."

As Sachin lay reminiscing, one of his favourite guards came to the cell door and told him he had a visitor. "Isn't it a bit late?" Sachin asked.

The guard shrugged and smiled.

Sachin jumped up. "Well, let's go then!"

In the visitor's room sat Anil, entirely incongruous and film starry, with his stylish clothes and radiant complexion. As soon as Sachin entered the room, Anil rose and smiled.

"You're looking well, Sachin!"

"Not as well as you, boy!"

"It must be either very good news or very bad news for you to come this late at night."

Anil shrugged and raised an eyebrow.

"Actually, I was just on my way to a party."

"Full of pretty girls?"

"Chock-a-block."

Sachin chuckled.

"Anyway, that's the good news for *me*. There's also some good news for you . . ." Anil continued.

"Tell me."

"Well, we shouldn't have any problems with our next project. As soon as you're out of here, we'll be ready to go."

Sachin took some time to absorb this; he had been hoping for this news but in his current position had not dared to think that it might actually happen.

"And when will I be out of here?" Sachin asked, lowering his voice.

"Soon. I'm taking care of that."

From then on, Sachin did not lie in his cell and reminisce. Instead, he started to look forward and imagine again.

VI

Anima knew that it was the orbitofrontal cortex that controlled impulsivity. As the brain developed from back to front, this meant that until one's mid-twenties, a person could be more prone to acting without due consideration and choosing immediate satisfaction over long-term gratification; this kind of behaviour was mainly associated with adolescents. However, even as a teenager, Anima had not so much been able to control her impulses but rather that she had not been hit by them in the first place. Whilst her friends had been reckless and impetuous, she had always followed a more calculated course of action. It was rare that any particular act felt overwhelmingly magnetic; she always had to weigh up the pros and cons of each possibility.

Perhaps that was why, a couple of months on from finding the incriminating text, she had still failed to question her husband about it. All probable responses seemed too obvious for her, too straightforward, too expected. Considering that the cheating game had been going on since time immemorial, the reactions to it seemed to be pretty limited. Surely the free market should have provided some competition for the bitter, vengeful virago and the desperate, feeble pleader? And the two main questions she was continuously asking herself were: What was there to be gained from saying something and what would be lost if she didn't?

Frequently, she imagined the start of the conversation:

"I've seen the text, you know."

"What text?"

"You know the one."

"What are you talking about?"

"Oh come on!"

"Honestly, I don't know!"

"The text from the girl you're having an affair with!"

But she could never imagine the end. She sometimes remembered the first line of a book she'd read, 'Either forswear fucking others or the affair is over.' Perhaps she could adapt that to, 'Either forswear fucking others or the marriage is over.' Maybe that should be her opener, maybe *that* would enable her to imagine the end. The problem was that she wasn't even sure she wanted such a renouncement! A man in his autumn years feeling the sun on his face again; did she really need or want to deprive him of that? Yet at the same time she felt keenly that things could simply not go on as they were, that something needed to be done.

She tried throwing herself into her work but her bourgeois patients, with their average lives and their average concerns and their average illnesses, made her feel more restless than ever. In the past week, her most outstanding—and depressing—case had been a morbidly obese teenage girl with an addiction to Kentucky Fried Chicken. Although she had also taken a meeting with a young man called Anil Thakur on behalf of The Lohia Hospital. Very charming. Very impressive. Shrewd, too: This is an opportunity to do something very important for the place you love. How do you know I love this place? Why would you have come back if you didn't?

But the opportunity to head up a brand new world class neurological centre, as exciting as it was, seemed very far away, a pipe dream. When she returned home that evening, Anima felt weary again: I became a doctor to tell people the patently obvious—stop stuffing your face with junk! All the back-breaking training, all the brain-bending exams, all the feet-numbing operations for *this*?

Everything seemed to be an effort: taking off her shoes, removing her jacket, washing her hands. A sudden depression weighed down on her, causing her limbs to become heavy and immovable, when what she needed was to keep moving, keep doing, keep performing; anything but stopping and facing up to what a wreck her life was becoming.

She shuffled slowly through the large house, so ornate and grand, so gilded and oppressive, and made her way to the formal dining room; out of some spurious sense of politesse, they took dinner in there, even though there were only the two of them. Despite her lethargy, Anima decided to make an effort and recount to The Professor the travails of her week. He seemed quite interested, nodding along whilst he chomped, raising his eyebrows now and then. She lightly mentioned the possible opportunity at the renewed Lohia hospital. He lightly responded: That sounds interesting. But when Anima had finished speaking, instead of addressing her concerns and despair, he replied with a slightly mocking sigh, "So the overweight are beneath you?"

Beneath me, Anima thought, *beneath me*! And what about what's beneath *you*—a girl young enough to be your *daughter*!

She took a large gulp of her gin and tonic and gazed at his

supercilious mug. In that moment, she despised him. His effortless condescension. His glib irony. His fluency in picking up on every tiny thing, things that could have been overlooked with just a little generosity of spirit, or a sense perhaps of, if not love, then of their lives having been spent more together than apart! But The Professor seemed to feel no sense of obligation towards anything but his own conceit.

"What do *you* think?" he continued, "Don't you think the increasing number of overweight children in this country is a serious public health problem which requires due consideration?"

I think you're a monkey—and that's an insult to apes, Anima wanted to say.

"Why does it matter what I think?" she shrugged. "You seem to have it all worked out yourself."

"Oh come now, it's not like you to take offence—answer the question," The Professor prodded, still smiling.

Anima stared at him. She was not smiling at all.

"It might be a serious public health problem, but, quite frankly, it's not mine—I have other problems to deal with. Like the one sitting across the table from me."

Wow, Anima thought, that just slipped out and nothing ever slips out of me! Maybe it's the heavy G!

The Professor was no longer smiling. Despite all of his little provocations, he had never been spoken to like this before. He fiddled with his food. A servant had appeared in the doorway holding a tray with dessert; the strained atmosphere held her in her place.

"Well, what are you just standing there for?" The Professor huffed in Bengali.

Timidly, the servant walked in and placed bowls of rice pudding in front of them.

"How many times have I told you I don't like rice pudding!"

The servant looked down at her feet.

"No need to take it out on her," Anima admonished him. "*She*'s not the problem."

Vaguely pleased that the servant had witnessed another, less agreeable side to The Professor, Anima squeezed her arm and smiled again.

"Have your own dinner now," she said.

The servant dithered.

"Everything's fine. We're done for tonight," Anima insisted, her comment as much directed at The Professor as at the servant.

After finishing dinner in silence, The Professor and Anima retired to separate rooms; he to the library, she to the drawing room. That was what money brought you, she thought—exemption from another's company. But when had that happened? The *wanting* to be apart from him? It could only have been since the text. Before that, they had not only sat in the same room in the evening after dinner, but even on the same sofa, with her frequently resting her feet on his lap. Sometimes, he would absentmindedly stroke or massage them whilst he read a book or watched TV. And years, years back, before Avik, sometimes they had even just retired to their bedroom straight after dinner! Now just the thought of him touching her made her skin crawl.

She lay down on the sofa, stretched her legs, and propped up her head on some cushions. She wondered what her husband was thinking. She knew that he had realised that something had changed in her, something irreversible, but did he know why? Did he even care why?

Suddenly, she jumped to her feet. Within minutes, she had called her driver and arranged for him to come over and pick her up.

As Anima waited for him outside the house, she smoked. Ever since that night, when she had filched a cigarette from the driver's stash, she had taken up the habit in earnest again. She smoked every day without fail. It now occurred to her that The Professor had not so much as mentioned this new addiction; although she didn't smoke right in front of him surely he had smelt the smoke on her? Maybe the only thing he was now interested in smelling was his new girlfriend's pussy. Or maybe the aroma of that was so pungent, it just superseded all other smells. That thought made Anima chuckle. Sometimes, it was very satisfying, despite her maturity and her sophistication and her poise, to be mean and petty and crude.

The driver, looking a little dishevelled, opened the back door of the car for Anima. She sensed from the way his shirt was half hanging out that she had interrupted him either having dinner or having sex.

"I hope I didn't disturb you," she apologised as she slid into the seat. "Have you finished your dinner?"

The driver smiled and cocked his head.

"It's absolutely fine, Madam," he said, amiably. "My wife's cooking is really bad. Now I can get a *kati* roll or something whilst I'm out!"

Anima laughed.

The driver was still holding the door open and looking towards the house.

"The Professor isn't coming," Anima said, "it's just me."

The driver couldn't hide his surprise; it was rare for a woman to go out on her own at this time. Even if she was a woman who could take care of herself better than any man ever could.

"You are going to a friend's house?" he asked.

"No."

"Then you are meeting a friend somewhere?"

"No."

The driver had run out of possibilities; he couldn't compute that she might be going somewhere on her own. Where did *anyone* ever go alone? He had three people living in one room; he could barely go to the toilet alone. He racked his brain: maybe she was going to the temple for some solitary contemplation? No, she wasn't the religious sort. He was all out.

"Where I am taking you, Madam?"

"To Kentucky Fried Chicken—you might know it as KFC."

Anima had never liked fast food and had indeed never set foot inside a fast food restaurant, even when her son Avik had been a child. As she sat at a plastic-topped table, she imagined what he might think if he could see her now. It wasn't inconceivable that he might think she was having some sort of nervous breakdown. Maybe she was. She hadn't told him anything about the text and the events of the past few months because how could she possibly articulate what was going on. *Darling, your dad and I have been drifting apart. Oh, and he's probably having an affair.* Even though Avik was now a grown man with his own life, she still felt the need to protect him. Besides, what was he going to do from eight thousand miles away in New York? And he had his own life to contend with. Not that she didn't long to see him. She remembered the days when, as a young child, he would crawl into bed with her and cling to her as if his life depended on it. Those days were gone. Sitting on a moulded plastic seat, under the glare of the harsh lights, Anima felt unbearably sad.

She sat for a few moments longer and then realised that she had to go to the counter to order. She was quite sure that the server had given her a funny look, maybe thinking that she looked out of place.

Once again seated at the plastic-topped table, she investigated what she had ordered by pulling it apart and then putting it back together again. She took a bite; it was actually very tasty. She laughed to herself. Other women her age were taking up hobbies like salsa dancing or painting or yoga. She was taking up junk food.

Again, she thought of Avik. She would have liked to share this moment with him, the absurdity of it. He had always enjoyed the absurd. The Professor, on the other hand, would have not been so amused. He would have found something clever to say and cleverness was the antithesis of absurdity.

Thoughts of escape, of reinvention, of reinvigoration and renewal flooded her brain. But where would she go? She had already decided that she could not go back to London. That part of her life was over and she could not revisit it. What about going to New York to be with Avik? She suddenly felt very possessive of him; he was no longer their son but hers alone. She wanted to go back to the days where he was in her womb, and it was the two of them as one. He grew in me, he's mine, she thought. Then a grotesque possibility hit her. What if The Professor had a child with his new woman? Then Avik would have a half-sibling. A lesser-sibling. She shuddered; don't go there. Besides, she didn't want to impose or impinge on Avik, add a dimension to his life that he had not envisaged. She would not lean on him. She would not relinquish her maternal power and become the child. Or maybe could not. Either way her strength had to come from within.

Just as she firmly told herself that she could not be the child, her heart was pierced with the fervent wish to be a child again. She wanted to go back to the time before duty, obligation, commitment, responsibility. Before she had even understood what those things were. Specifically, she thought of her childhood summers spent in her uncle's house in Balachuria. When her life was dictated by whether the weather was pleasant enough to play outside and all that the world required from her was a smile and the simplest of good manners. When she had been a little noble savage, spending time scratching patterns into the dirt with a stick, clanging together pots and pans, quacking at the ducks in the pond, marvelling at fireflies, inspecting the crap that was trapped under her finger nails. Oh happy days!

Was that house even there still? Did she have photos of it somewhere? When exactly had her family left it, never to return? She tried to take herself back in time, but all she could remember were certain snapshots. A suitcase being hastily pulled from under a bed, and dust filling the air. Lying in bed late at night, hearing her parents arguing in the bedroom next door. Her elder brother Pusan clambering up a Banyan tree and refusing to come down. Finding their white pet cat lying lifeless under a milkweed bush, blood coming out of its mouth. A peacock screeching from the roof. Yet she struggled to recall the narrative structure which accompanied these images. She knew why they had left: The Naxalites. But she knew this after the fact. Had she seen men with guns? Or had she just heard them talked about? It was as if there was a scar on her knee but she couldn't quite work out how it had come to be there. There was no one to ask now either; both her parents, her brother, and her uncle were deceased. Other relatives were long lost. This in itself gave those days some sort of mythic quality, the myth being built on the most innocuous but visceral of reminiscences—the smell of wet greenery after heavy rain; a man climbing up a coconut tree; a woman standing in the sunshine and washing herself using a water pump; a large, striped spider sitting high up on the wall of the latrine. She wanted to see and feel all of these things again. The closest there was to going back in time.

Anima returned to the car with a Potato Krisper, a packet of fries, and a Mango Burst for her driver, which he took, surprised and grateful. He hadn't eaten anything from KFC before but he was eager to try something new. After taking a quick look inside it, he carefully put it in the footwell, giving Anima another smile. She told him to eat it whilst it was hot; she wanted to take a walk. At this time, on your own? At this time. On my own.

Soon, she was standing outside The Grand, the fronds of the tall palm trees at the entrance swaying in the light breeze. Her wedding reception to The Professor had been held here. Six months after they had met—reaching for the same book, *Aranyak* by Bibhutibhushan Bandopadhyay, in a College Street bookshop—they had married. What was it called in those days? A *love marriage*. Maybe it was still called that in this part of the world. And the occasion had been perfect. No ominous signs. No telling glitches in behaviour. No doubts. No fears.

Not everything was foreseeable.

She went in. Took a seat at the table by the outdoor swimming pool. Ordered a single malt whisky. No funny look from the waiter.

She sipped her drink, slowly.

In their late middle age, she and The Professor had become people of minor qualities. Quite considerate, reasonably tolerant, generally well mannered, occasionally entertaining. In other words, they had acquired, through social osmosis and the passage of time, the quality of keeping up appearances. What else was left to them? Wasn't that life after all—half performance and half appearance? If you could just muster up enough energy to show up, you were still doing better than the billions already departed. Heart pumping, blood flowing, brain, if not quite *working*, then at least not completely dead—that was living. I'm still here! Wasn't that enough?

No, no, no, thought Anima. I'm not giving up. Not yet.

VII

Kolkata *may be bankrupt financially, but culturally, spiritually, emotionally, artistically, philosophically, ethically, and politically, her coffers are full!*

No, no, no, thought Devi. I can't say this. As artistic and profound as it sounded, it would not play well to a group of businessmen with whom she wanted to do business. What had she been advised? That she had to give confidence to investors. That before they got into bed with her, they had to trust her. That if she wanted to see the money pour in, she would have to show herself to be deserving of it, and that meant more method and less madness. More consideration, less rashness. (She had summarily dismissed the man who had given this advice soon after; the unnecessarily sexual get-into-bed idiom had sealed his fate.) And she really needed the money. And everyone knew she really needed the money, too. She sighed. She would have to put away her little composition and use it on another, more fitting, occasion.

Kolkata may have a chequered past, but with your help, her future will be glorious!

Hmmm. Maybe it was unwise to mention the past, especially when it was less than effulgent. And did the past even matter? Her enemies were always dragging hers up. Fine, so her family hadn't actually moved from East to West Bengal during Partition, and she hadn't actually been born in a fetid government-run refugee camp. (This one was figured out pretty quickly; for a start, if she had really been born during Partition then she would be ten years older than she claimed.) But she *understood* those sorry migrants, she *felt* their burden, she *sensed* their loss—because what was her early life if not one of instability and burden and loss! In spirit, if not in time, they were one! And then there was the issue with the school improvement project where the schools weren't, well, improved, and yet the money had been paid out to all and sundry for work not actually done. Fine; maybe she was account*able*, but she wasn't an account*ant*! Although maybe she didn't need the businessmen to be reminded of that fact either. Those kinds of people could be sticklers for details whereas she was more of a big picture person. A more symbolic person. A more metaphorical person. Her problem was that people could be so very literal sometimes!

She closed her eyes and leant back in her chair. She had another headache. They were becoming more frequent. She wanted to go to sleep. But first, she had to get this right. It could not appear that she was doing a U-turn, the most frowned upon of manoeuvres in the political arena. So what if only a few years ago she had camped outside The Grand Hotel to protest against a foreign firm's investment in some road-building project? That firm had been shady and underhand and in the pockets of the last government. She wanted to do business with good, clean American businessmen! People who appreciated her passion and her commitment and her unimpeachable mission to once again restore her Paschim Banga to its distant former glory!

As a girl, she had never once either thought or dreamt that this Herculean calling would be hers. From a lower middle class family, albeit a well-respected and valued part of the local community, her childhood days had soon been filled with the responsibilities of an adult due to the early death of both her father and her mother. Sure, her extended family had given her a monthly handout and a few of the neighbours had checked in on her but from then, her life had been filled with looking after her brother. For her, it had not been the innocence of childhood that had been taken away, but the carefreeness and the care*less*ness. No time to just see, to just feel, to just be. Nothing was just because. Everything was part of a greater mission. If she picked up a mango, she could not simply appreciate its velvety skin and its mouth-watering aroma, she had to figure out how soon it might go off and if there was a cheaper, larger mango at another stall. Enjoying the little things in life? There were no little things in her life! Purpose had been given to her heart, responsibility had been thrust upon her shoulders, determination had been ground into her bones. She had come early to the battle that is life. And unlike her peers who had two whole and functioning parents, her journey through childhood was not one of discovery, either of her surroundings or herself. Everything was clear to her from the start. It had to be. Ambiguity was a trap. Doubt was a trap. Indecision was a trap. She didn't have to run before she learned to walk—she had to fly!

The Future of Bengal is Bright!

Much brighter than she had ever expected hers to be. All she had imagined for herself was being her brother's provider and protector. And that was what her brother had expected, too. That was what everyone had expected! She had never been primed and pegged for greatness—unlike that indulged Mrs. Gandhi, who had stood on the shoulders of her father, the man who made modern India, the man who *was* modern India! No, she hadn't stood on anyone's shoulders mainly because there had been no one's shoulders for her to stand on! Both of her feet were—and always had been—firmly on the dirty ground. She was a grafter, that was for sure, but since when had hard graft been the basis of success in India? The home of good luck, bad karma, and dynastic indulgence. The place where everyone knew his or her place to the tenth of a millimetre. Granted, there was one similarity between her background and Mrs. Gandhi's—neither of them had been mothered. But that's where it started and stopped. Indeed, Devi prided herself on being *of* the people instead of just *for* them, unlike Mrs. Gandhi and all her supercilious ilk. Those sort of politicians were all in it for themselves whilst claiming to be anything but. Taking advantage of the public, by any means possible, be it sycophancy or treachery or just outright tyranny. Bastards of a feather! She alone—humble, truthful, virtuous—stood apart. Only *she* wanted to give the advantage to the common man, to give all the power to the people!

All Power to the People!

There was a diffident knock on her door. Devi checked her watch, an old Seiko, with a battered leather strap and a slightly scratched bezel and face. Another advisor had once suggested that she might want to, if not upgrade, then at least buy a new one, but why should she have? It still told the time correctly and that's what it was for—telling the time. No need for unnecessary extravagance. Extravagance was a kick in the teeth to the people who had little if not nothing. Her people! Style, glamour, grooming, it was all part of the same flippancy.

Nine. The conference would start in a couple of hours. And with the traffic, another problem for her to overcome, she would have to leave soon. She needed to be left alone to finish working on her speech. There was another knock.

"Come, come," she said quickly.

It was Nigel Gidney, her chief press officer, speech-adjustment aide and general sidekick. Nigel seemed to have a faint mark of something pink and chalky around his large mouth. Combined with his large nose and doleful eyes, there was something of the sad clown about him. He looked like he could be the proprietor of an old-fashioned hill town guesthouse, one that still served afternoon tea, and gin and tonics on the lawn in the summer months—the kind of place where his paternal grandfather, an English tea plantation manager, had met his grandmother, an Indian primary school teacher.

"Your stomach is still giving you trouble?" she asked with concern.

Nigel quickly rubbed at his mouth and made a gesture with his head which could have meant yes, no, or it doesn't matter either way.

"Simple diet. That is what you are needing," Devi advised, "like me."

A simple *life* is what I need, thought Nigel. Not a stressful one that involves needling and wheedling and coaxing and cajoling a woman into saying words which she has not personally conceived of. Then immediately, he felt shoddy for thinking this. She was a good woman with a good heart; which other great leader would have asked after his indigestion, even if, unknown to her, she had caused it in the first place. Besides, being fond of one's own ideas, perhaps sometimes unhealthily attached to them, even if they were wrong, was hardly an unusual trait, especially in a politician. And she had to have said the right thing at the right time and in the right way at some point because her listeners had voted her into power! He smiled graciously.

"Would you like me to read through your speech—I'm sure

it's perfect—but just in case . . ." He stopped. He couldn't think just in case *what* exactly. But better an incomplete sentence than a complete and completely foolish one. Devi frowned. Nigel twitched. Please don't ask me just in case what. Please. He needed another glug of Gelusil; since Devi had come into power, a lot of her staff were going hard on the pink stuff.

"Yes, you please be taking a read," Devi replied after a moment. "It is nearly done, I am just having to finish my closing paragraph." She held out a piece of paper. Quickly, Nigel took it with an almost apologetic smile.

The effort of trying to maintain that smile—with Devi's gaze firmly upon him—as he read through the speech, left Nigel in desperate need of somewhere to plonk his bony brown arse, but he knew that it was imperative to keep standing lest he sat down and never found the strength to rise again. He thought about clearing his throat, a gentle signal that what might come out of his mouth could perhaps be taken as criticism, albeit the mildest criticism of the most constructive sort, but he had learned from the past that Devi didn't really pick up on hints. If he cleared his throat, she would most likely offer him a menthol lozenge. Before he had a chance to speak though, she exclaimed, happily, "All power to the people! You are liking it?"

Huh?

"Yes . . .?" he replied, uncertainly, adding very, very tentatively, "But it's what the Black Panthers used to say. And I don't think a group of American businessmen particularly want to be reminded of that era in their history?"

Devi squinted at him as if she didn't understand what he was driving at.

"Also," he added, "it's what the People's Party of Pakistan use as their motto, and I don't think a group of American businessmen want to be reminded about Pakistan either."

Pakistan. Now her expression changed to a more open, thoughtful one. Pakistan, she understood. Pakistan was something all Indians understood.

Meanwhile, Nigel was thinking, too. He was thinking that he had absolutely no idea what any of this 'All Power to the People' had to do with encouraging a bunch of Americans to invest in West Bengal. The problem with Devi was that she was so prone to tangentialism, as Nigel liked to think of it. Stick to the brief? She couldn't be expected to stick to the brief. She was an artist! Artists and their bloody bullshit, it was the same the world over.

"Then what?" she finally said, her timbre ominous. Nigel receded into himself slightly. Sometimes Devi asking a question was far, far more dangerous than her giving an answer.

Then what? Well eventually, the sun will burn so brightly and give off so much heat that the oceans will boil and the ice caps will permanently melt and snow will disappear and life will be unable to survive anywhere on the surface of the earth, including in this room. That's what, Nigel thought, although he did not say this.

"What do you mean, Devi, by *then what*?" Answer a question with a question, buy myself some time, he decided.

"I am meaning," Devi replied, huffily, "what is the slogan?"

Nigel recognised a challenge when one was spat out at him. Tackle it head on? What, are you kidding? Avoid, avoid, avoid. Better to be a chicken than headless.

"I like the one you already came up with: Bengal Means Business!" he replied with as much enthusiasm and flattery as he could muster whilst his virility ebbed away. Who cared, there wasn't that much of it left anyway and besides, big balls were overrated. Ball-ache, meanwhile, was not to be underestimated.

"No, I am wanting a new one."

"Why?" The word slipped out of him like an unexpected fart. Quickly, he tried to cover it up by adding, "I mean, you cannot improve on perfection, can you?"

Devi looked into the mid-distance contemplating the linguistic and metaphysical possibility of improving upon perfection. Then nodded her head to the right and to the left, as if she had water in her ears.

"OK then," she conceded. "Everything else is alright, yes?" This in a tone that suggested that everything else *better* be all right.

Rock. Hard place. Nigel had already managed to push his luck through this smallest of gaps and was reluctant to try again. Yet some sense—of what? Integrity? Professionalism? Idiocy?—made him itch. And it was an itch that needed to be scratched.

"Well," he began, nervous, "I'm not sure of this bit about London . . ."

Devi frowned. That was one of her favourite bits. Kolkata *was* going to be the next London, so what was the problem with saying so? No need to be coy!

"What I mean is that I'm not entirely sure that using London as an example of a model city would necessarily endear you to a group of *Am-eri-cans*?"

Devi looked at Nigel, nonplussed.

"So perhaps we should use an American city instead?" he suggested.

Quickly, he tried to think of which city. Los Angeles—movies—Mumbai. Washington—government—Delhi. San Francisco—tech—Bangalore. All the good cities were taken up! Oh no, hang on one minute, what about New York, the ultimate metropolis!

"What about New York?"

"I am not liking New York. It is full of *aushobo* people."

That's how bad New Yorkers were. Devi couldn't even find an English word to describe them. Instead, she had used aushobo:

discourteous, rude, not so much misbehaved as *un*behaved. Not the kind of people you'd introduce to your parents, Nigel imagined. Although, of course, being New Yorkers, they wouldn't even *want* to meet your parents, as they'd have better, more important things to do. Nigel chewed on his lip. Maybe Devi had a point.

"What about Chicago?" he suggested. "That's where the President is from."

Devi pretended to mull this over although Nigel had had her at the P word.

"There is a river there? With a promenade? And somewhere for the people to be sitting-relaxing after working hard?" It was important to Devi that the people were able to sit and relax after a long day on the job, she was thoughtful like that. And if she had been the chief minister of Chicago, sure, it would have been a nice sentiment. But in Kolkata? Bengalis were famously averse to long working days. No two-hour lunch? What were they? Robots? Working hard was pretty much an affront to their humanity! These people need don't need more places to put their arses, they need to get up off them, Nigel thought. And to whom was she going to be telling all this sitting-relaxing stuff? He was suddenly quite annoyed at her guilelessness. Did she really think that some rich American executive was bothered about *sitting-relaxing* on the banks of the Hooghly river, eating a Kwality ice cream whilst watching the assorted crap float by? Keep calm, he told himself, be sensible, remain unequivocal.

"Chicago has everything, Devi," he replied, warmly and evenly, after a moment, "as will Kolkata."

After Nigel had left to gather his belongings, Devi took out her dolls. She seated all the Kens in neat rows (imagining them now as original American Kens) and then had Barbie stand on a book so that she could look down on them. She manipulated Barbie's arms into forceful, sweeping gestures, after which she made a number of Kens clap their hands together. Yes, the American boys would be amazed by her, she was sure of it.

In the car on the way to the conference venue in Salt Lake City, Nigel started thinking. Why do we have to aspire to be like another city? Why can't we just be ourselves, but the best version of ourselves? And why do I sound like I'm writing a twelfth standard politics essay at one of the more progressive schools which are popping up all over the place to cater mainly for the offspring of expats and the more enlightened middle classes? To his annoyance, the words started to swim in his head. *Why can't we just be ourselves, but the best version of ourselves?* They could have been the lyrics to a silly pop song. But there was something in them that made him purse his lips as he looked through the window at the fading colonial architecture of central Kolkata, streets and streets of beautiful Victorian buildings, now with their stucco work dirty and cracked and their paint faded and chipped. If the streets had been empty, they would have looked hauntingly beautiful, but Kolkata streets were never empty. Instead, with the animated peddlers and the brightly coloured fly-posters and the jostling pedestrians, they quietly faded into the background, consigned to the past. What was needed, Nigel thought, was a sympathetic restoration, a sensitive rehabilitation. Embrace the new but cherish the old! Respect history!

Whereas an hour ago, he had been all for pandering to and flattering the Americans, he now felt quite apprehensive about them. What did they know about Kolkata's past? More importantly, what did they care? He wished he hadn't said anything about Chicago. He wished he had had the guts to say that Kolkata should march to the beat of her own drum, however syncopated the rhythm. He no longer felt unequivocal about anything, he felt completely and utterly muddled. He thought again about his daughter. What kind of upbringing did he want her to have? One full of shopping malls and fast food and me me me? Now I'm being clichéd and silly, he told himself. But am I? *Am I?* Over the last decade he had noticed how the younger generation had started to speak English (Land of The Free) and not English (Land of The Queen). *What's up with the state of that restroom, dude? It's major league scuzzy!* Such satisfaction in managing to shake off the imperialism of one foreign culture only to willingly submit to another—do the math! And, according to a certain newspaper article he had recently read, although there had been a time when the American adaptation of the language had been infra dig, now it was becoming de facto. Well, at least Latin was still well if not quite alive.

"Devi . . ." he said tentatively.

"Yes?" she asked. In her current presentation, the sunlight on her face, the gentle breeze blowing through the car window causing strands of hair at her temples to flutter, she seemed quite serene and approachable. He was reminded of a photo of a black Labrador that had belonged to a minister in the past administration. The dog was famous for enjoying rides in the back of his master's chauffeured car, head tilted back, eyes half-shut, the wind blowing through his fur. It had been said that the dog was better fed than half the city's human inhabitants; his preference was for pork sausages from a shop in New Market. Devi, though, was a strict vegetarian. Meat, she said, was difficult to digest.

"I'm worried about the Americans . . ." Nigel said. He didn't need to elaborate further. Devi knew what he meant.

"Lots of people are worrying about the Americans," Devi replied, "but they are doing what I am wanting, I am not doing what they are wanting."

So that was that. Thank god for Devi and her certainty! Nigel's sense of relief was palpable.

They were now approaching Salt Lake City. Nothing at all to do with its namesake in Utah, it was built in the 1960s. It was a planned satellite town, conceived of to be home to Kolkata's business district, and backed by the chief minister at that time, Dr. Bidhan Chandra Roy. He was a man who had united Bengalis as much as Devi now divided them. A man who was to temperance what Devi was to temper. One of the only similarities between them was that neither of them had married. Nigel had heard the joke before that Dr. Roy (tall and incredibly handsome) hadn't married because so many women were in love with him that he couldn't choose, whereas Devi (short and not incredibly handsome), hadn't married because no men were in love with her to choose from. People could be so cruel. He very much hoped that Devi had never heard the joke. After all, underneath the thick skin, she was a woman, and a woman with feelings.

"All of this coming from nothing!" Devi exclaimed. "If Dr. Roy was able to do it, then I am able to do it, too!"

Although she didn't say so, she was secretly hoping that there would soon be a place named after her, in the same way that Salt Lake City was also known as Bidhannagar in Dr. Roy's honour. After all, she had taken it upon herself to rename streets after legendary personalities. And wasn't she the most legendary personality of all? She mulled over a few names in her mind and struck upon *Paramitapara.* Somewhere with lots of greenery and places to sit and relax. Perhaps to even meditate upon the life and teachings of the great Devi. Her vision was at once epic and idyllic. Well, I am a poet after all, she mused.

"You can definitely do it, Devi!" Nigel agreed. The 'from nothing' bit, though, he was less sure about. After all, the area had hardly been a wasteland. Indeed, the salt lake had been a very fertile fishing territory, full of catla and mrigal. So, not really *nothing*. But he didn't correct her.

Now, the gleaming new sci-fi buildings of Sector Five, glass and metal, came into view. Everything here appeared cleaner, crisper, more robust, the architectural equivalent of a good, firm handshake. It was a place that looked like it meant business. Devi started nodding to herself as they drove past the impressive edifices, home to a host of IT companies.

"It is good that the Americans are seeing this," she nodded, satisfied, "so that they are not underestimating us."

"We must not be underestimated!" Nigel agreed, his conviction belying his weedy frame.

"We are having great potential," she said solemnly. "We must be harnessing it!"

"We must harness our potential!" Nigel vowed.

"We must be showing the world that we are meaning what we are saying."

"We say what we mean and we mean what we say!"

"We are capable of achieving great things!"

"*Great* things . . ."

By now, Nigel was getting a little tired of all the fire-in-the-belly talk. He could almost feel the heat coming off her. Save it for later, he thought, I'm paid to be on your side, it's the Americans you need to convince!

"We must be resisting all obstructions . . ." she concluded, dropping her voice slightly.

"All obstructions must be resisted," Nigel confirmed, although his stiff, stilted tone had something of a 1980s robot about it.

But just as soon as the words had left his mouth, he chastised himself for being scornful of a leader who was so sincerely enthusiastic. What would he have preferred? Someone jaded, cynical, lukewarm? One of those out-of-touch elites who patted themselves on the back for doing the bare minimum, who had clocked off the job pretty much as soon as they'd got their foot in the door? And at least Devi never just went through the motions. She was motion itself!

And now it came into view: the site of the old Lohia hospital. There were materials and machinery everywhere—sacks of sand, cement, mortar, large blocks of concrete, ceramic tiles, copper and plastic pipes, pneumatic drills, angle grinders, impact wrenches. Then there was the everyday stuff: buckets, spades, hoses. It was a colony of activity, with groups of workers performing their jobs assiduously as ants. A man in sturdy shoes, a hardhat and a high visibility jacket, could be seen wandering about with a clipboard. Compared to many other building sites in the city that were filled with lungi-wearing hod-carriers, and scrawny men wearing flip-flops, dangling from shaky scaffolding and holding cables between their teeth, it looked like a model of health and safety; the scene could have been photographed for a glossy brochure for a construction firm.

Nigel knew what Devi's reaction would be and tried to pre-empt any blast, the power of which would probably shake the foundations of the nearby buildings.

"There was no misdeed or negligence on their part, Devi. In fact, as you might have read in the report, well . . ." he swallowed.

Her whole face was puckering. He needed to say something to straighten it out again before the wind changed and it stayed that way. Abruptly, he wondered whether she might be a good candidate for Botox. If she couldn't look angry, then maybe she wouldn't be able to *be* angry.

"It was investigated thoroughly and properly, and there was no evidence which allowed us to bring a case of culpable homicide . . ."

Devi had now stopped looking at the hospital and was instead glaring at her feet. Nigel could see the vein in her temple throbbing. He felt quite sick.

"So we weren't able to revoke the hospital's license . . ."

As it had turned out, the law had decided that, in opposition to

Devi's pronouncement, the directors of the hospital were neither terrorists nor murderers. They could carry on business as usual. She knew all of this already; she had been informed of it only a few days before. Nigel simply thought that if it was repeated enough times, she might, *might* accept it. Although if her wrathful expression was anything to go by, he doubted it. In the pit of his stomach, he sensed that the Lohia saga was going to go on and on and on . . .

The conference centre had been set up well, with a proper reception area where passes were checked, albeit in a somewhat haphazard fashion. To each side of the double doors leading into the main auditorium were large floral arrangements—gladioli, roses, lilies—with tinselly accents in the standard matrimonial style; well, in a sense, the Indians were looking to marry the Americans. In the corner, the floor-polishing machine had been abandoned; no one seemed to know where it should go. Nearby, on a table covered with a patterned silk cloth were neatly laid out colour booklets about West Bengal and Kolkata. The first page was a timetable of speeches, the rest of it half informational, half advertising. The print was a tiny bit fuzzy and the graphics rather childish, giving them a homemade quality. Amongst the promotions were a good few for goldsmiths; the hope was that the American men would take home gifts of jewellery for their wives and girlfriends. Around the edge of the reception were easels holding large photos of Kolkata monuments: the Gothic National Assurance building, the Neoclassical Raj Bhavan, the Gothic Writers' Building, the Corinthian Metcalfe Hall, the Neo-Mughal Victoria Memorial Hall, the Victorian Central Telegraph Office, and the Baroque Metropolitan Building. The facades of the buildings all looked extremely clean, not grey and smog-marked; the images must have been touched up. Neither were any people visible in them; the photographer was clearly not from the school of social realism. Indeed, if the photos were considered outside their context, it would seem to the viewer that they were in a refined and elegant European city. It was not clear whether this was the intention.

Furthermore, the air conditioning was on high, there were refrigerated bottles of water available, and the signs for the toilets (which had been cleaned once and then cleaned again) were clearly marked. Whatever else happened, the Americans would be cool, refreshed, and not bursting for a wee.

After the obsequious introductory remarks from the Mayor ("This is the only woman who can lead us all into a great future!") in which he would have deified Devi there and then if only he could have, came the speeches of the various ministers, all of whom were formally and comprehensively introduced, including the nitty-gritty of their education—doctorates and Master of Sciences galore. Urban Development; Power and Non Conventional Energy Sources; Commerce and Industries; Industrial Reconstruction; Information Technology; Labour; Science and Technology; Technical Education and Training; Public Enterprise; Backward Classes. Each ministry wanted their time in the spotlight. And as some of the ministers had more than one portfolio, there was an odd situation in which the same minister would have to be reintroduced for his different position ("And next we have Sri Rajiv Deb. Again."), at which point he would give a slightly different version of the speech he had given already. Some ministers, those who understood relevance and appropriateness, were better orators than others. None of them understood succinctness. There were plenty of stifled yawns, and not just from the Americans. Nigel, with Devi's handbag nestled in his lap, looked around and noticed a few flagging eyelids. There might even have been some light snoring. He worried that by the time Devi—the metaphorical fat lady—came on, everyone would be either tired or hungry and would pay little attention. But when her time did come, Nigel wished it hadn't.

She started off well, following her written speech quite closely. There was an encouraging geopolitical prediction about West Bengal being the hub that would join up East, South, and Central Asia, followed by some highlights of the local economy in appropriately puffed up language: readily available and flexible labour, unaddressed market needs, underutilised manufacturing capacity, and so on. This was language that the Americans understood; Nigel looked around and saw a few nodding heads. He allowed himself to relax a little.

Next, she spoke about Chicago. More nodding heads. Even some wide grins. Maybe it was a good idea, after all, Nigel thought. Well, flattery often was. And then, out of nowhere, a man stood up and bellowed, "Are you going to allow the Americans to be the next East India Company?"

Nigel's head shot around; what on earth? The man was old, short, white-haired, and wearing a stripy short-sleeved shirt. Those bloody pass-checkers. If they had been paying some attention, he wouldn't even have made it in! There was silence. Even better to hear his next question, "Are you going to allow them to rape and pillage our land? Are we going to be slaves again?"

Dear God, would someone just shut him up, Nigel thought. But no one did anything apart from look at the man with slack-jawed wonderment and in the case of some of the Americans, bemusement.

"Do you even know that the Black Hole of Calcutta was an imperialist lie? I've measured it myself, there is no way that one hundred and forty-six people could fit in that amount of space!"

Now, Nigel, running on horror and adrenaline, got out of his seat, scrambled to where the man was standing, then realising that he had never once in his life been involved in a physical skirmish and didn't actually know what to do with his hands, instead swung into the man's stomach with Devi's handbag, the only weapon he had. The man immediately fell to the floor and then the security guards were on him, dragging him away.

But what came next was worse. Just laugh it off and move on, Nigel thought desperately, picking up a few items that had fallen out of Devi's handbag—a comb, some papers, some mints. But Devi was in no mood to move on. She was amongst friends now—she seemed to have taken to the American boys—and she wanted to talk about what had just happened.

"That was a communist infiltrator!" she declared.

Nigel nearly collapsed right in the aisle.

Americans were likely to spontaneously combust from moral outrage if they heard the c-word. Even a hint that the communists might cause trouble would cause trouble. Why even mention that there were communists in, oh, a thousand mile radius? How far away was Vietnam from America and look what had happened there!

"That's what the communists are good at—trying to drag us backwards again! They are wanting to destroy my mission!"

Not even one communist then, but a whole bunch of them, Nigel thought. If only he could knock Devi over the head with her handbag!

"But I am knowing how to deal with them . . ." Devi reassured her audience.

She had completely lost her flow now, though, and had to rifle through her notes.

"Um," she said, "Er . . ."

The ministers were all looking at each other, and some were whispering roughly about what should be done. Voices were raised as disagreements abounded—the stingless drones were arguing about how to save the queen bee. Devi stood alone at the podium, isolated, harassed, enraged. What had started out, if not exactly slick, then at least reasonably professional, was now a shambles. The Americans were glancing at each other. Nigel, now running on pure shame, walked up to the podium, gently nudged Devi to the side and announced that it was time for lunch. As the words floated out of him, he felt like they were someone else's.

And. Still. It. Wasn't. Over.

As Nigel had bypassed both the rest of Devi's speech and the subsequent question and answer session, lunch still wasn't quite ready; food poisoning from undercooked chicken wasn't an option anyone wished to pursue. Instead, hastily arranged cool drinks were served in the reception. The ministers and various other civil servants and flunkeys did their best to mingle with the Americans and appear as on-the-ball and polished as possible, light-heartedly laughing off the case of the madman (better mad than a communist) and talking up their hometown as best they could in loose terms—special, distinctive, unique—which couldn't be queried.

Meanwhile, Nigel and the mayor tended to Devi in a small private room at the rear of the venue. The mayor, as ingratiating as ever, suggested that Devi give her full, unabridged speech *after* lunch. Shut up, you moron, Nigel thought. Devi, on the other hand, was in fighting mode.

"I am wanting to know who that man is!" she said viciously. "I am going to have him put in jail for indecent behaviour and trespassing!"

"There's time for that later," Nigel responded impatiently. "We need to think about the Americans now."

Devi's expression soured. What she wanted to think about was jail time!

Nigel was beyond caring for her feelings though. For once, she'd just have to put a sock in it.

"Devi, you're really going to have to work the room now," he impressed upon her. "Say nothing about the little incident which just occurred—"

"It was not a *little* incident!"

Nigel looked at her sullen face, exhaled, and then went on, "Say nothing about what just occurred, simply talk shop like investment opportunities, a huge talent pool, good labour relations, a stable political climate . . . And perhaps figure out a little toast which you can give at lunch—just a few light-hearted lines to let the Americans know that we can take everything in our stride."

"A tip-top idea," nodded the mayor. "A little toast!"

As Nigel walked down the corridor towards the reception, he spotted, in the distance, Manish Ray, the minister for backward classes. Manish was pouring something from a silver hipflask down his throat.

"Tally-ho," Manish said wryly, as Nigel stopped by him.

"Don't let Devi catch you!" Nigel whispered.

"Don't care, hope she does," Manish said stroppily.

"You don't mean that, Sir," said Nigel sympathetically.

"Yes, I do," shrugged Manish. "Although I must applaud your use of her handbag!"

Nigel said nothing and moved on.

In the reception room, he made his way around, surreptitiously listening to snippets of conversations, trying to assess the damage.

The conversations being held were painfully desultory. There was a question about the change of name from West Bengal to Paschim Banga for its administrative advantage in the state roll call. "So you wanted to be *quite* near the end, instead of right at the end?" Something else about whether the best golf club was The Royal or The Tolly. An entirely ludicrous to and fro about the pronunciation of the yoghurt drinks which were being served: "It's L-A-S-S-I." "Lassie? Like the dog?" "Dog? No, not dog. Lóʼsee." "Low-see?" And so on. The only vaguely investment-related conversation was between two Americans, uttered in low voices,

"You know that guy, minister of backward people or something? Well, what does backward mean? Retarded?"

"I can't say I know. Maybe. Or perhaps disabled?"

"Listen, I have no problem having a few handicapped people on the books—I'm a great believer in opportunity for all—but I can't staff a whole company with them. I mean, you can't have someone with cerebral palsy operating heavy machinery."

"Yes, but the problem is they're really big on quotas here . . . They even have a certain number of government seats allocated to the scheduled castes."

"Scheduled castes?"

"Yes, like toilet cleaners."

"They have government seats reserved especially for toilet cleaners?"

"Well, it makes sense if you think about it. They're used to the stink of shit!"

Nigel, who was never particularly hungry, pretty much completely lost his appetite.

Meanwhile, Devi was trying to *work the room*. Now that she had fallen out with the Marwaris over her comments about the hospital fire, she needed the Americans to get on board. Where else would the money for investment come from? And she may well have lost the Marwaris' votes, too. Less money plus less votes equalled flashing red hazard sign. Not that she was sorry about what she had said; no one should ever be sorry for speaking the truth! Besides, there was nothing to get voters as excited as American investment. It was the next best thing to actually moving to America. With that, she would have enough support from the rest to not care which way the Marwaris voted. As for their money, they could stick it up their mothers'—. No, no, no, I must not get worked up, she told herself, as she tried to smile and shimmy and sweet-talk, I must work the room!

Sachin did not look like Sachin when he emerged, three months after the fire. Usually clean-shaven, he now sported a luxuriant beard and longer hair, which gave him a more enigmatic, ascetic look than his usual, matter-of-fact short back-and-sides. Always thin but increasingly baggy, and with an advancing paunch, his body was now tauter, leaner, firmer, as if his skin had been taken off, neatly trimmed of excess, and then glued smoothly back onto his bones. His gaze, though still full of determination, was more contemplative. Instead of his workaday trousers and shirt get-up, he was dressed in a white cotton kurta pyjama suit; a small breeze caused the hem of the chemise to flutter in the wind like the thin petals of a *brahma kamal*. Overall, it appeared that he had not spent time in jail but in an ashram.

On the other side of the quiet street, Anil was waiting for him in a yellow patched-up Ambassador taxi, not the fancy black Mercedes. Sachin's driver, usually uniformed, wore his everyday clothes although his instinct was still intact; as soon as he saw Sachin, he rose in his seat to get out of the car and open the passenger door, but from behind, Anil put a hand on his shoulder and shook his head. Sachin opened the door for himself and slid into the back seat next to Anil. Anil nodded at him, pleased and impressed, and then put out his fist for a bump. Sachin, not knowing what to do, patted Anil's fist, which made Anil giggle. Sachin laughed along, too; he knew he was being teased, but coming from Anil, he liked it. Sometimes, being teased made him feel less alone in the world. And since Sharmila had stopped paying him any attention, it was nice to have Anil make him feel like a normal person with a heart and a soul and a sense of humour and not just an inaccessible, unfeeling tycoon.

The driver started up the engine, but within seconds of pulling out and turning the corner onto the main thoroughfare, he stopped again. A few metres in front of him, blocking the road was a cluster of journalists and photographers, throbbing with edacious energy. On the pavement itself gathered a very large assortment of men, around five hundred, in all shapes and sizes but generally of the same hue, much like the assorted broken biscuits which were put together from all the damaged packets, and sold off cheaply in non-branded, polythene bags. Starry-eyed, open-mouthed, pushing and shoving, they stretched their necks and focused keenly on the main jail door. They might have been teenage girls waiting for a pop star; that same pheromonal hysteria pervaded the air. Then the jail door opened, and a dark, scruffy man appeared, dressed in a tight, striped, short-sleeved shirt and a pair of flared trousers with creases down the middle of the leg. There were sweat patches fanning out from under his armpits. There was swagger in the way he walked. A huge cheer went up from the assembled crowd. Anil watched the man carefully and disliked him immediately.

As the man's fans manhandled him onto a makeshift podium, cameras clicking, crowd chanting, Anil rolled down his window so that he could hear what the man had to say.

"My faith in Devi is what kept me going!" he declared.

The man was Selim Shah; even though he was a Muslim, his faith in Devi seemed to surpass his faith in Allah. A pragmatist, then. A few months ago, during clashes between Devi's Truth Party and The Communists, Selim had attacked one Mustak Ahmed Attar—a senior leader within The Communist Party, a well-respected family man, a man of the people (to Devi's chagrin, she did not have the monopoly on this property), a reasonable man, a man who had lived his life with the kind of integrity that was in short supply amongst his cohort. In short, exactly the kind of man *not* to rough up if only for reasons of public sentiment. It was like kicking a loyal, old dog; even those who thought dogs were flea-ridden pests could not condone such behaviour. Mustak had been left with a severe concussion, two very black eyes, and a few cracked ribs. On hearing the news, Devi had suggested that perhaps Mustak had tripped up over a pothole; the roads in the area he was campaigning in were notoriously shoddy. Accordingly, she would set up a taskforce investigating the dealings of the civic agency responsible for handing out road maintenance contracts, as well as the contractors themselves; from now on, no more craters, only smooth roads!

Many thought that Devi was behaving like an abusive husband ("I didn't give her that black eye. She must have tripped in the shower!"), amongst them Mustak's doctor. From outside the hospital he insisted that tripping over a pothole or even falling into an extra large one could not cause the kind of injuries that his patient had sustained. When a journalist had told him, "Well, that's what Devi said," the doctor had replied, "Well, she may be a *goddess* but she's not a doctor!"

A day later, when Mustak's dose of heavy-duty painkillers had been lowered and he was capable of coherent speech, he accused Selim of being his attacker.

Selim was already well known on the political circuit as being a goonda, first for The Communists and now for The Truth Party. A former district superintendent of police, he was far more interested in dictating outcomes than following process. Rarely had the law been so loosely followed that not only was it not by the letter but neither was it in the spirit. It was used more as a rough—a *very* rough—guide. On top of this, he also seemed to have the power of knowing the answer without asking any questions—a man of some intuition! Add to that a dogged disposition and a *needs must* mentality, and he was the perfect enforcer. But he had gone too far, too often, and been ousted after a campaign headed by none other than Mustak, whose constituents had complained to him of Selim's brutishness. Selim had felt utterly betrayed. For years he had been keeping the Communist sister-fuckers happy by doing their dirty work—crushing dissent, stamping out protest, crippling resistance—but then, when it got *too* dirty, *then* they washed their hands of him. Where was their understanding? Where was their appreciation? Where was their fucking loyalty? He had cried like a baby and then, exhausted, fallen into Devi's welcoming arms. It was she who had overseen his rehabilitation and his reincarnation. No longer the man who had, in his khaki police uniform, been officer and overseer. Now, in his casual street clothes, he was not *a* man but *The* Man, and the most ardent of Devi's ambassadors. If support needed to be drummed up, Selim had a whole drum kit as well as other persuasive percussive instruments. He campaigned, he canvassed, he crusaded. He was here, there, and everywhere, with Devi on his lips. The leadership of The Truth Party admired his vim and vigour. After all, elections were won at grassroots level, and Selim didn't seem to mind getting a few grass stains. And if his efforts were a little too energetic, well, energy was simply the opposite of complacency, and in politics, it was complacency that was the precursor to defeat.

After Mustak's accusation, senior leaders within The Truth Party had gone on the counter-attack, insinuating that Mustak himself had arranged to be beaten up in order to put the blame on Selim. Despite the fact that arranging a serious head injury for oneself was fraught with far more danger than, say, a broken leg, the senior leaders, who, apparently did not have brains in their own heads must have assumed that Mustak's head did not contain one either.

This narrative came to a full stop a few days later when a video was posted on the internet showing Selim carrying out the attack; one of his groupies, young, flashy, and stupid, had filmed the event on his phone. He'd shown a few of his friends in order to impress them. Or rather, people he *thought* were his friends. Shortly afterwards, his phone was stolen.

The Communists now had their proof. Still, the leaders of The Truth Party dithered. There were murmurs of self-defence and provocation. It was only when Mustak, still in hospital, construed that the attack on him was part of a greater, overall political strategy, that the leaders realised that Selim would have to be dealt with. By the end of the day, the police had picked him up.

That night, he was put in jail.

The next day, he was bailed.

The Communists yelled.

The Truth Party did a passable impression of yelling back although they were actually wincing.

Selim was put back in jail. This time on non-bailable charges, including attempted murder.

The big question, though, was why had Devi allowed this risible spectacle in the first place? The sentimental reason—because she loved Selim. Although her tastes usually ran to men who were slightly womanish, who curtsied and gushed and truckled, and who carried her handbag when necessary, she found Selim's virile energy rather exciting. A little headstrong, perhaps a bit *mischievous*, but essentially a good boy. One of her loyal boys who deserved her loyalty in return!

The more hard-nosed reason—there was a national election coming up in a few months and she needed Selim to nudge any wavering voters in the right direction.

In any case, her view had been that Mustak, the silly old goat, was just making a mountain out of a molehill, or rather a subdural haemorrhage out of a minor cerebral contusion. Years ago, before she had seen the light and formed The Truth Party, and when she had been the regional leader of what she now referred to as The Other Party (If hers was the party of truth, then it figured that The Other Party was the party of lies) she had been attacked by a Communist party member whilst leading a rally (The Communists, meanwhile, were to her the party of eternal blackness where concepts such as truth and lies had no meaning). She, too, had been beaten about her head, but she had just taken it on the chin! Alright, maybe not, but she didn't like to dwell on the incident. Well, apart from when she could make political capital out of it by presenting herself as tough and tenacious, a survivor of the 'What doesn't kill you makes you stronger' breed. And so what if she did—she *had* been attacked! She *had* survived!

Anil noted carefully that even though neither Devi nor any of the leaders of The Truth Party had turned up to greet Selim on his re-entry into ostensibly polite society—they were tending to the Americans after all—Selim still seemed to be making his speech for their benefit. He spoke of his allegiance, "I entered this place a committed member of The Truth Party and I leave it a committed member of The Truth Party. My mind and my heart will always belong to Devi!"; his duty, "It is my job to ensure that the good people of this city are not blinded by the lies and deceptions of The Communists. And I will continue to do my job to the best of my ability!"; his obedience, "I will do what Devi tells me to do!" So, despite his serious transgression, he was not about to be cut loose. Devi clearly thought that he was a very important person. And that meant he was a dangerous person. Anil would have to keep tabs on him.

"OK," Anil said to the driver, "we can go now."

The driver, who had vaguely nodded off due to the heat and noise, came to with a jolt, and in a rush, mistakenly put the car into first gear instead of reverse. It lurched forward towards some members of the crowd, who at first instinctively retreated but then quickly started to move towards it, looking quite put out.

"Can't you see where you're going, you retard!" shouted one man.

Anil rolled up his window whilst the driver rolled his down.

"Now what are you doing?" Anil asked.

"He called me a retard!" the driver complained.

"Let's just go."

Grudgingly, the driver jammed the car into reverse and swerved it so that he could leave the way he had come. But just before he set off again, he poked his head out of his window and yelled at the man, who was now walking away.

"Donkey!"

The man turned around and started walking towards the car again but the driver put down his foot and they sped away.

In the back seat, Anil shook his head. But Sachin laughed with glee. It was good to be out.

In the *United Times of India*'s reception, a lethargic elderly man, who had slipped off his leather sandals under his desk, picked up the phone to inform Miss Ghatak that her visitors had arrived and then asked Sachin and Anil to sign in. Discordantly, behind him, was a large screen with The United Newspaper's homepage—sharp, slick, modern.

Seconds later, Miss Ghatak appeared. She glanced disparagingly at the reception man but he didn't pay any heed. Sachin had not seen Miss Ghatak since the day of the fire, when she had been splenetic verging on vitriolic. Now she seemed placid verging on flaccid; the way she took his hand so gently and shook it as if he were a holy man. He noted though that she took Anil's hand slightly differently—not gently as much as reticently. He said nothing though. He had been warned by Anil not to deviate from the very carefully constructed script.

Miss Ghatak ushered them into a meeting room and hastily removed a used paper napkin from the table, putting it in the bin. It smelled like someone had eaten lunch in the room. Or maybe farted.

"Please, please, sit down," Miss Ghatak said. Not just one 'please' but two, Sachin thought. Well, well. Sachin sat down. Miss Ghatak sat across the table from him. Anil, meanwhile, stayed standing, looking at the various framed news clippings on the walls, which seemed to have the effect of further unnerving Miss Ghatak. She cleared her throat but Anil didn't turn around, so she fixed her gaze on Sachin and smiled.

"How were the jail conditions? I hear the food in there isn't that good!"

"We're not here to talk about jail conditions," said Anil, without turning around. "Save that for one of your investigative reports."

Miss Ghatak swallowed, then started again.

"You must be delighted that you were exonerated of all the charges against you?"

"How can I be delighted when so many people died?" Sachin replied. "Yes, I have lost a few months. But they lost their lives. So there is no delight. Only relief that I am now free to continue to help the families of the victims. Being in jail was a minor discomfort compared to their pain."

Good, Anil thought, keep it self-effacing. The guru fancy dress accessorised with matching facial hair must have been helping him get into the mood. Well, if Devi could use her white sari and scrubbed face to convey her sober-mindedness and sincerity, then why shouldn't Sachin use a few props, too.

"And do you expect an apology or at least a retraction from the chief minister? She did call you a murderer, after all."

"Of course not. The chief minister was under a lot of pressure when she said that. And we can all say things we don't mean in the heat of the moment. I understand that her words were not a direct attack on me or based on any personal animosity but rather a reaction to what was a very sad incident. Her frustration was due to the fact that she cares, as do I. But I am confident that now the facts have been established, and *I* have been proven innocent of any wrongdoing, we can both look forward to re-establishing a happy and productive relationship."

Anil pressed his lips together for a moment. Fight fire with fire? Fuck that, he had thought, you'd end up with an inferno. Just piss on it instead. A torrent of soothing piss. Put the fire right out. Put *her* right out.

The interview continued for another hour. Both Sachin and Miss Ghatak kept glancing at Anil. Sachin to check he was saying the right thing. Miss Ghatak to check she wasn't saying the wrong thing. He had briefed them both well. At the end, when they all rose to their feet, he said to Miss Ghatak, "I think that was very valuable, don't you? After all, what's important is that Mr. Lohia had the opportunity to put forward his side of the story. After all, that's what free speech and democracy is about, isn't it . . .?"

Anil's tone travelled smoothly from straight to sarcastic, as if he were gliding down a polished bannister.

"We'll be running the story tomorrow," Miss Ghatak replied sedulously.

There was no need for her to add that it would be front page.

As Sachin and Anil stood outside the building waiting for the driver to pick them up, Sachin wondered whether he should ask Anil what exactly had caused Miss Ghatak's change in temperament from shrew to mouse. He wasn't sure he wanted to know because what he *was* quite sure of was that, whatever had happened, it hadn't been an organic change. He was right, too. As if Anil had read Sachin's mind, he confirmed cheerfully, "I just presented, how shall I put it, a convincing argument."

And what had been Anil's convincing argument? He had told Miss Ghatak that unless she rescinded her hostility towards Mr. Lohia and replaced it with a more *understanding* attitude, he would out her. Anil knew it was a tawdry threat. He didn't care. Or at least not enough to not make it.

How had Anil known though? He hadn't. But of all the journalists he was familiar with, she had just pissed him off the most by marching into Sachin's house. So he had decided to dig for some dirt on her. He wasn't looking for anything in particular, any dirt would have done. He had done a bit of quiet investigation himself, spoken to a few old boyfriends he had found on Facebook, realised he might be on to something, and then put a private detective on her tail.

Besides, Anil had put it to Miss Ghatak, wasn't it a bit rich to say that her life was dedicated to revealing the truth when she, herself, was covering up such a lie of her own?

Tapati Ghatak had felt sick to the pit of her stomach but what choice did she have? There was her work (of course the newspaper had an anti-discrimination policy in place and a code of conduct for all its employees but so far this had not given anyone the confidence to come out). The whispers. The looks. The being relegated to the middle pages, writing about some kid who had done especially well in his school leaving exams. It was already bad enough being a woman and fighting the men for the choicest scoops, but being a woman's woman?

As for her family, she couldn't even imagine how her parents would react—it was unimaginable for her, in the same way that people can't imagine their own death.

She had made her decision very quickly.

And now, Sachin's story—his countercharge—was going to be the front page of the most respected newspaper in the country, and that with the highest circulation. Anil had managed to stitch that one up nicely; he always had a needle ready, he just needed to find thread.

As for the fire, Anil had been prepared to exert whatever pressure was required on whomever necessary in order to get Sachin off the charges, but what had transpired had been quite unexpected, very welcome, and wholly gratifying. Of course, Devi had set up a quasi-governmental task force to investigate the cause of the fire but even before they had managed to agree on what exactly needed to be investigated and in which order, Anil had taken care of the situation. He, being more organised, more efficient, more decisive, altogether more effective, had pretty much started and finished his own inquiry, involving hospital staff, fire-fighters, health and safety auditors, engineers, sprinkler manufacturers, laboratory analysts, and arson experts. The conclusion derived from all their observations and examinations was that the fire had spread and caused such devastation simply because the sprinkler system had failed. And why had the sprinkler system failed? Because the pressure in the mains pipe from which it drew water was not high enough. And why wasn't the pressure high enough? Because the public water board had found that the mains water pipe in that area—old and decrepit—was leaking due to the high pressure. So had they replaced the pipe? No, they had lowered the water pressure. Much easier, much less expensive, and forget the people who were actually using the water. The hospital had never been notified of this. An administrative oversight, the water board said. A dereliction of duty, Anil said. The water board might not have started the fire but they had made sure it couldn't be put out. In effect, the disaster had been due to the actions of a state organisation. In short, it was Devi's fault. Well, if she could hold Sachin responsible for the fire, then why couldn't she be held responsible herself? What was sauce for the goose was sauce for the gander.

The driver pulled up to the kerb.

"You should go home, take some rest," Anil advised Sachin.

Sachin shrugged. He didn't want to go home. He didn't know what to say to Sharmila. They had not spoken once during his time in prison. He did not blame her for this, nor was he upset or angry. He just felt sad that the woman he had once shared everything with, he now shared nothing with apart from a house. In fact, prison had, in one way, been a relief. That sense of strain from each night going home and trying to find something, *something* to say which would elicit more than the most cursory of responses from her, that he had not missed at all. He didn't say this to Anil. Despite how close they were and how warm their relationship was, they never spoke of personal matters. Although Sachin was sure that Anil, with his keen sense of intuition and his perceptiveness, had a good idea of his domestic situation. So he replied, half-jokingly, "Well, I suppose I'm going to have to go home and face my wife at some point . . ."

"Well, that's the thing with wives," Anil said with a gentle smile, "they always have to be faced up to at some point. That's why I don't have one!"

And Sachin chortled and patted him on the knee.

As they drove south from central Kolkata, Sachin rolled down his window. After the monotony of his time inside, every single smell, even the bad ones, felt pleasurable to him. The scent of frying onions, fumes, dung, marigold garlands, incense, sewage, sap; he sniffed at them all with the keenness of a bloodhound. And he listened avidly to every sound; crows cawing, horns tooting, engines humming, people talking, radios playing. He was feeling quite relieved and relaxed. Things were just as he had left them. Suddenly, the car pulled to an abrupt stop, and Sachin was roused from his reverie. A khaki-uniformed policeman had just stepped into the middle of the road and put his hand up.

"What's going on?" Sachin asked, "Why has all the traffic stopped?"

The driver shrugged. Moments later, Devi's risible cavalcade came around the corner. At the start of her reign, she had insisted on travelling as if she were a normal member of the public, but her security team had insisted that for her own safety ("There are bad people in the world," they told her. "You don't need to tell me that!" she retorted. "I've spent my whole life fighting bad people!"), she should at least have a couple of police cars ride with her. The problem was *which* police cars should be used? The Kolkata police force had started to use the Haha Velocity sedan as their cruiser of choice, which wouldn't have been a problem if Devi hadn't come to power partly on an anti-Haha ticket. *I, and only I, am prepared to stand up for these farmers whose livelihoods will be destroyed if Haha builds their car factory on this land!* So to then use one of their cars in her cavalcade? Well, it seemed duplicitous, and duplicity wasn't part of her personal brand. Instead, whilst

Devi travelled in a Maruti Wagon R, petrol efficient, comfortable without being luxurious, wide-opening doors for easy entry and exit, the car which, according to its manufacturer, made 'you look a lot smarter than everyone else', her police guards drove in Mitsubishi Lancers—a nod to the Japanese. Such levels of consideration required for simply getting from A to B!

Anil rolled his eyes. Did people really buy this style (or lack of) over substance? Well, yes they did, that was both the problem and the point.

"Even she's being driven in a better car than me!" Sachin laughed.

In response, the driver revved the engine, and as soon as the cavalcade had passed, he released the brake so abruptly that the car flew across the junction, jolting Anil and Sachin forward. Once they'd landed back in their seats, Sachin frowned and said, his tone quiet and concerned, "The victims' families—we've done what we should?"

"Well," Anil replied, quite belligerently, "considering what we discovered, it's the Water Board which should be paying them compensation, but where are those *chutiye* going to get the money from—the whole city is bankrupt!" He reached out, touched Sachin's arm and softened his tone, "But of course we've taken care of them. In a few cases, we've even offered jobs—at an appropriate level of course, mainly in clerical positions, and in one instance, we've even made available funds to put one boy, whose father died, through medical school."

Sachin nodded, impressed and quite moved. All of his other advisers had been pushing him to do as little as possible. Just good business sense, they said, why incur more costs than necessary? People had notoriously short memories—they'd make a fuss then forget. Besides, they weren't in the business of humanity, they were in the business of business. Only Anil seemed to have a more comprehensive view that had people at its centre not its periphery. Which was surprising considering that Anil came across as the sort of person who didn't really need other people.

"Hearts and minds stuff," remarked Sachin. "It's as if we're fighting a war!"

"Well, aren't we?" replied Anil.

IX

For the last two weeks, Anima had been late for work every day. During the night, she wasn't sleeping well. When she woke up, far too early, she felt sick and tired. Then she would lie in bed, agitated, her mind racing, willing herself to go back to sleep for a few more hours. When she finally drifted off again though, just as it was becoming light outside, it was into a disturbing sleep in which she thought she was awake, but then realised that she was not. When she finally *actually* woke up, she had, in her mind, already woken up six or seven times. Her body felt near paralysed and she was exhausted. Something needed to change.

That, of course, was her problem—that something needed to change but she was not doing anything to change that something. For someone who had always had such control over her life, she now felt quite impotent. But why, she asked herself. I'm financially independent. I'm in good health. My only son is happy and doing well. I don't have a mortgage! In fact, I don't have any responsibilities to anyone! I'm free to do what I want. What's stopping me? What was stopping her was that, for the first time in her life, she simply didn't know what she wanted to do or what she *should* do. She was in a limbo of her own making. She had still not mentioned the text to The Professor. Perhaps the opportunity to do so had come and gone. Or perhaps it was her inclination to mention it that had disappeared. Her lethargy was overwhelming her.

And of course The Professor was continuing to be his usual self—congenial, droll, amusing, completely and utterly callous and self-centred. If only he could have seen inside her head!

She came down for breakfast ready and dressed. The Professor was still wearing his pyjamas, his skin creased, his hair dishevelled and sticky-uppy. As he lounged in his chair, Anima spotted that his pyjama shirt was straining at the buttons and through a gap between them, she could see his toneless, hairy skin. Thank god there's another woman, Anima thought, otherwise it would have to be me!

"Ready and dressed already!" he commented. "No rest for superwoman, eh, even at the weekend?"

The Professor left the house early during the week and didn't know about Anima's recent tardiness. It was only at the weekend that they ate breakfast together.

"Why waste the day?" she answered flatly, as she poured herself a glass of guava juice. "Too many wasted days and you end up with a wasted life."

"Philosophy so early in the morning!" declared The Professor, pretending to be bowled over. "I'll need some energy to deal with that!" He took a pronounced bite of his toast and chomped loudly. I hope you choke on it, Anima thought, as she sat down. She could still hear The Professor chomping. The sound drilled itself into her brain. For how many years can you have breakfast with someone before wanting to kill them? That's a philosophical question for you, Dear.

She looked at the items that had been laid out—toast, butter, various preservatives, cereal, muesli, milk, a couple of fresh fruit juices. Always the same, every Saturday morning.

As Anima knew, people were formed by repetition. The brain liked repetition, it liked mental shortcuts, it liked using up as little energy as possible. Depending on how you interpreted it, the brain was very lazy or super efficient, but either way, it was happy when you were living your life on repeat. But you *could* kick it into gear! You *could* be more than an accumulation of routines and memories and patterns of behaviour! You just had to break free of old habits and think consciously about what it was that you were doing.

"I think I'll have eggs this morning," Anima said, chewing on her lip.

The Professor looked up from his copy of *The United Times of India*. Anima could just tell that he wanted to say *On Saturday*? But that doing so would indicate a distressing level—to him, at least—of provincialism. No, he liked to consider himself the type of person who was open to eating anything at any time, that's how freethinking he was. So, he said, instead, "Do we have eggs?"

"Well, I don't know," Anima replied, her tone slow and glacial. "I better go and have a look." As she rose from her seat, she was quite amazed at the amount of poison she had managed to inject into such an inoffensive proposition. Maybe that's what marriage did to you or at least enabled you to do.

Fifteen minutes later she was back with an omelette, made with chopped shallots and finely sliced green chillies. The savoury smell was mouth-watering. As Anima sat back down, she noticed The Professor involuntarily lick his lips. And then it occurred to her that she hadn't asked him if he might want some eggs, too. He loved eggs, she knew that. But she simply hadn't thought to ask him and despite her earlier animosity towards him, she now felt quite mean and petty. That was marriage, too. At least for women. But maybe egg denial was where she needed to start.

Meanwhile, The Professor had been paying intense attention to the front page of *The United Times* and, news digested, he said to Anima, "Have you read this? About Sachin Lohia? He's out of jail, all charges dropped! Friends in high places, eh?"

"No higher than the people who put him in there in the first place."

"Ha, he offers you a job, and now you're his biggest fan!"

"A major trauma wing is being built, including a neurological unit. India's the head injury capital of the world, and he wants to create a world-class treatment facility. It's a pretty valuable thing to do."

"And I suppose a world-class facility requires a world-class surgeon?"

A little drop of acid in The Professor's tone. Although he had never had the candour to admit it, he had always been a little put out by the fact that whereas Anima was recognised as world-class by her peers, he was not. Anima was convinced of this.

"It becomes a world-class facility *because* it has a world-class surgeon."

Anima had never been one to boast but if The Professor had an inferiority complex, it was his to deal with.

"And a handsomely-paid position, too, I should think?"

Another drop of acid. And to think I felt bad for not offering him eggs, Anima thought.

"I have no idea, we didn't talk about money—but considering your contribution to our joint bank account, I certainly hope so."

Anima had never, ever said anything to The Professor about the quite substantial discrepancies in their incomes, nor about the fact that she had come into the relationship with family money and property whereas he had not. Neither had it ever occurred to her to mention it because she had never really thought about it. Until now.

"Life's not all about money," lectured The Professor, waggishly.

"Well, I suppose when you've spent most of your years living the good life on someone else's money, that's easy to say."

"I've never contributed anything?"

"You've contributed *plenty*, thank you."

All of this in such a light, frivolous tone, it could mean only that the words were not in jest at all.

Anima needed to get away. She could stay in a hotel or with a friend—Purnima perhaps—but these options seemed petulant and temporary to her, only one step up from slamming a door. A more determined and forceful action was required. Or was that being melodramatic? Overemotional? It was very difficult for a woman who had committed herself to reasonableness and proportionality to take any course of action that might raise eyebrows. She had the strong sense that people would gossip, that there would be speculation and comment and analysis and judgement. So what, she had to keep telling herself, so what. Let people find pleasure wherever they could!

In the cool, dark storage room, a very large, very hairy spider, having been disturbed, crawled over Anima's foot and then disappeared. Immediately, her body erupted in gooseflesh, and a fine queasiness travelled from the base of her stomach up to her throat. Her first reaction was to shriek for help, but she managed to keep her mouth shut. Where she was going, there would be no point in shrieking yet probably a lot more to shriek at. She better get used to it. Breathing out slowly, she rubbed at the bumps on her arms. Suddenly the word came to her—*horripilation*. She had thought for a long time that the 'horri' came from horror; she learned only later from Avik that it came from the Latin *horrere*, 'to stand on end'. She preferred her etymology, it was far more fitting.

She found a stack of boxes but when she tried to lift one, she realised it was far heavier than she had expected. She took a step back and told herself: don't give yourself a hernia! Then the adventure will have to stop before it's even started. That's how she was framing it—not as a departure but as an adventure.

She went through them all but couldn't find what she was looking for. What she had uncovered though was a load of junk—old kitchenware, old clothes, old electrical appliances. Old, old, old. But what to do with it? It seemed a waste of effort to put it all away again. And the sight of all the clutter all over the floor started to overwhelm her.

Calm down, she ordered herself, it's just my brain's reaction to multiple stimuli competing for neural representation, and my visual system has only limited processing capacity! The solution—just close my eyes for a few minutes.

Whilst her eyes were closed, she wondered: why do people hold on to things they no longer want or need? Why do people hold on to people they no longer need! Nostalgia or, even more feeble than that, hope—hope that they might be useful again in the future? Or were possessions just markers of time, a way to make sense of and remember your life? When I was ten, I had a bike. When I was twenty-five, I had a husband! Whatever the reason, Anima now had a strong urge to get rid of everything.

From a first floor guest bedroom window which gave her a good vantage point over the street, and sitting comfortably on the cushioned ledge, Anima realised that the passers-by in front of the house were looking suspiciously at all of the items laid out. She noticed though that a few people were walking backwards and forwards past the display. Finally, a hand-pulled rickshaw-wallah parked his rickety vehicle by the kerb and then shuffled his way through the small group of people. Without any qualms, he picked up a Teasmade, gave it a thorough inspection and then loaded it into the back of his rickshaw. She was delighted. He returned to take a look at a brightly patterned silk shirt, which he tried on over his torn white vest. Now, the others started to quickly grab items. There was even a little tussle between two matronly women over a flowery casserole dish. Anima watched the whole scene attentively and with pleasure. She didn't know why giving things away should fill her with so much satisfaction, but it did. Maybe it was because what had once been in the graveyard had now been given a new lease of life. Or because she had, right in front of her own eyes, created a little spume of happiness. Suddenly, she heard The Professor's voice, sweetly inquisitive, "You seem bored?"

Ah, Anima thought immediately, he's come to make amends, he's worried that I might take the money away—and then how will he afford to keep his other woman! The only thing I'm bored of is *you*! Instead, she replied, "I'm not bored, I'm thinking."

"What about?"

"Life."

By now, The Professor had joined her at the window and saw what was going on below. His expression darkened.

"Is this symbolic?" he asked mordantly.

Anima gave him a dismissive glance and replied lightly, "No, it's literal."

There was a small silence and then a change in The Professor's tone—more restrained if not completely conciliatory.

"You might have consulted me . . ."

"Why?"

"Well, just as a courtesy. Some of that was mine, too."

"You're right, that fondue set was yours."

She was making him seem petty and she was glad of it. The Professor had made a career out of making other people seem petty, so high above the fray was he that Anima imagined there were points at which people must have appeared as dots to him. Well, now you're becoming a dot to me, she thought, the process of dotification has begun!

There was another small silence and then yet another change in The Professor's tone, courteous but laced with a flinty, inquisitive edge.

"What were you looking for?"

"Looking for?"

"In the storeroom. You're not known for your ruthless Spartanism so I assume that the little clear-out was incidental?"

No point in denying the truth. Although she was very particular about how things appeared—flowers had to be arranged perfectly, the colour of the walls had to be just right, furniture had to be positioned just-so—she was quite happy to cram stuff in drawers and cupboards where they were out of sight.

"I was looking for some photos."

"Of what?"

"Avik. When he was a baby. I was feeling sentimental."

She felt compelled to add the *sentimental* to make the dig before he did. The Professor wasn't really one for family photographs. When they had been young parents and gone to other friends' houses and seen the posed family photos on the wall, he would, under his breath, quote Naipaul: *It was like a photographer's window in London, with the photographer's satire hidden from the sitter, who saw only the flattery.* Once she had heard this, she had been completely put off by those mannered photographs and had satisfied herself with just a few, casual snaps. As The Professor refused to appear in those himself, it would frequently just be Avik. Later, when they were on holiday or such, he would sometimes reluctantly agree to take a few photos of Avik and Anima together. Now, Anima thought, that might not have turned out to be such a bad thing. At least she wouldn't have to cut or scribble him out of the photos.

"You've spoken to him recently?"

"He called me at the surgery the other day."

"He's well?"

"Yes, he's very well. He's moving into a new flat, actually . . ."

Her casual articulation of this somewhat important news—to parents at least—belied her small delight in imparting it to The Professor. She knew Avik wouldn't have told his father. Indeed, when Avik had been growing up, Anima had rued the fact that he had never got on that well with him. For although there had never been any hostility between them, there had always been a level of formality. Now, she was quite pleased about this: our son loves me more. Because I'm the more loveable person!

"Oh, well, good . . ." The Professor replied disjointedly. "That's good . . . Anyway, the photos are in one of the armoires in the library . . ."

With this, he turned to leave.

"Where are you going?"

The Professor twisted his head around but spoke to the floor not her.

"Oh, just out for a little while," he replied, vague, imprecise.

"*Where* out?" Anima said, explicit, precise.

"Nowhere in particular, I just want to stretch my legs . . ." replied The Professor, now peering in Anima's direction, if not straight into her eyes.

You want to stretch your legs? I'll bet that's not all you want to stretch, Dear.

"Well, in that case, why don't you stretch your legs in the

garden? The marigolds need deadheading and the gardener's hurt his back," she suggested with a smile.

The Professor looked down and scratched the back of his neck.

"Actually, I was thinking of going to Bowbazar and having a wander around . . . I'll bring you back some *mishti* from Bhim Nag! That is, if you don't mind?"

"Why would I mind?"

The Professor shrugged sheepishly.

"OK, well I'll see you later . . ." he said.

Not if I have anything to do with it, Anima thought.

As soon as Anima heard The Professor leave the house, she marched to the library. The last attempt had turned into a lengthy, if pleasant, diversion. This time, she needed to be more efficient.

It took her little time to locate the few photo albums they had. First of all, she happened to open up the album containing Avik's baby photos but just as she was about to sit back and start reminiscing, she told herself firmly: no time for that now. Quickly, she found the album she was looking for—the one containing photos from her childhood. Again, the temptation was to gaze and reminisce but what she needed was a concrete pictorial representation that would enable her future not remember the past. Then she found the first of around twenty black and white photos taken in and around her late uncle's home in Balachuria. There she was, standing at the gate at the beginning of the drive that led down to the house. Over the gate was a painted concrete arch with some Bengali script written on it. Anima tried to make out what it said; it was only the house name—'Upabana'—not the address. But that was good enough. Then she spotted at the edge of the photo, on the property's boundary wall, some kind of painted symbol. She looked more carefully. It was half a sickle and hammer, the rest of it cropped off by the camera angle. This must have been near the end, before the trouble really started, before her family—apart from her brother Pusan—packed up and left. Pusan, of course, had stayed. Not forever. But long enough to cause pain and despair. And long enough to create another life, apparently . . .

How old was I? she thought. Ten? I was quite grown-up looking for a ten-year-old! Then a couple of her uncle—one with just her, one with her and Pusan. She could barely remember her uncle now. Instead of a complete, sequential life story, she could only recollect incidents in random order. What she did remember was that, to her, he had been a very kind, gentle man, patient, caring, nurturing. He had taught her how to ride a bike. He had taught her how to draw and paint. He had taught her how to look after chicks and puppies and kittens. (Anima recalled it being said by her parents that her uncle had always loved animals more than people. And now she was beginning to see how that could happen.) Another photo—one of the cat. The cat that had been poisoned. A slight shiver ran through Anima. It's fine, she told herself, that time is over, things are different now.

She also remembered that her uncle could be a scrupulous and austere man when it came to other people. Anyone who prepared or served him food had to be a Brahmin. Servants were not to speak to him unless he spoke to them and he banned Anima from mixing with the children of the servants. Even the children Anima was allowed to mix with—those whose parents were in higher employment than domestic service—had to come to her uncle's house, she was never allowed to go to theirs. To her, this had seemed vaguely unfair but not unreasonable. Now it made her feel quite uncomfortable. But back then, she had listened, not just because she was young but because she was the kind of person who listened. It had been Pusan who was the non-listener. And the questioner, too. Why this, why that—why, Uncle, do your pet animals eat better than your neighbours? She felt even sadder when she thought about Pusan and what had happened to him. So many accusations, so many allegations, so many insinuations—all of them coming from her uncle. When he was feeling generous, he would talk of a honeytrap: a poor, neighbourhood girl who had been set up by the Naxalites. She had, in no particular order, given Pusan some sob story about the injustices of her life, opened her legs, declared her love, and in no time at all, he had forgotten who he was and where he came from, and joined the enemy. When he was feeling less generous, he would say that Pusan was an inherently destructive and malicious boy, reckless, godless, worthless. A person who had no sense of the importance of tradition, of heritage, of culture, of birthright. A person whom the devil himself had fashioned out of flesh and blood! Giving up his charmed life to go and fight for those evil sister-fuckers and spread their propaganda—and for what?

And for what, indeed, Anima now thought. So many years Pusan had spent in the wilderness, away from his family, away from his friends, and what had he achieved? There was no grand endgame, no final line to cross or last hurdle to jump over. The life he must have lived, the things he must have seen, Anima thought, whilst I was in another country, living a settled life, concerned about only my family and my career . . . After more than fifteen years caught up in the maelstrom, Pusan had returned to the family home in Kolkata, a broken man who could not be rebuilt.

And of his rumoured other family? The Balachuria girl who had borne his child? Pusan could never be persuaded to acknowledge them, no matter how gently and persistently his parents asked him. Indeed, his silence on the matter was so resolute that in the end, it was concluded that maybe the reason why he had finally left Balachuria was because they had somehow died in the conflict and it was too painful for him to talk about them.

So his parents, with their connections and their standing, made sure that he was not bothered by the law, but this was his only relief. They tried their best to look after him, to bring him back to life, but they were aging and tired themselves. When her father was on his deathbed, Anima had gone home to see that the elder brother whom she had looked up to as a child was now an alcoholic shell, so crushed, so damaged, so utterly incapable, that she had arranged their father's funeral as if *she* were the first born son, going as far as having her hair cut off in mourning. When the time came for Anima to go back to London, her mother had told her: I'm very pleased that life turned out well for you at least. I must have done something right. Now Anima thought: yes, Ma, I thought my life had turned out well, too. I never saw *this* coming!

Anima looked at her watch. She had become distracted again. The past was always trying to sidetrack you away from the future! She had to keep moving. Quickly, she rose, tidied away the albums, holding on to the few photos she needed. She needed to pack a few things, too. What was the advice always given to abused women? Don't tell him you're leaving. Just grab the essentials and get out! OK, Anima knew that she wasn't quite a battered wife, but she was certainly an emotionally bruised one. And she knew that if she allowed herself to be dragged into a discussion with The Professor about their problems, to talk through their issues, to be honest with each other about their feelings, in short, to cling desperately to the cloying notion that what they had was worth saving, that all those years together had to count for something, well, then she knew she wouldn't leave because it would seem unreasonable and churlish. Even if it was precisely unreasonableness and churlishness which the situation required. No, for once, she needed to act before she thought. She needed to be impulsive and impetuous. No room for sense!

On her way to her bedroom, she phoned her personal

assistant and told her that she wouldn't be coming to work for the foreseeable future due to some 'health concerns'. The young woman immediately broke into sobs. Oh dear, Anima thought. She was a sweet girl, Anima was fond of her, and she certainly hadn't intended to upset her.

"Don't worry, calm down," Anima reassured her, "it's nothing terminal, it's just something which needs me to take rest for a while."

Was that too vague? Even if it were, she would be too deferential to ask anything further, Anima intuited. The assistant managed to calm down and take note of what Anima told her—the workload was to be split between the two other junior doctors she had recruited to the practice. If any patients wanted to know where Anima was, they were simply to be told that she was away on business.

"But that isn't the truth, Madam?" the assistant asked delicately.

"It's not a lie as such," Anima explained, "it's more of a fudge."

"A fudge, like the sweet?"

"No, a fudge like an evasion. Listen, don't worry about it, just say that I'm away on business and you don't have any more information."

A sullen silence. Anima could tell that the girl was not keen on a fudge or any other kind of misleading confectionary. "Can you do that?" Anima asked.

Finally, quietly, reluctantly: "Yes, Madam."

Anima wished that she hadn't had to concoct a sort-of lie to cover up another sort-of lie, but at that point she was trying to keep things as simple as possible. If she had told her assistant in the first place that she was going away on business, it would simply lead to more questions. Where, why, how long for, would travel arrangements need to be made, and could she please, *please* accompany Madam on the trip! Whereas informing patients that she was unwell would also lead to further questions. If they didn't start worrying that Anima might have passed on some communicable disease to them, then they would worry about the bad luck of having had an ill person treat them!

With that out of the way, Anima went to her bedroom to start to pack. But what did she require? She thought of the most basic elements in Maslow's hierarchy of needs—breathing, food, water, sex, sleep, excretion. Breathing? Her respiratory system was in good working order. Tick. Food? She was going somewhere where she would be able to purchase it. Tick. Sex? She was actively trying to avoid it but perhaps Maslow was working on a species level, not an individual one. Plus, he was a man. Sleep? Well, that's what she was hoping for. Excretion? Well, she had an arsehole. In fact, she thought, as an image of The Professor popped into her head, she had two arseholes; see related point about sex avoidance. So basically, she needed a working body and cash for everything else. And maybe some bedding and mosquito repellent. And perhaps a few good books. And maybe some candles and a torch in case the electricity wasn't hooked up. And some clothes and underpants. And what about medication? Well, apart from the alcohol and cigarettes. After five minutes of deliberation, she packed.

It was all so reckless and over-the-top! It was all so thrilling! Anima hadn't felt like this in years. For the last few years she had been winding down; the most excitement she had to look forward to was a possible wedding and, after that, a possible grandchild—although a grandchild who would be thousands of miles away. Now she felt like she was gearing up again.

Even if he hadn't seen the suitcase, the driver would have noticed Anima's change in demeanour and guessed that something unusual was happening. Although, he was still quite surprised when she told him where they were going.

"Why d'you want to go there?" he asked, before he remembered that his job was to drive, not comment on the suitability or otherwise of the destination. It was a mistake he sometimes made.

"There is a house there which belongs to me," Anima replied; the more elaborate, passive construction seemed appropriate.

The driver did not seem impressed. He just shrugged, opened the back door, and said, "Let's go then, Madam."

Anima was unsure how to read his reaction. Quickly, she slid into the back seat before she could change her mind.

"Don't worry, I'll pay you double-time," she said.

The drama of the morning combined with the gentle vibrations running through the car meant that, although Anima had planned on staying awake for the journey, she fell asleep within minutes of leaving the city perimeter, as the heavy start-stop traffic and the constant commotion gave way to the open country roads and only the occasional horn. A couple of times, she felt the car come to a stop, and then the driver's door open and close, and after a few moments, open and close again. She urged herself to wake up properly, to check what was going on, but her body was too exhausted to comply. Some time later, she realised that the driver had once again stopped the car. But this time, he came around to open up *her* door. She looked around her. They were on a remote road, not another person in sight. Darkness had almost set in, but in the dim light, she could tell he was frowning, staring at her. A little afraid now, she realised: I'm a rich woman. On my own. No one knows where I am. My driver is going to kill me and take the money. Maybe he will rape me, too, to serve me right for thinking I could go where I wanted and do what I wanted. Maybe it does serve me right. What a lesson! He reached out to touch her. Anima froze. This is a dream, she told herself, this is a dream. It's just glycine. Glycine released from my brain stem onto my motor neurons to paralyse me and stop me from acting out my dreams.

Then, she recoiled with such force that she hit the back of her head on the opposite window.

"Madam," said the driver, tentatively reaching out, "Madam? Are you OK?"

Anima shuddered violently and then looked around herself frantically.

"Madam," said the driver, again, "we've arrived."

The paint on the sign at the front gate had faded but it was the right place.

"Do you have sat nav?" Anima asked, slightly confused.

"No, Madam, I asked in the town. Everyone knows this house."

Anima inched herself forward, out of the car, and onto the road. The night-time insects were out; she could hear their whirs and fizzes. She noticed that the gate was bound together with a chain and padlock. She did not have a key. She had forgotten about keys; Maslow had made no mention of them in his hierarchy. After all that, they would have to go back.

"Shall we go?" asked the driver.

"Yes, I suppose we should," said Anima, utterly disappointed and furious with herself.

But instead of getting back into the car, the driver approached the gate, and unwound the chain. The padlock had not been clamped together. Anima realised that her life had just hinged on a difference of millimetres.

Standing outside the now slightly dilapidated house, Anima remembered she didn't have keys for the door either. She closed her eyes and tipped her head back to stretch the muscles in her neck. When she opened them, the driver had disappeared. Somewhere nearby, in the darkness, she could hear him taking a lengthy piss. If possible, she would have asked him to smash a window, but there were no windows, only wrought iron grilles and, behind those, wooden shutters. Then, she felt a presence nearby.

Her skin involuntarily erupted into goosebumps. *Horror*, she said to herself, *horripilation*. She remembered that her uncle always used to say that there were more ghosts in the countryside than in the city; they liked the peace and quiet. And more witches, too; *they* liked to hide in trees and behind bushes. Tie up your hair at night, Ani, lest a witch grabs a clump and puts a curse on you! It's fine, Anima chuckled to herself, I have short hair now, so there's at least one benefit to age-related thinning. Still, she slowly turned her head in the direction where she had sensed something. To her surprise—her city brain, her *adult* brain, having reminded her there were no such things as ghosts or witches—she saw a figure in the shade, under a tree. Dark, willowy, motionless. Her breath caught in her throat, Anima turned around again, and then stood very still herself. The driver reappeared.

"Madam, you look like you've seen a ghost!" he grinned. "Plenty of them around in a place like this!"

"You believe in ghosts?" Anima asked, feigning coolness.

The driver giggled, although there was a little gulp at the end, and he moved quickly towards the front door, then looked back at Anima for a key. So as not to come across as a completely disorganised fool, she had a good rummage around in her handbag, and then shook her head as if she couldn't fathom what might have happened to the key. The driver, who now seemed quite keen to get inside, gave the door a little shove with his shoulder, and then another, more forceful one. The door swung open.

Quickly, Anima and the driver carried out a quick assessment of the house. There was limited running water from a cold tap in the kitchen area, which coughed and sputtered out rusty water; electricity—the lights were very dim and flickered (who, she wondered, had paid the electricity bill?), but the mobile phone reception showed four bars, which Anima was bemused by. The driver had started to make insistent noises about how the place was in no fit state for Anima to stay, that they should drive back to the city—he'd have people sort out the house and then she could come back—but when she insisted that she would be staying, that she was quite capable of staying, that she *wanted* to stay, he simply replied that, in that case, he would stay with her, too. To that end, he would go to the local shop to buy some bottled water and snacks, which would at least see them through to the morning. The authority with which he decided this made Anima realise that although she was his boss, as a man, he felt that he needed to, in some way, take charge of the situation.

It was only when he had gone to the shops, that she thought: I wonder why no one else has moved in, this place has been empty for years. But she didn't dwell on this, and instead, as her phone had coverage, she decided to send a text to The Professor, out of courtesy and nothing else: *Dear, I've just come to Balachuria for a while to take care of some business here. Sorry for not telling you earlier. It was a last minute decision. Take care of yourself whilst I'm away. Yours, Ani.* She felt especial glee at writing the word 'yours', when what she had just done had implied that she was definitely not. But just as she was wondering what she would write if he replied—although she intuited he wouldn't, at least not straightway, he was far too cool and calculating—she caught a whiff of something in the air. Something ferrous. Sticky. Her surgeon's nose was familiar with the smell—it was of blood. As tempted as she was to ignore it, she knew she would have to investigate. Taking a deep breath, she followed her nose into what had been her uncle's bedroom. The smell was coming from under the bed. She swallowed and then knelt down and set the candle by her side. A straggly bitch was lying on her side, four tiny puppies trying their best to suckle at her teats. At her tail end, was a pool of blood. She was so weak that she had not even managed to clean up her litter; their fur was still covered in blood and amniotic fluid. Anima was wondering what to do when she heard the driver return. She called out to him and when he saw the bitch and her puppies, he immediately left the room, returning minutes later with a bucket of water. Anima's eyes widened with shock.

"No," she gasped, "we can't drown them!"

The driver frowned.

"No, Madam . . ." he said gently, "to clean them up."

After a perfunctory meal of bottled water and things out of packets, Anima and the driver retired to their respective beds. From her room, where they had managed to put together a makeshift bed for the bitch and the puppies, she could hear the driver, who was in the next room, speaking to someone—probably his wife—on his phone. She wondered what he was saying to her. Probably: my boss has gone mad. Well, she thought, sometimes it's good to go a bit mad. She checked her own phone. No reply. Am I running away from the problem, she thought. Well, why the hell shouldn't I? The one responsibility I have from now on is to take care of myself. And my dogs!

X

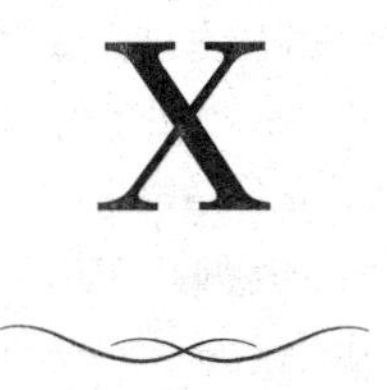

For breakfast, Nigel had consumed a quarter of a bottle of Gelusil, washed down with a cup of strong coffee. Devi had recommended a simple diet and what could be simpler than an antacid and a stimulant. Some nutritionists recommended eggs for breakfast, but *they* hadn't been woken up by a pre-dawn phone call from their angry boss, demanding that *they* attend an emergency meeting, and that *they* better have some answers! Eggs were no match for such exactions.

His wife, Shona had come into the kitchen, bleary-eyed and asked why he was up and dressed so early and where was he going? I'm going to hell, he thought.

And Devi had been in such a buoyant, optimistic mood yesterday evening. Then, she had been shuffling enthusiastically around her office, grotesquely filliped by her meeting with the Americans, as if they were the answer to everything. Her face had been contorting into all sorts of mad scientist expressions and her voice had been delirious. At least she had forgotten about the infiltrator and the handbag. But what had given him a headache was her complete lack of caution or circumspection. He had suggested briefing the papers that they had had interesting and positive preliminary discussions. She was having none of it. Tell them, she had ordered him, that the Americans are very impressed with us! Tell them that we have had concrete talks! Tell them that the Americans realise our huge potential and they want to be our partners! Is that what you think happened, Devi? Nigel thought. Because, what the Americans actually said, albeit in many more words and couched in far more reverential language, was a pretty equivocal 'we'll see'. But Devi was not one for slicing through subtleties. Her brain housed a chainsaw not a fine paring knife. But it doesn't matter, he had told himself, it doesn't matter. What matters is that she is in a good mood. In fact, that is all that matters.

Now all that mattered was that she was in a bad mood. A very bad mood.

As Nigel slid into the waiting car—Devi had sent her car for him, not so much courtesy as coercion—the driver passed him the day's newspapers. He could have gone online and checked already, but he felt he needed to hold the bad news in his hands, to make it as real as it could be. He braced himself. On the front page of *The United Times* was a large photo of Sachin Lohia, looking serene, the thoughtful elder, the man who had seen it all and was still filled with hope. Who does he think he is? Nigel thought. Desmond bloody Tutu! Then, even though reading in a moving vehicle made him feel quite nauseous, he read the whole article. News? thought Nigel. This is more like hagiography—quite apt considering Lohia's all-white saint's outfit! Then he noticed that there was a related story on page five. What related story? Hadn't enough been written about the man already! Miffed, he turned to page five, read the headline, squinted, then read the article very reluctantly but very carefully—Lohia's company had won a coal mining lease auction for a block in Balachuria. His company had not only been willing to pay a very competitive price, but it had also made a sound business case—not only would the coal be used in their steel and cement businesses, but they would be providing jobs, healthcare, and education for a whole community.

But Lohia had always been a nimble one, knowing when to twist and when to turn. The slippery sister-fucker! And underneath this superlative piece of news? The story of how the fire at Lohia's hospital was due to the Public Water Board having neglected their duty—and what was Devi going to do about that? She who had accused Lohia of murder. Again, Nigel rued her lack of caution. She was always too caught up in the moment, too say-what-I-think before think-what-I-say. No cool head on those dumpy little shoulders. In fact, sometimes barely a head at all, just a big mouth. And who was she going to blame all of this on? Now, there was no more careful reading. Now, there was just frantic flipping and scanning, as if his eyes were working at a checkout till. The Balachuria story had also made the front pages of two of the other major newspapers. One piece, in ostensibly the only pro-business newspaper in the state, suggested that Lohia might just be the man to return Kolkata to its industrial heyday, as long as governmental bureaucracy didn't stand in his way! The other, in a more left-wing paper, said that as long as Lohia had learned lessons from the sector's grubby and corrupt past, he had every chance of making it a success, adding that the patient and considered way with which he had dealt with his incarceration, bode well for his new project. They all covered his release from jail, too, in varying degrees. Much was made of his magnanimity. What an act, Nigel thought, shaking his head. Give the man a Zee Cine award, and whilst you're at it, give his press liaison an award for best screenplay! Feeling utterly down in the dumps, he managed to find the strength to take a look at the main Communist newspaper, and then wished he hadn't. They were leading with the story of how Devi, despite all her assertions of being against thuggery and political violence had not thrown Selim Shah out of her Truth Party nor even publicly disciplined him—*that* was the truth. This topped by an especially unflattering photo of Mustak Ahmed Attar, recuperating at home, his face gaunt and ashen, a walking stick in one hand. Dear God, what was this? Divine retribution? No, He wouldn't help out the Communists; they didn't believe him in Him. Although right at that point, Nigel wasn't sure he believed either. Then, to make his faith really waver, not only in God but in all that was good or just or right, he saw that the biggest-selling tabloid paper was leading with the story of Bhupati Koyal, a young man whose father had been killed in the hospital fire. Bhupati had believed that all was lost, until Lohia had put up the money to fund him through medical school, his one big dream. Once he was a doctor, he would not only be able to support his family, he would also be able to save lives! Accompanying the article was a photo of Bhupati, the picture of the perfect student, sitting on a wooden chair with his mother, sari *anchol* pulled over her head and a pained expression on her face, standing behind him with her hand on his shoulder. The caption: *God takes with one hand but gives with the other.* Oh please, why not just hand out awards for best dialogue, best director, best cinematography, and be done with it!

Nigel pressed his eyes closed, trying to black out what he had just read, but when he opened them again, he realised that *still*, it wasn't over, for the piece below was about Devi's . . . handbag. Receptacle of miscellany, security blanket, and . . . weapon. There was even a quick poll asking whether it was acceptable to hit someone with a handbag—64% said 'No', 31% said 'Yes', and

5% weren't sure. Nigel covered his face with his palms. It was an unmitigated disaster.

As for the Americans? Despite his ebullient briefing, there was no good news. Only cynical comments about her administration being all talk and no action, about her grand plans amounting to only that—plans, and about her failure to make a convincing case for West Bengal as an investment destination.

DEVI INVITES AMERICAN LAUGHTER INSTEAD OF AMERICAN INVESTMENT

PARAMITA PROMISES LITTLE TO THE AMERICANS AND DELIVERS EVEN LESS TO THE BENGALIS

WILL THE AMERICANS BECOME THE NEW MARWARIS?

AMERICAN INVESTORS UNIMPRESSED BY DEVI'S HANDBAG

There was even a snide opinion piece on how people elected the government they deserved, which just went to show time and again that West Bengal, as well as having the highest population of (self-certified) intellectuals in the world, also had the highest population of masochists. This, in the context of the American people choosing their leader on the basis of whom they'd most like to have a beer with—a naive mechanism, perhaps, but better than choosing on the basis of whom they'd most like to be punished by. Nigel took a deep breath and tried to exhale slowly. It was now apparent that what he was looking at was total belittlement. A complete and bloody hatchet job.

He hadn't known that all this would happen, he couldn't have known. Yet the whys and wherefores didn't matter right now. The shit was his to shovel, and he had better start shovelling before Devi drowned in it. He felt his temples throbbing, and even though he had showered only an hour ago and the air conditioning in the car was on high, he was now covered in a sticky film of sweat. He looked out of the window and then realised the driver was taking him in the wrong direction.

"Babu," he queried in Bengali, "where are we going? Writers' Building isn't this way. Is there a road closure?"

"I'm not taking you to Writers'," the driver replied, emotionless, glancing into the rear-view mirror, "I'm taking you to Devi's house. We're nearly there."

Any colour Nigel had left in his face, departed quickly. Devi's house. The dragon's own lair. He'd been there before, but that was for late-night bonding sessions, when Devi would combine social activity (poetry readings, singing, art appreciation) with political strategy (anti-Communist rants, anti-elitism rants, anti-anyone-anti-her rants). An early morning call-up was not for bonding, it was for blaming.

"Let me out," Nigel said to the driver, leaning forward.

"We're almost there," the driver said, not slowing down.

"I said, *let me out.* I'll walk the rest."

The driver narrowed his eyes and pulled over to the kerb abruptly. Nigel scrambled out, and the driver pulled away sharply, barely waiting for the door to click closed. Nigel watched him go and then squatted down, resting his hands on his bony knees. He was quite sure his stomach, his bowels, his bladder, his whole insides were about to evacuate themselves all over the street. I cannot shit myself, Nigel thought, I am wearing a suit.

The moment passed. Nigel looked up to see a skinny old man wearing a vest and lungi and carrying a plastic bucket staring at him, vaguely suspicious. Nigel smiled at him, his best 'Trust me,

I might be an Anglo-Indian but I'm just like one of you!' smile. The man did not respond. So, Nigel said in Bengali, with as much charm as he could muster, and in the hope of making himself seem, if not important, then at least credible, "Tell me, Dada, which way is Devi's house?"

The man jerked his head to indicate which way Nigel should keep walking. To Nigel's chagrin, he did not seem impressed.

Devi's house was in Behala. In neighbouring Kalighat, lived another female with a fierce temper: Kali, the dark goddess of death and destruction. And, as the joke went, there were days when the Behala Devi made the Kalighat Devi seem like a nagging housewife. Nigel feared that this was going to be one of those days. Wretchedly, he kept walking.

Devi's house was now in Nigel's eyeline, and accordingly, he slowed down his pace. Suddenly, he felt a tap on his shoulder and he spun his head around to see, Manish Ray, the minister for backward people, grinning.

"Let's go, let's go, let's go!" Manish said in mockingly singsong Bengali. "We don't want to be late for school. We might get the cane!"

Nigel did not even have to smell Manish's breath to realise that Manish had been up drinking all night. And he was quite sure that the man was swaying slightly, too. Either that, or he was standing still, and the morning's news had been so unbalancing that the world had stopped spinning and started oscillating instead.

"Actually, I think we're early," Nigel said solicitously, thinking as fast as he could. "So maybe we can go and have something to eat . . ."

"Eat?" smirked Manish, still speaking in Bengali. "Why would I need food when I have Devi's love to nourish me!"

Oh God, thought Nigel, oh God. This man is a liability. He is bad news and I have already had enough bad news this morning.

Now Nigel started to move quickly towards Devi's house but just before he could press the calling bell, Manish managed to catch up with him and put out his hand to grab Nigel's scrawny shoulder.

"Hang on one minute whilst I have a smoke," he drawled, rubbing his eyes. As he took one leisurely drag after the other, he seemed quite unbothered about the imminent bloodbath.

"You know, this house reminds of my student digs off the Iffley Road," Manish observed, back to his formal English.

"I'm sure that was a very nice digs," replied Nigel, uncertainly but earnestly, unsure of the word *digs.*

"It was a complete dump," snorted Manish, eyeing up the building. "I must say, she's taken this common people malarkey a bit too far, don't you think?"

Nigel shrugged warily, but this only encouraged Manish further.

"OK, OK, I understand," he continued, putting up his hands, "she doesn't want to live in the Raj, she thinks it reeks of pomp and ceremony. And I can see that living there might seem a little inconsonant. But doesn't she realise that living in the Raj is *precisely* what the common man would do if he had the chance! So, whilst ordinary people spend a good deal of energy trying to improve their lot, *she* spends a good deal of energy on assiduously neglecting material advancement. Let me put it another way—don't you think she's straining a bit for effect?"

Nigel wasn't really listening to Manish's monologue anymore. All he needed to know was that words were coming out of Manish's mouth and they were not flattering ones. She's standing by an open window, listening, Nigel thought, she's listening, and she's going to kill him. Today, this house will become an abattoir! But before he had a chance to tell Manish, in a clear and reverberating voice, that he wholly disagreed, and that he found Devi's decision to remain in the house in which she had grown up not only principled and befitting but also quite charming, Manish stubbed out his cigarette and said in a mock bark, "Right then; let's go! Devi Bo Beep has rallied her sheep!"

A lot of leaders make their subordinates nervous by making them wait and giving them time to stew. Devi, however, made hers nervous by not giving them any time to gather their thoughts. She ambushed them and then startled an answer out of them. So, as Nigel walked into her living room, even before he had a chance to locate a seat, she said to him, grabbing a handful of newspapers and shaking them at him, "Which people are being responsible for this?"

The first answer that sprang to Nigel's mind: *not me!* But before he could say anything, Manish answered, decorously pinching up his trousers at the knee as he took a seat, "Responsible for what? You taking a drubbing in the papers?"

Nigel furtively glanced around the room. In it were Partha Pratim Choudhury, minister of commerce and industry; Surajit Sinha, minister of environmental affairs; Insaf Khan, minister of power; and Rohini Poddar, minister without portfolio. Devi's favourites. For now. From their expressions, Nigel deduced that none of them were going to get on board with Manish. It was Devi who eventually scoffed, "And why I am being drubbed? What I am doing to be drubbed?"

"Well," sighed Manish, leaning back in his chair, "you were *there* at the meeting with the Americans yesterday. It was hardly an unqualified success. And your popularity's not at an all time high."

The man is insane, Nigel thought. And now Devi will cut out his tongue. Instead she replied, albeit defensively, scowling and crossing her arms, "I am not being a politician for popularity!"

Really, woman, Manish thought, your lurches from one populist position to another could make my head spin more than a triple vodka shot.

"Regardless," he continued, "along with all this Lohia news, it's a bit of a cluster fuck, isn't it?"

Everyone else looked at the floor pretending not to have heard. Devi was not familiar with the term 'cluster fuck' but she figured it out pretty quickly.

"You do not have to be using those sorts of bad languages," she told him, headmistress-y. "We are all bhadralok here!"

"Bhad*ra*? More like bhad*al*!" chuckled Manish.

"What is wrong with you?" Devi spat. "If you're going to behave like a chai-wallah, then go and make tea! Go!"

Tea duty might have seemed like a petty sanction for Manish's unmitigated effrontery, but Devi knew what she was doing. Belittlement often worked far better in shutting someone up than outright enmity. Besides, despite claiming to be proud of her humble background, she had no issue with using a lowly occupation as an insult. Manish rose to his feet, quiet now, if not quietened, and gamely made his way towards the kitchen. Nigel, keen to pre-empt Devi belittling him, too, offered to help Manish. "How many people does it take to make tea," she jeered, but she let him go anyway.

In the kitchen, Manish piped up again.

"You know what the problem is? The problem is that it is not Devi *of* The Truth Party, it is Devi *and* The Truth Party. Like Diana Ross and The Supremes. She's a solo artist. We're just her backing singers. We have to sing to her tune or we don't sing at all."

"But without Devi, we wouldn't be at the top of the charts, would we?" Nigel replied, wondering whether he had extended the metaphor correctly.

Manish mulled this over as he poured the tea.

"Well, in this part of the world, we do like our divas!"

In the living room, Devi was pacing so vigorously, that the trays of tea shook as Manish and Nigel walked back in.

"No, I am not accepting that!" she said to Partha Pratim, a slight, nervy man, whose whole body seemed to pucker under the onslaught. "We must be doing something! If you are not being capable, then I will find be finding someone who is!"

Partha Pratim looked down at his feet. For the last ten minutes, he had been elaborating on what the phrase 'cutting off your nose to spite your face' meant and why she should try her best to not carry out this act of surgery. However, she just did not seem able to grasp his objections.

"See," Manish mouthed silently at Nigel, as they set down the trays on the old, scratched coffee table, "Diana Ross!"

Partha Pratim now raised his eyebrows at Insaf, a heavyset, dour type, for support. Reluctantly, Insaf took up the cause, shaking his head and sighing, rather pompously, "Unfortunately, Devi, it's not your decision to make—the granting of coal mine leases is a function of one of our agencies, The Directorate of Mines and Minerals, not you personally. And The Lohia *Group*, not Lohia personally, won the auction through due process, as set out by the directorate. We have no right to interfere with the process unless we have very good reason to—it would make us look meddlesome. And even more importantly, in the context of the Americans or any other investors, it would make us look like we're difficult to do business with. In fact, it would make us look *anti*-business . . ."

"I am not being anti-business, I am being anti-corruption," Devi snapped.

Partha Pratim and Insaf glanced at each other, realising that at this point they had pretty much lost the battle. Now Devi turned to Rohini, a singularly snivelling and sycophantic sort—why else would Devi have a minister without portfolio, if not to make sure that said minister's loyalty was to Devi instead of her ministry—and griped, "The directorate is doing this only to upset me!"

Rohini cocked her head and closed her eyes for a second, thinking: yes, Devi, you're right, as always. Manish raised an eyebrow and then spoke, deadpan.

"Yes, the directorate's main concern is how to upset you. It's not how they're going to fulfil their remit which I believe is, wait, let me check," he tapped his phone screen a few times, "*towards systematic and scientific exploration and exploitation of mineral resource of the State to promote mineral based industries to encourage employment generation and to increase revenue earning.*"

Rohini looked at Manish askance.

"Anyone can look up a website!" she retorted.

Manish stared back at Rohini, amused.

"Yes, anyone can, but apparently *you* didn't," he quipped, causing Rohini to scowl.

Meanwhile, Devi was mulling things over in her head. Her beady little eyes were shooting all over the place, her nostrils flaring, her lips pouting. She looked very determined and hamsterish—a hamster with a plan.

After a moment, she declared, "We shouldn't be giving so much importance to the Americans; then they'll be getting too big for their boots. They should be chasing us to do business, not the other way around. We are not beggars!"

And with that, she sat down and crossed her arms.

Manish's hangover was just kicking in and he didn't want to make his nascent headache any worse, yet he took a deep breath, and said, carefully, "Well, if that's the case then why don't we take a completely different tack?"

Devi focused on him, so he continued.

"Do you remember that meeting you and I had a few months ago?"

"We are always having meetings and meetings and meetings!" she huffed. Well, you're not wrong about that, Manish thought, but went on gamely, "The one with the director of the rural livelihood . . ." he couldn't remember the man's full title, "*thing* . . ."

Devi kept staring.

"The one where funding was pulled because milestones were not met?"

Devi's expression soured, so Manish went on quickly.

"Do you remember that you and I discussed a public-private enterprise at the end? Something ambitious, something substantial, something that shows everyone 'Bengal Means Business'?"

"So?" said Devi, po-faced.

Everyone else seemed to wonder where Manish was going; they had to be sure before they would contemplate following. Good god, he thought, can't they work it out?

"So," Manish explained slowly, "what about offering an olive branch to Lohia?"

Devi's expression did not change. Olive, thought Manish. I could do with a Martini right now.

"We could piggyback on his coal mine project. We call the shots but they do the hard work. It would be a win-win situation. No foreigners would be involved, we'd win back the confidence of the Marwaris, and, most importantly, we would be improving the lot of your heartland—poor, rural people."

All the others scanned Devi's face to see how she might be taking this. They were now all excited by the possibility of a very rare win-win situation but dared not say so.

Devi was still thinking. As someone who had made a career out of struggling, whose career was indeed *based* on struggle, struggle was all she knew. A win-win situation? Immediately, she was suspicious. She deemed success without strife to be some kind of fiddle. Gradually, her expression changed. Now, she looked like she had a hair in her mouth. Someone else's hair. Eventually, she spoke, lifting her chin.

"I am always being a very fair and reasonable person. That is why I am always fighting injustice and lies and corruption, and that is why I am fighting a man like Lohia!"

So, there it was. The others tried not to show their disappointment; they were all annoyed with themselves for getting their hopes up in the first place.

"And," she said, smiling assuredly, "I am going to award the Banga Bibhushan to V S Aggarwal. That way the Marwaris will be liking me again!"

There was a moment's silence whilst everyone absorbed this, and then everyone apart from Manish nodded and told her that it was a very good idea, very astute.

Manish, however, interjected, "That's all well and good but what about Lohia and this damn mine? We start throwing our weight around with him, then we just look like we're hounding him—and for no good reason. That kind of behaviour does not encourage others to have confidence in this government's maturity or even-handedness. So are you going to let him get on with his business?"

The others looked down at the floor; had Manish actually just said *you*? In that tone of voice!

Devi glared at Manish with a ferocity which would make most people look away. But Manish just glared right back. Deadlock. Someone say something, thought Nigel. Anything.

Then, Surajit spoke for the first time, in a quiet, thin voice, which seemed at complete odds with his body.

"Ac-tu-al-ly, the project can't go ahead without my ministry granting an environmental clearance. And that in itself could take *years* . . ."

Devi liked this. She pretended not to, but her defensively folded arms opened up to rest on the sides of her chair. Leaning forward, staring straight into his eyes, she firmly said, "Yes! You must slow it down!" And then added, after a moment, with a sly smile, "After all, it is important that you are taking your time and doing your job properly . . ." And then, after another moment, "And what about that green army?"

"Which green army?" Surajit asked solicitously.

Devi scrunched up her face and focused her mind, but nothing came to her.

"What she means," Manish sighed, eyes half closed in pain, both from his headache and from the tortuous proceedings, "is Green Police."

"Oh, I see!" Surajit said with delight. "Green *Police*!"

"Army, police, doesn't matter. You must be going and speaking with them."

Surajit gave Devi a serious smile and nodded. "It will be done."

Now, back on the front foot, Devi became animated, getting into her groove, finding her rhythm.

"And the people? What about the people?" she asked keenly, looking at Nigel.

So far, Nigel had sat in a corner and kept quiet, willing himself to be unseen and unheard. He was feeling very lucky to be alive and he wanted to stay that way. So, he replied, vaguely, ". . . What people, Devi?"

"The common people!" she answered with gusto, adding, impatiently, "What are the people saying on the line?"

Nigel dithered. Manish, sensing his hesitation, answered instead.

"The people are fickle. Now that Lohia is out of jail and going around doing good deeds—of course for his own benefit but they don't see that—he's in their good books again. You, meanwhile, are not."

Devi pressed her lips together and stretched her dewlap. Now's my chance, Nigel thought, I'll elevate myself in her eyes by suggesting a solution.

"Devi, what I can do is employ some people to go online and put across another point of view—that Lohia is sneaky, that all of his *good person* antics are just an act. And that, at the end of the day, unlike you, he will do only what's good for him, not what's good for the people."

"Why we should be paying people to tell the truth?" Devi asked, annoyed.

They had had this conversation many times before: you have to pay people to tell the truth, because your enemies are paying people to tell lies! But she didn't care. To her, payment wasn't a fair exchange, it was just a form of corruption. But in the circumstances, instead of going through the merits of his solution yet again, Nigel thought it safest to crawl up her arse and hide there, so quickly conceded, "Yes, you're right."

Devi acknowledged this, drummed her fingers on the chair's arm, then said, firmly, "You must be arranging a town hall meeting and inviting the people. I will be telling them the truth. Then they will be knowing what's what."

Nigel's head emerged from her arse to say only one word.

"Yes."

Although what he really wanted to say was: No, no, no, no, no, no, *no*!

XI

Breakfast at Hyatt was providing Anil with a much needed counterpoint to the previous night, where he had woken up at two to find himself sharing his bed with a family of cockroaches. This despite the fact that he had told the caretaker seven times to make sure the garbage bags from the block were properly contained and disposed of so that they would not attract vermin. No matter; Hyatt was close enough to be a second home.

As soon as a long-serving waitress at The Waterside Café had seen Anil taking a seat, the first thing she had asked him after taking his order was whether he had slept well as he looked a little fatigued. A charming way of saying he looked like shit. Immediately, Anil was taken by her; she was very pretty, too. Ah, Kolkata—pretty girls, genuine thoughtfulness, attentive service, pretty girls . . .

"I've slept better," he smiled, "but how did *you* sleep? You're the one who had to be up at the crack of dawn!"

The waitress smiled coquettishly. "Very well, Sir, and might I ask how your parents are?" Anil's parents were well-known at Hyatt; when they were in Kolkata, they arranged for all sorts of parties and functions to be held there when they deemed their palatial home to be not palatial enough.

"My parents? Who knows? They're off on their travels again, Brazil at the moment I believe."

"How wonderful; I'd love to travel; I've never even left WB."

"Well, travel broadens the mind, but home is home."

Now that the waitress had mentioned his parents, Anil started to think about them. So are you back here for good? Really? he remembered his mother saying. Do you think anything is ever going to change in West Bengal? I mean, *properly change*? Some processes are irreversible, and some declines are permanent. After all, the phrase is *the rise and fall*, not *the rise and fall and rise* . . . And his father had added, why are you wasting your time here? Most people who have the chance, leave. Of course, it could have been London, New York, Kolkata, but it's not. Then why are *you* still here? Anil had countered, and what are *you* complaining about? Your life here seems pretty agreeable to me! Ah, but we're the decadent elite—we could waste money anywhere, it's just that it's easy enough to waste it here, and we're too lazy to move! But we don't represent anything, we're not the future, we're not what makes a place truly great. And this is a place which can never be made great again, its problems are intractable. That, I'm afraid, my boy, is life.

No, they're not right, they're just stuck in the past, Anil thought, as he ate his breakfast at the poolside table where he had relocated in order to feel the morning breeze. Because right now I am eating a croissant, which is light but rich, and moist but flaky, and a croissant of this greatness requires skill and diligence in its creation. And it was made right here. And not only that, but I am staying at a hotel for which the epithet *world-class* is no exaggeration. And there are plenty of pretty girls milling about! Sure, there is room for improvement—a lot of improvement—but we're hardly a lost cause.

Anil drained the last of his Assam tea and closed his eyes for a minute, considering whether he should go back to bed for a snooze when he suddenly sat bolt upright. *Newspapers.* He had completely forgotten. Just as he was about to go back to his room to fetch his tablet, the waitress reappeared and asked whether he would like another pot of tea; she was good. He accepted and asked her to bring him the day's newspapers, too. "Which ones would you like to read?"

"All of them."

Anil couldn't help but smile to himself as he read through *The United Times* piece on Sachin. Miss Ghatak had done a nice job. Not so fawning that it would arouse cynicism but still favourable enough to override any Bengali suspicion that Sachin was a rapacious Marwari who cared only for two things—himself and money. Now, he was both the emperor of largesse and the humble servant.

As for the coal mining project in Balachuria, so far, so good. The doubters, the defeatists, the depreciators, all would come forth—of that, Anil had no doubt—but for now, they were keeping their own counsel. The general mood, he sensed, was one of optimism and anticipation.

As for his adversary, well, she was being treated just how she deserved to be treated—with ridicule. From the start, she had claimed that everything she did, even hating people, was out of her love for humanity. But now her true colours were starting to show and her self-styled veneration of the common man was turning out to be closer to contempt for him, a contempt that was apparent in the way that although she claimed to do everything for him, she actually ended up doing nothing for him, or at least nothing worth doing. In fact, was her contempt not actually contained in the moniker *Devi*, which she clung to so fiercely? For a goddess relied on being worshipped, relied on the subservience of her devotees. If those people started to rely on *themselves*, then the deity became a relic. As Anil mulled this over, he saw a man in sports kit, a towel thrown around his neck, walking away from the gym building and towards him. Anil squinted for a moment and then realised that it was Taylor Nicholson, a classmate from business school, and not a classmate he had much time for at that. What the hell is he doing here? Anil thought.

"Hey! Buddy!" Taylor exclaimed, as he sat down next to Anil. "Long time, no see!"

Not long enough, Anil thought. And it's polite to ask before you take a seat.

"Taylor," he replied cordially, "what a pleasant surprise."

"Yeah, I know. What are you doing here?"

"I work here."

"For Hyatt hotels?"

"No, I mean I work in Kolkata."

"Oh, great . . ."

"And you?"

"I'm here with Telford & Co."

"The civil engineering guys?"

"Exactly. You know, obviously I'm not doing the creative or science-y bit myself, I'm just in sales and marketing. But even though I might not know a truss from a tread, if you ever want a bridge, I'm your man!"

Anil did not laugh at Taylor's phoney self-deprecation. Sometimes, he hated these business school idiots with their view of life as one big self-marketing opportunity.

"Good for you. And is that what you're doing here—building bridges, metaphorically as well as literally?"

Taylor chuckled.

"Literally as well as metaphorically," he repeated. "You're so funny, A-Neal!"

Then, he leant in, and said in a quiet, less jocular tone, "You know, there's a lot of red tape here, buddy. And even the basics—like power supply—are pretty hit and miss. Then there are the subsidiary issues, like the heat and then the monsoon, as well as the quality of the labour supply . . . I'm not sure if we can get comfortable with these kind of conditions . . ."

"I suppose it depends on your appetite . . ." Anil shrugged.

"For risk?"

"Not so much risk as, how shall I put it, inconvenience."

"Inconvenience!" Taylor chortled, adding solemnly, "Listen, we can deal with *inconvenience*—we just completed a project in Doha, where we had major concrete shrinkage, we were essentially road locked, we were in over a hundred degrees heat, and we were working at the pace of a retarded snail. *That* was inconvenient. But we knew that the government was backing us all the way and that, quite frankly, we were going to get paid. Here . . ." He leant back in his chair, sighed, then continued, with a frown which approximated thoughtfulness, "You know, you get the feeling that on one hand, people are keen to advance, but then on the other hand, you also get the feeling that they don't actually want to move on, that they're quite happy as they are . . ."

"Chronic ambivalence is a Bengali condition," Anil responded, quite tired of Taylor and wishing he would leave. But the waitress was bringing over Anil's fresh pot of tea, and Taylor took the opportunity to order breakfast himself. Oh god, Anil thought, he's just getting going. Before the morning's out, my ears will be bleeding.

"You know," Taylor started up again, as soon as the waitress started to walk away, "some of the women here are pretty darn hot."

Anil said nothing. The women here are far too good for you, he thought, you just stick to your native pussy.

Taylor, catching Anil's impassive expression, changed tack quickly.

"So, you know I was at this kind of conference thing yesterday, you know, with that woman *Davey*?"

It's *Devi*, Anil thought. She's not *that woman*, she's the chief minister of West Bengal. And that's not her actual name, you *gadha*!

"Sure . . . How was it?"

"Well, it was a bit chaotic . . ."

"We like to think of it as homespun," Anil smiled tightly. He might not have been able to stand the woman himself but he wasn't going to let a twerp like Taylor belittle her and, by proxy, his home.

"Homespun!" Taylor grinned.

The waitress came back with Taylor's breakfast, and Anil noticed how Taylor looked at her chest as she bent down slightly to put the tray on the table. Please just go back home, Taylor, Anil thought, there's nothing for you here. Suddenly, he rubbed his temple, then said, quickly, "Sorry—I actually have a meeting this morning, I must get going. But best of luck with all your projects and enjoy the rest of your stay here. And do stay in touch!"

And with that, he disappeared so quickly that Taylor did not even have the chance to call out: but I don't have your contact details!

For years, when at home, Sachin had been eating alone. He did use to ask Sharmila to join him, but either she didn't like the food that had been prepared or she wasn't hungry or she just didn't feel like it. Instead, she seemed to prefer to eat on the go, throwing handfuls of this and that into her mouth. In the early days of setting up their empire, being easy-going enough to eat what you could when you could, without fuss or ceremony, had been advantageous, necessary, even. But now, her unwillingness to actually sit down and enjoy a meal rather than just wolf down food on instinct, seemed unmannerly and unsociable. So, he was more than surprised when on Saturday morning, she joined him at the table, even taking a slice of toast from the rack.

He wondered what could have possibly precipitated the move. Even the night before, she had not seemed either bothered or bolstered by his return from jail. He had known that she would not visit him there, but could she not at least pretend that she was quite pleased that he was out of the damn place? After all, as it had been proven, he shouldn't have even been in there! Wasn't *that* cause for celebration? Sharmila, my love, he wanted to ask, are you actually a zombie? Although zombies could be sexy—they were in the late night movies Sachin watched—and the chance of Sharmila ever recovering any of her allure Sachin had long ago put at nil.

And then he noticed that she had put a newspaper on the table. A newspaper? He could never convince her to read the proper news. Her query: why should I? When he had answered that it was important to be well informed, she had retorted, why is it important? So that other people can say, oh, she's very well informed! The only things she liked reading were human-interest stories.

Wiping the crumbs away from her lips with the back of her hand, despite there being a napkin right in front of her, she passed the newspaper down the table to Sachin, asking, in a gentler tone than he was used to, "Is this your doing?"

Quickly, he scanned the page. The story was about Bhupati Koyal, a young man whose father had been killed in the hospital fire—and the article said that Sachin was now putting him through medical school! Sachin frowned for a moment and then relaxed: ah yes, Anil had mentioned this yesterday.

"Yes, that's right," he replied, putting the paper down. "Why?"

Sharmila cocked her head.

"It's a good thing you've done," she said firmly, and then left the room.

Sharmila had not said a positive word to Sachin in years. Shocked, his mind went blank for a moment and then he thought: is the real Sharmila back?

XII

For a week, the ghost had appeared. Mainly at night, but a couple of times at dusk, when there had still been enough light for Anima to confirm that it was definitely a she-ghost. At first, Anima had thought that it was the ghost of her brother—there was something about the spectre that reminded her of him—but then she had noticed the long hair and the clothing. This, of course, despite the fact that she didn't officially believe in ghosts or any other supernatural phenomenon. But living on her own, in a faintly familiar but still strange house with no human company, and just her thoughts and apprehensions and what-the-hell-have-I-done feelings to consume her, she was right on the boundary of her solidly grounded rationality. She told herself that it was just a strain of pareidolia—seeing a meaningful image in a random object. If a face could be seen in a cloud, or a man in the moon, then why not a woman in a tangle of trees? And she also knew that as she didn't have enough work to occupy her restless brain, her brain would then just make up things, as it disliked having nothing to do. Seeing a ghost was just a healthy expression of her brain amusing itself! But even *her* brain couldn't convince her of her brain's workings. So she had said to the puppies, which tussled and scrambled and rumbled around her feet, hey, what do you think? Do you think I should say hi to the ghost? She can't be that bad, right? After all, you little guys don't seem scared of her, and dogs are meant to be the best judges of this sort of thing! The puppies yipped and yapped. Yes, you should talk to her, they were saying. From pareidolia to anthropomorphia, Anima was on edge and on the edge. For two nights, she called out to the ghost, but no response. Fine, Anima thought, I would still rather live with a mute ghost than The Professor. On the third night though, the ghost spoke: Is this your house, Madam? Anima tried to remember what her uncle had told her to say to ghosts. Finally, she said: yes, this is my house, but you can stay here, too. The ghost came out of the shadows. The puppies, which followed Anima everywhere, raced untidily between the two of them. It's okay, Anima thought, she's clearly a friendly presence. Can I help you, Anima asked her gently, do you want to come inside?

In the kitchen, as Anima made tea, boiling water in an old pan on the single ring gas stove, as she hadn't yet managed to get hold of a kettle, the ghost told Anima that her name was Tipu Nath, and she lived a five-minute walk away. For a split second, Anima thought: oh, so you're haunting another place, too, and felt vaguely disappointed that her ghost had not taken up exclusive residency at her place. But then, just as suddenly, reason finally overcame emotion, and Anima realised that what she was dealing with was not a spirit, but a flesh-and-blood person. "Ha, you're real, I'm not going mad," she said, as much to herself as to Tipu. Tipu, not knowing what she meant, just smiled.

As Tipu had it, everyone in the village had been wondering who Anima was. She had been spotted the first night she had arrived, and a few times since then when buying groceries at the local shops, but she had not introduced herself and people had not dared ask—no one else apart from Tipu had been brave enough to actually come and find out. She said this quite proudly. There was even a joke going around, Tipu added, that Anima, who had seemingly appeared from nowhere, was a ghost. "Really," Anima smiled, "that's funny!"

Now, in the house, Tipu shed her initial reserve and bombarded Anima with questions—what was her name, where was she from, how was this her house, why had she come here? Although Anima did not usually respond well to an inquisition, she found Tipu's over-familiarity curiously appealing and answered her questions as plainly as she could. Tipu, accordingly, accepted Anima's answers without any further interrogation; there was something about Anima that made Tipu trust her immediately and fully. It was only after Anima's credentials had been established that Tipu informed her that firstly her grandmother, and then her mother, and then, finally, she herself had been taking care of the house since, as she put it, "Everyone went away a long time ago—before I was even born!" She said this in a voice that was at once reticent and candid; Tipu's own feelings on the matter would be decided by Anima's reaction.

Anima's heart immediately lodged itself in her throat. It couldn't be, she thought. It couldn't. It couldn't. Pusan's family in Balachuria were dead. No, no, no, *assumed* dead. She looked at Tipu carefully. Was there a resemblance to Pusan? No, not *really*. Her brain was just adding two and two and coming up with five hundred and six. Nevertheless, she couldn't help but ask, "Why did your grandmother and mother look after this house?"

"Because it needed looking after," Tipu replied plainly. "If you don't give a house a good sweep now and then, it gets eaten up by dust."

"Well, did they ever actually live here?"

"*No*," retorted Tipu, as if her mother and grandmother had been accused of squatting.

Realising that Tipu felt insulted, Anima continued lightly, "And who's been paying you to take care of the house?"

"No one," Tipu answered, clasping her hands behind her back and twisting and turning like a little girl.

Anima smiled. "That's very good of you. And how old are you, Tipu?" In Anima's judgement, Tipu still looked young enough to be asked that question.

"Eighteen, well, *nearly* eighteen."

"And how long have you been looking after the house?"

Tipu shrugged and then replied, looking down at the floor, "I used to come with my mum, now I come on my own."

"Why, where's your mum?"

"Not well."

"And your dad?"

Completely straight: "Yes, I have a dad."

As they both waited for the pan of water to come to the boil, Anima calmed herself down. Don't jump to conclusions, she told herself. In places like this, people are good, they see a beautiful empty property like this, they take care of it. Just because it needs taking care of. For no other reason. Remember that the brain likes to make connections where there are none. That's why there are so many conspiracy theories!

The water came to the boil and Anima made the tea. But Tipu seemed less interested in drinking her tea than in watching Anima crouch down to the mother dog, which was lying in a box lined with a woollen shawl, and gently stroke her whilst she lapped at a bowl of milk. Anima glanced up and noticed that Tipu wasn't even really looking at the dog; she was looking at the bowl of milk. Then it occurred to her that, in this place, fresh milk could be a luxury. And here she was, feeding it to a dog. She remembered a little scene from her childhood—she hated drinking milk, would have to have it forced down her by her mother or her ayah, but whenever in Balachuria, the other little girls who were invited around to play with her would cherish a glass of milk as if it were liquid gold.

"Would you prefer a glass of milk?" Anima asked, and then seeing that Tipu did but was reluctant to say so, she added, "I'm going to have one."

Tipu shrugged and said, "Well, if you're going to have one . . ."

As Tipu drank her milk (Anima's remaining untouched), she looked towards the dog and asked, "You're making her better?"

"I hope so . . ."

Tipu rubbed her lips together and then said, "She's my dog . . . Her name's Prem . . ."

"Oh," Anima replied, slightly abashed, "I'm sorry. She was here when I arrived. You know she's had puppies, don't you? Would you like to take all of them home with you?"

Tipu shook her head immediately. "No, you can look after them, they'll stay better here with you."

Anima smiled and went back to stroking Prem's head, although she could feel Tipu looking at her very, very closely. Finally, Tipu asked, "Are you a doctor?"

How could she have known? From just the way Anima was stroking a dog? Anima's gut instinct was to say 'no'. Saying 'yes' felt like it would bring with it a whole raft of obligations and responsibilities. But as a doctor, lying about it somehow seemed wrong. So, after a moment's quiet hesitation, she answered, "Er, yes."

Then, right off the bat from Tipu: "Can you make my mum better?"

"Er . . ."

She might have been a doctor, but she hadn't come to Balachuria to *be* a doctor. She had come to be alone, unbothered, free from responsibility. I came here to get away from things not to get involved in them, and I just want some peace and quiet, Anima thought. But she knew it would be churlish to say that, so instead fibbed, "Well, I'm not sure I have the time right now . . ."

Tipu looked at Anima, questioningly.

"I mean," Anima explained, moving her eyes around the kitchen, "I have so much work and stuff to do in this place . . . It's a very big house, as you know."

But Tipu already had an answer prepared.

"Your kind of lady shouldn't be doing that kind of work! You tell me what needs to be done, and I'll get in people to help you and make sure it's sorted out. *I'll* help you myself. And then you'll have time to be doing doctoring!"

And that was the end of that.

After Tipu had drained her glass of milk and left in a state of some excitement, Anima sat down by Prem and said to her: what kind of lady do *you* think I am? Just a silly lady who talks to animals, I suppose! And what kind of lady do *I* think I am? Apparently the kind of lady who allows herself to be outmanoeuvred by a wily kid! Absentmindedly, she reached for the glass of milk, took a sip, and then immediately grimaced, spitting it out over the floor. And definitely the kind of lady who still hates milk!

She has come, Tipu thought, skipping back to her house. Finally, she has come! All my life, I have been waiting for the person who is going to do, well, I don't know exactly what, but *something*. Because in this place, nothing ever happens! But not any more. I can just sense it.

"What's got into you," Tipu's father Kalyan asked her as she walked in, "and where have you been? I hope you haven't been hanging out at that old *raj bari* again, spying on that woman. If she catches you, she'll report you to the police for trespassing. You don't know her kind of people. They're different from us and they don't like us either." Tipu's face fell. "I'm only telling you this for your own good."

"Then why did you allow mum and I to go and keep an eye on the place?"

"That was when it was empty. It's not empty anymore, so you don't need to go up there." Dad logic—arbitrary but still compelling. Tipu said nothing and instead finished preparing dinner.

Anima was quite surprised by the alacrity with which Tipu arranged various works. Someone came to tidy up the garden. Someone came to fix the plumbing. Someone came to re-plaster the external walls and paint the inner ones. Someone even came to repaint the house sign. No one provided a quotation for their work at the beginning but neither did they ask for any money at the end; Anima would just ask Tipu what a reasonable price was and then pay that amount. Are you sure that's enough? Anima would check. That's more than enough, Tipu would reply, surely, pay them any more and it'll go straight to their head, you have to keep these kinds of people under control!

By the time Anima's driver came back a few weeks later he was quite surprised by the transformation, and also slightly put out. He had been hoping that Anima would be finding country life quite disagreeable—he had found that rich women could be quite whimsical—and would be ready to move back to Kolkata, where he thought she belonged. Instead he found her settling in, with a new set of people surrounding her. He felt slightly undermined, and grumped around the place finding fault where he could—nothing was as good as it was at *home*. He had rented a small van and brought with him a variety of items Anima had asked for, amongst them a large deluxe refrigerator, a fancy-looking kettle and matching toaster, a compact water purifier, a sleek air conditioner, and an elaborate steam iron (Anima had also been keen on a washing machine and a dishwasher, but they had agreed between them that the local plumbing would not be up to it) and was at pains to point out that she could not have found these things where she lived now. He was most put out though when she handed him a list of medicines to bring back next time (Tipu had suggested that payment to Anima's new staff might also include the occasional medical diagnoses and provision of drugs); he knew that they were not for her, that they were for the new people. Can't they go to *their* doctor, he complained, why should they hassle you? They're taking advantage of you, you know! They don't have a doctor here, Anima had informed him. Of course, she knew that he was upset because he felt his position in the household hierarchy had been lowered, so to alleviate his dourness, and serve her own interests at the same time, she asked him about The Professor. If there was one thing that universally made people feel useful and important, it was making them a conduit in a personal relationship. And, truth be told, although she was loathe to involve anyone in her personal affairs, she had no other option.

Since she had left a month ago, The Professor had only sent her the most perfunctory of texts, courteous as they were. How's that old house, are you keeping well, what's the weather like, that sort of thing. Enough so that he could not be accused of complete apathy but not so much that it indicated any genuine interest. And not one phone call. Although she had expected perhaps a tiny bit more concern, she put his initial coolness down to the fact that he didn't actually realise that she had left him. Denial? Perhaps. Or even more likely, she thought, a surfeit of self-absorption. First of all, she asked the driver how The Professor was and whether he was keeping well. The driver replied, briefly, that The Professor himself was keeping very well. Good, said Anima, I'm pleased to hear it. And does he have—how to put it so that she didn't sound expectant—any . . . message for me? No, Madam, the driver smiled. He didn't have to think about it. Oh good, said Anima, swallowing, I'm pleased that he's managing fine on his own.

Even if she didn't like to admit it, it was quite a kick in the stomach how easily her decision had been accepted by him. Of course, if he really did not know why she had left, then, by now, he would be desperate to know. It was actually his easy acceptance and his swift adjustment to the new conjugal paradigm that inculpated him; it was too easy and too swift. The Professor might have been accepting at first, thinking that Anima was coming back, but when she didn't, then shouldn't he have started to question what was going on? Your wife leaves the family home and you don't even ask her when she's coming back? Why not? It's because you know, you little, little man; you *know*.

When she had first arrived, in a heightened state of excitement, she had had grand ideas about endurance, stoicism, and detachment. She had also had ideas about herself, about what she was capable of, what she could rise to. She imagined herself as an emotionally self-sustaining unit, self-sufficient, self-reliant. Now she thought: there are only a handful people in this world that really don't need anybody else. Everyone else, well, despite the frustrations and the irritations and the exasperations and the botheration, we all still cling to each other and rub along. We would rather hear angry words or callous words or cruel words than no words at all. But The Professor was taking even those words away.

Now, she looked around and was relieved to see so many people around her—when they had first all started turning up to work, she had worried that she would be drawn back into a life of being responsible for others. But when the driver once again made mention of 'those people', she thought: better these people than that Professor.

After that, she committed fully to her new life. If The Professor wasn't a distant memory, she was determined to make him one. To that end, she turned on her mobile phone only once every few days to check, more out of professionalism than need. No more texts from The Professor. You're making me a memory, too, Anima thought. How on earth did we come to this? We came to this very politely, very restrainedly, and completely gutlessly, that's how.

So when she saw two texts from Avik, *Mum, call me!* and *Mum, where are you? Call me urgently!*, she was at first pleased, and then very worried. Immediately, she called him, not even bothering to check her watch for the time difference.

"Puppy?"

"Mum, where have you been?"

Avik's voice was upbeat; immediately Anima sighed with relief.

"I'm sorry, I'm sorry, I'm sorry, I've been a little preoccupied . . ."

"Why are you not in Cal?"

"You called home?"

"Yes, you didn't pick up your cell, so I had to."

"You spoke to your father, then?"

"Briefly."

What has The Professor said to my son, Anima thought. She would have to second-guess him. And she second-guessed that he would have not said anything that would incriminate himself at all. No, he would have said something vague, something that could not be contradicted. Fine, that suited her, too. After all, she did not want to involve Avik in her marital issues. Although, a tiny part of her wanted to blurt out: your father's a philandering imbecile! But she managed to restrain herself, and replied, "The pollution was getting a bit too much for me. I was suffering from one respiratory infection after another."

"Really?"

"Maybe it's late onset asthma . . ." she said reticently. This was the problem with lying. You could never just tell one.

"You're asthmatic?"

Avik sounded worried and Anima was immediately contrite. She had not meant to make him worry.

"I said 'maybe'," she explained quickly, "and I'm much better here, so there's nothing for you to worry about at all."

"And where are you exactly? Dad said something about an old family house?"

"It belonged to my uncle, he died when you were young, you won't remember him."

"The terrorist guy?"

This said so casually that Avik might as well have been asking if it was the guy who sold ice cream to the neighbourhood children.

"No, puppy, that was my brother—*your* uncle, not mine. And your uncle wasn't really a *terrorist* . . ."

"Well, cool, whatever. As long as you're fine."

It's funny how quickly my son has accepted my move, Anima mused. When children are young, you can't hide anything from them. They have these sensors, which pick up on absolutely *everything*. And then, when they grow up, they *want* you to hide things from them.

"I'm fine," Anima replied. "But what about you? Why the urgent text messages?"

"Well, Mum . . ." Avik said, his voice slowing, "I hope you'll be very pleased to hear . . . that I'm getting married!"

Anima wondered why the phrase was *mixed emotions*. Hers were individual and separate and not mixed at all. Brains were good at emotional lateralisation—they weren't indiscriminate blenders, they were incredibly clever and precise processors enabling you to feel many different things at the same time. Perhaps, she thought, *concurrent emotions* was a more apt description.

Because going through what she was going through, Anima had become quite reticent about the institution of marriage. If you've just been in a plane crash, it's difficult to endorse anyone else (indeed, not just anyone else—your own flesh and blood, no less!) getting on a plane, regardless of all the statistics about air travel being the safest kind. All she could think now was that her son was the only good thing that had come of her relationship with The Professor. She knew this could not be true—if it were, then she would have left a long time ago—but it was her prevailing sentiment, and one she could not shake off. But she knew that even if she suggested to Avik the slightest amount of caution or cynicism or just good old pragmatism about the venerated institution, she would be infecting him with the very bug that would eventually destroy the glue that held the thing together. And there was nothing to be done about that other than to keep her mouth shut, or rather to open it only to say bright and cheery things, which she didn't mean, at least not wholly and unreservedly.

And even more problematically, there was Avik's excited announcement that he thought it would be a nice idea to have some celebratory engagement drinks in Cal! Maybe at The Grand? Because although Avik didn't state it explicitly, it was quite clear that he expected that Anima would sort out the arrangements, that she would *want* to sort them out. And maybe a few months ago, before the text, and the falling apart, and the growing apathy, she would have. But now, even the thought of having to make plans and choose befitting menus and flower arrangements and entertainments and outfits and having to see old friends and play happy families with The Professor by her side, was completely draining. She just wanted to stay where she was and potter around her garden and snooze in the afternoon.

Of course, to Avik, she displayed only one emotion—delight.

Her son was getting married. And. That. Was. That.

But. That. Wasn't. Quite. That.

The terrorist guy?

Since the night she had first met Tipu, Anima had done her utmost to suppress the story of Pusan and the local girl who he had supposedly impregnated. That's how she was framing it now—they were no longer his family. Instead, a random, impregnated woman and the product of that impregnation. How cold and biological. Better that way though. Easier. What wasn't easy though was the question of why of all the people in Balachuria had it been Tipu's grandmother and mother who had looked after the house? She didn't genuinely believe her own 'They're just good people' answer. Surely, they must have had some connection to it. And what connection could that be? It wasn't a conspiracy if it was true! No; stop going there. Suppress, suppress, suppress. But the key to suppression was to completely, mentally and physically, remove yourself from the scene, not return to it and start digging around! It was not *asking* Tipu how old her mother was and then doing the math to work out whether it was possible that she could be her niece. It was not *asking* Tipu about her family in order to ascertain what had happened to her maternal grandfather—to be told that she didn't have one, that long before she was born, he had gone away and never come back. It was not *asking* Tipu whether she might examine Tipu's mother—in order to see if there was any familial resemblance. But despite her intention to bury it all deep in her brain, where even a seasoned psychotherapist would struggle to unearth it, Anima simply couldn't help but bring it all to the surface. It was the first time in her life, when she felt utterly controlled by instinct with her rational brain bringing up the rear. And she was shaken.

Bipin Baxi was very, very tired. Most mornings when he woke up, he thought about retiring. But the state retirement age for government employees was sixty. He had another five years to go unless he wanted to say bye-bye to his inordinately attractive pension. Five years! Another problem Devi refused to deal with was that the state's pension system was bleeding the place dry. Hers was one of only two state governments that had refused to join the National Pension Scheme, on the basis that it allowed its funds to be handled by private fund managers. And to her, private was a synonym for evil. She would not do a deal with the devil, even if it meant that money was freed up to spend on stuff like health and education. Better dogma than pragma! She was willing to suffer for her convictions and so were her people!

He went to the bathroom to turn on the geyser, and whilst he waited for the water to heat up, he wondered whether he was up to a field trip;

he hadn't been on one in over a decade. Indeed, in the last ten years, the furthest he had got away from his desk was the toilet on the ground floor, where he went every day after lunch, with a newspaper and a cup of tea. But Surajit Sinha, the minister of environmental affairs, had been quite insistent that Bipin carry out the initial determination himself. Why Sir? Bipin had asked. There are already in-depth assessments from the central government's Ministry of Environment and Forests, and the Ministry of Coal, and the National Environmental Appraisal and Monitoring Authority, as well as T G Associates, an independent environmental consultancy. They are all pretty much saying the same thing. So, in the first instance, why don't I just send a few members of my team to verify the facts? I'm sure your team is very competent but maybe they don't have enough experience to know what they should be looking for . . .? I trained them myself, Sir, so they know *exactly* what they should be looking for! . . .Yes, well, the thing is, those other reports, I don't really . . . trust them. Really . . . Bipin thought, as the matter became much murkier and much clearer all at once, well, I don't trust *you*, Sir!

Bloody politicians, Bipin thought as he soaped himself with a bar of cracked Cinthol. The fundamental issue, was that all politicians, regardless of their shade, always knew the correct answer—they just needed you to come up with the right data to support that answer! On that front, nothing ever changed.

This had been most apparent when Sinha, in cahoots with the minister for tourism, had come up with a hare-brained scheme to develop helicopter tourism in the Sunderbans, a place which had the distinction of being a UNESCO World Heritage Site, a National Park, a Biosphere Reserve, and most importantly and pertinently of all, a Tiger Reserve. Immediately, there was an outcry from anyone who knew anything about the area—both environmental activists and wildlife experts agreed that it was an absolutely moronic idea. Firstly, and very practically, even putting to one side any concerns about the environmental effect, the density of the green canopy would prevent tourists from getting an aerial view of any of the animals, especially the tigers, which would likely go even deeper undercover to get away from the noise of the chopper blades. That should have been enough to bury the idea. But both of the ministers persisted, because it was their prerogative to be persistently asinine. Roll up, roll up, you might not be able to see any tigers, but we have a couple of huge asses on show! So, then there came feasibility studies and impact assessments and ecological reports, all of which said the same thing—give up on this ludicrous scheme! The resources spent having to hammer home the point to two middle-aged men with massive egos could have been much better spent on conservation instead of conversation, but by then, Devi had become involved, and was backing the proposal as she had come to the conclusion that the Sunderbans was an ideal destination for international tourists with deep pockets and huge cameras. And once Devi had become involved . . .

Bipin broke out in a sweat just thinking about it, and had to turn the water to cold to refresh himself. The woman was so sure of herself that she thought that just one of her pronouncements was worth more than thousands of pages of expert testimony. Her certainty was beyond laughable hubris or megalomania. It was truly disturbing and dysfunctional. Even now, despite his own personal pleadings that the project be formally abandoned, Devi and her ministers would not be budged, unperturbed by how cloddish they looked. Instead, the project continued to eat up more and more resources whilst being stuck in a deadlock. So much wastefulness! So much unreasonableness! I don't even know why I bother, Bipin thought, and then he remembered his pension.

The three young members—two men and a woman—of his

team, whom he had chosen to accompany him, were already in the Maruti Omni minivan when Bipin finally appeared with his little suitcase and his tiffin box. He could tell they were amused—a younger person's amusement at an older person's impropriety; but exactly what form of impropriety he did not know. Maybe it was his tiffin box. Or his shoes. Or just him. He smiled at them so that they knew that even if he wasn't quite in on the joke, he was aware that there was one. The driver, who was vaguely snoozing, turned on the engine again.

"Balachuria, yes?" he checked.

"Yes," Bipin replied, sighing. He knew that his lack of enthusiasm was not a good example to set to the youngsters. But he could not help himself. And besides, wasn't it worse to pretend to be enthusiastic when you were anything but?

About a couple of hours in, they stopped at a roadside shack. The young ones asked for bottles of carbonated soft drinks, and sat down at a plastic table covered with a vinyl tablecloth. Bipin brought out his Thermos flask of milky coffee.

As the three of them waited for their drinks to be served, Bipin checked whether they had read all of the reports. They nodded but didn't offer any further comments or opinions. "What do you think?" Bipin asked them.

"What do *you* think, Sir?" replied one of the young men, straight-faced, although in his straight-facedness, there was a hint of contempt or at least insouciance; Bipin knew that the implication was that he was Sinha's puppet and would report whatever he had been told to report. The other two looked down at the table. What do I think, Bipin thought, what do I think? I think that all this environmental concern is coming more than a hundred years too late!

Because, as Bipin knew, by the early twentieth century, the British, with their agrarian invasion and their mentality of forest only as economic resource, be it wood for train tracks, or ponds for fisheries, had already wrecked the joint. At one point, the place had even been home to tigers and leopards, but they had been killed in order to make room for cultivable land. Deforestation, commoditisation, decimation—what was once moist tropical deciduous forest, supporting animals and humans, had became a semi-arid land, frequently suffering from droughts which caused crop failure, which caused nutritional failure, which caused disease. Many of the original people had had to migrate elsewhere, either to the tea plantations of Assam or the nearby coalfields. Those left behind scrabbled around for work and food, in the main eking out a living from farming small pieces of borderline fertile land, eating what they needed and then trying to sell the rest. Of course, to make matters worse, the British invasion had also resulted in different types of land tenure which had cemented the position of the grand estate holders, the zamindars, who had acted as intermediaries between the Indian peasants and the British. And for the zamindars' troubles? They had been paid in rent from an already diminished people who could barely afford it. So then, of course, came the Naxalites. Help the poor, working man? Well, that's what they said. But, in practice, they brought not food and jobs and security, but violence and danger and suffering. In short, the place had been well and truly *hajar-fucked*—and for a good while.

But so what? Bipin thought. No point in crying over dead tigers. Hand-wringing is a squandering of energy. What matters is now. And *I* am the now. Whatever anyone else was responsible for before, it is *I* who am responsible for what happens next.

"What do I think?" he answered. "I think that we have a job to do, and we will work carefully, diligently, responsibly, and *impartially*, and we will have some respect for the task in hand and for the people who live in this place!"

Once they had arrived in Balachuria, the rest of the day was spent with Bipin supervising his team in the scrupulous application of frame quadrats, soil kits, test sieves, nitrate strips, and the like. In the blink of an eye, after years of apathy, Bipin had found a new dignity and purpose, at least for the day.

As his team set about taking more measurements, and focusing on the minutiae, Bipin himself contemplated his surroundings, making notes about the place and its people. It was clear that although the village of Balachuria was hardly a hive of activity, it was functional, at least on a basic level. In the main thoroughfare, there was food in the local shops, both fresh and dried; the people were not ailing and diseased; there were a good number of bikes and a few motorcycles; most people seemed to have a mobile phone. There was even a garage and a small rice mill, although both were closed. But as he investigated a bit more carefully, it soon became apparent that the place was a nothing place, a place where nothing happened and nothing could happen because there was nothing really there. Groups of young men sat around, idle, passing time; they weren't even waiting for something to happen because they were resigned to the fact that nothing would. They should be at work, Bipin thought. But there was no work.

After Anima's initial overture that she examine Tipu's ill mother, Tipu had decided that she would wait until she had proven herself to be an indispensable member of Anima's staff before agreeing. She hadn't wanted to seem too eager, lest Anima think that she was only working for her in order to have her mother seen, after which she would continue to work only if Anima could make her mother better. It was important to her that Anima knew she was a professional and that personal considerations were entirely secondary!

Anima knew this and waited until Tipu herself brought up the matter of the visit, despite the fact that she was secretly desperate to see Tipu's mother's face and even more desperate to see that there was no familial resemblance at all! Though she also felt that it would be wrong, almost an abuse of her position, to visit Tipu's house as just a doctor, when she had another motive. To assuage this feeling of, if not guilt, then guile, she decided to classify herself as not just doctor but also friend; to that end, she went to the local sweet shop to pick up a box of *jilapi* to take with her. Anima was usually served as soon as she walked in, regardless of how many other customers were waiting. The first two times, she had protested that she was happy to wait her turn, but then she had grasped that she was not being served first just out of deference but because the other customers felt uncomfortable around her and wanted her out of the way so that they could continue with their banter. This time though, the two other customers who were already in there were having such an animated conversation with the owner that they did not notice her, so she hung back and listened.

The main gist of their discussion was that the 'kilipboard' people were back, and was this a good or bad thing? The owner was very suspicious of them; they did not say anything, they wandered around as they pleased, and most importantly, they had not visited his shop and bought anything, which indicated that they were arrogant city types who thought that his sweets weren't good enough for them! The other two men differed. One was indifferent, he thought that the kilipboard people were just doing kilipboard people type things—esoteric, cryptic things frequently involving strange pieces of equipment, but as they left things pretty much as they found them and kept to themselves, he considered them temporary and essentially harmless visitors. The other was excited—he believed that the kilipboard people had found something, he didn't know what, but something worth finding!

"What is anyone going to find here," the shop owner smirked, "there's nothing here. Same as there's nothing in your head!" Then he spotted Anima, and immediately the conversation dried up. She was a trouser-wearing city-woman and therefore probably more closely related to the kilipboard people than she was to them. Anima knew that their silence meant that she should get on with her business, so she moved up to the glass counter and requested a box of jilapi. She was tempted to ask about the kilipboard people herself but knew the shop owner would reveal nothing more to her, so she just paid and left.

Tipu had spent all day cleaning and tidying up the house in preparation for Anima's visit; Kalyan was not impressed.

"Does her ladyship spend all day cleaning and tidying when you go around?" he huffed.

"That's different," Tipu replied.

"And tell me why that is?" Kalyan answered.

It was left at that.

Nevertheless, he decided to stay for Anima's visit. When Tipu gave him a sideward glance, he retorted.

"What? Am I not good enough to meet the queen?"

Tipu said nothing but wondered why he wanted to meet Anima if he had already decided he didn't like her.

Kalyan sat on the daybed looking up at Anima—who was sitting across from him on a pink plastic chair (a piece of patio furniture without a patio)—with undisguised distaste and defiance. High up on the walls, surrounding them both, were posters of various gods and goddesses. There was not much else in the room—no books, no magazines, no TV, no trinkets, generally speaking, no stuff. Yet the room did not look purposefully empty, in the minimalist style, it looked like it was waiting to be filled. Anima wondered for a second where they kept everything and then realised that they didn't have anything *to* keep.

Neither of them said a word to each other. Every ten seconds or so, Tipu walked into this awkward silence and promised that the water for the tea was nearly boiling, until she decided that she could not wait any longer and instead brought out a tray with three glasses of milk and some Milk Shakti biscuits which were decorated with imprints of the cartoon characters Tom and Jerry.

With Tipu back in the room, Anima finally felt able to speak.

"Your daughter's been very helpful," she said to Kalyan. Kalyan shrugged, unimpressed, as if implying: more fool her.

Anima kept hammering away: she's very bright, she's very capable, she's very sweet, she's very impressive.

"Really . . ." Kalyan asked with an inquiring smile, "If that's the case, then why is she just your house-girl?" He had no need to add: people like you, you're all talk, but you like to keep people like us in our place. It was written all over his angular, accusing face.

"Dad!" Tipu said, but that was all she could come up with. Anima was not only quite surprised that she had been spoken to so rudely and frankly—she was used to the British way of being polite to someone's face and then denigrating them behind their back—but she was also stumped. She had a sudden urge to exclaim, actually, my brother was a Naxalite, he tried to help people like you! But she realised that would be absolutely self-defeating and utterly tasteless. So she composed herself and replied, gently and sincerely, "I'm just a start, your daughter is going to do a lot better than being just my house-girl."

Kalyan said nothing. Tipu, relieved that he had shut up, piped up, "Madam, you haven't drunk your milk?"

Anima's face froze although she tried to squeeze a smile out of it. She turned her head towards the glass. Immediately, she could smell the untreated milk, thick and richly dairy, nothing like the pouches of watery and highly processed skimmed milk that she bought in Kolkata. Her heartbeat slowed as she tried not to show her disgust. She was sure that she had already made a variety of micro-expressions, which an expert in reading faces would have picked up on, but hoped that neither Tipu nor her father possessed such sensitivity. It's fine, she told herself, my feeling of revulsion is simply pathogen disgust, a primal but not necessarily correct response to wanting to stay free of disease! But I *know* this milk is fine, I have been feeding this stuff to Prem, and she has been getting better not worse. Indeed, this milk is probably good for me, so I *should* drink it! Slowly, she raised the glass to her lips. Her hand was almost trembling. She took a sip and swallowed. And then immediately, all of her rationality and decorum left her, and she involuntarily wretched.

"Madam!" Tipu said, rushing over. "What's happened?"

Anima shook her head, focusing on not vomiting.

"Isn't the milk right?" Kalyan asked. His tone was not sympathetic.

"The milk's fine," Anima managed to say.

"Then what?" Kalyan pressed. "You don't like our milk?" He was smiling now, sweetly as a crocodile. In a place like Balachuria, Anima knew better than to say that she hated milk. In the city, not drinking milk would have probably been a nothing, an idiosyncrasy at most, but here, it was abnormal, it was like saying you hated babies.

"No, it just went down the wrong way," Anima coughed. But she could tell from Kalyan's still gaze that he was not buying it.

"Anyway, Tipu, aren't you going to introduce me to your mum?" Anima asked, having recovered her composure and desperate to get out of the milk room with the disagreeable man in it.

"Yes, Madam, come," Tipu said, indicating the corridor.

The corridor was only about six footsteps long, but at the third footstep, the house was engulfed by darkness.

"Tipu?" Anima said in the dark, but there was no reply. Anima's heart missed a beat. Again, she had that feeling, as she had had in the car, that she was in some sort of danger, that this remote place was a dangerous place. Now Kalyan's disagreeableness seemed like it might be closer to menace. And Tipu's amiability seemed like it might have been a ruse, a trap.

"Tipu?" Anima said again, swallowing.

Then after a second, a gentle light went on, and Tipu appeared in front of her, holding a lit candle. She was smiling.

"Don't worry, Madam," she said, "power shortage, it happens all the time."

Anima was about to respond that it hadn't happened at her house, but then remembered that was because she had a diesel-powered generator, which kicked in if the grid supply failed.

"Yes, of course, I know," Anima said.

They walked into the bedroom at the end of the corridor and Anima saw the prostrate figure in the bed heave itself into a sitting position as quickly as it could.

"Mum, Madam is here to see you," Tipu informed the figure.

Slowly, Anima walked over and then Tipu held the candle up so that the two women could see each other's faces.

This time, Anima's expression was closer to surprise than disgust, but the need to wretch was just as strong. For she felt that she was looking at her brother. Sure, the backdrop was different, the skin tone and the face shape, but the features were exactly the same. The Bengalis had a phrase for it: *boshono.* Sitting upon. Her brother Pusan's face was sitting upon Tipu's mother's face. That was the best way of describing it.

Anima's head almost exploded.

"Listen, Tipu," she said, suddenly very formal, "I can't examine your mother in this poor light, so I'll come back soon during daylight hours."

Tipu, unaware of why Anima had suddenly changed her demeanour, just nodded deferentially. And with that, Anima left, her breath so fast that she thought she might faint.

"Ta-ta, Madam!" Kalyan called after her disparagingly, but she did not even hear him, so loud was the sound of her heartbeat in her ears.

Surajit Sinha, fast car fan, skyscraper aficionado, and city dweller to the core, had never wanted the environment ministry. In the current climate, it really was the short straw. Still, he wanted to make his mark, whichever ministry was his. Because, for him, that was what it was about—making a mark, making a name for himself, and making an impression upon his great leader, Devi.

Unfortunately, his meeting with Green Police had not been as fruitful as he had hoped it would be. Indeed, if he were being completely honest with himself, which he was not prone to being, it had been fruitless. The two-person team they had sent him—and upon whom he had lavished Balaram Mullick sweets—had essentially told him that whilst they thought that his objective to stop the coal mine from opening in Balachuria was an admirable one, and one they fully backed in theory, in practice, they were going to do nothing to help him. Why? Well, said the young woman—who had already taken the chocolate *shandesh*, which Surajit had been eyeing up—the thing is, we just don't have the resources. We can pool resources, replied Surajit. We'll work with you, and provide you with money and people! Well, said the young man—who was about to take another piece of mango *burfi* but then thought better of it considering what he was about to say—the thing is, we're not sure if this case is high-profile enough. But the environment is the environment, Surajit replied, why does it matter what the profile, high, low, medium! Well—this from the young man again, as the young woman was still stuffing shandesh in her mouth—the thing is, sadly, that's not quite how it works. Our work relies on public donations and support, and the public needs, how shall I put it, a good story they can really get their teeth into. Now the young woman nodded, as she swallowed her last mouthful of chocolate shandesh. It's depressing, she continued, but the thing is that we can't take on every case that comes our way, we have to prioritise. And as it happens, right now, there are cases that will attract more press and more attention than this one because the scenario in Balachuria is just not that provocative. She looked at Surajit, wistfully. I don't know why you're looking so glum, Surajit thought, you're the one who's eaten all my chocolate shandesh and I'm the one who has received absolutely no return on my investment! The young man, picking up on the fact that Surajit was not satisfied, added: you don't know how sorry we are to have to turn this down, but the thing is, it's not like there are tigers whose habitat is about to be lost or that it's an area of outstanding natural beauty. He sounded genuinely sad that this was not the case—possible calamitous destruction was his real love. But it's still a coal mine, Surajit said, and I thought you people didn't like those? Oh, we don't, the woman piped up, we most certainly don't! But it's easier for us to do something about them in some cases compared to others. To put it another way, the young man said, if a fruit hangs lower, you can pick it more easily. Ah, those imperilled tigers, thought Surajit, although he said nothing. But we're very pleased you came to us, concluded the young woman, and the thing is, in the future, we'd love to work together with you—a man who clearly cares about the environment—so please don't hesitate to get back in touch. Yes, the young man added, the thing is, despite initial appearances, we're actually very keen to work *with* governments, not against them! Surajit gave them both a wan smile. He had heard enough. And Green Police realised that they had said enough, so with business cards exchanged, they left, trying their best to appear positive and, as they would have it, *forward-looking*.

Good luck! they both said as they waved goodbye.

Surajit had given them a cursory wave back, as he had risen from his desk. You know what the thing is, he had thought, slumping back down into his chair, the thing is that I'm screwed!

A couple of days after Green Police had given Surajit their nugatory assessment, Bipin knocked on Surajit's door.

"Come in, come in, come in!" Surajit said, hoping that Bipin was the bearer of better news than Green Police.

"Sit down, sit down!" he said to Bipin, who did as he was told.

"And what's that you have in your hand there?" Surajit asked, banging both hands on his desk, and gesturing towards the folder Bipin had.

Why is he behaving like such a buffoon, Bipin wondered. All this eagerness and idiotic grinning. What does he *think* this folder contains? He's the one who asked for it in the first place!

"It's the preliminary environmental impact assessment of the proposed coal mine in Balachuria," Bipin said, pushing the report across the desk. "You commissioned it, Sir."

"Oh, *that*!" Surajit replied, as if he had forgotten. "Good, good! So, what does it say?"

Bipin eyed up Surajit for a moment. You have the report in your hands and you're asking me what it says, he thought. You lazy swine. Although I suppose that's the problem with politicians—they ask for details but then they can't actually be bothered to read them. For them, everything has to be outlined, abridged, summarised. If it can't be quoted in a newspaper or used as a slogan, it's not worth their time. Most importantly, if it can't be explained to them, then it is always our fault for not being comprehensible enough, it is never their fault for not being clever enough to understand. Yet we allow them, these kings of casuistry, who do not understand the facts, who have no *intention* of understanding the facts, to lead us from one delusional state to another. More fools we.

"What does it say . . .?" Bipin asked, as if he did not understand.

"Yes, what does it say?" Surajit repeated, somewhat impatiently. "Give me the headline! The leader!"

"It says what the other reports say, Sir. Which is that, on balance, a coal mine would be a positive asset to Balachuria. So, you had no reason not to trust those other reports, Sir—they were factually correct and the conclusions they drew were both appropriate and legitimate. And we can go ahead and grant the environmental clearances required."

Surajit winced as if he'd just hit his funny bone.

"But yours is just a preliminary report, yes?" he said hopefully. "So you might come to a different conclusion once you have carried out a more in-depth assessment?"

Bipin looked at Surajit, cynically.

"It's possible, but it's very, very unlikely. So far, there has been no area in which an issue has been noted. Water availability, air quality, flora and fauna biodiversity, agricultural feasibility, local community—there's no apparent problem."

"I see . . ." Surajit nodded, rubbing his lips together and

drumming his fingertips on the table for a long, long time. "But as it so happens there are people who might disagree with your evidence . . ."

Bipin frowned.

"May I ask who disagrees?"

"The environmental agency, Green Police," Surajit replied, with a good degree of pomp, pushing forward a print out of an email towards Bipin.

Green Police? Bipin thought. You're comparing my clear-eyed, scientific people with a bunch of blinkered, dogmatic bullies? He was not insulted, he was incredulous. Sceptical, he read the email:

Hi Surajit,

I'm afraid we have bad news for you. Right now, the tribal people of Mooli, India, are being bullied into voting to build a coal mine, which will destroy their ancient forest and their ancient way of life. Instead of making a living by selling seasonal produce from the forest, they will be forced to work down a dark and dangerous mine!

Not only will this mine hurt the people, it will also hurt the wildlife. No more the chirrup of birds, the hum of insects, or the sweet call of animals. Don't let this happen. Keep the world a beautiful, peaceful place!

The mining company is pretending that the energy produced will be for local people but we know better—it will be for industry. We also know that there are some people in the government who have been employing nefarious tactics to force through approval for this mine.

The minister of tribal affairs has so far stood back and let the giant mining conglomerate call the shots. But if enough of us tell her that we will not let her get away with turning a blind eye, she will be forced to act. Because if there's one thing which she doesn't want, it's a national scandal.

The coal mine is not what local people want—and we *know* it's not what they want. So help us to make their voices heard and sign our petition at:
https://secure.greenpolice.org.in/save-mooli-forest

Use your voice and use it well.

Shanti Singh
Green Police Campaigner

PS. Dirty energy doesn't have to be India's future. In the state of Bihar, Green Police has worked with locals to bring reliable biomass electricity to the entire village, something the central grid had failed to do for the last thirty years.

"We could use this as a template for a press release of our own—swap the name, make some adjustments?" Surajit suggested glibly, as Bipin's expression became more and more disbelieving. "Don't worry, we'd leave out all that stuff about the government's underhand tactics—because obviously we *are* the government—but we could keep the same tone, that the mining operation must be stopped in the name of equality and fairness and peacefulness, indeed, in the name of beauty!"

"Sir, what does this have to do with Balachuria?"

"Well, it's the same kind of thing, isn't it? A coal mine in a rural area . . ."

To Surajit, there were two categories of place—urban or rural, possibly a third, suburban. For an environment minister, he had very little idea of geography, topography, geology, or physiography.

"But Balachuria doesn't have any ancient forest—any forest it did have was destroyed more than a hundred years ago, during British rule. And the people who live there don't make a living from the forest, because there is no forest to make a living from."

"Yes, but what about the dirty energy, hmmm?" Surajit said, becoming quite impatient. "And the social costs of coal mining? Like respiratory illness and so on and so forth."

"Respiratory illness is a possibility, of course," Bipin admitted, "but modern coal mines need not be as polluting as their predecessors and from what I can see, a very reasonable relocation plan is being proposed. Besides, we also have to consider what the social cost is of the locals *not* having a coal mine, which will bring them jobs and money. After all, why shouldn't the locals use their natural resources? Isn't that *their* advantage?"

Surajit declined to answer this, and instead, becoming increasingly exasperated, he said, "Well, what about giving them wind turbines instead? Or solar panels!"

Bipin raised an eyebrow. The Truth Party could be very volatile. At least The Communists were consistent, even if their consistency was derived from the fact that they consistently couldn't care less about the environment; everyone in the department knew what they were dealing with then. Now, Bipin decided, it is just a game of what's fashionable at any point in time. Today, they decide they like wind turbines and we all clamber about trying to find places to erect them. Tomorrow, they decide they quite fancy trying out rice intensification, and we're tasked with educating farmers about greenhouse gas emissions from paddy fields. They are all over the place and so, therefore, are we.

"There's not enough wind in Balachuria to make use of turbines. And solar panels are not as economically advantageous for that area. Plus, making solar panels is highly skilled work; there would be no jobs for the locals. With the mine, there would be. That is a consideration, too, is it not, Sir?"

"But Green Police have already stopped other coal mines in India!"

"Sir, I am sure you are well aware that the central government considers Green Police to be a threat to national energy security. As West Bengal only just about produces the amount of power supply it needs, I would be wary of associating too closely with an organisation which could make that problem worse."

"Yes, and I'm sure that *you* are well aware that the Supreme Court just cancelled all coal mining licenses issued since 1993!" Surajit retorted petulantly, pointing his finger at Bipin.

Bipin cleared his throat.

"That was because of corruption and the lack of proper process, Sir," he replied patiently. "In fact, the main problem was that the government didn't make as much in revenues as it could have because the coal blocks were sold off on the cheap. The court's decision had very little to do with the environment, and it certainly had nothing to do with Green Police, whatever they might claim. And *this* coal mining lease was awarded to The Lohia Group through an auction—a completely separate and new process."

"But Green Police—they don't care *how* the lease is granted," Surajit replied, agitated, his hands fluttering about the place, "and they're very popular, you know. There are always photos of them with smiling villagers and film stars and people like that, so we don't want to fight them, do we?"

Surajit leaned back in his chair, exhausted, excited, worked up.

And completely baffled as to how he'd managed to manoeuvre himself into such a corner. I thought I was being clever, he thought, but I have been a fool. I should have just taken the report and left it at that. Instead, this crummy old civil servant is calling the shots—and calling the shots is my job!

"Sir, are you telling me that Green Police have officially stated that they are against this mine on environmental grounds and that if you grant the requisite clearances for the project to go ahead, they will oppose you?"

Surajit dithered. He was very, very tempted to lie. The truth, that Green Police had turned down the opportunity to work with his ministry, was deflating if not downright humiliating. But he wasn't confident enough that he could carry it off. And Devi would be furious if she found out that he had knowingly lied (lies which turned out to be based on misunderstandings of facts or gaps in knowledge or plain stupidity, however, were more acceptable). Instead, he avoided the question completely and changed direction.

"Well, it was very good of you to come, Bipin," he said, and now, he was neither eager buffoon nor restless inquisitor but steely politician, "but I don't think this matter is a priority. After all, you have various other concerns, like the arsenic mitigation scheme and the rice intensification programme to focus on, and I know that you have limited resources—although, of course, we did manage to increase your departmental budget for this accounting year."

He stood, and Bipin, slightly perplexed, followed.

"Anyway," Surajit said, bizarrely calm now, "thank you for this report, I'll take the time to read it properly and thoroughly before drawing any conclusions about our next steps. But in the meantime, you should concentrate on more pressing matters for the environment ministry. Rest assured, if I need any more information about this little mining project, I'll be in touch."

After the meeting with the minister, Bipin had spent the rest of the day bristling, becoming more and more agitated by the minute. He was no troublemaker but the way in which the minister had tried to manipulate him, had really infuriated him. He told himself it was nothing new. Politicians always had their own agendas and were always trying to push them, regardless of the evidence presented to them—their careers *relied* on manipulation, sometimes of the most guileful sort—but Bipin could not shake off the feeling that the minister should not be allowed to get away with it. He again thought of his pension. The reason he had risen so high was because he was compliant, accommodating. He had always put ease and security above principle. That was the truth and he knew it. Sure, he had also carped and complained about his bosses, moaning about their senselessness, their hypocrisy, their sheer idiocy, as much as anyone else. He had even put up a fight now and then, but when it came down to it, he knew when to shut up and keep his head down. The Argumentative Indian? he thought. Only in my lunch break! But again he thought: he can't get away with it! But with what exactly? What was *it*? Being misguided, being duplicitous, being a downright fibber? That was all par for the course. Why rock the boat now? Well, because he had to. He had no interest in power himself, had never wanted to rule over others, had in fact always been happy enough for others to lord it over him, but he did not want some smarmy, self-serving politician to deprive a whole group of people of their choice—and in the name of environmental preservation. It was just one con too far.

He flipped through the other reports again, and then concentrated on the one from T G Associates. Good old Tapan. Even at university, he'd always been the most ambitious and driven. He wasn't all showman though, he was an excellent scientist, too. Bipin respected that. Later on, as Tapan's company and wealth grew, some of his other classmates, who had gone into less well-paying jobs, mainly in the public sector, would grumble about Tapan's conduct and cast aspersions on his integrity. So very Bengali, Bipin thought. Anyone made any decent money and it had to be due to some kind of crookedness. It could never be due to diligence and astuteness and flat out hard graft (a concept which his public sector colleagues and their 5 p.m. home-time were not familiar with). Bipin had never bought into such hearsay. As far as he was concerned, it was just the expected steam coming off a hot brew of envy, resentment, and spite. In fact, many years ago, when Tapan had called him to offer a job, he had considered taking it. In the end, he hadn't, only because he considered his government job more secure and stable. But perhaps it was finally time to take a risk.

XV

The home of communications agency, William & Ray, was situated on the top floor of a new and purpose-built office in Salt Lake City, even though the rather antiquated-sounding company name might have suggested an office located in some crumbling old colonial building in the north of the city. The company, however, was actually only five years old and had been set up by Lalima Manna, a graduate of Jadavpur University. She had purposefully wanted the name to sound old, because, to her, old implied reputation, lastingness, and prestige. It had been formed by putting together Fort William, her favourite building in Kolkata, and Satyajit Ray, her favourite film director. But it wasn't only the name that marked out the company. Whilst competitors were busy chasing the modern urban consumer's digital rupee, concentrating on strategies like social media optimisation and digital content creation, William & Ray had decided to focus its attention on a different audience—the poor, or as the lingo went, the *under-served.* Because, when it came down to it, there was still money to be made out of them. You just needed to be patient. After all, a person was an individual but a group of people constituted a market.

Cynical? Well, as far as Anil was concerned, it was even more cynical and patronising to not consider the poor as a market, to exclude them from the world. There were people who considered him an exploitative and unscrupulous opportunist, a person who put people before profit, a person who knew the price of everything and the value of nothing, a person who, in short, embodied the worst traits of humanity bar perhaps paedophiles and rapists. Well, as far as Anil was concerned, it was those people who were the real enemies of the poor, with their duplicity and hypocrisy and sanctimony. So there was nothing to be done apart from going to war against them. Of course, the enemy's objective of keeping poor people in their place had been going on since ancient times, but now it had metamorphosed into something far more insidious—now poor people were ostensibly enabled to achieve their own goals and exercise their agency through outside advocacy and assistance. And if that resulted in them remaining poor and uneducated and deprived, then so be it! We have no right to patronise them! But, in reality, the poor couldn't have been patronised more—for they were just pawns, a cheap but emotive way of making a point, of asserting a position about the world, much like having a charity direct debit or buying a certain type of coffee or subscribing to a particular blog. They were being used, as they always had been, albeit in a different, subtler way. And that's what he had to battle against—the illusion of goodness. So when Anil had been considering which agency to use to persuade the Balachuria locals that a coal mine in their locality would be a positive, life-enhancing thing, he knew whom to turn to. It also did not hurt that Lalima Manna was *hot.*

"This is just an initial mock-up," Lalima said to Anil, as she looked at the giant computer screen in front of her, with Anil standing behind her. "Although, I'd appreciate it if you didn't ask for *too* many changes. They're rather time consuming, and I need my beauty sleep. Otherwise I wake up looking like a *chucho*." But the world's most attractive chucho, Anil thought. Just that morning he had received an email from his business school classmate, Avik Shastry, informing him of his engagement and his celebration drinks in Kolkata at a soon to be confirmed venue. Anil liked Avik—he was an all-round nice guy, what the Americans would call *regular*. (Well, apart from his wealth, which was highly *ir*regular.) His fiancé Paige, though, Anil didn't like at all; she had also been at business school with the two of them. To Anil, she was a regular pain in the ass. One of those superior, patrician types who used the auspices of duty and conscience to be condescending. Indeed, so keen was she to *check her privilege* that her whole way of being had become deeply corrupted and falsified. She was anti-herself. A person who came with an inbuilt apology but was really apologising for nothing. A person who claimed to care for those less fortunate than herself but wanted them to stay less fortunate so she could continue to seek out some phony personal redemption. A person who was a series of carefully edited (just like her wardrobe) postures and gestures. As far as Anil was concerned, *she* was definitely one of the enemies. And even though Anil didn't usually feel competitive with Avik, he was very keen on taking Lalima to the engagement drinks as his girlfriend. For a start, she was about twelve times better looking than Paige, which he found especially gratifying. This is my home turf, he thought, I rule here!

The problem was that not only was he not sure about having a relationship, he wasn't sure *how* to—at least one of those conventional, long-term ones, which were meant to be good for your physical and emotional health, promote societal cohesion, and ensure you lived longer. He'd always been one for a more extemporaneous, impromptu type of exchange, simply because in the past, he had never seen the appeal of stretching out over a course of months, years, sometimes even a lifetime, what could be said and done in an evening or occasionally a few weeks. Neither had his parents put any pressure on him or made any enquiries after his romantic life, even when they had started to be invited to the weddings of their friends' children. A few years ago, his father had asked, quite casually, Neal, are you a homosexual? To which Anil had replied, deadpan, not yet, Dad. His father had just nodded gamely. And his mother had recently told him a story about a friend of hers who had actually lost her hair because of the thought that her son might never marry, but Anil was quite sure that this was because she thought that losing one's hair over *anything* was ludicrous. So as his own parents seemed unconcerned by his conjugal prospects, the impetus to make a change to his personal life had become even more negligible. Most of all, though, Anil simply enjoyed work more than he enjoyed women; although they both made their demands, he found the former to yield more satisfying, satiating, and lasting results. But now, with the advent of Lalima—and the appearance of Avik's email in his inbox—Anil had wondered whether a rethink was in order. After all, he really did like her. She was sarcastic and cynical and captious and wry and salty; all the qualities which men usually did not look for in a woman but which Anil ate up. And behind her soft, full mouth, was a mean tongue.

"What are you thinking about?" Lalima said. "Whether you turned off the cooktop? I personally spend a lot of my day thinking about that. Along with lights, hairdryers, geysers, occasionally other small personal electrical appliances, like my toothbrush. I mean, has it been going zzzzzz all day long?"

Anil came to.

"I don't cook," he smiled.

"I'm sorry, of course you don't," Lalima said. "You're a modern Indian executive with no time to cook! Or, you know, you're a man . . ."

Anil smiled again but did not reply; he was concerned that there might have been some truth in what Lalima had just said. Instead, he looked at the screen. At the top of the page, in Bengali script: Future Balachuria, Your Balachuria. Underneath that, an artist's watercoloured sketch of the health centre that was part of the Balachuria coal mine proposal. It looked very modern—whitewashed concrete, clean straight lines—as if it would house the latest equipment and the best treatment facilities. In front of the building was a doctor in a white coat with a stethoscope around his neck, talking to a couple of white-uniformed female nurses. They, too, looked modern, and cool and calm and professional. All the whiteness gave the impression of cleanliness and composure and control. For this was no jerry-built surgery, understaffed and underfunded, with sick, coughing patients queuing in the dank corridor to see the one, harassed doctor who seemed to be operating with machinery from Victorian times. No, this was premium, modern healthcare!

"The key is emphasising what the benefits of the mine will be, not what the mining itself will entail. That's why the sketch of the health centre is on the front cover. And it is a *health centre* not a hospital. Semantics, of course, but the former sounds more positive and holistic." Lalima looked over her shoulder at Anil for a response.

Anil smiled waggishly and then shrugged.

"Oh, I don't know. A sweaty, coal-smudged miner might have some kind of macho appeal? You know, a hardworking man providing for his family!"

Lalima raised an eyebrow and examined Anil carefully.

"What?" he said. Now it was Lalima's turn to shrug.

"I'm trying to imagine you down a coal mine," she replied, "I can't see it."

"Oh, really?" Anil said. "What about our dear Devi? Can you imagine *her* down a mine, actually doing an honest day's work?"

"Her white sari would get dirty and that would never do," Lalima replied.

"Quite . . ." Anil agreed, sighing.

"Are we decided then," Lalima continued, "that we'll keep the health centre on the front cover?"

"We'll see . . ." Anil replied. "Show me what's on the inside first."

Lalima clicked to come to the first double spread. FUTURE BALACHURIA, YOUR BALACHURIA: WHY CHANGE CAN BE GOOD. On both sides, there were simply captioned images. On the left, photos showing Balachuria as it was. On the right, sketches showing Balachuria as it could be. It was nicely, shrewdly done; there was no question that the presentation of 'Future Balachuria, Your Balachuria' was anything but an improvement on present Balachuria.

A hardworking teacher does her best with limited resources. A photo of the current school, where a ragtag of scruffy children were being taught outside, under a tree, by a tired teacher holding an out of date, dog-eared textbook. *A proper education is for everyone and benefits everyone.* A picture of a modern classroom, with neatly uniformed, standardised children sitting at desks, surrounded by shelves of books and even a couple of computers, and being addressed by a smiling, enthusiastic teacher!

Poor sanitation leads to your poor health. A piece of sandy barren land, covered in a dishevelled pile of plastic detritus (bottles, wrappers, broken utensils), and god only knew what other sorts of waste, being pecked at by malignant crows and tatty dogs.

Public parks and green spaces improve your physical and mental well-being. An elegant, orderly green park, complete with trees, flower beds, and a children's play area; mummy-daddy standing under a tree and watching their daughter as she ran around. Even the crows had been replaced by a couple of incongruous but graceful white spoonbills, and the manky dogs had been reimagined as a small, bichon frise type of canine, which sat at mummy-daddy's feet. Anil smiled at the corner of his mouth. The artist had perhaps gotten a little carried away or maybe he just liked silly, poufy dogs. Anil pointed at the spoonbills and, more specifically, their long legs.

"Aren't they waders?" he asked Lalima.

Lalima scrutinised the birds.

"So?"

"Waders need water. Where's the pond or lake?"

Lalima looked at Anil, sardonically. Whilst she was amused, she was also impressed by his attention to detail.

"Would you like me to ask the artist to add a body of water?" she said.

"Yes, please do. And ask him to get rid of that ridiculous dog. If he wants to put in a dog, tell him to draw a proper one."

"Pro-per-dog . . ." Lalima said, as she wrote it in her notebook, slowly and deliberately enough to be slightly mocking.

Anil smiled indulgently at her—maybe he should ask her out—and then went back to looking at the last set of images on the pages, those of the main street.

Locals struggle to negotiate the unwelcoming market street and many shops fail to make a profit. A dusty, dirty road, next to a cracked pavement lined with crummy little shops, frequently open-fronted, with crummy painted signages. In front of the sweet shop (the fading sign read 'Na di i s') was a hand-operated water pump, with a scrawny child squatting in front of it, holding a plastic bucket. And, quite fortuitously, for the photographer, if not his subject, a middle-aged woman had been captured tripping up in the street and dropping her groceries into the filthy gutter. *Entrepreneurs flourish when local businesses are rejuvenated, boosting the local economy and providing a more enjoyable shopping experience.* A clean, smooth tarmac road next to a widened, tree-lined paved area, almost a promenade. The shops remained, but now they were all glass-fronted, with proper, professional-looking signages ('Na di i s' had become a pink neon 'Nandini's'). The water pump and the scrawny child had been replaced by a painted bench, upon which sat a healthier version of the boy, eating a box of Nandini's sweets. The middle-aged woman had risen again and was now carrying a shopping bag as she chatted to a friend. Edging into the sketch was the nose of a small family-type hatchback, which looked a lot like a Nano. Anil frowned.

"What?" Lalima asked, trying to read Anil's expression. "Is the car a bit too space age for the setting?"

Space age. Anil smiled at Lalima's usage of the phrase and then shrugged. He wasn't sure. And his phone had started to ring in his pocket. Fishing it out, he looked at the screen. It was Tapan Ghosh. He frowned.

"Please; go ahead and take it . . ." Lalima said.

"No, it's fine," Anil replied, putting the call through to voicemail, even as he wondered why Tapan would be calling him. As far as he was concerned, they were all done and dusted. "Let's carry on. Where were we?"

"The car—in or out?"

Anil contemplated this for a moment more. In future-future Balachuria, they would most likely hanker after pedestrianisation as they tired of motor vehicles and the congestion and pollution they brought with them, but right now, cars were still an aspirational and positive thing. One step at a time . . .

"In."

Lalima nodded and then clicked to go to the second double spread, the real meat of the matter—the coal mine itself. BRINGING NEW JOBS TO BALACHURIA: WHAT WE CAN ACHIEVE TOGETHER. This time, there was more text, but it was neatly set out in a number of boxes. In the first box, the hard stuff—the amount of investment that the coal mine would bring to the area, the number of jobs it would provide, and the expected rise in per family income. The numbers were in bold. Anil nodded as he read through them. In the second box, a little blurb about how the coal mine would directly lead to the reliable, sustainable, and affordable supply of electricity to the area—and the benefits of this. Anil's nose twitched.

"What does *boost in productivity* and *increased educational outcomes* actually mean to the man or woman on the street? In fact, women really benefit from electrification; they can use electrical appliances instead of having to do everything by hand, they can store food in a fridge instead of having to go out shopping for groceries every day," he told Lalima. "You need to make this tangible."

Lalima nodded.

"Sorry, you're right," she replied. "So, we're talking about less time spent on household chores which enables more leisure time, and also time for engaging with your children."

"Yes, and also more prosaic things: lighting when you want it—being able to read in the evening; fans or AC to keep your house cool—so you can sleep better; watching TV! The things we take for granted."

"Understood."

"OK, but you need to make sure that whatever you write, it's direct and compelling. It has to make someone think: I need that. Electricity isn't a brand like Apple, so there's no inbuilt lust. No one thinks, I really, really have to have that new electricity seven. So you have to get buy-in another way. Yes?"

"Got it. Make people lust after electricity."

Anil laughed, and then read through the text in the third box, which was about subsidised housing for the coal mine workers, and the related facilities, such as a gym.

"What about the relocation? Do you want me to sandwich that in somewhere?" Lalima asked.

"This is all about good news: you have to reel them in first. Then you mention the relocation," Anil replied.

"They might not be educated, Anil," Lalima pointed out, "but they're certainly not stupid. They'll realise that some residents will have to be relocated. And we don't want to be accused of patronising them."

"It's not about patronising them," Anil said. "It's about disseminating the information in an order which will encourage consensus, harmony, and the best possible outcome for everyone."

Lalima leant back in her chair, tapped her pen against her notepad and thought about this. Finally, she shrugged: "OK, you know best." Together, they looked at the copy in the final box, which was a paean to coal—*the black diamond*—and how only it could save India from a severe power crisis. *Do your part! Secure India's future!*

"I like that," Anil said. "It's like war propaganda: do your part."

"Well, it is war, isn't it? That's what you said."

Anil smiled and then switched his focus to the images, looking at a photo of a man wearing a hard hat, against a backdrop of industrial machinery.

"What's in the mid distance?" he asked.

"I don't know. Why?"

"Well, why is that man staring into it then?"

Lalima chortled.

"Men are always staring into the mid distance. Maybe they think some hot girls are about to appear there," she said.

Anil guffawed.

"Fine," he said, "but find a more appropriate stock image. I think that one's from a chemical plant, not a coal mine! And that sketch of the mine is incorrect, too—it will be an underground longwall mine not a surface one, I want that to be explicit. I can do without all of that *ugly gash in the landscape* flak. Granted, it won't be pretty—industrialisation never is—but it's not like we're going to be blowing the tops off mountains."

"We're not blowing the tops off mountains?" Lalima said. "But I thought we were properly evil, like Blofeld. I've even just gone and bought myself a white cat! Now what am I going to do with it? It's not even large enough to make a coat. A small muff, maybe . . ."

Anil grinned.

"Back cover?" he said.

Lalima clicked. The back cover was blank.

"It's a pictorial representation of the inside of Devi's head. I thought you'd like it."

"The problem with the inside of Devi's head is not that it's empty, it's that it's full of *gobor*," Anil said.

"I'm sensing that now is not the time to discuss the many uses of gobor, like fertiliser, building material, fuel . . . Right, then. We can either keep it as matter-of-fact as possible—give them the times and dates of the workshops, community meetings and so on, along with contact details. Or we can be more emotional."

"You? Emotional?" asked Anil, feigning surprise.

"Personally, never. Professionally, only if I have to be."

"And what does emotional mean in this context?"

"It means telling people: listen, we are not the mining mafia. We are not going to walk all over you and your rights. We're not going to ruin your lives whilst we make a fat profit from your misery. We're a legitimate, respectable company and we operate responsibly and accountably. So work with us, not against us."

"Mining mafia?" Anil sighed. *"Really?"*

"You know how it is. There are plenty of unscrupulous *haramjada* out there—survival of the most ruthless and all that."

"I'm unscrupulous and ruthless," Anil replied, poker-faced.

"Of course," Lalima agreed, "you're a businessman. But those guys make you look like Babaji. Anyway, understandably, you then get stories spreading about corruption and coercion and violence—I read recently about a guy from a village having chillies shoved up his anus by some crooked policeman, because he had dared to complain that his crops were being destroyed by the acid mine drainage—and the next thing you know, you have someone from the Civil Liberties Union turning up and making a fuss. That's if you're lucky. If you're *un*lucky, you get the Naxalites turning up and blowing up the place. And then it's pretty much game over."

"But what does that have to do with our project? We certainly have no plans to fuck anyone over—that's not the point. The point is quite the opposite, in fact."

"Well, that's very nice for you, Mr. Harvard Business School, but it's all about association. People will be suspicious as soon as they hear the words coal mine. More importantly, there are people, like our dear Devi, who will take advantage of that suspicion, encourage it even, in order to push their own agenda. So why not be upfront and say: we know you might be suspicious, we *understand* why you might be suspicious, so tell us what we can do to build trust. Basically, prevention is better than cure."

Lalima looked at Anil for a response but he said nothing.

"You're thinking about the bum chillies, right?" she asked him, finally. "Well, if you're interested, there's this joint I've heard of. Don't worry, not in Sonagachi, a respectable place just off Park Street . . ."

"You know, I *am* thinking about that poor guy's arse. The

police can still be pretty brutal here with their lathi charges and their rubber belt beatings and their bum chillies."

Before she could respond, Anil's phone started to ring again. Rolling his eyes, he looked to see who was calling. Tapan, again.

"I better take this," he said.

When Anil had been scouting around looking for an environmental consultant to report back on Balachuria, he had been tempted to use one of the big players like Arup or WSP Global. Granted, they were expensive, but they were also reputable, dependable, and trustworthy. But in the end, he had convinced himself that he needed to use a smaller, home-grown company, lest The Lohia Group be accused of being in cahoots with some huge, faceless, global corporation—which could not possibly care for the well-being of the people of West Bengal (well, how could they, if they didn't even bother to have a local office) and which would, somewhere down the line, have a vested interest in the outcome. So when T G Associates had submitted their quotation for the job, Anil had actually given them proper consideration and invited Tapan Ghosh to a preliminary meeting.

Anil disliked Tapan. Within minutes of meeting, Tapan had started going on about China for some reason. They had more nuclear warheads, they had higher literacy levels, they lived for longer, they had won more gold medals at the London Olympics! And before anyone said what about press censorship in China, well, actually, the real statistics showed that it was India in which journalistic freedom was more curtailed. And just when Anil thought Tapan had finished with his Sino-tribute, which was apropos of nothing, Tapan had added—and this was the fact he was clearly most impressed by—do you know that the Chinese import more than ten times the number of luxury Swiss watches that the Indians do! Anil had thought: well, why don't you fuck off out of my office and go to China, then, if it's so much better? It's only up the road! Although, by looking at that hideous diamond-studded Rado on your wrist, and that huge ruby ring on your finger, and that chunky gold chain around your neck, it looks like you've been doing well enough out of India, even if she's not quite up to your standards. And then, to top it all off, Tapan had shown Anil a photo of his plump, not-that-pretty wife, called Dimple or something. She should have been called Neck Rolls or Fat Tits, Anil had thought as he smiled, a smile that Tapan had misconstrued as appreciation.

Yet, despite Anil's immediate antipathy towards Tapan, he didn't say thanks but no thanks. Because, as aggravating and charmless as Tapan was, he served Anil's purposes. First of all, he was not only an Indian but a Bengali—and Bengalis felt more comfortable with their own. Secondly, he had experience of local politics, and shrewdness in knowing which facts to communicate and how to communicate them. And that was just as important as the facts themselves. Thirdly, and most importantly, despite many attempts by assorted agencies—legal, political, environmental—to discredit him at various points, his reports were very rarely overturned or dismissed. For, notwithstanding his gauche comportment, he was an expert in his field, his social unwieldiness hiding a meticulous and nimble scientific mind, and his transparent greediness surprisingly having no impact, or at least very little, on his professional probity. So, if Anil had a problem with Tapan, it was one of style not of substance. And that's how Tapan's company had come to be given the job of putting together the Environmental Impact Assessment of opening a coal mine in Balachuria. And it was this assessment that had been a major contributing factor to Anil deciding to forge ahead with the project. And now Tapan—whom Anil had hoped to have nothing to do with once the report had been handed over—kept calling him. And Anil was feeling quite uptight about this, for a variety of reasons, relating to both style *and* substance.

"Mr. Ghosh, what can I do for you?" he answered, his tone clipped. "I trust everything's fine?"

Of course, Anil knew that if everything was fine, Tapan probably wouldn't be calling but he thought that just by saying it, Tapan would be encouraged to *make* everything fine.

"I am quite certain it *will* be," Tapan replied.

Anil could not help but sigh. Even though he knew that there was absolutely no chance of the project going ahead free of political opposition or outside interference or just turmoil of some variety, trouble was never less exasperating because of the certainty of it. Here we go, he thought.

The way Tapan put it, Devi's minister of environmental affairs, Surajit Sinha, whom Anil had pegged as a nitwit in a Nehru jacket ever since he had proposed some ridiculous and unworkable tiger tourism scheme in the Sunderbans, was going to try and block the coal mine in Balachuria on the basis of its environmental impact. Dirty energy, harmful to health; to Anil's ears, it was like the annoying noise of a buzzing gnat, which needed to be swatted. Dead.

"Is this a problem for us?" Anil asked sharply, cutting Tapan off.

"Well, Bipin—"

"Sorry, who's Bipin again?"

"He's the Chief Environment Officer at the Environment Ministry, very senior—"

"And how do you know him?"

"He was a college classmate—"

"And *why* is he coming to you with this information? I assume it's not just out of the goodness of his heart?"

Now, Tapan's tone changed and became less sing-song, more stiff.

"Bipin's information is absolutely good and fine. He even told me that the government is engaging Green Police on this issue."

"Green Police!" Anil groaned, closing his eyes. "You cannot be serious?"

Tapan did not offer up a response, so Anil sighed.

"OK, and your Bipin, what does he want?"

"Well, by coming to me in the first place, he has done you a grand service. Now you can deal with the situation from a position of power. Otherwise, you would be in real trouble. You know yourself how difficult it is to secure environmental clearances even without any additional interference."

Tapan's amiable tone had now disappeared entirely. In its place was a colder, flintier inflection, which Anil noted.

"Well, I'm very grateful to him, so please do tell me what I can do for him in return."

"Well, he's worked very hard for many years, and for not much in the way of pecuniary reward. I actually offered him a job with my company many years ago but he didn't take it, despite the fact that he would have earned much more—that is the kind of person he is, very dutiful, very civic-minded, very dedicated to public service. But despite this, now all he really has to look forward to is his pension—"

"Yes, I think I get the picture," Anil interrupted. "How much does he want?"

There was silence.

Bengalis were very funny about money, Anil thought. On one hand they thought that showing too much concern about the stuff was vulgar but on the other hand, they didn't seem happy to live a life of complete denial. What they wanted was a *seemly* amount of money. So when it came to money matters, Anil had learned to be very circumspect and careful. There was always the pretence about not having any figure in mind, when, in fact, there was always a very particular number to be reached. Although even when that number was reached, there could be no outright acknowledgement of this—*if you think that amount is right, then that's the right amount!* Usually, Anil would be willing to go along with the whole charade, but today, he had neither the time nor the energy nor the inclination.

"Mr. Ghosh, I asked how much? I'm sure the gentleman has some sort of number in mind."

"Well, you know how it is here. Everyone is very quick to make a big fuss about everything and then, just as quickly, it's forgotten. There's always the promise of investigations and inquiries but definite conclusions are very rarely reached; it's always a bit of a *makha-makhi* as we say. I used to like to think that this was due to some kind of open-mindedness but now I've realised it's simply to do with a lack of tenacity and guts. We don't have the stomach for finality, you see, we prefer iterations. Perhaps this is a Hindu thing, considering our belief in reincarnation."

"Mr. Ghosh, I absolutely one hundred per cent agree with you, but what I need from you right now are some tangibles," Anil said desperately, looking at his watch.

"Please, may I finish?" Tapan said.

"Of course . . ." replied Anil, closing his eyes.

"Well, as I was saying, our people enjoy making a fuss. They enjoy being indignant. Above all, they enjoy the sense of virtue which disapproving of others gives them, but they are far less bothered about following through. Our media is especially guilty of this. One week, one story dominates, the next, you would never even know that the story existed. Isn't that right?"

"You couldn't be more right."

"So, whilst Bipin might be a hero for coming forward with the truth, he'll be a hero for only a week or perhaps a month. After that, he'll be forgotten. And whilst in the short run the government might have to face some difficult questions, it is very likely that in the long run, it will be business as usual for them, and that Bipin's position as a public servant might become untenable. You know how these things are. They might not be able to outright fire him, but they could make his life difficult—"

"And we could make it easier, yes?"

"Not only could make it easier, but perhaps *should* make it easier, considering how he's willing to help you out?"

"I'm sure he has his own reasons for speaking out and I doubt that it's because he wants to help *us* out, Mr. Ghosh." As soon as Anil had said this, he regretted it. No point in being antagonistic in such a situation. Negotiate, don't alienate, he told himself.

"Regardless of why he wants to speak out, if he does, it *will* help you, that is correct?"

They were going around in circles. The point needed to be come to.

"Yes, you're right Mr. Ghosh, it most certainly will help us out. And not only would we encourage—", Anil had suddenly forgotten his name, "—your friend to speak out in the interests of honesty and scrupulousness, we would also like to reward him for his undoubted integrity in whichever way he sees fit."

"Well, that's very good of you, Anil," Tapan said, a measured warmth returning to his voice. "I didn't doubt that you'd understand the situation."

"Of course," Anil replied, tonguing his teeth. If there was one thing he could be relied on to do, it was to understand *situations.*

"Well, let me speak with Bipin, and then perhaps you and I can talk about the details later on. I know I can rely on your word to take care of our friend."

My friend. Our friend. We're all friends! Anil thought.

"Of course. I'll look forward to hearing from you in due course."

"Important?" asked Lalima, as Anil walked back in.

"Probably," Anil shrugged. "Unfortunately. Or maybe fortunately."

Lalima raised an eyebrow.

"I love it when you get all cryptic on me," she said.

"I'm not being cryptic, I'm waiting and watching," Anil explained as he wondered whether she was flirting with him.

"That's what all the coolest guys do, you know—wait and watch," Lalima laughed, adding, "Right, back to prevention being better than cure."

"Oh, yes. And what kind of prevention did you have in mind?"

He was suddenly aware that he had made the question sound carnal in nature, or at least it sounded that way to him: Lalima, if we're going to have a sexual relationship, what would you like to use to prevent sexually transmitted diseases or unwanted pregnancy? She seemed to smirk for a second and Anil was quite sure she was about to say KamaSutra Contoured or Manforce Banana flavour (for 'the monkey business' no less!) but then she replied, straight, "I was thinking about someone actually going and talking to the locals. The literacy rate in the area is around forty-five per cent. Which leaves the majority requiring someone to actually go and explain things to them—you know, a roadshow type thing. Then again, I suppose you could argue that it's the people who are literate who will have the most say or, rather, influence over what's done."

"OK, well let's arrange that. You look into a suitable venue and so on, and I'll look into who we should put upfront."

"You don't fancy speaking to the locals yourself? But I thought you were a man of the people!" Lalima teased.

"For the people, dear, *for* the people," Anil replied. "Speaking of which, what are the *people* saying?"

Lalima shrugged. "You know how it is. You can't please everyone all of the time."

Anil pulled up a chair to Lalima's desk, sat down, and folded his arms.

"Go on," he said.

"Well, there's some low level but insistent grumbling—all online at the moment, nothing in the proper press, and no meetings or rallies or anything like that."

"Grumbling about what precisely?"

"Coal mining—the epitome of evil. Exploiting the environment, exploiting the poor, exploiting the political system, et cetera. And all because of greed and avarice. Capitalism at its nastiest. Of course, what we need, *comrade* Anil, is a revolution. Power to the people!"

"How original."

"You don't expect originality from the comfort of an armchair, do you?" Lalima said sarcastically, soothingly. Anil bristled, but then seemed to calm down, only to lean forward a moment later, jabbing his finger in the air.

"All those commentators don't really care," he said, infuriated. "They're the type of people who say they care for humanity, for the environment, for this, for that, but what does caring mean? Taking ten minutes during their lunch break to make some pithy criticism about evil corporations. The kind of evil corporations, which in all likelihood, have made their own lives cushy and pleasant and undemanding. Of course, when they're sitting there, tapping away, do they bother to ask themselves: hang on, how is my computer powered? Oh yes, electricity. And where is seventy per cent of electricity in this country generated from? Oh yes, coal! But I don't like coal so I shall spend the rest of my life looking for the ultimate environmentally-friendly, renewable power source. Oh, hang on, I'm not actually that clever myself, but hopefully someone else will find the solution. Until then, I will live in a biodegradable yurt, travel atop a goat, and use my own shit as fuel to cook my dal. Actually, that seems too much like hard work, and I quite like my evenings free so I can sit in my air-conditioned flat, watching my TV and pulling out cold beers from my fridge, all of which run on, well, coal-powered electricity, but anyway, that doesn't matter because I've done my bit. I've written a comment and that proves I care!"

"Why are you getting so worked up?" Lalima asked, slightly surprised. "They're just commentators, after all. And as you've said, they're not actually *doing* anything."

"I'm worked up because these self-righteous idiots try to make people like me look like the bad guy, the guy who's only out for himself, whereas all *they* actually care about is the number of likes they receive! Refresh the page, refresh the page—look, another idiot has given me the thumbs up!"

"So, I'm extrapolating from what you're saying is that I should set up a Facebook page for the Balachuria coal mine, and invite people to like it? Although we could, of course, just buy likes."

Anil threw his head back and laughed.

"Ha. Yeah. Love for sale, right. Whilst you're at it, why don't you set up a Twitter account, hash tag LoveDirtyCoal, and buy some followers."

Lalima gave Anil an empathetic smile.

"Ignore the critics," she said gently. "They're very passionate and involved for an afternoon. Then they'll move onto something else tomorrow. It's like the intellectual equivalent of a one-night stand, in fact, not even that, a handjob."

Anil shrugged, not disagreeing, but then said, still slightly bristly, "Do you know what would be good for this planet? I mean *really* good for it? If people didn't exist. No more rich people, no more poor people, no more people full stop. No more consumption, no more pollution, no more waste!"

"Yes, but as we *are* here," Lalima replied, "however unfortunate that might be for the planet, perhaps we should get on with the job? Now, I was thinking, can we do something for the locals, you know, give them something?"

"Like what?"

"What about a free health check? You know, a taster of what's to come."

Anil mulled this over for a minute.

"Sure, something like that could work, why don't you work out the details . . ." he said, then added, quite seriously, "Listen, you are going to get this brochure done on time, aren't you?"

Lalima smiled.

"I hope you're not calling into question my dedication, efficiency, or *ceaseless* professionalism?"

And Anil smiled back: Of course not.

Tapati Ghatak frowned when she saw who was calling but answered anyway. A good source was a good source even if they were also a complete *kutar bacha.* And the best journalists didn't hold grudges. They rolled with the punches, went with the flow, saw where the story took them, and tried to avoid clichés!

"Yeah?" she answered with a calculated insouciance, though it was clear to both her and Anil where the balance of power lay. "You have something for me?"

"Why else would I be calling?" Anil replied.

"Maybe you want to take me out for a romantic dinner," Tapati said.

"Well, I do like a woman with a sense of humour . . ." Anil laughed, not being one to hold a grudge himself. "And I do have a proposition for you, but far more interesting than dinner with me."

To lie or not to lie? This is what Surajit had been mulling over as he had been driven to Devi's office. Of course, if he had been asked outright whether he would ever lie to his boss, he would have said, of course not. They were grown-ups with mutual respect for one another, they could be frank and forthright with each other, they had the same aims, they shared the same vision, they held the same beliefs, and so on and so forth. But, in truth, he was scared shitless of her, his underlying belief being that he should do whatever and say whatever stopped her ire from being aroused. So when he arrived in Devi's office and she asked him bluntly what progress he had made with the Balachuria coal mine affair, he had lied pretty quickly, figuring that with a bit of clever this-way-that-way, he would subsequently be able to turn that lie into the truth or something close to it. Besides, Devi never listened that carefully, so if it all went tits-up, he could always count on the classic excuse of there having been a miscommunication. He hadn't noticed, until it was too late, that Nigel, Devi's little lapdog was sitting in the corner of Devi's office, making notes. What he had said was now in writing. The written word. A record of what had been said. Every good politician's nightmare. God, did he hate those Anglos—jobsworths, every single one of them. Full to the brim with their misguided sense of British heritage and everything that came with that—authority, standing, probity. Disgusting food, too. What decent-palated person could eat Mulligatawny soup?

So, now it was in writing—damn the alphabet, damn it!—and the government had an official standpoint: the Balachuria coal mine would likely have a devastating impact on the environment and its people, according to the initial report from the Environment Ministry, and their position was backed by Green Police. Nigel was nodding. I'll prepare a press release, he had said determinedly, we should get it out as soon as possible, no time to waste! Devi was nodding, too. She was very pleased. Now this is what you call progress, she had said, her little beady eyes shining, you've done well! Surajit automatically smiled broadly—a Pavlovian response to praise from Devi—until he remembered that what he had said was pretty much the opposite of what had happened, and that the current state of affairs was categorically not progress. It wasn't even regress. What it was, was a massive error with the potential to become a complete fuck-up! I always try my utmost, Surajit had said, utterly dry-mouthed. Then he had scuttled out of Devi's office and asked his driver to take him home as quickly as possible.

As he pressed the calling bell to his flat, he tried to decide what his opening gambit to Bipin should be, and the tone. Should he play the boss: you'll do as I say if you know what's good for you. Or the collaborator: we're in this together and I'm saying this for the good of both of us! Civil servants liked rank and order. But Bipin had now proved himself to be a bit of a freethinker, and in Surajit's experience, freethinking often became runaway thinking—and that's when it became really dangerous and took a lot more resourcefulness and energy to hobble.

Finally, his housekeeper, a fussing, middle-aged woman, opened the door. He had a key himself, but preferred doors to be opened for him. Devi might have insisted that she and her party were servants of the people, and encouraged them to shun any trappings, animate or inanimate, which indicated an attachment to social status or wealth, but Surajit couldn't bring himself to get rid of the little things. Like servants. If he had been his usual self, he would have asked her what had taken her so long, but with his current preoccupation, he marched right past her, not even hearing her call out that he had a young lady visitor and that she was waiting in his study for him.

Indeed, he didn't even notice his visitor until he had poured himself a glass of Amrut, sat at his desk, found Bipin's direct office number in his governmental phone directory, and picked up the phone. He was just about to dial when he saw a pair of women's shoes in the corner of the room, then moving upwards from the shoes, ankles, calves, skirt—a whole woman and an attractive one at that. Was she a present from someone? No, he thought. Sadly, those days, when he was a businessman, were over . . . More likely, he decided quickly, she was looking for an internship; the environment ministry was a big draw for postgraduates interested in a career in politics. Well, good on her for being so enterprising as to come to his home—not just a pretty face, after all!

"And who are you, then?" he asked, using the polite form of 'you', in his best benevolent voice, and putting on his most avuncular expression.

The young woman reciprocated with a contemptuously nubile smile. "I'm Tapati Ghatak from *The United Times of India* and I've come to ask you about the Balachuria coal mine."

Now, Surajit frowned and simpered at the same time. That boob Nigel must have already informed the press without even pausing for enough breath to eat a bowl of Mulligatawny soup. Usually, Nigel could be trusted to be found on the back foot or thereabouts, but now, when Surajit least needed it, he was all ready-steady-go. "Ah yes," Surajit said, nodding and sighing, "*that*. Well, it's my job to make sure that any business venture in West Bengal respects our environment and our people first and foremost. And I can't ignore the evidence presented to me, even if other people with their own interests would wish me to."

Tapati nodded in what looked like agreement, which warmed up Surajit nicely and caused him to continue. "You see, unlike our predecessors, The Truth Party does what's best for the people, not what's best for our pockets. Unlike them, we're not in cahoots with certain big businessmen! We can't be bought!"

"Would you say then that you're anti-business?" Tapati prodded.

"No, no, no," Surajit replied, shaking his head vigorously. "We are not anti-business, we are anti-corruption. We like business very much, but we are pro only good, honest business, business that is good for the people and for the environment, not business that is only good for certain businessmen's bank accounts!" He leaned back in his chair, very pleased with his answer and that the journalist had not caught him out.

"So, you're not generally anti-business but you're specifically anti a certain businessman?" Tapati asked, scribbling something in her notepad, then looking up, enquiringly.

Surajit shifted in his seat. Suddenly he realised that he might have been better off getting rid of the woman from the start.

"What kind of nonsense is that?" Surajit rebuffed her with a nervous grin, getting up from his chair. "I don't make things personal, my decisions are based on facts not emotion! Anyway, it's been very nice talking to you, dear, but I have a lot of work to do, so I'm afraid we'll have to leave it at that. If you have any more questions, please feel free to contact my office." He got up, opened the study door and gestured for Tapati to leave but she remained in her seat.

"So, it's nonsense that you tried to railroad a very senior civil servant from your ministry into slowing down the process of issuing an environmental permit for the Balachuria coal mine? Even though all evidence, including that from your own department, indicates that the coal mine will not only bring a whole raft of economic and social benefits to the local community, as well as going a good way to securing a much needed electricity supply for the area, but will result in only limited degradation to the environment?"

Surajit went completely blank. How did she even know what had happened with Bipin? Had Bipin told her? No, he wouldn't have had the gumption. Besides, *why* would he? What did it matter to him? But then if *he* hadn't . . . Surajit was roused from his speculation by the sound of Tapati tapping her pen against her notebook. Suddenly, he became quite irate at her cool effrontery.

"Who told you all these falsehoods?" he asked her angrily and without thinking. "I demand to know!"

"*For the record*, are you denying that you asked anyone in your department, for no good or proper reason, to slow down the process of issuing the environmental permit for the Balachuria coal mine?"

"Why would I ask anyone to do that!" Surajit spat. "What are you talking about!"

"Yes or no?" Tapati pressed, unmoved by his indignation. "Did you or did you not ask for the process to be slowed down? And if you did, why did you? Is it because of a personal vendetta against Sachin Lohia?"

"Is that what he said?" Surajit raged. "Because if it is, I'll sue him for defamation!" Any good sense that Surajit might have had, had been replaced by pure, angry adrenaline.

"Yes or no?" Tapati repeated, much less hormonally. "Do you, or indeed this government, have a personal vendetta against Sachin Lohia? Is that why you decided to slow down the process? Or was it not your decision? Were you indeed asked by someone *else* within the party to slow down the process?" That *else* was the word that pissed right on Surajit's fire. Now he became stone cold.

"I have no further comment," he said without emotion. "Please leave."

"You don't want to defend your actions?" Tapati asked candidly. "Or at least explain them? Or is it someone else who needs to do the explaining?" That aggravating, alarming, awful *else* again. And despite his current sticky predicament, Surajit had not forgotten that the golden rule of The Truth Party was 'Always save Devi's arse, lest you wish to bring upon yourself her vengeance and wrath!'.

"Madam, please leave before I have to call security!"

If Surajit had been thinking prudently, he would have, on Tapati Ghatak's exit, made straight for the phone and called Bipin to find out what had been said and to whom, and next, to call Nigel to apprise him of the rather regrettable situation. That damage had already been done was undoubted, but damage could always be limited. That's what he had learned during the media-coaching course run by Nigel—although, admittedly, he hadn't been paying much attention, believing that media coaching was on a par with health and safety training and fire alarm drills. But with some imagination and chicanery, even a misdemeanour of colossal proportions could be refashioned into a forgivable lapse or an error in judgement, or best of all, just a misunderstanding. Yet before that transformative process could take place, a frank and comprehensive disclosure would need to be made about the metrics of the transgression, and as that would involve explaining himself to Devi, Surajit preferred to bury his head in the sand.

XVI

Balachuria: Minister Sinha Caught Obstructing Due Process

I should buy shares in Pfizer, Nigel thought, as he gulped down another mouthful of Gelusil; he had now moved on from the *Original* to the *Xtra Cool* variety. Of course this had had to happen right on the day of Devi's Town Hall meeting. Just when I thought we were in the clear, two months after that Lohia got out of jail and caused such a fuss, I've got this to deal with. The Hindus are right—there is a god for everything, including a god for good timing. And right now, that god is laughing at me.

Preparation for the town hall meeting had already been tough enough. There was never enough money to put together a slick show, it was always a bit make-do. And whilst that might have suited Devi's particular stamp of rough and ready down-to-earthness, sometimes Nigel wished she would come across as a bit more polished. However, the fact of the matter was that she was cheap. She never had the budget for anything other than more white saris. It was always: how can we be spending money on PR and this kind of luxury, when we need to be spending money for the betterment of the people? After all, money is not growing on trees! No, Devi, you are right. Money is not growing on trees nor anywhere else in this place. But PR is not a luxury, it is your bread and butter, it is about your *Public Relations*, that is, your relationship with the public. He sometimes wondered whether she actually realised that it was two letters—P and R—and that they stood for something, or whether she thought it was *Peeyar* or some such. Yes, my Peeyar man is very good at holding my handbag!

And now that arrogant, duplicitous shit Sinha had done this. Nigel had already called him several times to find out exactly what he had said and when and to whom, but he wasn't answering his phone. As for the civil servant, whom Nigel had figured to be Bipin Baxi, well he wasn't answering his phone either. And in between phone calls, he was trying to mollify Devi, who was lurching from screaming that one of her favoured ministers had purposefully misled her to declaring that the article was just another part of The Great Communist Plot against her, and whose knickers had become fully twisted in the process. Another job for the Peeyar man, then—to untwist and smooth knickers. And in between phone calls and knickers, he was trying to finalise arrangements with the television interviewer who was insisting on some post-show analysis conducted amongst the audience which Nigel had learned, from bitter experience, hardly ever went in Devi's favour especially amongst an educated, urban audience who were not so easily convinced by her blunt rhetoric and lofty promises. *So Reshma, were you satisfied with Devi's answer to the question about youth unemployment? No, not really, I don't think she has offered any real solution, because she doesn't seem to understand that her government doesn't create wealth and jobs, the private sector does. Well, that's definitely an interesting point, Reshma. And Gautam, what did you make of her performance? It was very energetic, wasn't it? Yes, she was very energetic—in the way that a lunatic is energetic!* Stick her in front of a load of poor farmers, fine, but the town hall audience would be made up of students and middle class professionals and, worst of all, Bengali intellectuals. She had once been a breath of fresh air for them but now they tended to turn their noses up at her as if they had sniffed a public latrine. Of course Nigel had done his best to try and stop her from doing the event at all, first by suggesting that she already had a jam-packed schedule and wouldn't she be better off focusing her time and energy on more productive activities (Although what, he thought, did politicians actually *do* apart from talk a lot?). But Devi was having none of it. She had insisted to Nigel that she had to make time for her people, show that she was accountable to them, that she was keeping them informed. Not for her the quiet corridors of power and behind-the-scenes manoeuvrings. No, she was all for candour and veracity. So, his next tack was to try and persuade her that some of her audience would be cynical at best, hostile at worst. Of course he softened the blow by adding that she would have many supporters there, but sadly, the voices of discontent were always the loudest. However, this approach backfired completely. No one liked to shout someone down more than Devi did. Bring on the doubters and the detractors, she had said. She didn't get to where she was, and coming from where she had, without getting into a fight or three. And who was Nigel to forget that! And to add to his woes, neither would the TV presenter agree to stick to the list of pre-prepared questions. Instead, she wanted to use them as a springboard in order to keep things spontaneous. Why don't you springboard up my bum, Nigel thought miserably. No doubt the spontaneity would lead to a question about Surajit Sinha and Balachuria, even though

Nigel had told the presenter categorically that Devi would not be answering questions about that topic until all the facts had been gathered. After which Nigel had then had to gently impress upon Devi that should she be asked any questions about Surajit Sinha and Balachuria, her only response was to be that she would not be answering questions about that topic until all the facts had been gathered. However irate or indignant or upset she was, it was imperative that she remained courteous, collected, and cool. He had even tried to go through a practice run with her, pretending to be the TV presenter and asked her leading questions.

Now Devi, I'm sure you must have seen the story which was on the front page of *The United Times* this morning, as I'm sure a lot of people in the audience have as well. Would you tell us exactly what has been happening with Minister Sinha and the proposed coal mine in Balachuria? (Smiling sweetly) I'm sorry, Bidisha, but I will not be answering questions about that topic until all the facts have been gathered.

Does that mean you don't know what one of your own ministers has been up to? And are you saying that he acted behind your back? (Bristling slightly) The point is that I am not yet knowing if Minister Sinha has actually been doing any wrong and I must be giving him a fair hearing, also. That is why I will not be answering any more questions about this topic until all the facts have been gathered.

So, you're implying that the very senior civil servant, at the environment ministry who came forward with these allegations about Minister Sinha, is a liar? (Suddenly explosive!) Who is lying! It is your kind of people! Media people! Always trying to stir up trouble!

After which, Nigel, heart still quailing, had tried to point out to Devi, very, very delicately, that her *reaction* was exactly why it was important to stick to the scripted 'I will not be answering questions about that topic until all the facts have been gathered', without any unrehearsed but seemingly innocuous enhancements. Only to be met by a look of pure scorn and outraged silence from her. So then, terror-stricken, and cowed, he had said: well, I think we're all set then! He had tried. What else could he do apart from down more Gelusil?

And now Priyanka, his skinny assistant was waiting by his desk. He could tell from her expression that she had not managed to make contact with Sinha. Looking at her timorous face and shrinking frame, he realised that he should have tasked someone more robust with the job. Besides, although she always did everything she was told, she had never had much resourcefulness. Don't worry, he sighed, even before she'd had the chance to explain, we'll just have to fly blind, I suppose . . .

Down the corridor, Devi sat in her office, so incensed that she could barely focus on the notes she had made for the town hall meeting. Once more, she was being conspired against. Right from the very start she had been conspired against! And why? Because she was *worth* being conspired against, that's why! Because they were scared of her and what she was capable of! Because she was a person of substance and principle and conviction! Because she had vision! Because she had truth on her side! *The* truth!

And now she was being told to practise her responses, to temper her reactions, in essence, to deceive. And for what purpose? So that she could be just like the last lot? All bogus concern and slippery lip service. All liars! The people deserved better than that. As for the voices of discontent, which Nigel had deigned to remind her of, well, she knew exactly to whom they belonged—those self-appointed pundits who believed that their freedom of speech and right to say clever, spiteful things was more important than the progress and betterment of the masses. And that kind of pundit needed to be put in their place, not appeased.

Of course, when she had been in opposition, those same pundits had latched onto her as a fresh and vital force in a stagnant system. A clear, honest voice, a beacon of light, bright enough to lead the way out of the darkness! Yet as soon as she had been elected, the rumblings of dissent and dissatisfaction had begun because those pundits thought a deal had been done; whilst in opposition, it was deemed fitting that she was aggressive and combative and ready to hitch up her sari and wade into the morass. Once she was elected and no longer on the warpath, they had expected that she would shed her belligerence and emerge as a new person—softer, more complaisant, altogether more genteel—as befitted the position of chief minister of West Bengal! Yes, that is what they had expected—her becoming one of the establishment.

Why, only recently, there had been a clamour over the fact that she had not turned up to meet the American ambassador to India. Apparently this was rude, ungracious, a major disgrace. Well, why should she have turned up? She had never said she would. It had just been assumed. Just as on a previous occasion, the American Secretary of State, a showboat if ever she'd met one, had assumed that it was *she* who would control the agenda. So, after the photo call, in which the Secretary had coerced her into a quite awkward, semi-embrace ("I think we can do better than a firm handshake. Let's leave the macho formalities to the men!"), they had taken lunch ("Let's enjoy this wonderful food. We can wait until later to talk shop!"), then finally got down to business. And the Secretary's first point? After some ingratiating opening gambit about how pleased she was that The Communists had finally been ousted and that the Americans could therefore once again resume relations with West Bengal, which was not only full of economic potential, brimming as it was with some of the country's brightest and best graduates and a highly trainable workforce, but also, the gateway to the Far East market and, last but not least, the real intellectual and artistic centre of India. After *all* this butt-kissing blandishment, the Secretary's first point had been about . . . supermarkets! The Secretary wanted India to allow supermarkets in, multi-brand retail, to be technical and precise. Devi had already made clear her feelings about foreign supermarkets getting a foothold in India, invading the country with their chilling chiller cabinets and their eerie fluorescent lighting and their antiseptic wide aisles. They would squeeze out the small traders with shoestring operations, and drive down the prices paid to already hard up farmers. *Her* traders and *her* farmers! Moreover, they would change the culture of bustling markets, which provided nourishment for both the body and soul! Instead of picking a squawking chicken to be slaughtered on site, people would pick up a plastic container with parts already neatly delineated. Simple, nutritious home-cooked meals would be replaced by pre-packaged pap, full of artificial flavours. How could it possibly benefit people to replace real flavour with artificial ones? Indeed, in time, people would forget how to cook altogether, and how was that progress? No, as far as Devi was concerned, foreign supermarkets were as welcome as polio. She was right and there was no way she was going to change her mind. The Secretary was either very foolish or very arrogant—or both—to think that she was going to persuade her otherwise! And she was going to tell the Secretary as much until Nigel had suggested that perhaps, in the interests of diplomacy, an affable equivocation would be better than an outright and hostile dismissal. So, still miffed, she had mumbled that the Secretary had raised some interesting points (as if!) and that she would certainly consider them (no chance!). And where had this delicacy got her? To a press release from the Americans, much quicker off the mark than the dolts working for her, stating that the Secretary had indeed discussed the issue of supermarket-entry with the chief minister and that she had been open and responsive. Discussion? What discussion? Yes, she had respond*ed* with the little courtesy she could muster, but she hadn't been respons*ive*. And as far as being open was concerned, well, yes, she hadn't stormed out of the room, but that was only because she had been told such behaviour might come across as churlish. And for her efforts? She had been made to look like a suck-up, and worse than that, a hypocrite. How would her people trust her if it looked like she was saying one thing to them and then quite the opposite to the American bigwig? A clarification was needed, an apology was required! But an apology was not forthcoming. For a whole week she had waited, only for Nigel to bring the daily news that there had been nothing further from the Secretary's office; after her two-day trip to West Bengal, the Secretary was done and had swiftly moved on to other matters. So when Devi had been informed that the American ambassador was visiting, she had behaved in kind. What was wrong with that? Why the outcry? Did they expect her to be grateful and beholden? To smile like a simpleton and to hell with self-respect? And all the talk from the pundits about her being an embarrassment, a discredit to her office? It was simply because they had failed to mould her. They had believed that she would dance to their tune if they played loud enough. They were wrong! Does she not realise what a fool she's making of herself? they said. But they were the fools for expecting that she would suddenly lose her integrity, lose all sense of herself! Admittedly, she was not the consummate politician—but neither did she want to be, for to her, that would be the ultimate insult. Her politics were those of instinct and honesty! And now Nigel was telling her to deny that instinct, but what was left of her if it was taken away?

Of course, all this wouldn't be happening if it wasn't for that scoundrel Sinha. She'd pegged him as a schemer from the start, always thinking of himself instead of the people. A charming schemer, for sure, with his genie-like *your wish is my command* deference, but a schemer all the same. Well, he hadn't fooled her. But she had had no other choice. Politicians like her, with her altruism and profound sincerity, were a rare breed, even within her own party. In fact, the breed was completely endangered—there was only one like her, and that was her! And if the last lot had their way, she'd be extinct! Furthermore, she had no doubt that it was they who were behind this farrago. After all, they had always been in league with Lohia, handing him the juiciest contracts and most lucrative business in return for his patronage. And Balachuria had been a closely run seat between them and her in the panchayat local election. It all added up.

If only she could replicate herself and send out an army of clones, all carrying firm, structured handbags, which could be used to clobber the enemy over the head. This thought pleased her, and for a moment, her mood lifted until she remembered that she had the town hall meeting that evening and it came crashing down again. They'd be out to get her, that was for certain. Well, let them try, and then they'd really see what she was made of!

Her fingers were twitching. Her feet were tapping. She needed her nervous energy to dissipate. Her dolls. Furtively, she brought out Barbie and a Ken. That Sinha! Ken received a slap around the face. The scoundrel! Ken bent down and begged Barbie for forgiveness. The good-for-absolutely-nothing! Barbie gave Ken a good kick in the balls (well, where his balls would be if he were an anatomically correct doll).

She felt much calmer and steadier after that.

XVII

Not quite as pithy or amusing a headline as it could have been, Anil thought, as he looked at the front page of *The United Times*. Of course, it was a serious paper not a tabloid, so even though a header along the lines of SINHA CAUGHT SINNING or SINHA IN MINEFIELD OVER MINE or SINHA TREADING ON HOT COALS would have tickled him, he was perfectly satisfied with what was a clear summary of the situation. Reading on, he came to the conclusion that Tapati Ghatak had quite a talent for sticking the knife in—as well as the main meat of the story, she had added to the case against Sinha for obstructing due process by digging up some dirt from his past incarnation as a businessman, when he had been accused of trying to derail an investigation into unsafe practices in one of his garment factories. So much for the businessman who had become a politician because he wanted to 'give something back'. More like the businessman who had become a politician to get away from something. Not only that but one of her colleagues had written a scathing piece about the two Green Police activists whom Sinha had tried and failed to get on board. The man was a college dropout (it being such a rarity in India that there was an explanation of the term given in a box: a *college dropout* is a student who withdraws before completing a course of instruction. Reasons for dropping out are insufficient motivation or not being prepared for the rigours of academic work; stress; or family issues including financial problems. The term is an Americanism from the 1920s, and although college dropout rates are significant in America, they are not so in India.) and the woman had at some point suffered from a mental illness, or as the journalist had put it 'been committed to a mental facility'. So both were implicated as being, in their separate ways, weak-willed, feeble, and altogether unreliable—and they were whom Sinha had turned to for assistance. Yet another lapse in his judgement. Anil almost felt sorry for the two; they couldn't have known what was coming. And he wondered where the journalist had found the information. Well, Anil had his methods and he guessed that the journalist had his, too. What they had in common though was ruthlessness and the willingness to do whatever it took to get the job done. And the job *had* been done. Sinha was being buried alive under a pile of ignominy.

Feeling quite upbeat, Anil folded the newspaper, put it down in the seat next to him, and switched to his phone to see if any comments had yet been made on the online version of the article.

Ratnabali (Kolkata), 3 July 2013, 8:32 a.m.

They say they are for Truth, but only too happy to resort to Lies when it suits their purposes! The mine would be a very good thing for the locality but it seems Devi wants to stop it from going ahead and is using one of her ministers to do her bidding. Is this democracy?

Biswajit (Kolkata), 3 July 2013, 8:50 a.m.

This is no surprise. Devi promotes herself as honest and transparent and trustworthy, but underneath the very thin veneer of high-mindedness, she is petty, bigoted, and self-centred. I have no doubt that all the blame will be laid at Sinha's door, but let's not fool ourselves. All of Devi's ministers are just her puppets.

Krishnan (Mumbai), 3 July 2013, 9:18 a.m.

Well, you guys voted her in! Is it any wonder that whilst places like Mumbai go from strength to strength, Kolkata remains in the doldrums? It's because our politicians support our entrepreneurs instead of trying to put them out of business!

> Gautam (Kolkata) replied to Krishnan, 3 July 2013, 9:22 a.m.
>
> Why don't you keep your businessman Ambani and we'll keep Devi. Let him enjoy looking out over the Mumbai slums from his palace in the sky, but luckily for most poor Kolkatans, they have someone who actually cares about them.
>
> Krishnan (Mumbai), replied to Gautam, 3 July 2013, 9:25 a.m.
>
> I was waiting for the old Kolkatan leftist jealousy to rear its head, it didn't take long! That's the

problem with your type, you're like a bucket of crabs. As soon as one almost reaches the top, it gets clambered over by another and then they both fall to the bottom.

Kush (Kolkata), 3 July 2013, 10:13 a.m.

I think it is a shame that every time it looks like some sort of progress is going to be made in WB, there is something to hinder it. Always conflict, never collaboration. And who loses out? We do. We thought by finally booting out the Communists we were going to move in a positive direction but maybe that is not written in our fate!

Anil nodded to himself. So the commentators were, in the main, blaming Devi for the stunt. Well, good, because he had absolutely no doubt she was behind it. There was no way that Sinha would have tried to block the environmental permit being issued if Devi had not required it, be it blatantly or surreptitiously. Of course, it was early enough in the day, and no doubt more of the Devi apologists and stalwarts would soon make an appearance, filling the comments pages with their ifs and buts and hows and whys but Anil had drawn first blood. As for the Ambani jibe, well, fair enough, that man was so indiscreet, it was embarrassing. But Lohia was hardly in the same camp; for an incredibly wealthy Indian, he led an almost austere life. Sure, he had a few baubles, but, all in all, his tastes were relatively modest and certainly not flashy enough to attract either attention or criticism. His Rolex wasn't even diamond-studded!

In any case, the gist of the general response to the article was a further fillip to Anil's good mood, and it was with a replenished sense of optimism that he asked the driver to take a detour by the hospital grounds.

There had been a reasonable amount of discussion over the design of the whole unit, with the hospital's management insisting that they simply rebuild the hospital in the same nondescript, blocky style. But Anil, who was not on the hospital board (nor indeed the board of any of Sachin's other businesses, as he found directorships cumbersome; he preferred to be agile, adroit, and as independent as possible, reporting to only Sachin) had seen an opportunity to make a statement about the kind of place Kolkata was, and had managed to convince Sachin to agree to a grand reinvention rather than just a standard rebuild. As Sachin had been in jail at this point, Anil had simply put it to him that rebuilding in an ambitious, imposing, eye-catching style would be an act of defiance, boldness, and determination all rolled into one. Furthermore, Anil would oversee the redesign process so that the hospital's management would not have to spend their time doing so. As Anil had predicted, this approach appealed to Sachin's sense of illustriousness (and gave him something to dream about whilst stuck in a dank, grey jail cell), and once Sachin had agreed, the rest of the board, of course, acquiesced.

Always keen to give people a chance, Anil had come up with the idea of running a competition, which was promoted to final year students at the best architectural courses in India. Along with the prestige of winning the commission, there was also a hefty cash prize. Of course, he had then been inundated with entries, most of them insipid, derivative, or downright ugly, but acting with his usual purposefulness and decisiveness, he had soon picked the winner: a Miss Krishna Valiathan, a South Indian studying at Sir J J College of Architecture in Mumbai. Her design, somehow seamlessly combining the elegant curves and intricate patterns of Mughal times, with the bold, determined lines of the Brutalists had stood out immediately. The renewed Lohia Hospital would now not only be a centre for excellence in healthcare, it would also be a landmark!

And now looking at the space where the hospital had once stood, the wreckage having been removed and the ground levelled, Anil, always committed to the art of the possible, envisaged that with Dr. Acharya at the head of the hospital's new neurological unit, it would become a world class centre. First, patients from all over India would come. And then from Asia. And then some day, the whole world! He needed to contact Dr. Acharya again, tell her things were progressing nicely. He could take her the prints of the new design, he was sure she would be as impressed by it as he was. Or would she consider that pushy? After all, she hadn't seemed like a woman who would take to being pushed. Very gently nudged, perhaps . . .

He was running late; he would have to give proper consideration to the matter later. Dr. Acharya was central to his grand plan and would have to be handled carefully and accordingly.

There was an unfamiliar car in Sachin's drive and Anil squinted at it, wondering whose it might be. There was also a driver in the car.

"Go and find out to whom that car belongs," Anil told his driver. He wanted to be prepared for whomever he might bump into in Sachin's house. A moment later, his driver returned and told him through the open passenger window.

"Bhupen Mandal."

"Yes, but *who* is Bhupen Mandal?"

The driver looked blank for a minute and then turned to go back and ask. "No, no, forget it," Anil shook his head.

"It's not a problem, Sir, let me go and ask!"

"No, honestly, there's no need. I'll find out soon enough."

Despite being a very regular caller, Anil was subject to the same treatment as any other visitor—made to wait in the marble floored hall whilst his arrival was announced by butler to front-of-house maid to valet to Sachin himself. Sachin had told Anil that this made his staff happy as they felt included, but it sometimes occurred to Anil that maybe Sachin just enjoyed the theatre of it all. Indeed, it had also occurred to Anil that Sachin was somewhat like a politician with his predilection for pageantry and fanfare. But, no, Sachin was far too good to be a politician!

The butler returned and smiled fawningly.

"Mr Lohia is ready to see you. I'll show you through to his study."

I know where his bloody study is, Anil thought, as he followed the butler who was walking at a slow, magisterial place, can we just stop this charade, and I can get down to business and you can buttle off!

As Anil was led into the study, he was surprised to see another man sitting across from Sachin. He had momentarily forgotten about Bhupen Mandal.

"Ah, Anil!" said Sachin brightly. "I have just been telling Bhupen about you!"

Anil reached out to shake the man's hand and nodded politely. Bhupen, who looked like he was in his fifties, clean-shaven and with neatly groomed greying hair, was wearing Indian dress—kurta pyjamas with a Nehru-collared waistcoat and an embroidered scarf over one shoulder. Yet, despite his genteel appearance, Anil sensed something of the gangster about Bhupen. Anil made his handshake perfunctory and withdrew his hand as soon as he could. Meanwhile, Sachin, who seemed to be thoroughly enjoying his reinvention as humble and holy, at least from a sartorial point of view, was sporting a white temple-ready short tunic with loose drawstring trousers. And Anil suddenly felt quite out of place in his collared shirt and suit trousers, as if he had missed the dress code at the bottom of the invitation. But more than that, he felt that he would not be made party to whatever had been said between the two men before he had arrived, and that whatever would now be said in his presence would be adjusted accordingly. And he still couldn't figure out who Bhupen was although he was quite sure he knew him or at least of him.

"How wonderful I am, I hope?" Anil replied, glancing at Bhupen.

"Of course!" declared Sachin, turning to Bhupen and saying, "Didn't I say he was a funny man?"

Bhupen waggled his head.

Yes, I'm fucking hilarious, thought Anil, and who's this other joker?

"If you have business to finish," Anil said, gesturing towards the door, "I'm happy to wait."

"No, no," Sachin shook his head. "We were actually waiting for you. I have been telling Bhupen about the situation in Balachuria but obviously you know more than me!" Then he turned to Bhupen again and added, "Anil is the details man."

More head-waggling from Bhupen.

Now Anil tried to deduce who Bhupen actually was—clearly of such standing that it was expected Anil *should* know. Someone in the public eye, then? And someone in the public eye who would be interested in Balachuria?

"Maybe we can be of help . . ." Bhupen said softly, and again, Anil sensed something thuggish underneath the civility. And help? What did that mean? Then Anil realised who Bhupen was. He was the West Bengal president of The Sevak Party, the Hindu nationalist party that, despite its national success, had so far fared reasonably poorly with the Bengalis. However, recently their situation had started to change and mainly because of Devi. She, put out by their rise to national power and afraid of what that might mean for her locally, had tried to ban them from holding a political rally in front of one of Kolkata's major landmarks, where she was sure they would attract too much attention. On what basis? On the basis that the rally would create traffic problems. In a city known for its intractable traffic problem, this was disingenuous if not downright laughable. However, the municipal authority had upheld the ban, leading to a whole lot of outcry and even more column inches.

DEVI DISHEARTENS WITH OFFENSIVE DISPLAY OF DISDAIN FOR DEMOCRACY

DEVI SHOWS SUPERCILIOUSNESS OVER SEVAK RALLY

DEVI THE DICTATOR!

And then, almost inevitably, the Kolkata High Court had overturned the ban, and there had been even more column inches, and photos of Bhupen Mandal looking suitably smug. The Sevak Party was becoming a threat very much because they were perceived to be a threat. Soon, they were hoping to overtake The Communists as Devi Enemy Number One!

Anil already had his hands full with Devi and her merry band of meddling men; he had no appetite for managing yet another self-serving politician. Sachin knew this, so why on earth had he invited Bhupen Mandal into his home? What was he thinking? My enemy's enemy is my friend? Whatever the reason, Anil was most displeased. It was imperative that the project go ahead on its own merits, without any political glad-handing or arm-twisting. Only then could it live up to its true potential. This Bhupen character would have to be written out, even if it upset Sachin. Sachin would get over it. He'd gotten over far worse. Indeed, Sachin's resilience was one of the qualities Anil most admired.

"That's very generous of you but I think we're managing quite well so far," Anil smiled politely.

Sachin and Bhupen shared a rueful look, which seemed to Anil as if it was filled with pity for him, as if the truth would have to be broken to him gently. Anil did not appreciate this look. So he said, now more pointedly, "Besides, I'm sure you have more important matters to campaign about."

Bhupen smiled and shook his head.

"What is more important than job and wealth creation for our people!"

Then, he turned again to Sachin and said, with such jest that it could only be meant seriously, "Votes for us, profits for you!"

Anil waited for Sachin's response—surely, he wasn't going to let Bhupen get away with such a crude summary—but Sachin seemed to just absorb his comment, and then Bhupen added, slowly, emphatically, and completely unnecessarily, as if he were speaking to the mentally lacking, "*Mu-tu-al* benefits . . ."

Anil, now fully irked, was quite ready to tell Bhupen to stick his benefits right up his *mu-tu-al*, but his sense of professionalism, and of self-preservation, considering Bhupen's mafioso air, tempered his feedback.

"Well, naturally," he said, "but let's conserve our energies for the moment, shall we? For all we know, once the environmental permit is issued, the project might progress without any further impediments." Of course, he did not believe for one minute that this was true.

"You mean *if* the permit is issued," Bhupen said, smiling.

"No, I mean when," Anil shot back, tacking on a smile so brief, it could have been mistaken as a twitch. He might have been wary of Bhupen, but he wasn't going to just stand there and be patronised.

Bhupen threw his head back and laughed, then told Sachin,

wolfishly, flicking his chin towards Anil, "He really is a funny man—and optimistic!"

Yes, thought Anil, but I'm about to have a sense of humour failure. He turned to face Sachin with an expectant expression.

Sachin, sensitive to both Anil's and Bhupen's egos, but not threatened by either of them, played the we're-all-grown-ups-here card.

"This is a very important project for West Bengal," he reminded them. "It's as much to serve its people as it is to serve ourselves. So we must be careful, prudent, and above all, united. We certainly don't want to make ourselves susceptible to any accusations of internal conflict or rivalry. That would be an unnecessary—and unnecessarily sad—outcome." All of this in the most gentle of voices with the most winning of smiles. Only a lout would object.

Damn, thought Anil, I've got to give him credit. Grace, economy, feeling—he really did learn from that Magdalen student. And not only learn but really take on board. He probably practises in the mirror.

Damn, thought Bhupen, but he's the one with the money.

"Anyway," Sachin went on, "I just wanted the two of you to meet each other. We can get into the details later on."

Suddenly, the butler reappeared and Sachin asked him to show out the esteemed gentleman.

Esteemed gentleman, Anil thought, well that's definitely not me, and he finally plonked his bottom down in his favourite tub chair with an expressive sigh of comfort.

Esteemed gentleman, Bhupen thought as the butler ushered him out, I really do like this Sachin man, he is a person with manners and taste, and he recognises quality when he sees it!

"So," Anil asked Sachin, as soon as the door had been closed on Bhupen, "what's the deal with the Mandal fellow? He seems a bit shady to me."

"Shady?"

"You know . . . underhand.

Sachin laughed. "When you're in this game, you have to work *under hands*. At least for some of the time."

"Well, that may be so but why are his lot bothering with Balachuria?"

"Were you not listening? Votes for them, profits for us!"

"Why do there have to be votes for them? Why not just profits for us!"

Amused laughter from Sachin. But as he went on to tell it, in a place where politicians were still trusted to do what was best for the people, despite plenty of evidence to suggest the contrary, and where businessmen, especially Marwaris, were still assumed to be liars and swindlers, despite plenty of evidence to suggest the contrary, it was a prerequisite that any business deal of consequence had to be backed by a political party in order to gain popular support. It didn't really matter which party, it only mattered that someone who was ostensibly in the service of the public had given the project their backing. In this particular case, Devi and The Truth Party were quite obviously out! Meanwhile, Sachin's old allies, The Communists, were too busy licking their wounds to get involved. And the trusty old Other Party had lost the plot and was wandering around in circles, chasing its own tail like a demented dog. Which left Bhupen and his Sevak crowd.

Anil was not convinced. "Why do we need any of them? Our case for the mine is strong enough on its own. We don't any politician to back us."

"That's just the way things work here," Sachin said, matter-of-fact.

"Well, maybe it's time for things to work differently."

"Now you're being foolish."

"I've just seen a rat!" declared Sharmila loudly, in colloquial

Bengali, as she walked into the study, stood in front of Sachin, and crossed her arms, surly as a washerwoman. She glanced briefly at Anil but did not bother to otherwise acknowledge him.

Anil stared at her broad, squat form and the untidy way in which her sari was shoved into her petticoat and the dense roll of back fat and thought: *Aré baap!* He had seen her a few times before, also in the house, but only ever in passing. And he had been too preoccupied on those occasions to pay much attention. Besides, Sachin had never mentioned Sharmila, and if your boss doesn't mention his wife, then you certainly don't take it upon yourself to ask after her! But Anil was still rather taken aback. He hadn't expected a lithe young beauty. He knew that in India, it wasn't the done thing for a rich, powerful man to replace his wife with a younger, faster model. He just kept the latter in a nice little flat, gave her pocket money, and made promises he had no intention of keeping—in return for being called 'Uncle' with all the benefits that uncle-dom proffered. But, still, neither had he expected *this*.

For the first time ever, Sachin appeared slightly flustered.

"Why are you telling me?" he asked, quite prickly, also in Bengali. "Why don't you ask one of our people to sort it out!" Then turning to Anil, he spoke in English, adopting a very proper tone, "Excuse us . . ."

Anil shook his head: not at all. He wondered what Sachin was more embarrassed about—the rat or his wife.

"Why should I tell your staff?" Sharmila said coarsely, sticking out her neck and placing her hands on her hips. "It was *you* who invited the rat in!"

Ah, okay, now I get it, thought Anil; I like this woman.

Sachin grit his teeth. After years of such apathy from Sharmila that he had genuinely considered getting a dog for the attention and affection, she had recently, ever since the news article about the hospital fire, started taking an interest in him again. Honestly woman, he thought, your timing couldn't be worse.

"The gentleman to whom you're referring is very highly regarded," Sachin replied politely.

"Highly regarded, my arse!" Sharmila spat, and Anil had to keep himself from bursting out laughing. "You should know better. All he does is spread shit. And once he's stuck himself to your bum, you'll never prise him off! How much is he asking for, anyway?"

"He's not asking for any money," Sachin answered curtly.

"Oh, brother!" Sharmila sniggered. "I'm sure a lot has changed since my day, but one thing which will never change is politicians asking for money!"

"I'm telling you, he's not asking for money."

"What *is* he asking for?" Anil interjected, his tone airy and innocent.

Sharmila turned around to look at him; although he had spoken in English, Sharmila had sensed what the question was, and she turned back to Sachin for an answer.

Sachin did not like being put on the spot, especially by people who were meant to be on his side. He was their boss, after all. With wifely intuition, Sharmila knew not to bother pushing him for an answer, though she was too impish to leave the matter entirely. So, instead of saying anything further to her husband, she turned around to Anil and said in her ribald way, "Leave it. When he gets himself into trouble because of that rat, then whom will he run to? Pest control—*yours truly*. Just you wait and see . . ."

And with that, she was off.

Sachin exhaled. The truth of it was that he hadn't yet come to any particular arrangement with Bhupen. Of course, it was implicit that when it was opportune, a mu-tu-ally beneficial understanding would of course be reached. What he had been hoping was that he would first persuade Anil to get on board with his pragmatic approach—to succeed, Balachuria needed the backing of a politician. He certainly hadn't counted on Anil being so dead against it! And now that the preliminary overture had been made to Bhupen, it would be very, very difficult, not to mention potentially dangerous, to retract. Because although Sachin had dealt with numerous difficulties in the course of his life, that did not make Bhupen Mandal someone to be toyed with. And he had to remember his position as a Marwari, too. He might have been one of the biggest employers in the state and set up numerous philanthropic ventures to aid and improve the city's lot, but a Bengali politician could turn against a Marwari businessman in the time it took to slurp a cup of chai from a tiny clay cup. And it didn't take much to turn the Bengalis against a Marwari, regardless of how the Bengalis had benefitted from his presence. All that had to be brought out were the age-old insults—Marwaris were uncultured, tasteless, money-grubbing, greedy, an insular lot who spent their time counting their money and chewing paan. Whereas, of course, the Bengalis were cultured, tasteful, money-resisting, ascetic, and broad-minded (if not quite broad-minded enough to actually and truly appreciate all that the Marwaris had done for their state). And then, *then*, that same politician would have the shamelessness to ask the Marwari for support when he needed it. And the Marwari, always aware of his subaltern status (drilled into him by the rejection from all of Kolkata's elite members' clubs), would feel compelled to acquiesce. It was a disgraceful situation. It has to change, Sachin thought. Credit where credit is due. Recognition where recognition is due. Respect where respect is due!

Meanwhile, Anil had been struck by inspiration. He had been pondering who should address the Balachuria people at the roadshow—who would least alienate them and best be able to herd them through the gate. Sachin may have once been suitable, many moons ago, but now, in his current incarnation as His Serene Highness (Billionaire Businessman), he, on his own, would be too far removed, far too out of place, far too much to persuade a bunch of poor country folk that his mine would be valuable to them. What he needed was a down-to-earth sidekick. But Anil putting in an appearance himself was tricky—his spoken Bengali wasn't natural enough. His parents had always spoken in English with him, his schooling had been in English, so the only opportunity he had ever had to speak Bengali was with the servants and outsiders like taxi drivers and shopkeepers; the repertoire in which he was really fluent was limited. And then there was his physical being—the height and the fairness—it was clear that his background was an entitled one. Which might outright offend a group of people who had never felt entitled to anything. So he was out of the question. Then he had considered Lalima—she was eloquent, forceful, convincing. But she was far too good-looking. And whilst her sex appeal might have been just about acceptable in the metropolis, in Balachuria, the men would be so distracted by her appearance that anything she said would be lost. Meanwhile, the women just wouldn't be able to trust her and would probably be too busy whispering about what kind of woman Lalima was (certainly not *their* kind of woman) to listen to what she was saying. So, Lalima, sadly, was also unsuitable. He'd even considered Tapan. Briefly. Very briefly. Just for long enough to remember his diamond-studded Rado. And then, as the obvious contenders had been ruled out, he had been left feeling a little stuck. Until Sharmila. The First Lady of My Arse! What a gal! Straightforward and straight-talking, no airs and graces, and despite her husband having gazillions in the bank, still wearing a cheap, synthetic sari, and looking like she ate promotional multi-packs of biscuits for a living. Just when he was in a spot of bother, she had made a perfectly timed entrance. Why shouldn't he be optimistic!

XVIII

"Do you think I'm wearing too much lipstick?" Bidisha asked. "I don't want to look like a clown next to Devi. She never wears even a touch of blusher, not even for TV."

"*She*'s the clown," retorted the make-up artist as he worked some more eyeliner into Bidisha's lash line, and then inspected his handiwork.

"Sshhh! She might be standing right outside!"

The make-up artist dabbed a little smidgen of gloss onto Bidisha's lower lip to make the most of the bright lights of the stage. "So, what are you going to ask her about?"

"The usual stuff—what has she been doing for us, what she plans on doing next."

"And what about that coal mine thing?"

"Well, her press officer has said no questions about Minister Sinha and Balachuria."

"But you *are* going to ask her about that, aren't you?"

"Of course!"

A mixed bag, Anil thought as he craned his neck from his front row seat to see who else was coming through the door—many groups of students; a few families (only in Kolkata, Anil thought, would an evening at a politician's town hall meeting count as appropriate entertainment for a 'family night out'); a good number of elderly couples; some young professional types. Soon enough, there was just standing room. Then, as the lights in the hall were dimmed, and the stage lights were turned on, the presenter came on stage, which had been set up with two chairs and, in between them, a table carrying two glasses of water. Anil recognised her from one of the early evening news shows, Bidisha something. Not one of the hardest hitters, and she always wore too much make-up to be taken completely seriously but certainly no walkover either. There was a smattering of syncopated applause; no one seemed to know whether it was necessary to clap the presenter. Bidisha didn't seem to care. She nodded, grinned, and then introduced the audience to Devi, with the preface that the Bengalis were very lucky that they had a chief minister who was always prepared to come and meet with and take questions from the electorate, whilst the chief ministers of other states would always try to wriggle out of facing an open, honest, and people-led audit!

Nigel, standing in the wings, let out a silent sigh of relief. He had almost had to prostrate himself in order to convince Bidisha to start off the session with that introduction.

"Why have they sent *that* girl—the one who always wears too much make-up!" Devi whispered to him as she stood at his shoulder and peered at the presenter. But before he could answer, it was time for Devi to walk on.

Bidisha waited for Devi to take her seat and then sat down herself. The chairs were positioned at an angle, so that they were slightly facing each other, but just as Bidisha was about to start speaking, Devi got up, and moved her chair so that it was directly facing the audience. Then she sat back down again, giving the audience a great, big grin as if she had done something quite hilarious and perhaps even a little bit naughty. Anil noticed that, bizarrely, she was holding a mobile phone in her right hand, and that the phone had a Hello Kitty charm attached to it.

"Are you comfortable now, Devi?" Bidisha asked courteously.

"I do not want to be sitting in the dais, I want to be sitting in the down with the people," Devi said, smiling for effect.

What the fuck is a dais, what the fuck is an *in the down*, and please the fuck don't come and sit next to me, Anil thought.

Some of the audience laughed at this. Phew, thought Nigel, I hope it continues like this. Suckers, thought Anil, it better not go on like this!

Bidisha started gently questioning Devi about her last six months, and Devi gamely trotted out a list of pre-prepared statistics and facts—air conditioning on buses; bank lending to micro, small, and medium enterprises; the provision of a twenty-five thousand rupee grant to unmarried girls who were in full-time study or vocational training; better acoustics in a famous music hall. Combined with the sticky heat which could not be dissipated by the feeble old fans, and due to the fact that he had not had the time to take his usual refreshing early evening shower, Anil started to feel quite drowsy as Devi eagerly droned on and on and on . . . Then, suddenly, after a small but pointed pause, she told the audience, very proudly, that of course one of the most important achievements was that West Bengal was no longer a power-deficit state. As she told it, there had been huge capacity building in the last three years and Bengal had received third position in Best State Power Utility Award! Now Anil was quite awake again. There are awards for this kind of thing, he thought, bemused, like the Electricity Oscars? And then, more disgruntled:

sure, that's all well and good, but what about the fact that we're *at* capacity; there's not enough power supply for anything more! Is *just about enough for now* something to be proud of?

Nigel, meanwhile, was aghast. He had pleaded with Devi not to mention anything energy related. Of course you're right to be pleased, he had said, and of course it's an extremely important achievement! But perhaps we just put out a press release lest Bidisha is given an opening to broach the subject of Sinha and the Balachuria coal mine? But Devi had either forgotten his warning or, more likely, didn't care to heed it. Now you're asking for it, he thought, grimly.

"So . . ." Bidisha began, "That's all great, but perhaps we could talk about a less positive matter . . ."

Devi stopped smiling but didn't scowl outright. Instead, she came out with a stoic expression, which implied *If we must.*

Here we go, thought Nigel, here we go. He closed his eyes, and wondered where he'd put his bottle of Gelusil.

"Let's talk about the matter of political violence and specifically the case of Communist leader Mustak Ahmed Attar. Now, Selim Shah was put in prison, having been found guilty of assault but you've still allowed him to remain a member of your party—why is that?"

Nigel opened his eyes. *What?* A question about Shah hadn't crossed his radar. He hadn't prepared Devi for this at all. She would have to deal with it free-form, and there was nothing more unnerving than a free-form Devi.

"I am not believing in goons and thugs," said Devi, dismissively, as if that answered the question. She folded her arms as if to underline that was the end of the matter.

Body language, thought Nigel, body language!

"Well, I'm sure that you don't believe in goons and thugs, but how can you align that belief with the fact that a man who you know has committed an act of violence against one of your political opponents is still a member of your party?"

"That is all in the past," huffed Devi. "I want to be talking about the future!"

"Yes, we shall definitely talk about the future, but as—and I think I can speak on behalf of everyone in this room—we want the future to be free of political violence, can you please tell us how you're going to make that happen when one of your own party members is a convicted thug?"

Suddenly a woman jumped up and raised her hand. There was a slight murmur from the crowd, and Anil turned his head to see what was going on behind him. Ah, cometh the hour, cometh the heckler! It was better than free *nimki*.

"You always say that The Truth Party is against violence but isn't it the *truth* that you rely on violence just as much as anyone else? In fact, since you came to power, hasn't political violence been on the rise?"

"If there is being an increase in political violence, it is because of the others not because of me," Devi sniffed. But the girl went on.

"Then why is it being reported that you use goons to rig election results?"

"It is because one section of the media with their vested interest is behaving like this, always carrying out personal attacks against me!"

"I'm not personally attacking you, I'm just asking you a question about why political violence is on the rise. Doesn't everyone have the right to exercise their democratic freedom?"

Now Devi's expression turned ugly.

"I am telling you, you are a Communist cadre. I will not be answering to Communist cadres. I will only be answering to the common person."

"I don't belong to the Communist party, I'm just a student."

"A student where?"

"At Jadavpur University."

"Everyone at Jadavpur University is a Maoist!"

Both the girl and the rest of the crowd seemed quite amused by this and there was a little bit of tittering, which ruffled Devi further, causing her to slip into speaking in Bengali.

"That girl is speaking rubbish! The Communists were conspiring to murder me and now she is telling me about violence! This whole thing is a plot! The Communists have planted her to try and cause trouble and to denounce me!"

"But I don't have anything to do with The Communists," the girl said, now looking quite distressed herself. "I'm just a student. And I'm not trying to denounce you, I'm just asking you a question."

"I won't be asked questions by so-called Maoists!" Devi shouted, switching to English again, as she started to rise from her seat. "Or so-called people! All I am saying is that I don't like goons or guns!"

Body language, thought Nigel, body language. Though he was well aware that her actual language—and the volume at which it was being uttered—was just as much of a problem. But he needed to try and keep calm enough to give her a pep talk if she stormed off.

What the hell were *so-called people*? Anil thought. And why was she shouting? Though she was right about not needing to be elevated on the dais. Not with a voice like that. No, she needed to be lowered. Into some subterranean chamber. Perhaps, for extra certainty, a subterranean vacuum chamber. Suddenly, the impulse to say something overtook him, and he stood up.

"Have you considered, Chief Minister," he said politely, "that with all the murder conspiracies and the personal attacks and the plots against you, you might be suffering from some kind of delusional paranoia? And if not that, have you considered that you might just be really unpopular?"

Devi's nostrils flared and she promptly stood up.

"He is another Maoist!" she declared, raising her hand in his direction, the Hello Kitty phone charm swinging wildly.

"I'm not a Maoist, I'm a strategy consultant," replied Anil, laconically, which garnered a good few laughs from the audience.

"Yes, a strategy consultant for the Maoists!" screamed Devi. "I will report you to the police!"

"OK, OK," said Bidisha, "let's move on, shall we? And perhaps we can wait until the end for questions from the audience."

The girl sat back down, now looking quite diffident. Anil also sat back down, not sure why he had drawn attention to himself but not too concerned about it either. Devi gave them both death stares. Her own arse was still hovering a few centimetres above her chair in anger. So Bidisha said to her, soothingly, "Shall we continue?"

Devi shrugged stroppily, plonked herself back down, and slouched.

Oh, for the love of God, Nigel thought, body language, BODY LANGUAGE!

"Well, perhaps we can now move on to the small topic of Environment Minister Sinha and his attempt to prevent an environmental permit being issued for the proposed coal mine in Balachuria."

Nigel's heart lurched. He had been concentrating so hard on the traffic accident in front of him, that being rear-ended hadn't occurred to him.

Devi looked up to the ceiling, as if she were bored, and then shrugged.

"I will not be answering questions about that topic until all the facts have been gathered."

"I haven't asked you a question," Bidisha said, deadpan.

"Yes, well, I am telling you that I will not be answering questions about that topic until all the facts have been gathered."

"So, there's nothing you would like to say about the situation?" Bidisha asked lightly.

"What I would like to say is that I will not be answering questions about that topic until all the facts have been gathered."

At this, she swung her feet like a young girl and smiled coyly.

Oh god, Nigel thought, she's *playing*. This is what happens when you miss out on a childhood.

"You won't mind me asking but don't you think the audience deserves a bit more from their chief minister than such a non-response?" Bidisha asked, still courteous.

"I'm a professional, aren't I?" Devi said, smiling again at the crowd for effect, but this time the smile was a little more stretched.

That might be stretching it, Nigel thought.

A professional idiot, Anil thought.

"Well, if you don't mind me saying, for a professional, you don't seem particularly concerned about what might turn out to be a very serious transgression by one of your senior ministers?"

Devi's face curdled. And then after a second of hate-filled silence, she exploded.

"Of course, I am caring!"

Even Bidisha was taken aback by the sheer volume of the blast and momentarily forgot what she was going to say next. But by the time she had gathered her thoughts, Devi, inexplicably, had a smile on her face again.

"The important thing in this matter is that we are needing to respect the verdict of the people," she said, unprompted.

Bidisha furrowed her brow and then asked, ". . . But the people of Balachuria haven't yet given their verdict."

"If you are a simple person then you have to be struggling. I am of this soil," Devi said.

Oh no, thought Nigel, on the verge of collapse, she's doing that thing where she just steamrolls questions out of the way. The end is nigh.

Oh no, thought Anil, get your act together Bidisha, don't let her get away with this simple person shtick.

"Well, there is no doubt about that," Bidisha said hesitantly, "but—"

"Status matters," Devi interjected. "The rich and powerful—and we know who they are in this town—are always trying to rule the common man! So it is my duty to protect him!"

"Of course, and that is an honourable duty, but—"

"And when I said 'Slow down' to Sri Sinha, what I was actually meaning was 'Don't be rushing—give the project ample time'."

At this, she looked quite smug; she was very pleased with how she had managed to put a positive spin on the matter. Ample time. Nice one.

Nigel pressed his palm to his forehead and closed his eyes. How many times had he told her not to offer up information? But instead of stepping around the dog turd, she had stepped right in it. And who was going to have to clean up the stinking mess?

Anil was delighted that she had accepted liability for asking the issuance of the environmental permit to be delayed, despite her contingent and cack-handed attempt at explaining *why* she had done so—ample time, his arse—but was also dismayed that a person in such a position of power possessed such a malevolent kind of stupidity.

Bidisha pursed her lips and then leant in towards Devi and asked, sternly, "So you are admitting that it was you who asked Sri Sinha, the environment minister, to slow down the issuance of the environmental permit?"

Devi's face fell. Now that it had been put like that, it didn't sound so good. The realisation that she had opened a can of worms hit her hard and then she responded the only way she knew how. By screaming.

"If you are not letting me speak, then I am going to leave!"

"But of course you may speak," Bidisha said, unclear as to what Devi meant. "Please, go ahead."

Devi looked at the audience who all looked back at her expectantly.

"This is all a Communist plot, all of it!" she yelled, standing up and leaning forward to straighten out the hem of her sari. As she did so, Anil noticed a stray grey hair sticking out from her parting like a lightning conductor. Well, she'd need that in the storm she'd just created!

"What is a Communist plot?" Bidisha asked earnestly, which seemed to enrage Devi even more, causing her to shout even louder.

"You, *you* have been planted to ambush me! You tricked me! Well, I am not a sitting duck!"

And with that, Devi marched off the stage, leaving Bidisha next to an empty chair.

"Er, sorry about this . . ." Bidisha said to the audience, which had started muttering and was fast becoming antsy. "Let me see if I can sort out this . . . situation . . ."

As soon as Nigel saw Bidisha approaching, he simply shook his head. She stopped in her tracks, seemed to think to herself for a moment, then started up again. Nigel shook his head again. It was over.

An hour later, in his hotel room, Anil's ears were still ringing. But he was also filled with energy. The town hall meeting had been a disaster and he had to capitalise on that as quickly as possible. Buzzing, he phoned Lalima, half expecting that she wouldn't pick up out of business hours. But within two rings, she had answered, so he delightedly explained what had just happened and told her that the promotional brochure for the Balachuria coal mine had to be dispatched urgently in order to show the people (those simple people of the soil!) what spoils awaited them, before Devi regrouped and tried to stick another spanner in the works. He was sure that she would be as excited as he was, so was surprised at her light, breezy 'sure'. Plus, he had been hoping to keep her on the phone a little longer.

Casually: "So, you'll be working on it first thing tomorrow morning?"

Dryly: "Anil, I'm in the office working on it right now."

He was in love.

"Oh, well, great . . ." he replied, trying to keep her on the line long enough to strap on a pair and ask her to Avik's engagement drinks. "So, er, do you need any further input from me?"

"No."

Completely in love.

"Right then . . . Well, um . . ."

"Bye, Anil."

"Er, yes, bye for now . . ."

Phone call over, Anil found that his crackling energy had been replaced by a more twitchy energy, which he needed to release. He thought about going to the gym but that might just energise him further. There was only one thing for it. He slipped his shoes back on.

"Where's Rahul?" Anil asked the man who was standing at the concierge desk.

"Sorry, Sir?"

"Rahul, the usual concierge."

"Oh he's been taken ill, Sir, and gone home for the evening. I'm Apu, can I help you instead?"

Anil wasn't sure he could. He wondered whether with Apu he should play it straight or go wink-wink.

"I need a . . . mass-," inflection or no inflection—Apu was showing no sign of being a wink-wink sort of guy—no inflection it was then, "-age."

Actually, what he needed was a mass, swooping inflection, *euse.* A technicality but an important one.

"No problem, Sir," Apu said, warm but business-like. "The spa is closed for the day now, but I can arrange for a therapist to come to your room. What kind of massage would you like?"

Therapist. So, Apu did understand. Thank god for that. Anil was just about to reply, when Apu reeled off, "Hot stone massage, aromatherapy massage, Swedish massage, Balinese massage, deep tissue massage, or back massage?"

Oh. So, Apu didn't understand. Now what? Anil was becoming increasingly tense, but the tenser he became, the more he needed that massage!

"Oh, and of course," added Apu, "couples massage. If you have a partner who would enjoy a massage, also."

Couples massage? Is that what you're meant to ask for nowadays, Anil thought. He took a deep breath and tried to recalibrate. He could just go to the bar. If there was one thing common to all cities, it was *therapists* in fancy hotel bars, looking for business.

"You know what, Apu, I think I'll just go and have a drink," Anil said, with a smile.

"Surely, Sir," Apu said. "Enjoy your evening."

And Anil was quite sure that Apu had a smirk on his face.

An hour and two martinis later, Anil was back in his room with 'Milly'. Easy. He'd had a hard day at work. He deserved this. And 'Milly' was no Lalima but she was agreeable. Indeed, he was feeling quite pleased with himself as 'Milly' kneeled at his feet and unzipped his fly. Then he looked down and saw a lone grey hair emerging from her parting. A grey hair at twenty-five? 'Milly' had clearly fabricated her age as well as her name! And then his mind's eye immediately jumped to Devi's grey hair, that lone grey hair, standing out from her head like a lightning rod. He tried to quickly remove this vision, but instead it started to mutate, until his head was jammed with an image of a vituperative Devi scowling away at him like a rabid dog. And despite the best efforts of 'Milly, the twenty-five-year-old', it was game over before it had even started. Damn that grey hair! Damn that Devi! Damn her, damn her, damn her!

XIX

Gucchi *Mattar*, *Chingri Malai*, *Sarson Mahi* Tikka, home-smoked *Hilsa*, grilled *Bekti*, Lobster Thermidor!

There was always so much thought required if you wanted to do things properly. And Avik's engagement drinks had to be done properly, especially since he had casually informed her that a good number of his own friends would be flying in for the occasion. What a privileged life these young people lead, she thought, jetting around the world to go to parties! And without any genuine sense of just *how* privileged. But she supposed that her own life, in its way, had been filled with certain advantages and exemptions, too. And if she sometimes felt a little guilty about what had come her way without having to work for it, she didn't feel *so* guilty that she would deny her own son a lavish affair at one of the ritziest hotels in town. She took another look at the menu. She had asked Avik whether he wanted an 'international' menu as the lingo went, which actually meant a Western one, or an Indian one, or a bit of both. Whichever, Mum, I trust your judgement. This refrain, *I trust your judgement*, Anima had heard frequently, not only from her son, but also from many others. She had never particularly tried to cultivate this quality of having trustworthy judgement, but it seemed innate to her, and she sometimes felt it quite a burden, because it forced her to actually spend time thinking, mulling, considering, whereas sometimes she would have just liked to shrug her shoulders, like everyone else seemed to, and say: don't know, don't care, don't ask me!

Flowers. All white roses, perhaps? Or varying types but still all white? Or varying types in one colour, maybe red? Or mixed bouquets? In a strict vase formation? Or a more loose arrangement? What would Paige like? Should I bother to consult her? Or is my judgement trustworthy enough in botanic styling, too?

Ever since Anima had been to Tipu's house and seen Tipu's mother, Isha, who was her own brother Pusan's daughter, she had been feeling stunned. Paralysed. But she was not the proverbial deer in the headlights. She was the car, shining her headlights on the deer, her foot hovering over the accelerator, not knowing whether she should just reverse and get out of there at full speed! And what she also was, was Tipu's great aunt. Tipu was her great niece. She was related to Tipu! Tipu! Her housegirl! Who called her Madam. Who came to her house, sometimes to work and sometimes to just while away the hours. Yes, Tipu and Isha (and even Kalyan!) were family. Sometimes, she wondered: didn't they realise themselves that they were family? Didn't Isha ever wonder why it was she who had continued to look after the house? Didn't Tipu ever wonder? Was the past really so hazy and fragmented? Couldn't either of them add it all up? And if they, simple and innocent as they were, couldn't, then what about Kalyan? He was sharp and perceptive. Surely he knew? Yet he had not said anything either. But regardless of their seeming unawareness, that family living down the road, that sorry lot, with their pathetic little house and their pathetic pink plastic chair, were *her* family. And Anima had a duty towards her family . . . Duties like arranging engagement drinks at The Grand!

The premium drinks package included Bagpiper, McDowell, Royal Stag, Antiquity, Hercules, Old Monk, Contessa, White Mischief, Magic Moments, Blue Riband . . . I haven't tried any of these brands before, she thought. Does that matter? The super premium package at least has names I know—and that Avik's friends will know, too. But no Champagne included, just Prosecco. I guess I should go for the luxury drinks package then, and if I'm going for the luxury, then I might as well upgrade to the vintage champagne, too!

Kalyan knew what the score was. Of that, Anima was certain. Maybe he couldn't prove it, maybe he didn't *want* to prove it, but on a deep, fibrous level, he knew. If he had been the crafty, conniving sort, slowly but surely he would have used Tipu to inveigle indulgences from her, starting with a little bit of extra cash for fixing this and improving that, and then moving onto larger and larger requests, perhaps a car, perhaps a house! And then, if she refused, he would threaten to expose her and she would be disgraced—the rich, old woman who was denying her own family a better life! Or if he was bold enough, he might have outright played the poor relation card and asked upfront for a bung, protection money—to protect Anima's reputation. Or if he was frank enough, he might have just declared to all and sundry that a rich relation had come into town, and wasn't that good luck! But now she realised why he wouldn't say anything: he was too self-respecting. And as far as he was concerned, being related to Anima was nothing to be proud of.

But even if she herself had wished to acknowledge kinship out of a sense of goodwill and honour, she had Avik to think of. And of course his wife-to-be Paige. A woman whose pedigree made even Avik's look slightly shabby. And whilst they would both claim to be happy, she knew that, deep down, it would cause them great unease. Or maybe they would be completely fine and take it in their well-heeled stride, and really, it was *she* who found the truth an embarrassment. She, who had always thought of herself as being above, if only slightly, such considerations of status and standing. Perhaps she should just invite Tipu and Kalyan and sickly Isha to Avik's engagement drinks! Wouldn't that be a real scene! No, of course she wouldn't do that, it would be unnecessarily cruel to all parties. Although, they would probably still end up meeting each other because, despite Anima's best efforts to convince Avik otherwise, Avik was now insisting that he and Paige visit Balachuria. Why? Anima had asked. There's nothing to do here! Well, if that's the case, Avik replied, what are *you* doing there? Well, I meant nothing here for you and Paige to do, and the reason I'm here is precisely because there's nothing to do. I'm at that age now, darling! Oh, stop with the *I'm old* nonsense, Mum, besides Paige wants to see the summer house. Puppy, it's not a summer house in the sense that Paige thinks of summer houses . . .

Lighting. Should the pool be floodlit? Perhaps some fairy lights—white or coloured? In the palm trees around the pool? And what about some tea-lights floating on the pool? Or is that too much?

"Madam?"

Anima turned around with a start to see Tipu grinning at her. For a while now, Tipu had stopped knocking and started letting herself in instead, and Anima didn't have the heart to explain to her concepts of privacy and politeness. Instinctively, Anima tried to push The Grand's hospitality brochure out of sight. Tipu seemed to squint at it, as Anima moved it, but unlike usual, she did not blatantly ask 'What's that?'. Indeed, she seemed to be far more interested in the brochure she held in her own hand, and which she now brandished with glee.

"What's that?" Anima asked, nodding at it.

"Didn't you get one, Madam?"

Madam, Anima thought, *Madam*. Shall I tell you what I really am, Tipu? Your great aunt. What's that in Bengali? *Dida*? Should I tell you that's how you should be addressing me?

"I don't know, Tipu," Anima said, glancing at the pile of papers on her desk. "What is it?"

"A very good thing is happening!" Tipu said excitedly, her phrase imbued with such innocent enthusiasm that it could only arouse a sense of misgiving in Anima.

"Oh?" said Anima gently, "And what's that?"

"They're building a coal mine here!" Tipu exclaimed. "And," she added, much more impressed, "a very nice park. With a lake."

Anima raised an eyebrow and reached out for the brochure, which Tipu handed over with energy. Anima started to read . . . So Balachuria was sitting on a coal bed! And now, some company, Lohia or something, wanted to start mining. Lohia . . . wasn't that the name of the hospital where she had been offered a job? She couldn't quite remember, it all seemed so long ago . . .

"So?" Tipu said impatiently.

"Wait!" replied Anima with a smile. "I'm reading!"

And what was this company offering in return? A wholesale makeover of the town, it would seem. A health centre, a new school, a park, a shopping promenade, and, of course, most importantly, jobs! Proper jobs, which would make Anima's employment of casual labourers seem inconsequential.

"Well?" Tipu asked, almost beside herself with eagerness.

"Wait!" replied Anima, again with a smile. "I'm still reading!"

She was now taking a closer look at the drawing of the health centre. It looked very impressive. And then Anima thought: it's just a drawing. These are all just flat drawings and flat words on a flat page. But I expect Tipu must be awestruck . . .

"Very good . . ." Anima concluded vaguely, handing back the brochure.

Tipu pouted a bit. She had been expecting more.

"I'm going to take my mother to the health centre," she said defiantly, as if the centre had already been built.

Anima felt a pang of guilt. Since she had visited Tipu's house, Isha's poor health had been on her mind. Her niece's poor health. She had subtly encouraged Tipu to improve her mother's diet—by sending her home with Tupperware filled with mutton or goat curry which she had purposefully cooked too much of—thinking that Isha might have been suffering from anaemia. But there had been no improvement. "How's your mother doing?" "Same-same", and Anima knew that Isha needed to have proper tests run to diagnose exactly what was causing her malaise. Yet, although Anima was more than willing to pay for Isha to go to the city and be seen properly, she was extremely reluctant to offer lest she offend Kalyan and his sense of self-sufficiency ("Do you think I can't take care of my own wife?") as well as increase his already quite obvious antagonism towards her ("What? You think you can just come here and buy everyone by throwing your money around? The big lady from the big city!"). On the other hand, she was well aware that Tipu was wondering why she didn't call in a favour ("But you're a doctor! If you don't know what's up with my mum, then at least one of your doctor friends will.") or at least just hand over some cash ("You're always keen to pay your workmen above the odds, so why can't you cough up a few quid to have my mum seen to? Besides, that amount of money wouldn't mean anything to you; I thought you were meant to be the big lady from the big city!").

Her head suddenly ached at the convolutedness of it all, and she rubbed at her temples. Tipu noticed but she was in no mood for sympathy. She had come over brimming with excitement but Anima had responded so tepidly that it bordered on heartlessness as far as she was concerned.

"When the mine opens I'm going to get myself a job there," Tipu stated plainly.

"You're not going to work for me anymore?" Anima said jokily, but softly.

Tipu looked at the floor. She hadn't even thought about that. And now she felt foolish that of all people, she had come to her current employer to gloat about her future employer. To her mind, there was no doubt whatsoever that she would be working for The Lohia Group. She had no idea about resumes or past experience or interview technique. She was simply of the mindset that if there were jobs going, she'd go and get herself one. Hmmm. Tricky. Now what.

"I was joking," Anima reassured Tipu, seeing that she was looking quite rattled, and remembering that Tipu frequently did not understand comments made in jest. "Of course you should go and work for them."

Immediately, Tipu looked up and responded to Anima's endorsement by asking, very seriously, "They're going to make this place better, aren't they?"

"Well," Anima began, really having no idea and, based on what she knew of the world history of mining, bending more towards the conclusion that the townspeople might well end up paying a very high price for getting involved in such a venture, "I would hope so . . ."

But to Tipu, even such a half-hearted embrace was good enough, and she immediately leapt on it by saying, "So, you'll come with me to the roadshow? The gentlepersons from the company are coming here to talk to us, which is very good of them, isn't that so?"

Anima could not help but be amused by Tipu's ingenuousness, the *gentlepersons*, the *very good of them*, the very bloody unlikely that either was true. Poor old Tipu, always assuming that those above her were somehow better than her, which couldn't be further from the truth.

"Well, you should definitely go!"

Tipu's lips involuntarily trembled. She wanted Anima to come. She *needed* Anima to come. Because Anima was a doctor and the big lady from the big city and that meant that Anima was clever and important and what Anima thought was clever and important and that meant everyone else had to listen to Anima, even her dad, who thought he was much more clever and important than Anima, but he was an idiot, because he really wasn't!

Anima looked at Tipu's eager little face. Her great niece's eager little face. Tipu did not try to further her case. Instead, she remained silent as Anima seemed to reconsider.

"Alright," Anima agreed, finally. "I'll go with you."

Tipu grinned with delight and in that grin, there was that ingenuousness again, an ingenuousness which sometimes made Anima worry for Tipu's safety.

"Now, are you finally going to make some tea?" Anima chided her jovially, and Tipu happily dashed off to the kitchen, although Anima was quite sure that as she did, she had glanced again at the hospitality brochure from The Grand, which was still peeping out from within the pile.

As soon as Tipu had disappeared from sight, Anima gave it a good shove so that it was properly covered up. She had no idea why she was so bothered about Tipu seeing it considering that Tipu had clearly intuited from the start that Anima was A Woman of Means. But perhaps the vague 'of means' was what Anima felt comfortable with. Perhaps A Woman of Lobster Thermidor at Two Thousand Two Hundred and Fifty Rupees was a clarification too far.

As she heard Tipu playing with Prem and the puppies in the kitchen, she took another look at the brochure. *Do your part. Secure India's future!* Despite Tipu's energy, Anima felt tired. She had come to Balachuria to get away from it all, to tune everyone and everything out. But with Avik and Tipu and their demands and her obligation to meet those demands, she instead felt as if she was stuck between radio stations, picking up the kind of exasperating noise that made her want to throw the radio out of the window.

Persuading Sharmila to speak at the roadshow had been less difficult than Anil had thought it would be. He had imagined that she might get sniffy and all 'Why me?' and 'What's it got to do with me?' on him, and then he would have to coax and cajole and flatter her ego. But instead she had signed up to the gig immediately, as if she were just waiting to be asked, and Anil had been rather surprised, but pleased, by her eagerness. See, that wasn't so hard, he told Sachin, with a smidgen of satisfaction; Sachin had warned him that getting Sharmila involved might not be such a good idea. At this show of success, Sachin had nodded and smiled, but kept schtum.

Trying to persuade Sharmila to adhere to a pre-prepared script, and to say the necessary, the all-important, the significant, the compelling, the—how else can I put this, lady, just say what you're told to say!—had been an exercise in pointlessness of the most frustrating kind. It was like trying to pull a superliner along with a rowing boat. As far as Sharmila was concerned, she knew what to say. How do you know what to say, Anil had asked her.

Because I do. Okay, well, perhaps we could discuss what you're going to say? I don't need to discuss it, I know what I'm doing. Do you, thought Anil, *do you*? He had to go back to the boss.

Listen, he said to Sachin, I don't mean to be unprofessional but would you mind having a word with your wife? Sachin shrugged with a smile: I could but it's your project after all. When did I say it was my project? When I suggested to you that you don't involve my dear wife, what did you say to me? That it was my project, Anil sulked. And? And that you should trust my judgement . . . So? So I'm on my own, you're not going to help? Ha, ha, no, you're not on your own; you have Sharmila as your sidekick now! Oh come on, Sachin, I messed up, I admit it, but you have to help me! She'll only say what she wants to say! Sachin laughed. Well, of course, did you think she was just going to be your mouthpiece? No, not mouthpiece, more like director of oration . . . Sachin roared with laughter. Help me! Anil pleaded. What did they teach you at your fancy business school about how to deal with difficult characters? Pay them to quit, but I have a feeling that's not going to work with her! It's quite a conundrum, isn't it? Sachin grinned. Anil noted that Sachin had said the word conundrum with relish. Fine, Anil said, I'll sort it out somehow. I'm sure of it, Sachin replied, that's why you're my number one guy!

But despite Anil's best and varied efforts, Sharmila would not listen. And as Anil, Sharmila, and Sachin were driven to Balachuria, Anil thought: this is going to be an epic failure. Sharmila is going to humiliate me, she is going to humiliate Sachin, she is going to humiliate The Lohia Group, and she is going to humiliate herself! I've had lapses in judgement before, but this is up there with the time I microwaved an egg still in its shell. I should have just cancelled the event, but no doubt, Sharmila would turn up anyway lugging her own soapbox. What a pickle I've got myself into. Maybe I could persuade the driver to have an accident, not so terrible that any of us are seriously injured but bad enough that we are incapacitated and cannot make it to the roadshow. He glanced at Sharmila, who was leaning back comfortably in her seat, contentedly eating a packet of biscuits. Actually, *that*'s what I should have done, Anil thought, I should have poisoned her biscuits!

"You're very quiet," Sachin said to Anil. "Everything OK?"

"Of course," Anil lied. "I'm really looking forward to this, fingers crossed it will be a success."

Sharmila, able to make out what the two men were talking about, now leaned forward and said, gruffly, mouth half full, "Of course it will be a success, you two stop fussing and just leave it to me!" And Anil was left staring at the tiny flecks of chewed biscuit which had shot out of Sharmila's mouth and been deposited on his trouser leg.

When they arrived, a crowd had already begun to gather at the sports pitch (a flat piece of dried out earth where the children played football, cricket, and sometimes kabaddi) where the event was to take place. Anil had arranged for tea and samosas to be served. People were always more receptive when they were fed and watered. And the general mood seemed keen and lively; people, some of them holding the brochure, were so busy talking amongst themselves, that they barely noticed when Sachin's car pulled up. The three of them disembarked from the car and surveyed their surroundings.

"A good number have turned up," nodded Sachin, pleased.

"I think William & Ray did a good job with the brochure," Anil replied.

"Is that all there is to eat?" Sharmila said loudly, looking towards the refreshments stand. "Samosas?" Anil said nothing. On the stage, the sound engineer tapped away the microphone and said, repeatedly, "Testing, testing, one-two, one-two!" You needn't bother, thought Anil, this one doesn't need a microphone.

As they stood surveying the scene, Anil noticed a man hovering nearby trying to catch his attention. Anil put his hand up and smiled. "Ah, you must be Radesh!" Radesh, the events manager, came forward and shook Anil's hand.

"Very good to meet you, Sir."

"Anil, please just Anil. This is Sachin." Sachin and Radesh shook hands. "And this is Sharmila." Sharmila just stared at Radesh's hand, so he politely withdrew it.

"Shall I show you to your seats?" Radesh asked.

"Good idea," said Sachin, turning to Anil, "but where is Jagganath?"

"Sorry, who?"

"Jagganath, our group HR director."

Oh fuck, thought Anil, I've been so busy worrying about what a mess Sharmila is going to make, I've completely forgotten about the others! Where are they?

The others were from The Lohia Group's Board—the HR director; the health, safety, ethics and compliance director; and the legal director. The latter two were new recruits after the hospital fire had resulted in their predecessors absconding and Anil had therefore had a good amount of influence in their appointment: unlike the previous holders of those posts, the new two were blue-chip, tried-and-true, and had a profile on LinkedIn.

"Don't worry," Anil replied breezily. "They're on their way."

As soon as Radesh had guided Sachin and Sharmila away, Anil dashed to the edge of the venue and pulled out his mobile phone to call Jagganath. No reception. We really are in the middle of nowhere, thought Anil. And people had started to sit down. I am going to do my nut if *Juggernaut* doesn't bloody well turn up, the fat *boga*, Anil thought. And as for the other two . . .

Jagganath was from the previous era when Sachin had handed out executive positions to his chums, regardless of their suitability for the job. As Anil understood it, Jagganath had been Sachin's first employee, when aged sixteen, Sachin had bought a rusty old minibus and started transporting people around the local area. Jagganath had been a good bus driver—speedy, safe, and reliable. Then, a few years later, when one minibus transporting people around the local area had become a small fleet of lorries providing ground transportation through West Bengal, Bihar, Jharkhand, and Odisha, Jagganath was promoted from driver to the human resources director, responsible for sourcing long distance lorry drivers for Sachin's logistics business. And as the story went, he had got them driving longer and faster than anyone else by supplying them with a special herbal amphetamine-type drug which he had concocted himself. Soon, there were some routes for which there was no point competing; Lohia ruled those roads. And by ruling those roads, whole new avenues of business opened up. So, there was no doubt that Jagganath had played his part in building a multi-billion-rupee company. But Anil, whilst appreciating that, would have preferred to see Jagganath handsomely paid off, and replaced with someone more polished, more proficient, and altogether more professional. Sachin was loyal, though. Sometimes, too loyal . . . Where are they? Anil thought again, when a Maruti Omni minivan rattled up, and out poured four young women and four young men, all of them dressed in white shirts and khaki trousers, and looking vaguely military. Oh god, thought Anil, I asked Juggernaut to request his people look neat and professional, not like the fucking Territorial Army. Well, let's hope these Balachuria folks respect a uniform! The squadron leader nodded politely to Anil and then started handing out pens and clipboards to his team. Anil was keen to digitise and would have preferred them to take details by a handheld device but knew that the people were more likely to trust hard copy; this was ink-and-paper country. Having completed his task, the squadron leader stood aside and nodded again at Anil. There was something so earnest about the lot of them that it took Anil a moment to compose himself and not laugh. Then he said, "You have the template, yes?"

They all nodded.

"Good," Anil continued, "and remember, I want as many details as possible. Our aim is to find out in as much detail as possible what our future workforce looks like, because that will impact directly on what kind of training and apprenticeships we'll need to provide and which jobs can be done by locals and which ones will have to be staffed by outsiders."

The group all nodded as one, seriously and vigorously.

"Right then," Anil said in a brisk voice, which did not belong to him but which suddenly came out of him, "off you go!"

Suddenly the squadron leader piped up. "Sir, the goody bags are still in the van."

"I'll sort that out, you lot go on."

Ah yes, the goody bags, it had taken he and Lalima ages to decide what to put in them. Although they had initially conceived of them as cheap and tacky, they had later decided that they would be far better received than an offer of a free health check; people seemed to have a silly, almost childish, fondness for doodahs. And goody bags were, after all, close-ended. A health check, meanwhile, might throw up the possibility of high blood pressure or heart disease or worse. So, in the end, they had plumped for a ballpoint pen, a notepad, an umbrella, a key ring, a small credit card sized vanity set which comprised of a mirror and comb, a bottle opener, and a cotton handkerchief. All items were logoed with The Lohia Group logo, which was an L shape with an elephant standing within it, its back legs on the horizontal, its front legs on the vertical, all navy blue. Are you trying to rebrand the whole place as Lohiaville, Lalima had joked. Better than Shitsville, Anil had replied.

As soon as he'd finished instructing the van driver where to unload the bags, a black Mercedes Maybach rolled up, and Anil rolled his eyes; he had asked Jagganath to come in a suitably discreet vehicle. After all, Lohia, Sharmila, and he himself had come in a tough but unshowy Toyota Fortuna. After a moment, Jagganath rolled out, followed by Nalin, the health, safety, ethics, and compliance director and then Onkar, the legal director.

"Gentlemen!" Anil exhaled, "Where have you been?"

Jagganath looked oblivious to Anil's exasperation.

"We stopped for a cup of tea."

"There's tea *here*!"

"I do beg your pardon," said Jagganath in Bengali, grinning, "but I'm getting old now and when I get thirsty, I can't wait. It's like when I need a wee, I can't wait then either!"

Anil remained expressionless but noted that as Jagganath was looking for a laugh from his colleagues, Nalin and Onkar smiled, although in both cases it looked more like a wince. Anil knew that although they might not respect him, they respected the length of his tenure. He recalled that Juggernaut had once made a joke about the length of his tenure to a young secretary. Anil chose to wipe this recollection from his mind; he was already having enough trouble keeping it together.

"So, you know what you're saying?" Anil checked with Jagganath. Unlike Sharmila, he had been quite happy to be told what to say.

"You told me what to say, I'm saying it. Unless you've changed your mind. You have to pay me extra if you have, ten rupees per word!" He grinned at his own joke and again looked at Nalin and Onkar for encouragement. Again, they smiled politely. Anil also smiled, albeit through gritted teeth.

"Don't worry, I haven't changed my mind. Now, shall we go?"

As they started walking down the side aisle towards the front row, Jagganath couldn't resist adding, "Damn, I was counting on that extra money for a cup of tea on my way home!" He was very pleased with himself, even if no one else was.

Everyone seated, Anil was pleased to observe that he had a full house and there were people standing around the edge. Indeed, he had purposefully told Radesh to set up fewer chairs than the number of people he anticipated would turn up. Because it wasn't just about numbers, it was about the appearance of numbers. Empty chairs indicated disinterest. People standing around the edge implied eagerness. Radesh was now on the stage introducing the session and The Lohia Group. He started off smoothly, describing The Lohia Group as it was on the website. Although he spoke in Bengali, he dropped in English phrases such as 'one of the largest diversified business conglomerates in the country', 'a well-deserved reputation for excellent business practices', 'a world class company which aims to deliver high returns to all its stakeholders', blah, blah, and the audience seemed to be listening. But it was when he started to speak more colloquially and spontaneously, saying "Tell me, has another reputable company like this, a lakh lakh company, a pukka company, such a prestigious company ever come to our town to talk with us before? Since when has anyone been interested in us!" that the audience really started to engage, leaning forward in their seats and focusing. Of course, the spontaneity was planned by Anil, too. He had asked Radesh to start off scripted but then to appear as if he had just decided to speak his own mind so that the audience would think they were getting the real story. Looks like they've started to get on board, Anil thought, let's hope Sharmila doesn't have them scrambling to get off!

Next up was Sachin. And even Anil was quite in awe of him now, because if he was acting then it was some act! The doggedness, which had first attracted Anil to him, seemed to have disappeared entirely to be replaced by a more meditative aspect. Maybe *that*'s what he's doing on stage, Anil thought: meditating. Maybe any minute now he's going to start floating!

For Sachin, the event was like some sort of bittersweet homecoming. He had spent years and years trying to get out of the kind of town Balachuria was. The kind of place where everything—ambition, desire, passion, energy—was attenuated, until just getting through another day was seen as a success. The kind of place where it was seen as conceited and, more than that, pointless to want more. But the kind of place where they were also mesmerised by those who had 'made it', and those who had made it were always the people who had left. And then, everyone who was left behind would say "He might be a bigwig now but this is where he grew up and this is where he was made!" and point out to their children "So it goes to show that even if you come from a small place like this, you can still prosper if you work hard enough!". But despite the cynicism, Sachin looked at his audience, all agape that a man like him had come to their town, that a man like him even knew their town existed, and he felt for them—for their struggles and their lassitude and their boredom and the sheer monotony of their daily lives. A phrase that a Chinese business partner had once used now came to him—a journey of a thousand miles begins with a single step. Well, what if the road was circular, and you kept stepping only to find yourself right at the start again? Wasn't that life for these people? All those years stepping, stepping, stepping, but at the end having moved nowhere . . . And so, without notes or any real preparation, he simply thanked the audience for giving him the opportunity to come and speak with them and then gave them a little philosophical speech about the nature of aspiration and striving and motivation and incentives and, of course, rewards—both physical and mental.

Anil was impressed. There was none of the awkwardness in

Sachin that usually showed up in businessmen who had become used to speaking to bankers and investors but had suddenly been put in front of an audience of ordinary people. And neither was there any sense of superiority yet his authority was clear. Anil was also beginning to think that maybe Sachin wasn't acting anymore, that maybe he really had changed. And that maybe Sachin was getting a bit philosophical and wishy-washy and soft? Anil dearly hoped not. If there was anything bound to cause problems for a business, it was a leader who was getting metaphysical. Save that for your autobiography! Anil thought.

As he considered this, a loud voice jolted him back into the present. Sharmila had taken the stage. Anil felt quite queasy and wondered whether he should just go for a walk but forced himself to stay.

"I bet you're all wondering what I, the boss' wife, am doing addressing you! Well, I can tell you one thing from the get-go—he might be the head honcho now, but he wouldn't have got here without me, so I know what I'm talking about it when it comes to business, and pretty much everything else in life. No, really, he might have worked his way up to the top, but it was whilst holding my pretty hand. And secondly, I cut through the crap and tell it like it is; I'm not one of those fancy suited-booted office types who'll try to win you over with big claims and grand declarations. Yeah, you should feel relieved you got me and not one of those city slickers . . ."

Anil looked around and was surprised to see that the audience was responding, and positively! For whereas Sachin had elicited a quiet reverence, Sharmila was eliciting chuckles and guffaws and general positivity and good humour. I misjudged her, Anil acknowledged; she *does* know what she's doing. She knows these people in a way I never can. As he continued to look around, his eyes stopped at a woman who was literally head and shoulders above everyone else. With very short hair, and from the exposed skin at the back of her neck, Anil could see she was almost white. Well, she's certainly not from around here, Anil thought, I wonder who she is. Hopefully not a journalist. Or even worse, one of Devi's crones! I must keep an eye on her and make sure I catch up with her before she leaves . . .

Anima gestured to Tipu to hand over her brochure—which Tipu had been carrying around with her as if it was a security blanket—and started to fan herself with it. She could see from Tipu's expression that Tipu did not approve of it being used in such a way, but despite the sun having gone down for the day, it was still hot and Anima's skin was itching, especially with all the layers of sari covering her legs. If only I could wear a pair of shorts and a T-shirt, I'd feel so much cooler, she thought, but wouldn't that give the people here something to talk about. They've already plenty to say about me! But apart from the itchiness, she was quite enjoying herself. It was rather like being at an open air theatre and watching some amateur comic drama—the woman standing on stage was a real hoot!

"So, here it is—you lot have a coal field, and luckily for you, my husband wants to mine it! Now, I can see plenty of you are clutching your brochures and I don't want to bore you and repeat what's in it, but a coal mine here means jobs and money for you."

Sachin smiled. After a long time, he was remembering why he had married Sharmila. And it delighted him to see her back in her element. Sometimes, he wondered: If I hadn't met her, would I even be where I am? He remembered one of his first acquisitions—a river sand company. His lorries had been transporting the stuff and it was Sharmila who had said to him: listen, the old man who owns the sand company is on his last legs. Now he can either put his idiot son in charge and the company will get run into the ground within a few years or you can offer him a good price for it. But how will

I persuade him? Sachin had asked, you know how it is, fathers like to leave their businesses to their sons. Leave it to me, Sharmila had replied, and had then got back to Sachin within a few days with what the old man considered to be a reasonable price. But what did you say to him to convince him so easily, Sachin had asked. I told him exactly what I told you, Sharmila had replied, what else. And it was from her that Sachin had first learned that one gram of frankness was worth ten kilograms of bullshit!

"I know what you're all thinking," Sharmila said, "I know. You're thinking, why should I listen to a rich man's wife? Well, look at me. Look. At. Me. Do I look like someone who's going to live a life of luxury off the back of your hard work? Well, do I? I'm telling you, if anyone knows the value of hard graft and making your own way in the world, it's me. Do you think I was born with a silver spoon in my mouth? No. I was born with a wooden spoon in my big gob! I'm one of you. And I know how tough life can be. But I didn't expect anything from anyone. What god gave me, I used, that's all! And most importantly, if I saw an opportunity, I took it. So, let me say it again—this mine is a life-changing opportunity for you. You'll have a good roof over your head, you'll have good food on the table, you'll have money in your pocket, and most importantly of all, you'll *feel* better. Because that's what working hard does—it gives you mental satisfaction and sets your mind free! Now, there will be some people who will try to convince you otherwise, who will try to poison your mind by saying that this mine will not benefit you. But the truth of it is this—those people want to keep you in your place because it's better for them! Yes, that's right: they're thinking of themselves, not you! So that's what *you* have to do: think of *your*self! Because if you don't, who will? Anyway, I've said a lot and your ears must be stinging by now, but if there's only one thing which you remember of what I've said, it's—"

Just as Sharmila was about to summarise her speech, there was a kerfuffle at the back, and hushed voices, which caused more and more of the audience to turn around, until pretty much no one was looking at Sharmila and pretty much everyone was standing up and looking behind to figure out whom they should be looking at. Then, from an entourage of heavy-duty bodyguards emerged Bhupen Mandal. The audience started buzzing with excitement now. The real rock star had arrived after the warm-up act. Anil chewed on his lip. He had not anticipated this at all.

"Who's that man?" asked Anima, scrunching up her eyes.

"He's Bhupen Mandal," exclaimed Tipu.

"Yes, but who's Bhupen Mandal?"

Tipu had stopped listening to Anima because now Bhupen was speaking.

"Please," drawled Bhupen, lapping up the attention, "no fuss, no fuss, please everyone sit back down. I'll be just fine here at the back, please let the good lady carry on." He theatrically unfurled his arm towards the stage and gave Sharmila a courteous bow.

You wanker, thought Anil. You. Complete. Wanker.

Is that Amitabh Bachchan, thought Anima, what on earth is he doing here? I thought Tipu said his name was Bhupen something or other. Damn, I wish I'd brought my glasses!

I had to invite him, Sachin thought, guiltily, but did he have to make quite such an entrance? Who does he think he is? Amitabh Bachchan?

My husband invited him, of course, thought Sharmila, and he didn't even have the courtesy to tell me. Both Bhupen and he are shits. Complete. Shits.

But, just as Bhupen had known, the audience was not just going to sit back down. No, now that he was here, he would have to speak. So, feigning reluctance—shaking his head whilst pretending to be stuck to the ground—he eventually allowed two supporters to take him by the hand and lead him onto the stage where he gave Sharmila an apologetic namaste with a bowed head and then drew himself up to his full height and grinned at the crowd; people cheered loudly.

"I just came to support a new business venture which will bring prosperity to you good people." More cheers, which Bhupen calmed down by patting his fingers against the air. "Tell me, why shouldn't you have a slice of the pie? Why should you have to just sit and watch whilst other Indians get on?" Lots of agreement from the audience, which spurred on Bhupen, "As you know, my party's first priority is job creation! We support enterprise and investment and above all, involvement! So get involved!" Wild acclaim.

Sharmila, almost boiling with rage, realised that the moment was over and no one would be listening to her anymore. Bhupen, she decided, wasn't even a shit. He was a shit *stain.*

In the free-for-all which followed, with goody bags flying around and Bhupen holding court and Jagganath ditching any vestige of respectability and trying to corral the crowd by shouting "Over here! Over here! Over here if you don't want to miss out!" and Sharmila angrily stuffing her face with samosas whilst she dreamt of throwing her cup of tea (multiple teaspoons of sugar) in Bhupen's face and Sachin wandering around like some mystic, and Nalin and Onkar trying not to get crushed, Anil tried his best to locate the woman he'd spotted in the crowd, when he felt a gentle tap on his shoulder.

"I thought it was you . . ." Anima smiled, looking slightly perplexed.

Anil couldn't have been more surprised if his own mother had shown up and tried to think of a socially appropriate way of saying 'what the hell are you doing here?'. Then he remembered what the acceptable phrase was.

"What a pleasant surprise!" he said.

"Likewise!"

So, she doesn't know what the hell I'm doing here either, Anil thought.

"What brings you here?" he asked.

"Oh, I have a house here. And you? Don't you work for the hospital?"

"Oh, The Lohia Group has a lot of interests—steel, chemicals, agriculture, construction materials, logistics, packaging, and now, coal mining, which we'll vertically integrate with our steel and cement businesses."

"And of course the hospital," Anima reminded Anil.

"Well, the hospital isn't so much an interest as it is a philanthropic venture enabled by the other businesses . . ." Anil explained, immediately aware that he was sounding like a corporate dick.

"How . . . decent of you," Anima replied, immediately aware that she had unintentionally come across as sarcastic. Trying to make amends, she added, "Because, of course, a lot of businesses just exploit people but don't give anything back." Now she realised that she had implied that, despite its philanthropy, The Lohia Group still exploited people, and she tried again to rectify the situation by adding, "Not that I think that The Lohia Group exploit people, I'm sure you're very fair and square." And she was back to sounding sarcastic again. Better just shut up.

She cleared her throat, hoping that Anil would change the subject, and he, knowing what was required, said, "So, when will you be back in Cal? We could have lunch, talk a little more about the opportunity at the hospital?"

So the opportunity was still there. Anima felt a little tingle on hearing this. She had barely thought about it since their initial chat, but now that it had been mentioned again, she realised how interested she was.

"Actually, I'll be in Cal for my son's engagement drinks in a few weeks. He's coming over from America."

Anil frowned for a moment, then tentatively asked, "Avik?".

Now it was Anima's turn to frown. "Yes, how did you know that?"

"He's a very good friend of mine from business school, I've been invited actually, The Grand, yes?"

"Er, yes, exactly, The Grand. Well, what a coincidence . . ."

"Quite. But Avik's Shastry and you're Acharya."

"Oh yes, I kept my maiden name after getting married." She was very tempted to add 'And considering the situation now, thank god for that!'

"So, what do you think?" Anil asked.

"About Avik getting married?"

Anil laughed. "No, I meant the proposed coal mine. But sure, about Avik getting married, too, Paige is a nice girl . . ."

"Yes, she's a very nice girl. Do you know the two of them are going to come here?"

"Where? To Balachuria?" Anil clarified, surprised.

"Yes, that's what I thought . . ." Anima said, raising her eyebrows.

"No, sorry, I didn't mean that—" Anil apologised.

"Oh, it's quite alright, I thought exactly the same," Anima reassured him amiably, "but apparently Paige is insisting!"

"Maybe she wants to work down a mine," Anil said waggishly.

"Can you imagine . . ." Anima laughed.

Just then, Tipu bounced over, goody bag in hand. As soon as she laid eyes on Anil, they shone even more. Anima knew exactly what Tipu was thinking and felt quite poignant; a man like Anil would never be interested in a girl like Tipu. But Tipu was far too naïve to realise that. As far as she was concerned, if she could get a job with The Lohia Group, she could get a man like Anil! Anil was also looking between Tipu and Anima with what Anima thought was a fair amount of interest. Suddenly, she was very concerned that Anil had noticed a certain amount of facial similarity between the two.

"Oh sorry," she said quickly, then switching to Bengali, "this is Tipu, my . . . er, my, friend. And Tipu, this is Anil, he works for The Lohia Group—and he's also a friend of my son, Avik."

"I see . . ." said Tipu, slightly shy, but delighted with both the designation of 'friend' and also the fact that she had been introduced to a very handsome man who not only worked for The Lohia Group but was also Anima's son's friend, which made him an all-round winner. Indeed, she'd never come across this quality of man in Balachuria before. She had to impress him!

"So, tell me," she said to Anil, coyly, "where exactly is this mine going to be? I hope it's not too far from my house, because, you know, I only have a cycle to get around, no car . . ." She was hoping to sound casually confident and just a little bit cute.

Anil dithered for a moment and then said to Anima, "Do you mind translating? My spoken Bengali has become quite poor from disuse."

"Of course," Anima replied, explaining to Tipu what was going on.

Oh no, thought Tipu, there's a language barrier between us but no matter, love will conquer all!

"Well, there's no mine yet, just coal. We have to construct the mine first."

Anima translated and Tipu immediately replied, "So where exactly is this coal?"

"Well, I don't have the map with me but it might even be right under where we're standing now!"

Again Anima translated. Now Tipu looked quite excited, as if she had been told that she was standing on gold.

"Here!" she exclaimed. "Right here?" And then she turned to Anima and said, "Is that the truth? Are we standing right on the spot?"

"Well, perhaps not *right* on the spot—" Anima said. Then she stopped for a moment and frowned, saying to Anil, back in English, "So the coal is under a residential area? People will have to move?"

Too late, Anil realised his mistake. How many times had he told everyone in his employ to avoid any conversation that confirmed that people would need to be relocated. If anyone asked, the standard response was that details would be confirmed once the venture had gained general approval and been permitted by the local council.

"Those kind of details will be confirmed once the venture has gained general approval and been permitted by the local council," he said falteringly, tacking on jokingly, "I don't suppose you're a member of the local council, are you?"

"No. I'm not," replied Anima lightly, well aware that she was being fobbed off but not wishing to push the matter considering she was speaking with one of Avik's good friends and in front of Tipu. Dear, sweet, the-world-is-a-good-place Tipu, who, despite not understanding English, might well cotton on to a change in tone. Then an awkward silence which Tipu filled by asking, blithely, "What's going on?" and looking first at Anima and then at Anil.

Anima then looked at Anil as if to say 'why don't you answer her?'.

"So," Anil said brightly, "do you have your CV with you, Tipu?"

Anima dutifully translated without any hint that Tipu was also being fobbed off. Tipu shook her head. She had never heard the word Seevee before but she wasn't about to let Anima know that, at least not in front of her Future Balacuria, Future Boyfriend!

"Well, why don't you bring it to Avik's engagement drinks, you can hand it to me then," Anil said encouragingly.

Anima swallowed. Of course, Tipu had not been invited. And she would not be invited either.

"I'll tell her," Anima said in English. "Anyway, we better be going."

"Okay, great, well I'll look forward to seeing you again soon!"

"Likewise."

And Tipu looked quite perturbed as she was led away gently but firmly by Anima—and without a chance to say a proper goodbye to her prospective husband!

Back in his hotel room that night, Anil went over his conversation with Anima. There had been something in her tone that had suggested she might turn moralistic. He sincerely hoped not. And yes, he had been a little bit cagey about the fact that people would have to be relocated but was it really such a big deal? Although people could be very funny about their homes and having to move. Even if their homes were complete holes and you were offering them something a hundred times better. As far as Anil was concerned, such attachment was baffling. And worse than that, uneconomic! But my great grandfather and my grandfather and my father all grew up here . . . Yes, you all grew up here without running water and sanitary facilities, you all literally pissed in a pot! But this is where I've made a life for myself . . . *What* life! He tried to put this possible issue out of his mind. The roadshow had gone as well as it could have, and what happened next, happened next. Right now, he had other matters to deal with. Quickly, he typed an email to Avik: I trust that it's alright to bring my girlfriend Lalima to the party? Well, Anil thought, it wasn't a lie, just a future truth.

Manish's hangover was as rotten as they came. In fact, it was so bad he didn't need a hair of the dog, he needed its whole coat! Only a few days ago, he had been summoned to Devi's office for a right old arm-twisting. He had been hoping to stay under the radar and continue to trudge along with his little upliftment projects which were to do things like encourage female literacy and increase bank credit facilities, which were a perpetual work in progress.

But with the Slow It Down debacle, that had all come to an end. She was a ruthless one, all of her party knew that. Of course, Sinha had resigned, as everyone had known he would, only after elaborately and exhaustively blaming himself for misinterpreting Devi's instruction to slow it down, which was of course a clear instruction to give the project the time and consideration it deserved. And it was a grave error, *his* grave error, that he, despite knowing Devi to be a fair, impartial, and above all, honest person, could misinterpret her requirement. And that was that, because if Sinha himself took all the blame, it was not possible to then apportion some of it to Devi. She was, therefore, blameless. And all those journalists who had come down like a tonne of bricks on her for being petty and spiteful and having a personal vendetta against Lohia? Didn't they look foolish!

Inside the party, it was agreed that Devi should now just have the environmental permit issued and buy herself some goodwill—which she could certainly do with. The Sevak Party were already making plenty of noise about how they were the party of business whilst The Truth Party were the party of busybodying. Devi's response: it is good to be keeping your body busy; better than just sitting around passing comment. And in a separate to-do, The Communists were accusing Devi of aiding and abetting murder since their man Mustak Ahmed Attar had died, due, they claimed, to the injuries caused by Devi's henchman, Selim Shah, though the inquest into his death was still to take place. Devi's gruff response? He was an old man. Old men die. Nigel was desperate for her to at least pretend to have some sympathy, and to show people that she was, underneath it all, a person with a heart, but her response to him: Has anyone ever had any sympathy for me? No, I've always had to get by with people taking potshots even when I've been beaten up!

Still, her closest ministers suggested, nay, begged her: put the whole Balachuria matter behind you. But she was having none of it. No, she was persistent. As persistent as a bad case of Athlete's Foot, Manish thought. And now she had roped him into the whole charade under the auspice of properness and due process. As she put it, she couldn't have those poor, tribal people ridden over roughshod by some megalomaniac. Lohia is not a megalomaniac, woman, Manish thought, you are! He had tried to reason with her: but those people don't come under my remit, they're not tribal, they're just standard issue! How do you know, she had said, you have to go and establish that. And no, he couldn't use census data, and no, he certainly couldn't ask for the assistance or input of some NGO (especially not one staffed by crazy people like that Green Police duo!), and no, he couldn't send someone else, he had to go himself to give the project the right amount of importance. Oh no, thought Manish, here we go. I'm next for the chop.

So a trip to Balachuria had been hastily organised, and Manish had yesterday met with the local council (a Truth Party seat, albeit only narrowly). At the beginning of the meeting, the council had been very excited—matters at a state level and at a town level did not coincide frequently—and they were delighted to be paid a visit by one of the big boys, but their excitement soon turned to perturbation when Manish started to explain exactly what he was doing there. Yes, of course they knew about the proposed mine but why was he going on about tribal people? Way of life, Manish replied, we have to preserve their way of life. What way of life, came the response—is sitting around passing time a way of life? Mining—now that's a way of life! Besides, *which* tribal people are you talking about? Listen gentlemen, Manish said, I have orders from our dearest Devi to make sure that the tribal people of Balachuria are protected. Protected from what? Destruction of their way of life. But we've already said that there is no *way of life*, because there's hardly anything called life here—and there are no tribes, well, apart from the tribe of people idling away! For god's sake, thought Manish, if you're all going to be so reasonable and sensible it's going to be very difficult to work with you. Well, he persevered, do you think any of the locals consider themselves to be forest-dwelling people? The councillors were offended. What do you think we are, said one, monkeys? There is no forest here, said another. Right, of course not, Manish said vigorously, but perhaps there are what could be considered *Heritage People*.

Heritage people, they frowned, what are they? Well, replied Manish, you know, the people who do hand-weaving and that sort of thing, handicrafts, woven blankets, wood carvings—the kind of people who make items for the Cottage Industry shop in Kolkata! No, replied the council, sternly, no heritage people here. Manish had, once again, felt himself failing. So he had tried playing the Devi card again. You know that Devi sent me because she wants to make sure that you're properly taken care of, she doesn't want you to think she's forgotten you. But by now, the cynicism had set in. The local council were only ever remembered at election time. After that they were left to their own devices. And even those who were most devoted to Devi knew that she had done little for them despite her promises; it always seemed to be someone else's turn to be given her attention. She had asked for their support, their loyalty, their patience, and in return? After her campaign had secured the seat, she had never been seen again, except on TV when she was always somewhere else but Balachuria. Yet now, here was one of her ministers giving them the old *we're in this together* spiel! Best for them? Best for herself, more like. If they weren't afraid of being expelled from the party, they would have sent him and his handwoven tea-towels packing. But they knew Devi came down hard on anyone who defied her, so instead they were suitably equivocal: we're just representatives of the people. There's no point in coming to us, you must go to them. Perhaps carry out a survey! And Manish knew then that he was half way to being wholly screwed.

Of course, he had not communicated the outcome of the meeting to Devi, assiduously avoiding phone calls from her little lapdog Nigel, who had left umpteen yippety-yappety voicemails instead. But at some point he would have to tell Devi that, as per usual, the project was a work in progress, and he needed more time. But then he had thought: perhaps, for once, that was exactly what Devi wanted—someone who was going to stall and drag his feet and play for time. And maybe that was precisely why she had chosen him to go. Was she that sly? Absolutely. Immediately, he felt better. The local council's charge to go directly to the people might actually have turned out to be in his favour as far as slowing down the process was concerned. If Devi's strategy was to leave no stone unturned in her bid to defeat Lohia, then this stone would be turned very, very slowly. Then he thought: hang on, so she has chosen me for my *in*competence. Now, he felt lousier than ever, especially as his hangover had lurched into a hitherto unknown domain of pain. And he had to get out of bed and get ready for his lunch meeting with People For . . .? He couldn't remember People For what. Oh god, oh god, oh god!

As Anil (still living in Hyatt despite the cockroaches in his flat being long gone), took a leisurely breakfast and polished off another dosa, he wondered what tack he should take with Manish. He knew all about Manish's trip to Balachuria, although he didn't yet know the outcome of it. Maybe he should wait to find out what had happened before deciding his approach . . . He could call Priyanka for a heads-up but would she take his call whilst she was in the office? For all Anil knew, she could be standing right next to her boss Nigel. Although Anil was quite sure that Nigel would never suspect whom she was speaking to.

Anil had spotted Priyanka on the night of the town hall meeting—trailing behind Nigel, as he trailed behind Devi, who was marching towards her car. Nigel had got into the car with Devi, but Priyanka had been left standing on the pavement. And then the presenter Bidisha had come out and called "Priyanka, do you have a minute?" and Priyanka had dithered and then shaken her head and run away. This girl Priyanka is afraid, thought Anil, she doesn't know what to do. She needs to be told.

So, under the pretence of being a journalist who wanted to

profile up-and-coming women in the public sector, he had taken her out for a milkshake at Flurys. And as soon as she had started sucking on the stripy straw, he had revealed who he was. And as soon as she had heard that he worked for The Lohia Group, she had stopped sucking. Listen, Anil had said, you and your boss Nigel must have been having a pretty difficult time with Devi over the whole Balachuria business, no? Priyanka had been reticent at first to even answer the question. It seemed disloyal, somehow. But finally, she had admitted that yes, morale was rather low in Devi's public relations department, lurching, as they were, from one drama to another. Well, wouldn't it be better for everyone, yourself included, Anil suggested, if at least the Balachuria matter was taken care of? I mean, let's be frank, you have other things on your plate! Priyanka was tentative: I suppose so . . . but how? Well, if you tell me what Devi is planning next with regards to Balachuria then we can try to sort out the matter in private, behind closed doors, instead of the whole matter becoming more fodder for the press—and more of a headache for you and for Nigel. Priyanka had still looked doubtful. So Anil had said, getting up to leave: listen, I'm sorry, I shouldn't have bothered you, I just thought that, for once, it would be an idea to dispense with the drama and just try to work together to smooth things out! At this, Priyanka had rubbed her lips together. The drama *had* been getting to her—and not just her but everyone, especially her boss Nigel who seemed like he was permanently on the verge of a breakdown. Indeed, the only person who seemed to thrive on the drama was Devi, maybe that was why she went around creating so much of it! Anil pretended he hadn't noticed the slight shift in her comportment and said, if you could at least not tell anyone about this, I'd be grateful, and thank you anyway for your time. He was just taking the bills out of his wallet to pay for the drinks when she said: exactly what kind of thing would you like to know? Oh nothing secret or confidential, I mean, certainly no details—I don't need to see memos or anything like that, I just need a general idea of what can be expected next . . . I mean, I'm guessing that the environmental permit isn't forthcoming . . . is it? Priyanka made a gesture, a sort of shrug-head shake combo. Listen, Anil bolstered her, you're not going behind Nigel's back, if that's what you're worried about. Still, she looked doubtful. And you don't want him to have a heart attack from all the stress, do you?

After a few rings, Priyanka picked up and answered his question in a flat, almost disinterested monotone, which would arouse no suspicion in the office should anyone overhear. And her message was simple: there was no news from Manish. That can mean only one thing, Anil thought, Manish has nothing positive to report. There's my *in* with him.

Manish quickly took a look around the other diners at La Cucina to see if there was anyone he recognised, and more importantly, anyone who might recognise him, and then put on his glasses and pretended to consult a page in his leather-bound notebook, which actually contained his measurements and the contact details of his tailor Haider, at Barkat Ali & Brothers.

"So," he said regardfully, "you work for 'People for People'."

As he leaned in, Anil smelled the soury sweet aroma of last night's alcohol. Priyanka had been right about that. Nice of her to throw that in for free.

"Actually," Anil revealed calmly and evenly, "I work for The Lohia Group."

Manish froze and then, after a moment, he replied, "I don't think it wise that I speak with you, considering current goings-on." He said this ruefully; La Cucina had the best wine list in town. And it had taken a lot of energy and application just to put on his trousers.

"Surely, there's no problem with listening? It's not as if you have to act on what you hear, Sir?"

That was just the excuse Manish needed—Gin and Tonic, here I come—and he concurred, as if it was Anil's logic which had cemented his staying, "Well, yes, I suppose you're right, and in any case, I'm rather interested to hear what you have to say."

"Well, that's just fantastic, Sir. How about we start by ordering drinks?"

Manish dithered as a vision of Raging Devi flashed before his bloodshot eyes. "I'm not sure I should be drinking alcohol whilst in my capacity as a government minister . . ."

"Oh, well of course, that's quite understandable, Sir. I hope you won't mind if I have a little aperitif?"

Manish dithered again. "Oh," he bumbled, "well, if you're having one, then I shall have one, too—it would be rude not to!" For Manish, the only thing more painful than a hangover after an all-night bender was having to stay dry whilst watching someone else drink.

"Oh, that's very good of you, Sir," Anil smiled. "I'm going to have a gin and tonic—and for you?"

"Same, same."

Anil smiled again and scanned the room, as if he were looking for a waitress and then said to Manish, "Please excuse me whilst I go and order." Then he strolled over to Mim, one of his favourite waitresses.

"Hey, Mim. You're looking very pretty today, you should wear your hair off your face like that more often."

"Oh, thanks, Anil." Anil was now a long-term resident at the hotel, and had developed quite a rapport with various members of staff, and insisted that they call him by his first name. "That's very nice of you to notice! What may I do for you?"

"Just a drinks order for now. For me, a sparkling water with ice and a slice of lime. For my guest, a gin and tonic—double, no, *triple*—also with ice and a slice of lime."

"Surely," Mim replied with a smile and without batting an eyelid.

Halfway through his tenderloin of beef and a bottle of Cabernet Sauvignon (and a second gin and tonic on the house as the appetiser had been delayed for some reason), Manish fancied that he, as a slightly old and tired mucker, was holding his own very well against the young whippersnapper Anil. Anil, meanwhile, sensing that Manish had wholly loosened up due to the influence and was now, in fact, pretty much under it, decided to drop the niceties. Indeed, to gently preface the change in approach, he had dropped into the conversation that Manish and he had attended the same Oxford College and wasn't that rather a turn-up for the books!

"Now," he said, calm as ever, but with a harder edge, "come off it, Manish, they're not tribal people, and you know it and I know it." Indeed, Anil had made very, very sure of that. He had even paid a Harvard Professor of Anthropology to establish that fact as Anil knew better than to mess with tribal people in India.

"Self-identification," Manish replied with a grin, "self-identification, we must ask the people if they consider *themselves* to be tribal."

"And if they considered themselves to be pink-arsed baboons, would they be pink-arsed baboons?"

"Ah, taxonomy and philosophy collide!"

"This is just another one of Devi's delaying tactics," Anil sighed, spearing a piece of crispy potato, "and you're just doing her bidding."

"Not at all, dear boy, not at all," Manish said with largesse. "This is about the preservation and protection of our ancient heritage; that we must advance is not in question but at what cost? As you know, India has always been the home of diversity and tolerance."

My tolerance for your bullshit is waning, Anil thought, but he continued jovially, "Oh, for god's sake, Manish, you're talking as if Balachuria is a world heritage site—whereas it's currently a veritable shithole.

Manish chuckled and took another swig of wine. "One man's shithole is another man's chamber of defecation!" He spluttered a little bit at his own joke, and Anil noted, with distaste, that little specks of red spittle had hit the table.

"OK, let's say that these pink-arsed baboons decide that they no longer wanted to indulge in pink-arsed baboonery and do pink-arsed baboon type things. Instead, when they are asked if they fancy working for a billion-rupee conglomerate, which offers great working conditions, healthcare and pensions, they leap—as baboons are wont to do—at the chance. Would you have a problem with that?"

"Well," chuckled Manish, "maybe the baboons leap because they don't understand the proposition properly? Or maybe, it's not so much that they leap of their own volition, rather that the branch they're sitting on is cut off, and they have to either leap to another one or fall to the ground?"

"So, what you're saying is that the pink-arsed baboons don't really know what they want, or rather what's good for them, so you're around to ensure they make the right choice? You don't find that attitude a little bit, how shall I put it, paternalistic? Or maybe it's not even as well meaning as paternalism, maybe it's just a matter of manipulating pink-arsed baboons and turning them into dancing monkeys, as it were."

Manish chuckled again, thoroughly enjoying himself. "You're too young, you haven't been around long enough to understand."

Playing the man, instead of playing the ball. Anil knew then that Manish was finished. A shame. He had genuinely believed that Manish might have been open to reason and reasonableness. Oh well, he had tried. "Well, maybe you're right. Maybe I am too young, and maybe I haven't been around long enough to understand . . . Maybe I'm just naïve!"

"Oh, don't worry about that, dear boy. The naivety will soon be kicked out of you!"

"Well, tell you what, to say thank you for at least giving me the time to hear me out, why don't we have a bottle of Port to remember our Oxford days?"

Manish couldn't resist. He loved a little bit of nostalgia. So, Anil ordered a bottle of vintage Port and they both raised a toast, "To naivety!"

Tapati Ghatak no longer frowned when she saw who was calling. In fact, she answered the call with eagerness.

"Do you have something for me?" she asked readily.

Anil laughed.

"Slow news day?"

"No news day. So what do you have?"

"Well, do you know that, at Devi's behest, Minister Ray was in Balachuria just a few days ago to see if he could find some tribal-type people—because obviously building a coal mine in their 'hood will destroy their culture and their ancient way of life."

"*Are* there tribal people living there?"

"No, of course not, it's just another one of Devi's time-wasting exercises. And I need to send a message that such time-wasting is not acceptable."

"So, what do you want me to do? I hope I don't have to go all the way to Balachuria for this."

"You just have to pop down the road to Hyatt, room 126, in the name of Miss Milly Rudra."

"Who is Milly Rudra?"

"You'll find out when you get there. And take a photographer."

XXI

Sachin peeked over the top of his newspaper as Sharmila trudged into the dining room and dropped herself into a chair at the opposite end of the mahogany table. The butler went to pour her a cup of tea but she waved him away with irritation, and poured herself a cup, stirring in her multiple sugars with such vigour that the tea became a whirlpool. The butler, undeterred, moved forward again to unfold the white linen napkin at her place setting and drop it into Sharmila's lap, but instead, Sharmila grabbed it from him and blew her nose on it. Then, leaving the napkin in a crumpled heap, she reached out and grabbed a slice of toast from the rack and started to chomp on it dry. The poor butler tentatively pushed the butter dish and the silver-plated condiment tray towards her, but she steadfastly ignored them, and when he, aghast at her uncouthness, offered to butter her toast himself, she gave him such a filthy look that Sachin suspected that his balls may have jumped back into his body. She had been like this since their Balachuria trip and the incident with Bhupen Mandal.

Sharmila had hated politicians from the early days when a local councilman in their town had offered them a helping hand in getting their logistics business off the ground. I want to see your business flourish, he had said, so let me help you avoid the usual pitfalls in terms of things like rules and regulations, legal compliance, and all that guff. That way you can concentrate on growing the business. How much do you want? Sachin had asked him, smartly and straightaway. Oh no, no payment, besides you wouldn't want anyone to think that you were bribing me, would you? No, I'm happy to help you for free. Just remember me when you're a big shot businessman. Sachin had excitedly reported this back to Sharmila: he doesn't want anything from us, he just wants to help us out! Really, replied Sharmila, he doesn't want anything—but everyone wants something, don't they? He just said to remember him when I'm a big shot! Really? Sharmila had shrugged, slightly dubious, but then acquiesced, well, if you say so . . . And then, mellowed, she had gone to see the councilman to thank him for his generosity. That's quite alright, my dear, he told her, the only way our little town will flourish is if we all help each other, isn't that right? She was just about to leave with a smile on her face when he had told her, actually there is a little thing you might do for me. Sure, Sharmila agreed, what's that? And it turned out that the little thing involved Sharmila lying down and spreading her legs. In the past, Sharmila had been in no way averse to leg-spreading and other related manoeuvres but only ever on her terms. And there was no way in hell that she was putting out for any man other than her husband, let alone this lecherous old man. I'd rather shag your dog, the damn thing is always humping my leg, anyway! And off she went, to report what had happened to Sachin.

Sachin was outraged—how dare that man treat his wife with such disrespect—but Sharmila herself had been far more nonchalant. Let's just see how this plays out, she shrugged. Within a few days, a couple of Sachin's lorries were set alight and wrecked, soon after which, the councilman came to pay him a visit. What a shame about your lorries, he said, but as you know, there are a lot of vandals in this place. It's mindless, isn't it, their destructiveness. Sachin gritted his teeth and asked, is there anything you can do to help me? You're best off reporting this to the police, the councilman said. Sachin knew very well that the police would be in the councilman's pocket and it would be of no use going to them. He grit his teeth harder and asked, are you sure you can't help? After some further tedious to and fro, the councilman pretended to relent: OK, OK, as you're so desperate, I know someone who knows some goondas who could keep an eye on your vehicles—but it'll cost you. How much? Sachin asked wearily. The councilman smiled.

Sharmila did not smile when Sachin told her what had happened. We're not paying him, she said, and that's that. Sachin tried to impress upon her that there was no other option but she insisted that there was always another option. You just recruit your own lads to look after the lorries, she told him. A few days later, there was the expected run-in with the councilman's thugs, and the police were called. The police are going to side with the councilman's thugs, Sachin moaned. But to his surprise, the police sided with his lads! See, said Sharmila. What did you do? Sachin asked Sharmila. Everyone has dirt on them, even the Police Chief, Sharmila shrugged. And after that, everyone knew that Sachin was the new name in town. And Sachin knew that he better listen to his wife—because she was a woman who knew what was what.

Of course, in the successive years, he had gradually forgotten this. But now he was remembering again and he was truly sorry that he had involved Bhupen Mandal in the Balachuria matter. For if Sharmila intuited that Bhupen was a rat, then no doubt he was. And not only that, but Sachin had allowed a rat to steal Sharmila's thunder. No wonder she was in such a grim mood. But what to do? Sharmila was notoriously resistant to softening in the form of gifts. Romantic dinners, fancy jewellery, shopping sprees, exotic holidays—no dice. Although now, he appreciated her difficultness. For once the money started to roll in, wasn't it far easier, not to mention predictable, to enjoy the razzmatazz? Indeed, wasn't it wonderful that Sharmila was so comfortable with where she'd come from and who she was that, despite Sachin's best efforts, she had refused to take an interest in antique French furniture and expensive wines and couture clothes and classic literature and the theatre? That sort of determination had to be applauded not looked down on. Before, he had believed her refusal to change was her failing, but now he realised that it was possibly her greatest asset. All these years he had been trying to lift her up, lift her *out*, but finally he understood that right *in* it was where she wanted to be. Yet just at the moment when she was back in her element, she had once again been lifted out of it. But how to make amends for such an insult? And not only that one incident, but also the years of misunderstanding. The years of patronising her. The years of trying to get her to fit in (And fit in with whom? The vacuous, shrill wives of rich men? And fit in for what? Social acceptance from snobs?). Well, he had to try. He had to start somewhere.

"You'll like this story," he called down the table to her. Sharmila glanced up, so he continued, "One of Devi's ministers, Manish Ray, you know the one for backwards people, well he's been caught liquored up and with his pants down with a whore in Hyatt hotel! Front page! And get this—in the last paragraph it says that he was recently in Balachuria to persuade local councillors to vote against our proposed coal mine. I had no idea!"

"Why is that on the front page? It's hardly news, everyone knows politicians are scum."

Sachin laughed. "That's for sure."

"I don't know what you're laughing about," Sharmila quipped, "you're getting into bed with one of the filthiest of them all, you might as well be sleeping in the sewer!"

Good, Sachin thought, at least she was spitting out her grievance now instead of just chewing on it with her dry toast. "You're not wrong, but I was only trying to help Anil, I want his project to succeed."

"First of all, that Anil lad is a lot shrewder than you—he's a real operator if I've seen one—so you don't need to offer him your help, you should just let him get on with it. In fact, I wouldn't be even vaguely surprised if in some way, he's behind this minister story. Didn't he say during our journey to Balachuria that he was staying at Hyatt? Coincidence? I don't think so. And secondly, you think his project will succeed if you involve a rat? All these years of experience, and you're still an idiot!"

Sachin was delighted to be insulted; at least she was engaging with him. "But you know how it is in this place, if you don't get them on side, they tend to get in your way!"

"Yes, but you have to use your judgement when deciding whose arse to kiss—and that's one thing you've always lacked, good judgement!"

"I've got this far without good judgement," he smiled.

"You're *very* lucky."

"Well, I suppose I was lucky to marry you," he teased.

"Damn straight. If you'd married one of those hoity-toity ladies that you're so keen for me to emulate, you'd be putting in the hours at the office whilst they screw their personal trainer at The Hindusthan Club and spend all your cash on Park Street!"

"Is that right?"

"Yes, that's right!"

"Well, let's say, for argument's sake, that I've been foolish in involving Bhupen, what would you suggest I do?"

"Ha," Sharmila sniffed, "what did I say—that you'd soon be asking me to sort out the situation."

"So, sort it out."

"Nah," Sharmila shrugged, "too late, we're going to have to wait it out for a while now, we have to see what a rat eats before we can poison it. And let me tell you something else, if you ever let that dick upend me again, I'll have your balls!" And with that, she poured herself another cup of tea and stirred in her sugars.

Although to most men a conversation that ended in a threat to his genital area might be considered a disaster, to Sachin it was a great success. It meant that Sharmila had, in her own way, forgiven him! As for Anil . . . For the first time, Sachin was slightly worried. If Sharmila was right, and he was behind the minister's downfall . . . No, he couldn't ask. If Anil was indeed behind it, then he hadn't told Sachin for a reason, and whatever that reason was—most likely the desire to keep his boss free from any accusation of wrongdoing, should the whole thing blow up—it had to be respected. But still, Sachin wondered whether Anil knew what he was doing. Really knew. Or had he fallen into the trap of thinking he was playing a game, which required cleverness and cunning, but had no real consequences, that he could simply walk away once he got bored? Sachin sincerely hoped not. Because that would be a mistake. A very big mistake.

Standing outside Devi's office, Nigel's palpitations were noticeable bordering on full-blown arrhythmia. He should have mentioned Manish's fondness for a drink to Devi (and, come to think of it, he shouldn't have even bothered with the genteel innuendo 'fond of', he should have told it as it was. Manish was a complete and utter boozehound.) as soon as he had learned of her intention to involve Manish in the Balachuria affair, which had already become a convoluted mess. But he hadn't. And why hadn't he? Because it wouldn't have made any difference. And why wouldn't it have made any difference? Because the woman never listened. And of course, once again, *The United Times* had stuck the knife right in.

There had been a time, a better, more civilised time, when the papers would have come to him first, to verify the facts, ask for the other side of the story, perhaps be convinced to keep quiet or at least indulge in a little trading: I'll keep this story under wraps if you give me something juicier . . . But now, there was no gentlemanliness, instead there was just ugliness (and the truth was frequently so, so ugly!) followed by more ugliness in the form of scathing tweets and scabrous cartoons and twenty-four-hour news programmes flashing up photos of an inebriated Manish with his private parts blurred. A pixellated penis! Was there absolutely no limit to how far these bloodthirsty journalists would go nowadays? Lord, have mercy, Nigel thought, or at least give me the strength to deal with this palaver. And then for a moment, he switched to being furious with Devi. For after what had happened with Sinha, it had been gently suggested to her by anyone who dared to pop their head up above the parapet, that in the name of pragmatism, of prudence, of practicality—in the name of good politics!—that she swiftly move on and distract people with other, more positive issues. For example, the IT Parks that were apparently going to be built, providing thousands of jobs. Or the apparent project to clear the railway tracks of the shanty-dwellers and move them somewhere safer. Sure, neither of those things were quite as *apparent* as a minister with his pants down but anything but

Balachuria. Anything! But Devi wouldn't budge. She was stuck right where she was. Maybe, thought Nigel, she worked on the basis of a stopped clock—it was still right twice a day. But once again, he was overwhelmed by the feeling that although she might be stubborn, intractable, contrary even, her heart was in the right place, and, as always, his fury faded and he once again tried to put on his practical hat—a hat which was about to fall apart at the seams from overuse—and tried to think how he might fix the problem. So he read through the article again, this time very, very carefully, to see exactly what they were contending with. And then he noticed the journalist's name. And he frowned.

Devi was absolutely beside herself. Even her folder of yellowing paper clippings failed to buoy her. Those halcyon days, when she had first surged to power on a tsunami of the people's righteous anger and frustration and desperation for a better future, seemed a long, long time ago. Now it seemed that the wave was about to turn and drown her.

She should never have trusted that Ray. She had been suspicious right from the start when he had jumped ship from The Communists to join The Truth Party. Sure, the Commie ship had been sinking at that point, and Ray's move was considered by most to be a pragmatic step by an old codger who was rather attached to the appurtenances of government and didn't fancy the scratchier existence of opposition life. But Devi had believed him when he had told her that he wanted nothing more to do with The Communists and nothing more than to oust them from power. That having been on the inside, he had seen that they were no longer interested in anything other than self-interest. And he had buttered her up further, pointing out that it was completely hypocritical that The Communists were so ready to denounce her credentials, always alluding to her status as a lower middle class woman, when real communism was about gender equality and the absence of class! And, he had added, he was beginning to find it completely tedious hanging out with a bunch of old men, with their old ideas and their old ways of doing things. He wanted fresh! He wanted new! He wanted change! He wanted . . . Devi! And she had believed him. Why shouldn't she have? Because everything he had said was absolutely true. And if his colleagues could not fully comprehend that the people might hand Devi the reins of power—believing that power of that sort could be wielded by only upper middle class men—then they were soon going to find out that times were changing.

And now, times had indeed changed and Devi herself could not have predicted where she would end up—with yet another of her ministers humiliating her. When she had been battling her way into power, she had frequently visualised herself as paddling up a fast-flowing river, the strong current against her, trying to reach its source high up in the mountains. Now, she realised that her visualisation was wrong—she had actually been paddling downstream through rapids and white water, only to cascade off the edge of a waterfall into the plunge pool below. That was what being in power was like: being plunged into a pool of cold, swirling water and barely being able to work out which way was up and which was down, let alone breathe! More than ever, she felt unfocused, no, not unfocused but focused on so many things that it made her head spin. And all because she was trying to protect the people from a voracious industrialist who was a puppet of The Communists. Or was it the other way around? Oh, who cared which way round, they were all in it together and all against her!

Now the press were making out that she was recalcitrant, mulish, perverse even, and granted, the way in which her intention was being acted on might appear to be antagonistic, but the intention itself was good, it was pure, it was right! Yet it was being distorted for the sake of column inches and readership numbers and airtime. And the mud that was being slung at her—that she was using tribal people as an excuse, that, just like everyone who had come before her, she was happy to use the powerless as pawns in her game and then discard them when they had served their purpose. Use them? Discard them? Wasn't it she who had gone out of her way to shine a light on their conditions? Had she not been the one to hitch a lift to one of their settlements and eat their weird bugs and roots food and see how they really lived? Had she not always been their supporter, their defender, their queen! This was now her righteous narrative and she genuinely believed in it.

And then, more mud—Ray had been caught with a sex worker, one of Devi's neglected women who needed protecting from unscrupulous men, and wasn't that an irony. God did she hate irony. And irony's chums—sarcasm and wit and ridicule. They all had it in for her!

But how had this all happened? Again, she thought of Ray and his silky words and earnest pledges to her. And suddenly it all became clear. Ray was a Communist agent. They, anticipating her rise to power, had planted him so that he could bring her back down to where they thought she belonged. Politics in West Bengal had always been treacherous, full of double agents and hidden agendas and subterfuge, but this, *this* was an abomination! And that's why she had, from the start, been so utterly right in not wanting to give the enemy any room to manoeuvre. She had to stamp them out. Stamp and stamp and stamp until they were entirely obliterated.

"Nigel," she screamed, "come in here immediately!"

The rant went on for over half an hour. God, thought Nigel, she's nearly twice my age but she has more than double my stamina. I should be inspired by her. I barely have the energy to tie my shoelaces yet here she is ranting and raving and running a state of a hundred million people whilst still finding the time to paint and write poetry. Incredible.

Devi was insistent that Nigel brief the press about the Communist plot to bring her down and to expose Manish as a plant.

"But," said Nigel, tentatively, "we're just speculating, aren't we?"

"It is not a speculation," Devi spat, "it is a fact!"

It's a fact in your head, Nigel thought, it's not a fact in the real world; Devi often conflated the two. "Listen," he said, trying to distract her, "I have another idea . . ."

"And what is that," Devi huffed, still very attached to her Communist plot exposé idea.

"Well, I've noticed that the journalist who revealed the Sinha story is also the one who revealed the Ray story, and that can't be a coincidence."

"She must be a Communist, too," shouted Devi. "Just have her arrested and put her in jail!"

"Have her arrested and put in jail for what?"

"For what? For what? For troublemaking and muck-raking. For lying and misleading! For undermining the democratic process and destroying the integrity of the press! That is for what!"

Nigel nodded sympathetically, though he wasn't sure that any of Devi's indictments were criminal in nature. Or maybe they were. Either way, Nigel concurred, "Well, that would of course be the right thing to do—and this journalist certainly deserves to feel the full force of the law—*but* I was thinking that we might take a more low-key approach and try to work with her rather than against her?"

"Why are you suggesting that we work with the enemy? Am I looking like a desperado?"

Desperado, thought Nigel, where on earth did she pick that one up from, clearly she doesn't know what it actually means.

"Of course you're not desper*ate*, you've never been desper*ate*, but I thought that there might be an opportunity here to turn an enemy into an ally. I could go to her and give her our side of the story, an exclusive of course, and promise more juicy insider gossip?" But Devi had completely lost interest.

"Just sort it out," she said roughly.

"Sorry?"

"I said sort her out!" Sort *her* out or sort *it* out, Nigel wondered, there was potentially a police investigation between the two. But in the mood Devi was in, he didn't dare to ask for further clarification.

In his office, Nigel mulled over the issue further. Sometimes, he just felt like giving up. He was exhausted. And it was in this state of mind—tired, stymied, desperate—that he picked up his phone, winced, then dialled. Then cancelled. Dialled . . . Cancelled. Dialled . . . Cancelled. Five more times before he let the call connect and heard Selim Shah say "Hello? Hello? Is anyone there?"

Tapati Ghatak was feeling quite on top of the world as she walked up the stairs to her parents' flat where she lived with them and her younger brother, Raju, who was still in school. It was through him that she had met her girlfriend—his maths teacher Miss Himani Samaddar. Raju was taking extra maths tuition and on one occasion, when his mother had been unable to take him to Miss Samaddar's house, Tapati had taken him instead. And that's how the affair had started. No longer Madam or Miss Samaddar but lovely, wonderful, darling Himmy. At a glance, Tapati and Himani were an unlikely couple. Whilst Tapati was fast and fiery and ambitious and more more more, Himani was softer, gentler, nurturing, happy with her little world, concerned mainly with her students and their well-being. All the same, Tapati was madly in love with Himani and tried to put out of her mind that she couldn't publicly acknowledge her in the way she would have wished. Indeed, Tapati had just been at Himani's flat celebrating her piece on Minister Ray. The editor of *The United Times* was delighted with her scoop and although he had alluded to just how she had managed to come across such a succulent story, it was a rule to not ask about sources. Now, feeling professionally successful and personally satisfied, she opened the front door with a grin on her face and called out happily, "I'm home."

"We're in here, Tapati," her mother called back, "you have a visitor." A visitor whose presence has made my mother use my proper name, she thought, that's weird. She went through to the dining room, and saw, sitting at the table a strange man, gulping down her mother's homemade rice pudding.

"Where have you been?" her mother smiled politely. "I tried calling but your phone was off. This gentleman is here on newspaper business," she added seriously.

The strange man gave Tapati a knowing smile as if he was fully aware of where she had been. Immediately, she felt sick. She racked her journalist's brain to see if she could place him, and suddenly it occurred to her that she might have seen him parked outside Himani's block of apartments when she had gone in. Now, she felt doubly sick.

"Hello," she said, not sure whether to pretend to know him in front of her mother. Who knew what he had told her? "How are you?"

"Fine, fine," said the man, grinning. "Your mother is a wonderful host, and her rice pudding is the best!" Tapati's mother bowed her head in embarrassment and gave a little smile.

"Oh, it's nothing. If Tapati had told me you were coming around, I would have prepared something much more elaborate!

Anyway, I'll leave you to it. Sorry, my memory's terrible, what did you say your name was?"

"Selim," the man smiled.

Selim, Selim, Selim, Tapati's mind raced, and then she knew who he was. Triply sick.

Anil was in bed with Lalima. He had invited her out to celebrate the Ray story and the date had gone superlatively well. Indeed, he was feeling exceptionally pleased with himself, when he noticed his phone light up. Tapati Ghatak was calling him. It was always the other way around. He guessed he better pick up.

"Hello," he whispered, then, "OK, OK, just calm down and hang on a minute." As quietly as he could, he slipped out of bed and went into the sitting area of his suite.

"Has he actually threatened you, physically?" Anil asked.

"No," Tapati replied, sounding harassed, "he doesn't need to, he knows."

"He knows what?"

"*He knows what you know!*" Tapati said, and Anil could sense the tiniest bit of bitterness and loathing in her voice.

Anil didn't know how to respond and he suddenly felt quite disgusted for having blackmailed Tapati himself. Especially as he considered her almost a friend now. This was the problem with becoming emotionally attached to people—you became emotionally responsible for them, too.

"I don't care about myself anymore," Tapati said tightly, "but her life will be ruined. She's a schoolteacher, you know. Parents will say that they don't want a woman like that teaching her kids. They'll get rid of her."

"They can't get rid of her, that's illegal!"

"Don't be so naïve, you know exactly what the situation is here!"

There was a circumspect silence from Anil, and then he asked, "But what's the point of the threat? What does he want from you?"

"He wants to know the source of the Sinha story and the Ray story because he wants these stories to be cut off at their source."

Now the silence from Anil was tense. "What did you tell him?" he finally asked, quietly.

"I haven't told him anything. He's given me a week. After that, he's promised to start spreading the news and being the gentleman that he is, he also said that if he felt like it, he might pay my girlfriend and me a personal visit to see if he can convince us to *switch side.*"

On hearing this threat of sexual violence, Anil responded angrily. "Why don't you just expose him? Write a big piece about political violence, implicate Devi, it'll be huge." In his voice was a hastiness Tapati had not heard before. Now, it was her turn to be calm.

"First of all," she replied emotionlessly, "there's no implication for Devi, she can simply say that he was acting of his own volition, and considering that he's already been to jail for her, and still remained loyal, I have no doubt he'll take whatever she dishes out. Secondly, if I write about it, then I end up revealing my own personal circumstance. That's the whole point of blackmail, isn't it?"

There was silence at the other end. Then, finally, in his usual smooth tone, Anil replied, "Just leave it to me."

"Why, what are you going to do about it?"

He didn't speak.

"Anil?"

Anil put the phone down.

He stood on the balcony and looked up to the sky for

inspiration. This was his fault and he knew it. And he was not one to shirk his responsibilities. He thought about calling Sachin but he knew that it was best not to, lest he implicate him in some catastrophic mess. Anil knew that he could easily move on, move away, within months he'd have a lucrative job in London or New York (it would be easy enough to dismiss the incident as the deplorable politics of doing business in a third world country, "You know what it's like in those places", and that would suffice) and could put the misadventure behind him, but if Sachin was embroiled, it wouldn't be so easy for him. He'd emerged victorious after his first stint in jail, but a second stint might be his undoing. And without Sachin at its helm, it was a very strong possibility that the whole Lohia Group might sink, with thousands of people losing their livelihoods. God, Anil said to himself, what on earth was I thinking setting up Ray like that! This is not a game! But if he could not call on Sachin for help, then whom could he call? And then, a dark, unwelcome intuition came to him—Bhupen Mandal.

As Anil slipped back into bed, Lalima roused.

"Who were you talking to," she asked sleepily.

"Oh, it was just a business call. Go back to sleep."

Lalima cuddled up to him and then woke up outright. "You're trembling. Are you ill, shall I call a doctor?"

"No, don't call a doctor. I'm just cold, don't worry." Lalima wrapped her arms around him to warm him up, but despite the heat from her body, Anil shook for the rest of the night.

Within a week, Tipu's excitement at the prospect of a job at the Balachuria mine—and, concomitantly, a boyfriend in the shape of Anil—had been trampled on till it was almost obliterated. And by her own father. It was only due to her extraordinary optimism (which her father called stupidity) and her idealism (which her father called naivety) that she managed to remain positive and find ways to keep the faith in the brightness of her future.

What had happened was that Tipu, in her excitement, had mentioned to her father that they might be standing right on top of the coal. Really, Kalyan had retorted, well if that's the case, what do you think they're going to do with us? They'll have to move us, won't they? And where do you think they'll move us to? A five star hotel? Tipu had no answer so Kalyan had answered the question for her: they'll ship us out wholesale to some nasty compound, where we'll live cheek by jowl and choke on the fumes from the mine. Won't that be paradise!

And of course, Kalyan took his job as town harbinger very seriously and had soon spread the news about the prospect of being forcefully relocated and, relatedly, being treated as second-class citizens in their own town, and being stripped of their rights to self-determination and freedom and emancipation!

Now Kalyan was well known as a cynical, grumpy fucker, but plenty of the town thought that sometimes, cynical, grumpy fuckism was what the situation required. Too much optimism could leave you burnt. Indeed, a good number of them remembered years ago when the Naxal lads had come to town, all swagger and promise. And look how that had turned out! Kalyan had been only a ten-year-old boy then but he was still bitter about what they had done to the place, had done to him! No, the bright lights of The Lohia Group had almost blinded the townspeople but Kalyan had reminded them in time to be wary and untrusting.

And then of course there had been Minister Ray's visit. That the local councillors had been insulted by the stated purpose of his visit and sceptical about Devi's real reason for sending him was very quickly forgotten now that Kalyan's pessimism had started to spread. No one wanted to be the gullible idiot who had been bowled over by some pie-in-the-sky talk and a free samosa or two. Now, the tune was quickly changed—Devi had sent Minister Ray, and Devi was innately trustworthy because she was out for the people unlike Lohia who was a Marwari businessman, and, by definition, out for himself. The particulars of Ray's visit, the whys and wherefores, were not discussed further. That Devi had sent him was enough to indicate that something was up. And there was not even an elaboration of what that something was. *Something* was enough to raise suspicion. And once suspicion had been raised, it was almost impossible to erase. The proposed mine had quickly gone from being good news to bad. As for Ray's indiscretion, the townspeople were not vaguely affected or interested. As far as they were concerned, that was just the kind of thing city people did.

There was still a large minority though, who were not so quick to change their minds. These were mainly the younger folk, boys and girls in their late teens and early twenties who weren't old enough to be bitter, and who were young enough to believe that change was possible, and necessary! Tipu started to rally them, tell them their voices needed to be heard and shouldn't be drowned out by the negativism of the naysayers. Wisdom of the elders? More like the crabbiness of old age. Caution of the more experienced? Simply the ignorance of those stuck in their ways. She, dynamic as ever, held a meeting, told the kids that they needed to stick together, that they needed to be organised, coordinated, assertive. They couldn't let this opportunity pass them by. Another one like it might never come, and then their humdrum lives would go on as before.

Kalyan reacted to his daughter's moxie with amused negativity. Those city folk really have you fooled, don't they, he told her. Well, be careful what you wish for, because those businessmen don't care about your dreams, they care about their profits—and they won't mind trampling all over you to get what they want. And then what was your dream will become your nightmare.

Tipu said nothing in response. As far as she was concerned, negativity was the worst possible trait, especially in a father. What kind of father went around wrecking his kid's dreams? Forget 'you can be anything you want to be!'. With him, it was more like 'what's the point in trying to be something? There's nothing in this place to be!' Apart from a miserable bastard like himself! Well, this time, she had had enough. She was going to leave home. Because, finally, for the first time in her life, she had somewhere else to go. Anima's.

Anima greeted Tipu's decampment with restraint, being warm enough to imply that she was, of course, welcome, but not so enthusiastic as to endorse her decision to leave her family home. But despite Anima's reaction, Tipu's mere existence was really testing how decent a person she was. The person she thought she was—moral, conscientious, principled—knew that the right thing would be to acknowledge her kinship with Tipu and Tipu's family, and for god's sake, help them out! Tipu needn't pin her hopes on the damn mine; Anima could whisk her out of Balachuria and put her in a decent job within a week. Yet her truest self was telling her: get out of this situation and quickly. This Tipu girl will end up bringing you nothing but grief and complications. Just scram. And don't leave a forwarding address!

In order to resolve her conflict, she tried to reduce herself to her brain functions. My prefrontal cortex is in control of my impulses, and it is telling me that the socially appropriate way to behave is to show compassion and consideration and generosity. This part of the brain gave rise to civilisation—without it, we'd all be animals! Yet, my amygdala is making me feel fear and anger and telling me to get out of here. This part of the brain is what has ensured the continuation of the human race—without it, we'd be no more! Which part of my brain shall I rely on? I don't know! Why is my brain not telling me which part of my brain to rely on? Maybe I should just pretend I've had a stroke and then I won't be accountable for what I do or don't do. Maybe with all this stress I'm going to have a stroke! The inner monologue was at such a pitch, she felt her head was about to explode. She felt like letting out a very, very loud scream. But she didn't think that to be socially appropriate.

Tipu had no idea of what was going on in Anima's head. To her, Anima was the same as ever—calm, reliable, to be counted on. As far as she was concerned, Anima was different from all the other grown-ups she knew—she listened, she encouraged, she supported. She didn't dismiss or, worse, laugh at Tipu's ideas and plans. Indeed, Tipu had no doubt at all that Anima was the best person to advise her on how to ensure the Balachuria mine actually happened. And there was the matter of the Seevee thing, which Anil had asked for, whatever it was. And then there was also the matter of Anil. Well, Anima would be able to help her with it all!

Anima really, really did not want to get involved with anything to do with the mine. Instinctively, she knew that her actions would result in tension and acrimony and she had had enough of that in Kolkata—that was why she had left the place. And knowing that Devi was involved in the matter made her even more wary as she was intrinsically not a political person. She'd already had quite enough of politics with a small 'p', and she certainly didn't want to get involved in politics with a capital 'P'. But what could she do when Tipu had come to her with such earnestness, such spirit, such certainty that Anima would do right by her! She would be crushed if Anima made her excuses and declined to help, even if the excuses managed to somehow convey that it was in Tipu's best interests that no assistance was forthcoming (perhaps it could be construed as 'character-building' Anima mused or 'empowering'). Inaction was an action in itself!

Anima had also realised that Tipu had absolutely no idea about due process. To her, everything was just a matter of determination—if you wanted something enough, you could will it into existence. So, by her reckoning, whether or not the coal mine opened in Balachuria was simply a battle of wills. And with Anima's will—which she considered to be made out of better quality material than everyone else's—on her side, she couldn't lose. The concept of actions having to take place within a predetermined framework to give them legitimacy was completely foreign to her. Neither did she seem to grasp that everyone *could* have their say, but who got listened to was a very different matter, and in this realm, Anima's voice didn't necessarily count for anything of consequence. It might have the power to annoy others—'Who does she think she is, turning up and sticking her nose into our affairs?'—but no more than that. Yet Anima felt that she could not unload all of this on Tipu, and instead she did her utmost to approach the issue in as professional a manner as she could.

"Listen," she said to Tipu, "I will help you but you have to give me time to think through things properly."

Tipu seemed to agree to this, and nodded respectfully, but then she blurted out, "How long will you be?"

Anima could not help but laugh. "How about you give me this afternoon?" she asked jokingly. But Tipu considered this very seriously and then agreed.

After a while, with the clock ticking, Anima realised that she didn't have a clue what to do. She pursed her lips and wondered who would have a clue and then she thought of Saradindu Mitra, her lawyer friend.

"Hello?" said the voice.

Anima recognised it, but it wasn't Saradindu's, it was The Professor's. Slightly disorientated, she replied, ". . . It's me, how are you doing?"

Using pet names seemed jarring considering their circumstances, but using first names seemed inappropriate.

"Oh, hello . . ." replied The Professor, having taken a moment to recognise his wife's voice. "Yes, I'm OK, and you?"

"Yes, I'm OK, too . . ."

She couldn't think of anything else to add.

"So," The Professor filled in, "I'm guessing you want to speak with Purnima, yes?"

"Actually, no, I need to speak with Saradindu, I have a question for him."

"Oh?"

"Yes, it's to do with the proposed coal mine in Balachuria, you might have read about it in the newspaper?"

"Yes, I'm familiar with it," replied The Professor in a tone that implied he was familiar with everything it was necessary to be familiar with. "Are you considering a new career in coal mining?"

"Yes," answered Anima, tonelessly, "so can you pass the phone to Saradindu, please."

"Er, actually, he's just nipped out for a moment . . ."

"Oh; well please ask him to call me back as a matter of urgency."

"It's an urgent matter?" asked The Professor as if it couldn't possibly be.

"Just ask him to call me," Anima said irritably.

"Of course."

"Thanks."

Anima was about to say a terse goodbye when The Professor started up, "So what do you make of this proposed mine you want to talk *urgently* to Saradindu about, are you for it?"

Anima knew that if she said she was for it, The Professor would inform her why she should be against it, and vice versa. He was a contrary bastard.

"I'm neither for nor against it," she said coolly, hoping that her neutrality would neutralise him.

"Ah, sitting on the fence—neutral. Well," mused The Professor, "I suppose even someone as faultless as yourself has to look after their own interests some time . . ."

"Sorry?"

"Well, it's The Lohia Group which has offered you, what I'm sure is a well remunerated job, at their hospital, isn't it?"

How had he even remembered that? He clearly had a memory like an elephant. A sarcastic, sanctimonious elephant.

"Perhaps well remunerated in your book," she replied, feeling wonderfully mean. "Not really for me. Family money, remember."

"How could I forget."

"Yes, come to think of it," Anima went on with no idea where the words were coming from, they were just spilling out of her, "now that I don't live in Cal anymore, I was thinking of selling my house there. Besides, you must get lonely rattling around in that place all by yourself, you could get a flat or something, much cosier."

"As you wish," replied The Professor, flatly.

Yes, thought Anima, as I wish. Too damn right.

"Anyway, I'll see you at Avik's engagement party next week," she ended airily. She was about to add 'The ones I arranged and am paying for' but it was unnecessary. Her point had been made.

"Of course."

"Well, bye then."

"Bye."

She put down her phone and then checked her watch. Hang on a moment. It wasn't even four o'clock yet. And Saradindu hadn't retired, he still worked—he was still *at* work. He hadn't nipped out. He was at the office. *Er, actually, he's just nipped out for a moment* . . . Er? 'Er' was hesitation. 'Er' was making up a lie on the spot. So why was The Professor at his house when he wasn't home? But Purnima—her dear friend, Purnima—was at home, wasn't she?

Missing you. Can't wait to see you again . . . P xxx

P wasn't for Polly. It was for Purnima.

Anima went blank for a minute or two. And then she thought: good job that Tipu was putting me under pressure, otherwise I wouldn't have made the mistake of calling Saradindu at home. And then she thought: Purnima? *Purnima*? But she's not even pretty! It all makes sense, the grown woman acting like a teenager, sending her paramour the message 'Missing you' whilst on her way to him! God, husband having affair with best friend, it's all so obvious. And then she thought: why is this happening to me? I don't deserve this double betrayal! Those bastards. I'm going to get even with them, just wait! And then she thought: don't be silly, I'm too old for revenge, besides I have my only son's engagement party to look forward to and no one, not even his father, is going to ruin it for me.

It was during this period of apparent equanimity that Avik called. Anima and he were having a very upbeat and excited conversation about the imminent party, when Anima's voice broke.

"What's the matter, Mum?" he asked, concerned.

"Nothing, Puppy, nothing."

"Well, there's something wrong, I can hear you sniffing."

"Honestly, it's nothing."

"Mum!"

"I really can't tell you."

"Tell me what? Now you *have* to tell me!"

Silence.

"Your father's having an affair."

Silence.

"I don't want him at the party; in fact, I don't want to see him at all."

"Oh, Puppy, don't be silly, he's still your dad; I knew I shouldn't have told you."

"I said I don't want him there."

"But what are you going to say to him? You mustn't tell him I said anything to you, he'll think I put you up to it!"

"I won't; I'll just tell him he's not welcome."

"Oh, but you mustn't, he'll be devastated!"

"Good."

XXII

Two huge urns of gladioli, magnolias, lilies, and roses marked the entrance to Avik and Paige's engagement party at The Grand. Pink-tinged lotuses and white candles floated on the pool. Fairy lights twinkled in the fronds of the palm trees whilst stems of tuberose circled their trunks. Waiters in starched white uniform glided around holding trays of delectable canapés or coupes of vintage champagne. A small stage had been set up for a sitarist and tabla player, who were sending dulcet sound waves into the balmy evening air. The guests themselves seemed to be hovering, as if they were high on luxury. Lavish was not the word. Sublime was perhaps closer.

For the umpteenth time, Anima smiled and said, "Thank you, that's very kind," to a guest who had come up to her to congratulate her on such a sensational party, and to those who asked about the Professor, her pre-prepared answer of, "Yes, it's a such a shame that he couldn't make it, but he's been taken ill. Well, I suppose he'll see the photos!" But her mind was on other things. Tipu, mainly. How difficult it had been to pack her bag for the trip, whilst Tipu sat on her bed and asked her question after question about Avik and Avik's wife-to-be and their engagement party—would they come to Balachuria and if they did, would she meet them, and how many guests would be at the event, and who were the guests. And all the time, Anima had been telling herself: just invite her, what harm will it do, she'll be absolutely delighted! Then she would think: no, I can't. I just can't.

And then there was the mine, the bloody mine. Which was always at the forefront of Tipu's mind. She had not forgotten about Anil asking for her CV, and Anima had spent the last couple of days helping her to pad out Tipu's Curriculum and make her Vitae seem far more impressive than it actually was. For example, she was no longer Anima's house-girl, but her Domestic Affairs Administrator; skills and responsibilities—assessment of key projects, cost-benefit analysis, procurement of tenders, management of direct reports. Tipu doing the grocery shopping for her mother—Head Buyer; skills and responsibilities—logistics, budgeting, negotiation of credit terms, relationship building with vendors. Well, thought Anima, why not, nearly everyone exaggerated on their CV. Besides, didn't exaggeration itself show keenness? And Tipu had even insisted on adding her own finishing touch—a photo of herself, fully made up, and looking quite unlike her usual fresh-faced self. Anima had guessed at first that this was what Tipu thought a young, professional working woman would look like. Then she had realised, no, it wasn't that, it was what she thought Anil's girlfriend would look like. And Anima had felt a deep pathos for Tipu and thought: and that's why I should invite you and exactly why I won't. But what was far worse was that, despite Tipu asking her numerous times whether she had heard back from her lawyer friend, Anima had told her no, and to be patient. Whereas the truth of the matter was that she had heard back from Saradindu very quickly and his finding had sent Anima reeling.

Most of that land is yours, not those people's, he had told her, without ceremony. Really, Anima asked incredulously, how is that possible? Why are *you* so surprised, Saradindu replied, nonplussed, you come from a family of landowners, and your uncle was the largest zamindar in Balachuria, and of course he had no children of his own, your brother was—well your brother's best not mentioned—so he left everything to you in his will, surely this makes sense? In fact, wasn't this the answer you were expecting, don't you remember? No, Anima exclaimed, *no*! She had genuinely thought those days of landowning were over. And she had no interest in being a landowner. Indeed, she had had it in her head that many years ago, the government had taken away land from rich zamindars and redistributed it. She had no idea why she thought this, perhaps it just seemed sort of equitable. In any case, the grand old house in Kolkata was already verging on preposterous but just, *just* about socially acceptable, although comments had been jokingly made that if she ever felt like it, she could take just a few rooms for herself and turn the rest into a tourist attraction, like the Marble Palace which was down the road. But landowning? It seemed ludicrous. Are you absolutely sure, she asked. Sarandindu did not appreciate being questioned. As a lawyer, I don't have a habit of saying things unless I'm sure, he huffed. Anyway, I have copies of all the deeds and so on, I'll bring them to Avik's engagement drinks, shall I? If you could, that would be much appreciated, Anima replied. She had to see it with her own eyes.

There was a tap on her shoulder. Anima turned around to see Saradindu and Purnima smiling at her.

"Before I forget," Saradindu said, handing over a folder.

"Thank you so much for looking into the matter so quickly," Anima nodded, "please do send me your bill."

Saradindu shook his head. But Purnima did not seem pleased at his gesture of generosity.

"Fancy that," she said, smiling saccharinely. "Owning all that land. Lohia will have to pay you a pretty penny for it! You'll be a rich woman. Well, rich*er*."

Anima eyed her up. Isn't it enough, she thought, that you're having an affair with my husband? I would have thought that the guilt would have at least made you behave nicely to me, but you're so envious that you still have to take a swipe at me. All these years I didn't realise that my best friend is actually a bitch! She glanced at Saradindu to work out whether he knew that his wife was having an affair but from his proprietal and proprietorial arm around Purnima's waist, Anima knew that he didn't. She was very, very tempted to throw a cat among the pigeons, maybe hint at something a bit too cosy between The Professor and Purnima, see the look on Saradindu's face, and wipe the smile right off Purnima's. But then, remembering where she was, at a joyous celebration of love, she said brightly, "Will you please excuse me? I just need to take care of something. I'll catch up with you both later. Please eat, drink, and be merry! And Saradindu, thank you, again!"

Ever since his phone call to Bhupen Mandal, Anil had not been able to go into work. He felt ill. Even though he had asked Bhupen only very vaguely if he might help out with the situation, he knew what he had *actually* asked for. And the thought of a man being physically assaulted at his behest had completely shaken him. The visceral imagining of the pain, of hard fist or knee or booted foot meeting soft flesh, had made him want to vomit. For whereas financial persuasion and emotional manipulation had felt justifiable, the leap to violence had left him feeling unnerved.

He needed to pull himself together and just get on with it. Take it in little steps. Have a shower. Shave. Put on one of his best suits and his handmade shoes. Look like he was going somewhere. Then go there!

"Could you squeeze in just a bit tighter," said the photographer, making a gesture with his hands. "Yes, you, madam, yes, in the green jacket." Click-click-click. "Thank you! And perhaps now one of just the bride and groom-to-be. Madam, yes you in the grey sari, could you please just shimmy a little to the right. Please be careful not to fall into the pool though!"

Anima stepped out of the way—being careful to avoid falling into the pool—only for Paige to lurch at her seconds later with a horrified expression.

"I'm so sorry about the photographer, he was rather rude!"

"I didn't think he was rude at all, just to-the-point, and to-the-point is fine with me. But where did he come from? The photographer I booked is over there."

"Oh, I hope you don't mind, but I invited my own, too, for the party pages of a lifestyle magazine I contribute to. Just a little bit of fun!"

What's fun about having your photo featured in the party pages, Anima thought, the fun is *being* at the party.

"That is fun!" Anima replied. "And I'm sure your sari will look great in the photos."

"Oh, do you think so? I wasn't sure whether I should go bright or subdued, plain or print, and I ended up with a bit of a mish-mash. You know, I was so stressed when I was getting ready that I was tempted to just wear a dress but Avik insisted that I should wear a sari. I guess I should have checked with you . . ."

Yes, you really should have checked with me, Anima thought, your sari choice is dire, you have no idea about what constitutes stylish and tasteful in this sartorial arena at least, and you're showing *far* too much of your stomach.

"Don't be silly, Paige, you look wonderful. Avik was right to insist you wear a sari—it suits you!"

Now Avik joined them and looking around himself, at the guests, the food, the flowers, the splendidness of it all, he said, with feeling, "Wonderful, Mum!"

"Yes, thank you so much, Anima," Paige added. "This really is something. And I'm so looking forward to coming to Balachuria, too!"

"Oh, so you're definitely coming?" Anima had been half-hoping that they might have changed their plans and decided to go somewhere like Kerala instead.

"Of course!" Avik smiled, and then said excitedly, "Look who's here!"

Walking towards them were Anil and Lalima.

"Wow," Avik continued, "that must be Anil's girlfriend!"

Paige said nothing and instead looked away for a moment.

Then followed effusive introductions and greetings and congratulations and compliments until Anima broke the felicitations and said, "Oh, before I forget, Anil, I have something for you," and with that, she handed over Tipu's CV.

Anil squinted at it as if he weren't sure why she had given it to him.

"You remember? The young lady you met in Balachuria?"

"Oh yes, of course. I just didn't recognise her from the photo!"

Now Avik peered over Anil's shoulder and stared at the photo, "Mum, don't you think she looks like someone we know? Who does she look like?"

Anima shrugged, wondering why she had chosen a moment when her son was around to present the CV. The stress of it all was clearly making her lose her head. Then Paige also looked at the photo and laughed, "Avik, I reckon she looks a bit like you!"

Everyone but Anima laughed.

"Mum, is there something you're not telling me . . ." Avik joked.

"Actually," interrupted Anil, sensing Anima's unease—though he couldn't work out why—and wishing to capitalise on it, "I have something for you, too."

He handed over a slim folder of papers; he had been planning to hand them over in front of Avik and make the most of the sense of obligation that came with family.

Right on cue, Avik asked, "What's that?"

"Oh, they're the plans for the new hospital," Anil explained casually. "I've asked your mother to head up the neurological unit. It's going to be world class—as long as your mum agrees!"

"That's so cool, Mum!" Avik said, pleased and appreciative. "So much for a leisurely retirement, eh?"

"Well, quite . . ." Anima said modestly. The job at the hospital had been on her mind but she did not want to upstage Avik and Paige by asking more about it. Yet, despite her sensibility, she could not help but add to Anil, "And I'm sure you'll be able to find something for Tipu once the mine goes ahead?"

"Of course!" replied Anil, smartly, "We're always on the lookout for talent!"

"Mine?" asked Paige, with a raised eyebrow.

"Yes, Paige, a mine. You know, one of those things which people go down so that they can extract substances from the earth's crust. In fact, I believe that's how one of your ancestors got rich isn't it? Mining?"

"Oh god, Anil," drawled Paige, "is this another one of your little projects?" She turned to Lalima and elaborated, "At business school, Anil was always obsessed with *real* work. He thinks real work is mining and construction and building and making stuff. He thinks that what we do is just sitting around."

"I do sit around a lot," Avik admitted to Lalima, "but at least I'm in an office. She," he said knowingly, pointing at Paige, "often works from home!"

"Yes, the world's greatest civilisations were built on *working from home*," Anil commented. Lalima laughed and Avik joined her. Paige noticed this and then said, airily, "Anil's one of those idealistic types who thinks he's going to change the world."

"Well, everyone changes the world, don't they, Paige—just by being in it?" Lalima replied coolly, adding after a considered pause, "Obviously, some people for the better. And some for the worse."

Anil and Avik looked at each other; something passed between them. Paige and Lalima looked at each other; something passed between them. As the eldest, and officially most mature of the group, Anima decided that it was her job to diffuse what was fast turning into an unpleasant situation. Forget falling into the pool, at this rate, someone might get thrown into it!

"You two," she said to Anil and Lalima, "haven't had anything to eat yet, and neither have I, shall we?"

And with that, she guided Anil and Lalima away.

"Give me another one!" Manik Majumdar said to the man serving the grilled tiger prawns. There were now six huge prawns on his plate and room for little else.

"Don't you want some salad?" his wife Debolina nudged gently.

"Salad!" Manik scoffed, "Who comes to The Grand to eat salad!"

Debolina looked away, embarrassed. With a few too many

glasses of champagne in him, her husband had turned from quiet and proper to loud and boorish. Of course, at home, he would never have drunk champagne. He was too frugal—prudent, as he liked to put it. But when it came to enjoying someone else's hospitality, there was no stopping him! He was one of those people who was always happy to take up an invitation but never happy to issue one. Debolina had brought this up with him many a time but his jovial answer had always been that why should they bother hosting when they had friends who were better placed to do so. As Debolina gave the server an apologetic 'Please don't mind him' look, Manik turned around to the man next to him and repeated, "I ask you, who comes to The Grand to eat salad?"

"Sorry?" Anil said, distracted, holding his plate out for some bekti fish.

Anima, next to Anil in the line, heard Manik's familiar voice, and popped her head around Anil.

"I thought it was you!" she smiled.

"Ah, Anima," Manik declared, "you are a vision! A paragon of beauty!"

Anima laughed this off whilst Debolina tried to slowly step away and fade into the background. But it was too late.

"And Debolina, I'm so pleased you could make it. I haven't seen you in a while."

Gingerly, Debolina stepped forward and as she did, Anil and she caught sight of each other. There was an intensely uncomfortable silence, but Manik was too tipsy to notice, and instead said to Anima, "And who's this young fellow? A fine quality suit he's wearing—I can tell these things, you know!"

Yes, you've always been able to tell these things, Debolina thought, but you've never wanted them for yourself. I suppose you think that's some sort of tribute to your integrity. How long can I bear this I'm-a-humble-man routine for!

"Oh, sorry, this is Anil, and this is Anil's girlfriend, Lalima. Anil's one of Avik's friends from Harvard, but he works here in Cal, now."

"Ah, Harvard," Manik sighed rapturously. "Motto: veritas. The truth."

"Oh, not the proper Harvard. I went to the business school—the Harvard for second-hand car salesmen."

Lalima and Anima laughed at Anil's self-deprecating remark, but Manik continued, quite seriously, "And what is your profession now?"

"Actually, Anil works for The Lohia Group," Anima answered, getting fed-up of Manik's interrogation, mainly because her food was sitting on the plate going cold whilst they stood and talked. "Listen, shall we move, we're holding up the queue here."

They all moved, with Anima, Anil, Debolina, and Lalima hoping that the group would be broken by the flow of other guests, but somehow they remained stuck together and ended up at one corner of the pool.

"So, The Lohia Group . . ." started up Manik, "do you actually know Sachin Lohia?"

"Yes, I do," Anil replied, curt but polite.

"A proper Marwari, eh?" Manik jested, nudging Anil with his elbow.

"What's a proper Marwari?" Anil asked, quite seriously.

"Oh," smiled Manik, "you know . . ." He rubbed together his thumb and first two fingers.

"Manik's a very simple man," said Debolina, bitterly. "He doesn't believe in money."

"Of course I believe in money," Manik laughed. "I just don't believe that it's the be-all and end-all!"

"I assure you that Sachin Lohia doesn't believe it's the be-all and end-all either," Anil said.

"What a loyal employee!" Manik announced, patting Anil on the back, and then continuing in a conspiratorial whisper, "Now tell me, what's happening in Balachuria? I have a feeling the auction was rigged! And considering that our own Tapan Ghosh was involved in preparing the environmental report, I have no doubt whatsoever that the whole thing is shady! What say you to that, Sir?"

"Manik," pressed Debolina, "stop it. This is not the time or the place." She looked at the three others and apologised, "Sorry, my husband is always trying to uncover corruption and bribery where there is none, he's one of those conspiracy theory types!"

"What?" laughed Manik, completely oblivious. "I'm just joking! We're all having fun, aren't we?"

Anima, Anil, and Lalima said nothing, but still Manik continued.

"I said to my wife here: how much did they pay *you*?"

Bloody hell, Anima thought, has he drunk a *case* of champagne? I knew unlimited booze was a bad idea.

"Yes, and I said to you," Debolina replied through gritted teeth, "that the point of an auction is that it's transparent."

"She can't take a joke!"

"Maybe she doesn't think you're funny?" Lalima suggested, with a fleeting smile.

"Maybe she doesn't think I'm funny? Ha, ha, ha, that's funny!"

Next thing, Manik was in the pool. And he didn't seem able to swim. Anil glanced at Debolina. Had she pushed her husband? Anil couldn't tell.

"Can someone please help!" Anima shouted.

Quickly, a waiter slipped off his shoes and jumped in. By now, all the other guests were turning around to see what was going on. The waiter managed to drag Manik to the edge and one of his colleagues pulled him out. Slowly, Manik rose to his knees, dripping and dishevelled, whilst the waiter ran off to find a towel. The event was over as quickly as it had started.

"See, now that," Lalima whispered to Anil, "*that*'s funny."

Presently, Debolina came closer to them and observed, without emotion, "I suppose it's a good thing that he didn't drown. It would have ruined such a nice occasion." And then she walked away, leaving the good people of The Grand to tend to her sopping husband.

"No," Anil whispered back to Lalima, "*that*'s funny."

They were both laughing—and it was the kind of laughter which occurred at the beginning of a relationship when the participants thought that they would be immune to the tribulations of long-term coupling—when Anil suddenly remembered that Manik had mentioned Tapan, *our* Tapan. First Debolina. Then Tapan. A small world. The smallest world. The ittiest bittiest tiniest world.

"Shall we go?" Anil asked Lalima, casually.

"What? We only just got here. Why? Who else is here that you don't want to bump into?"

"Else?"

"Oh, come on," Lalima said, poking her tongue into the side of her mouth. "I saw that look between you and, what was her name . . . Debolina? She works at The Directorate of Mines, yes? Interesting."

"Interesting? What are you implying?" said Anil, trying to smile.

"What are you hiding?" Lalima replied, smiling back.

"Me? Hiding something? But you know me. I'm Mr., how did Debolina put it, Transparent!"

"Fine," Lalima shrugged, licking her lips.

"So, shall we go?"

"No," Lalima smiled. "And, FYI, you can't bribe me to make me, either."

And Anil was left in her wake as she swanned off towards the bar, leaving him to feel quite unsettled and quite in love.

It was at the dessert table that Anil finally came face to face with Tapan's wife, the neckless Dimple, who was piling up her plate with an assortment of sweets. Oh god, Anil thought, if she's here, he's bound to be close by. How on earth am I going to be able to persuade Lalima to leave before I bump into him and he says something inappropriate? I know, I'll just tell her we're going. No, that won't work, Lalima's not the kind of woman you *tell.* Maybe I'll just go. Say I'm not feeling well.

"I saw you, and thought, no, it can't be, but it is!" Tapan said, tapping on Anil's shoulder from behind. "Dimpu, Dimpu, come over here and meet one of my clients!"

Dimple glanced over at them, smiled, but then went back to what she was doing.

"Oh, Mr. Ghosh, how nice to bump into you," Anil replied noncommittally, scanning around for Lalima.

"Everything's going very well, isn't it . . ." Tapan said conspiratorially.

"Yes, this is a lovely occasion," Anil replied, without batting an eyelid.

"Oh yes, it certainly is! But what I meant was that—" Tapan began to clarify.

"I said, it's a lovely occasion."

"Ah, I understand," Tapan wiggled his head jovially. "No shop talk!"

"Exactly," Anil smiled stiffly. "Anyway, I'm terribly sorry but I appear to have lost my girlfriend so I better go and find—"

"But," Tapan interrupted, as if he hadn't heard a word that Anil had said, "I have some information which I think you might find very interesting . . ."

"Why don't you call me?" Anil replied hastily. "Just drop me a line and we'll arrange to talk, yes?"

"It's top secret!" Tapan said, eyes gleaming.

"Well, in that case, you better keep it that way!"

Tapan laughed raucously. "That's funny! So, do you want to know?"

Anil stared at Tapan for a moment. The man has no idea. No. Idea. At. All. How he has got this far in life is beyond me, he thought. Or perhaps his cretinism is just a ruse. Maybe under all the bluntness and fatuity, he's an evil mastermind.

"Go on, then," Anil said indifferently.

"Well . . ." Tapan began, stringing it out, "sources have it that most of the land in Balachuria belongs to one person. Makes your job easier, doesn't it? You have only one person to win over! Well," he added with a smirk, "apart from our beloved Devi . . ."

Anil disliked Tapan so much that his reaction was to say 'Oh', whatever information Tapan had imparted, but then he realised that what Tapan had said was actually meaningful. Damn Tapan and his usefulness—first Bipin, now this! Despite being an irritating boga, he did, even unasked, keep coming up with the goods.

"Really?" Anil replied, careful not to sound too interested. "How do you know?"

"My wife told me."

Your wife, Anil thought, *your wife*? That neckless wonder?

"She must be very important to be in receipt of such crucial information!"

Tapan accepted this with a dip of his head.

"One of her friends told her—in confidence, of course!" he elaborated without any sense of irony at all. "And this friend knows because her husband is a top class lawyer who specialises in land use . . ."

"Wow . . ." Anil replied, thinking: I thought my Legal Director Onkar was meant to be all over this sort of crap. Obviously he's not quite as meticulous and thorough as he thinks he is. Does a LinkedIn profile count for nothing!

"And this lawyer was consulted by the person who owns the land," Tapan boasted. "And they're both of my acquaintance!"

"Gosh," Anil smiled, "that's some coincidence!"

Tapan didn't like this so much. It most certainly was not a coincidence; it was because he was an exceedingly well-connected man who moved in the right circles. He demurred by looking down and shrugging.

Don't go cold on me now, Anil thought. Now you've started, you better finish.

"Of course," Anil rectified knowingly, glancing around with a raised eyebrow, "we all know that there are no coincidences . . ."

At this, Tapan warmed right up again, with a big grin. Now tell me who it is, Anil thought. And then, abruptly, Anil understood it was Anima. Who else could it be? It was a simple enough deduction.

"Actually, tell you what, Tapan," Anil said hastily, "you better not tell me. I wouldn't want you to break any confidences."

"Oh, no need to worry about that!" Tapan laughed.

"No, really," Anil said, very seriously, "I don't want to be responsible for any misdemeanour. Enjoy the rest of your evening."

"Shall we go?" Anil said to Lalima. Lalima sensed the change in tone.

"What's happened?"

"Not now."

It was only when they had been in the car for ten minutes, and Anil had told the driver that he'd be grateful if the driver could stop asking questions about the party and just drive, that Lalima broached the subject again. She had never seen Anil look quite so serious.

"So . . .?" she asked tentatively.

"You know Avik's mother, Anima? You met her tonight. She's the one I've offered a job at The Lohia Hospital."

"Yes?"

"Yes, well, she also happens to be the largest landowner in Balachuria."

"And . . .?"

"*And?* The Lohia Group offers a top notch job to the person who will have to sell their land in order for the mine to go ahead?"

"So what? It's a coincidence."

"You know, the funny thing is, it really *is* a coincidence. But it doesn't look that way, does it? It looks like we're trying to buy her off. And I don't think she's the type of person who'd respond well to what she might think is bribery. And if she doesn't agree to sell, we're screwed. And if she doesn't take the job, we're screwed."

"She seems like a very astute, level-headed woman to me. I'm sure she'll sell *and* she'll take the job."

"Well, that's the best bit—if she *does* sell and she *does* take the job, then that's Devi's dream come true! She's been against this mine from the start because of some personal vendetta against Sachin, and so far she hasn't been able to make anything stick but if it looks like The Lohia Group and Anima are in cahoots, then it's game over! Think of how it will be portrayed. And then this damn party at The Grand of all places—all that one per cent type stuff. Because, no doubt, Devi, the tireless champion of the underprivileged and disenfranchised, will make some massive controversy out of it all, and then, once more, we're screwed."

"Anil, what has gotten into you? You're completely losing your cool over nothing. Rich and powerful people are connected to each other the world over. That's what keeps them rich and powerful. So the fact that there is this connection between you and Anima is neither surprising nor suspicious. It's just a fact of life. Of course, Devi won't like this fact of life and she'll make a fuss but making a fuss is what she does. But her objections will just be put down to the resentment of a woman who promised so much and yet has delivered so little. As for a private party at The

Grand, how on earth is Devi going to find out about it? And even if she does find out, so what? Does she get to dictate where people should celebrate? We live in a democracy. Another fact of life that she might not like, but a fact all the same."

"Yes, but she always pits herself as the servant of the everyman against the mercenary likes of, well, the kind of people who go to parties at The Grand, or even worse, throw them. And people really buy into it—enough people to put her in power. She can't be dismissed so easily, Lalima."

"I'm not saying she can be dismissed *easily*, Anil, but she's not unbeatable. The woman's not bulletproof!"

The woman's not bulletproof, Anil repeated in his head, as they drove over the Park Street flyover, above them the glittering stars peeping through the smoggy night-time sky, below them the glowing red and white lights of the ever-present traffic.

That's exactly what Bhupen Mandal had said.

XXIII

"Selim Shah has been killed. His body was found this evening by his mother."

After he had vomited violently and uncontrollably, it was Nigel who broke this news to Devi.

Devi had stared at him with disbelief, then distress, then fury.

"Arrest them!" she screamed.

"Arrest whom?" Nigel asked, quaking.

"The leaders of The Communist Party! This is their doing!"

"The police are already making enquiries," Nigel briefed her, "but so far, there are no solid leads . . ."

"The police do not need to be making enquiries when I am knowing who is responsible!"

"We need to give the police evidence," Nigel whispered, looking at his feet.

"I am giving them plenty of evidence," Devi retorted. "My whole life story battling against those goondas is evidence! Mark my words, they will not be getting away with murder this time!"

Then, without warning, Nigel had thrown up again, all over Devi's floor.

Shortly afterwards, once he had managed to compose himself and drank enough Gelusil to cover up the acrid tang in his mouth, he had arranged an emergency meeting at Devi's house to discuss the slaying of Selim Shah, Truth Party strongman, and Devi acolyte. The only way in which he had managed to function was to entirely suppress the fact that it was he who had been in touch with Selim about the journalist at *The United Times*. On one hand, he couldn't believe that a journalist—and a female journalist at that—would have the nerve to kill Selim, or at least have him killed. On the other hand, he couldn't believe that his phone call to Selim had absolutely nothing to do with Selim's subsequent death. So the only way out of the quandary was to buy wholesale into Devi's accusation: it must have been The Communists! Arrest them all!

The scene in Devi's homely front room was suffocatingly tense. The only people there—the only people Devi now trusted—were Nigel, Partha, Insaf, and Rohini. There was now another detail: Selim had been found hanged. And this seemed to have aggravated Devi even further; there was something mocking and contemptuous about a hanging, a good old-fashioned beating to a pulp would have been more respectful! What everyone in the room agreed was that The Communists had ordered the killing of Selim Shah in revenge for the death of their Mustak Ahmed Attar. But that was the only thing that was agreed. So far, Partha, in his nervy, mousy way, had suggested that they do, well, nothing really. After all, Selim Shah had been to jail for assault, and did The Truth Party really want to be seen shedding tears over an ex-convict, dead or alive? Especially as Devi had said so much about ridding politics in West Bengal of violence and bloodshed, the kind of activity Selim had specialised in. She could, of course, say that she was saddened by the death of a party member, but in the way that she would be saddened by the death of *any* party member. No more than that. Let others speculate about the hand The Communists might have had in his demise.

Devi had almost spat on him and his circumspection. A loyal—the most loyal—party member is murdered and he was suggesting moderation? What was moderate about being murdered? Anger was needed. Action was needed. Angry action was needed! Rebuked, Partha duly backed down and retreated, wondering why he ever bothered speaking up.

Now, Insaf, the matter-of-fact man, stepped in.

"It's a heinous crime," he concurred, "but we must leave the police to investigate the matter, and we must not be seen to be trying to interfere or influence their investigation. After all, it has not even been established whether Selim Shah was killed due to his membership of our party or whether the motive for his murder was completely unrelated to us and actually due to his activities as a private citizen. For all we know, he could have been killed because another man found him having an affair with his wife. We can't just *assume* that The Communists had him assassinated. Yes . . .?"

Devi gave him a look as if he were a complete fool. "That is exactly what we are assuming!"

"Yes, of course, in private, that is what we're assuming—that is what we *know*!" Insaf mollified her, "But when we are asked for our reaction, it would be prudent to keep our knowledge to ourselves, and say that we trust the police to find the perpetrator, or perpetrator*s*, of this crime and bring them to book, and of course, that in the meantime, we will assist the police in any way we can. We must all appear to be the same as every other citizen, that is, not above the law, and certainly not trying to alter its course. And then, when the police do indeed uncover that The Communists ordered Selim's murder, the accusation will in no way be compromised by what could be seen as undue pressure from ourselves."

Nigel liked this approach and found himself nodding, but Devi was having none of it. With an astonished look, which sent her eyebrows scurrying into her hair, she snapped, "Are you going to be going to Selim's mother and telling her this wishy-washy sitting-on-our-hands nonsense? Is this how the party of the people is treating people? Is this how the party of truth is telling the truth of what has happened? Is this how my own party is wanting me to be double-dealing and hushing up? Have you no shame?"

Shame? Perhaps not, thought Nigel. Sense? In spadesful. But what good was sense in the face of such zeal!

Insaf out for the count, Rohini now stepped in. "You're quite right, Devi. One of our own people has been murdered by those Communist thugs. And obviously we must do *something*. We are not the party of sitting around doing nothing! We are the party of action!" Hmmm, thought Nigel, debatable. "But," continued Rohini, "we have to do the fitting thing—take the *right* course of action, the one which will best honour Selim's contribution to our party."

Devi stopped pacing and seemed to mull this over. Good god, thought Nigel, has Rohini made Devi see sense? Finally?

Devi couldn't believe her ears. A man who had dedicated himself to The Truth Party, a man who had ensured its rise to power, a man who had been to jail due to his unerring commitment to conquering the party's enemies, *that* man had been murdered for his devotion. And instead of gratitude, instead of recognition, instead of the retribution which he so thoroughly deserved, her dastardly lot were advocating detachment—all with an eye on saving themselves. Could none of them be relied upon to stick their neck out even a millimetre for the sake of a fallen comrade? No, she would not allow such despicable selfishness in her presence. It was against everything she stood for.

"All of you," she ordered, "get up and put your shoes on. We're going out." No one dared ask to where. Instead they all rose from their seats and put on their shoes as they had been told.

Even at one in the morning, the streets were not deserted but they were quiet enough for Devi and her band of apprehensive followers to be given nary a second look. The people who were up and about at that time had more pressing matters to give their attention to, like finding somewhere to sleep or have sex.

After a while, Nigel realised that they had fallen into a line behind Devi and that no one had said a thing. She is leading us to be executed, he thought. That's how it is in the movies—single file, heads down, silent. We are to be executed for being deplorable, self-serving fuckers. Only Devi had the heart and soul to want to avenge Selim. The rest of us were all trying to sweep his death under the carpet. I deserve to die. When the bullets spray me, the blood that seeps out of my body will be a lurid pink like Gelusil . . .

"Devi, Nigel has fainted," Insaf called out. Devi stopped, looked behind her, and frowned.

"How many times am I telling him to eat properly," she lamented as she walked towards Nigel's buckled form, which was propped up in Insaf's arms. She crouched down and tenderly put her hand on his forehead. "He has a fever coming, he needs to go to hospital."

"We're in Shyambazaar, which is the closest hospital?" Insaf asked.

"R G Kar," said Devi, with certainty. They all shared a furtive glance. The state-run hospitals were notorious for having shortages of doctors, with many of them choosing to pursue more lucrative and cosy positions in the private sector, and in the dead of night, the three of them doubted whether Nigel would receive the best treatment possible—that is if he received any treatment at all and wasn't just left languishing in the waiting room. Because they also knew that Devi, with her sense of fairness and integrity would not pull any strings to have Nigel tended to more quickly. Even if she herself had been about to drop dead on the spot, she would have waited in queue to be seen. Because that was what being for the people was about—it was about waiting in line with them and not using your power and status to wangle yourself to the front, however deleterious the outcome. And they had to respect that because that's what they had signed up for when they joined The Truth Party. So they said nothing. A state hospital it was. Besides, they justified, if Nigel himself was conscious, he would have also wanted to be taken to a state hospital because to do otherwise would be bad PR and if there was one thing they couldn't afford, even more than an ailing Nigel, it was yet more disparaging press.

"So," Rohini asked, scanning around for a taxi, "how are we going to get him there?"

"Shall we call your driver?" Insaf asked Devi, hopefully, already quite exhausted.

"What for I am going to be waking up my driver for at this time?" Devi chided him.

First integrity, thought Insaf, now self-sufficiency. They were all good and well during working hours but in the middle of the night, they were a bit much. What was needed now was convenience and ease. And a snack of some sort, preferably deep-fried. Meanwhile, Partha seemed jittery and was looking around himself. Unlike Devi, he had lived in a gated compound for most of his life and whilst he was happy to try and improve the lot of the street people, he wasn't quite comfortable being amongst them, especially at night, when they apparently turned a bit feral. And whilst Kolkata had always been known for being safe, especially for such a huge city, why take a chance? They needed to get inside or at least get moving. Suddenly, a young boy scampered towards them, and Partha instinctively started to run away from him. Rohini gasped in terror and clutched at her chest, whilst Insaf, still with a murmuring Nigel in his arms, just froze. Only Devi was completely unfazed.

"Isn't it a bit late for you to be out on your own?" she asked the boy.

"I've lost my cat, have you seen him?"

"Don't you be worrying about your cat. Cats are liking to roam around at night, he will be coming back to you in the morning, so you be getting on home."

The boy looked at Devi and gauging her natural authority, he nodded at her and then scampered back into the alley from whence he'd come.

Now, Partha, Rohini, and Insaf tried to seem composed but Devi could tell that they had been scared. She looked at them despairingly. These are my closest advisors and what a pitiful bunch they are. No guts! And always looking to me to come up with a solution. And then people say that I'm autocratic but what choice do I have? Would people really prefer these numpties to run things? I'm the only safe pair of hands around here!

"I will be taking Nigel to the hospital," she declared with a sorrowful shake of her head, "you lot be going home."

"But how will you take him?" Rohini asked.

"You be leaving that to me," Devi replied dismissively, thinking, *that and everything else.* And she started to walk towards a cycle rickshaw whose puller was curled up sleeping in the seat. Devi gave the puller a shake and he stirred, glimpsed Devi, and then pushed her away, telling her grumpily, "I'm sleeping, go away." But Devi persisted. This time the driver sat up and scowled, "Seriously, lady, I ain't going anywhere at this time. You have two legs, so walk!" But Devi kept talking and after a moment, she called out to Insaf.

"Bring Nigel over here."

"He can't go to hospital in a rickshaw," Rohini whispered, as Partha bent down to lift Nigel's legs.

"Do you want to go home or not?" Insaf hissed back. "Besides, it's her show so let her run it how she likes!" Nigel was carried over to the rickshaw and amid his murmurs and moans, wedged into the seat. Then Devi indecorously wrestled her handbag out of his closed hand so that she could take out her purse and pay the puller. But then, to their surprise, the puller sat down on the curb, counted the money, then looked up at Devi and nodded.

"Hey, stop being so insulting," Partha told him. "The lady's given you the right amount, you don't need to count it."

"Who asked you?" the puller retorted.

"Forget about me," Partha huffed, hoping to re-establish his credibility after his cowardly run-for-it, "don't you realise who this lady is, she's our beloved leader De—"

"Hush!" Devi snapped at him. "This good man is doing me a favour, what need is there for you to be getting involved?" And with that, she hitched up her sari and straddled the bike. "I'm off," she said, matter-of-fact, and started pedalling.

Hello Dad,

I'm really sorry to drop this on you, but I think it would be best if you didn't come to the engagement party. I was speaking to Mum and it's quite clear that something has happened between the two of you and that things are not quite right at the moment. And I just don't want things to be awkward at the party—for any of us.

Besides, as Mum has gone to the trouble of arranging everything, it wouldn't be right to ask her not to come, instead of you. Paige and I will of course try to see you on this trip, perhaps on our way back from the Andamans.

Avik xx

Pranab Shastry thought it quite ironic that as a Professor of English, he couldn't quite think of an English word to describe how he felt. Perhaps the German language with its proclivity for sticking words together would have been better, then he could say he was 'angrysad'—which was a different proposition to angry *and* sad. And who was at the root of this pain—his wife, Anima. His brilliant, brainy, beautiful wife Anima. Oh yes, he had plenty of English words to describe her and he'd got to only the second letter of the alphabet. And there was another b-word which was apt for her, too . . . And maybe even a c-word, come to think of it!

No, Pranab, he told himself, don't be so crass, don't stoop so low! How he would have loved to say to her: and tell me, my dear, what injury did I cause you that you were *so* aggrieved you felt the need to persuade our only son to stop me from attending his engagement party? How many times had he read that email from Avik? He'd lost count. It was just so civil that it would seem churlish to do anything other than accept it. As if not accepting it would prove the point about the kind of disagreeable person Anima was having to deal with. Yes, the subtext of the email was clear: do not make a fuss. And the real kick in the teeth? The line about him not being able to uninvite Anima because it was she who had arranged everything. Even if *I* had arranged everything, he wanted to shout at his son, you would never have uninvited your mother—because you have always loved her more!

His thoughts went back to Anima. Wasn't it enough that

you left me without any explanation? *Wasn't that enough*? But he knew that even if he asked her, he wouldn't receive any explanation because Anima was one of those people who was beyond explaining. And beyond explanation, too. Of course in the beginning, it was this aloofness that he had found so captivating. There was something so measured about Anima, so precise. There were never any slip-ups from her. No, she was perfect. That had been the draw and now that was the catch. Loathsome perfection! The kind of perfection that made others feel imperfect.

He knew that was what others would say: well, if Anima has left him, she must have her reasons. And if Anima told Avik to leave out his father from his engagement celebration, then she must have had her reasons for that, too! And Anima's reasons—whether stated or not—were never called into doubt. Moreover, when Anima did something, it was assumed that it was the right thing to do—because if it was the right thing to do, Anima did it. Damn circularity! He had spent many years of marriage assuming that, as well. Even when he thought that maybe she should take another course of action, better question himself than question Anima. She who could not be questioned. And from whence had that unimpeachable unquestionability come? From the old money, the grand house, the finest schooling, the distinguished career, the whole damn shebang. Even a terrorist for a brother hadn't put a dent in that pedigree! In fact, it had enhanced it because it had just highlighted that despite the same upbringing, her brother had failed miserably to make the world a better place, going so far as to take lives, whereas what was Anima doing? She was saving lives, that was what! Yes, life had just been one success after another for her.

And his life? One success after another? No such luck. He'd had to toil and endure and fight to get to where he had. He remembered when he had first moved to England because Anima had wanted to for her career. Of course, she had got off to a flying start. Meanwhile, he, a wide-eyed, brown-skinned man—and he was far browner and more obviously Indian than she, and his spoken English far less natural, because unlike her, the language had not been spoken at home—had had to bear the petty, everyday racism of his colleagues and the petty, everyday politics of academia, and the petty, everyday discourtesies of Londoners . . .

No, Pranab, don't look back in anger, he told himself, and don't blame your wife for things that had nothing to do with her! Then, of course, Avik had come. Yet, despite the fact that Anima had not wanted a baby any more than he, the baby had wanted Anima more than him. Not just during the breastfeeding infant days when it would have been physiognomically impossible to even try and compete, but even after that—during boyhood, puberty, adolescence. And why was that? He had not been less loving or more severe. He had tried to get in as close as possible but his overtures were rejected. He had not been less interested or more self-centred. He had not been any less a father than Anima had been a mother! No, Pranab, he told himself, parenthood is not a competition, and if our son should have, for whatever reason, bonded more with his mother, then just be pleased that he has found such a friend in her, if not me! But the fact remained that he could have stomached all of this if only he could have been open with his wife about his wretched feelings. But Anima, even in her role of wife, came across as not someone to open up to, but someone to impress. Because she, who was the maestro of the brain, who knew from where each impulse sprung, who could give back feeling with a scalpel, who could control expression with her prescription pad, *she* had no emotion herself. She was an android. There was no other explanation. India was desperate to join the space race elite, but forget that, it had produced the world's first fully functional human robot, one who could even give birth! No,

Pranab, don't be so crude and vicious, he told himself, if you are unable to control your own emotions, then don't transfer your inadequacies onto your wife by disparaging her. See a therapist!

Over and over and over he went through the same conversation in his head. Over. And. Over.

He knew he shouldn't do it. But then he went and did it anyway.

And it felt good. Much better than anything had felt in a long, long time.

Nigel was feeling terrible. Much worse than he had felt in a long, long time. The doctor at his bedside seemed cheerful though.

"You had a nasty stomach ulcer," he grinned. "Did you know that?"

Nigel shook his head.

"Right at the site of a blood vessel, too!" he elaborated, adding brightly, "That's bad luck!"

You don't know what bad luck is, Nigel thought. Try being me and you'd have a better idea.

"So I carried out a little surgery to repair the affected vessel and stop the bleeding!"

A little surgery, Nigel thought, as opposed to what—a lot of surgery? He just nodded.

"Of course, we explained all this to you when you were admitted," the doctor said, now more stern, "but you were quite confused, so I thought it best to explain again, now that you're compos mentis."

Compos mentis, Nigel thought, I haven't been compos mentis in a long time, more like compos *de*mentis.

"Thank you very much, Doctor, I'm extremely grateful," Nigel said. "When will you discharge me?"

"Discharge?" The doctor laughed. "You young men nowadays, always on the go! No, it's best that you're under supervision for a couple of days and then home for at least a couple of weeks' bed rest. Speaking of home, shall I contact your mother to let her know that you're out of surgery and awake?"

My mother's dead, Nigel thought. Hang on, is this all a bad dream?

"My mother . . .?"

"Yes, your mother," the doctor repeated slowly, looking carefully at Nigel in case he was showing signs of being confused, "the woman who brought you in?"

Nigel was blank for a moment, and then it all came flooding back—Devi and her execution march.

"Oh yes . . ." he replied, looking around him, suddenly wondering whether the doctor was actually his executioner. Maybe this was all a ruse and tomorrow there'd be an item in the news about how he had unfortunately died due to complications arising from surgery! He had to get out of there.

"You're looking a little unsettled, Nigel," the doctor said, leaning in. "Are you OK?"

"You stay away from me!" Nigel trembled, leaning away from the doctor.

"Hmmm," the doctor said, frowning. "Are you in pain, Nigel? Perhaps you just need to sleep . . . I can help you with that."

"You can't put me to sleep!" Nigel yelled, "I'm not a dog, I'm a human!"

"Of course you're a human," the doctor replied soothingly. "Now just take it easy . . ."

He retreated towards the door and called something down the corridor, and within seconds, a nurse came scurrying back with a loaded syringe.

"Now then, Nigel," the doctor said, approaching him with the syringe, "this is going to help you. So don't worry, you'll feel much better after a good rest . . ."

For a moment, Nigel wriggled around, trying to free himself of the tubes and machines he was hooked up to, but it was of no use.

"Just a little scratch," the doctor smiled, as the surprisingly strong nurse held Nigel's arm straight.

Then they both stepped back and inspected him. These are the last faces I'll ever see, Nigel thought, no longer upset, no longer agitated, no longer anything, really. And within a few minutes, he had drifted off.

When he came around a few hours later, his first thought was simply puzzlement that he was still alive. Or maybe he was just dreaming he was alive. No, if he was dreaming, that in itself would necessitate him being alive. So he must be alive. But whether he was dreaming or not was uncertain. What he needed to do was check what was going on in the world. If things had deviated too much from the norm that would be the tell-tale sign that he was in a dream. But how could he check what was going on in the world when he was in a hospital room with no TV and he had no idea where his phone was? Presently, the doctor walked in.

"Ah, good, you're up. How do you feel now?"

"Much better, thank you, Doctor," Nigel nodded. "Um, I don't suppose you know where my things are, I mean, my clothes and personal possessions—like my cell phone?"

"Ah, your cell phone . . ." the doctor joshed. "Can you imagine, you've lasted a good twelve hours without it—that must be some record!"

"Yes," Nigel snapped, quite unlike him, "do you know where it is or not?"

"Hmmm," the doctor replied, eyeing him up, "I can see that you're feeling *much* better. Anyway, I shall ask the ward sister about the whereabouts of your belongings and have someone bring them to you."

"That's very kind of you, thank you, Doctor," Nigel replied, quickly chastened.

About an hour later, still not one hundred per cent certain that he wasn't in a dream, Nigel was surprised to see the doctor return with his clothes and a plastic bag containing his wallet and phone.

"Oh, it's very kind of you to bring those things yourself. There really wasn't any hurry . . ." Nigel said, still feeling guilty about his earlier outburst.

"That is quite alright," the doctor replied, handing over the items. "Actually, it's been brought to my attention who you are and who the woman is that brought you in. I should have recognised her, but it was very late at night and although I registered a similarity, it didn't occur to me that it could actually *be* her."

Nigel carefully noted that he had refrained from referring to Devi by either that moniker, or her first name and surname, or her position as chief minister. She was just 'the woman'. Clearly the doctor was not a fan.

"Well, I'm sure she won't take it personally!" Nigel said feebly.

The doctor didn't even pretend to acknowledge the joke, and instead burst out, as if he'd just received an electric shock.

"Does she have any idea how many doctors are needed to properly run a large hospital like this? We need highly qualified specialists. That means we need the working conditions to attract them and the money to pay them! Do you realise that in the whole state there are only two specialists in surgical oncology on the payroll? The rest are at private hospitals, which only the rich can afford! Of course, I do the best I can, but I'm one man, and an old man at that. Do you know how many doctors—good doctors—I've seen come here and then leave to join the private sector at those fancy hospitals? But instead of fixing this problem, she's building super-speciality hospitals in the middle of nowhere. Why is she doing that? *Why?*"

Nigel didn't know. And his tummy hurt. And his head hurt. And, really, everything hurt. But, through the pain, he tried to recall the press release that had been sent out about the matter.

"Er, the hospitals are being built in order to make advanced healthcare facilities available in the remote interiors of the state," he stated, hoping he'd got it right.

The doctor looked at him with incredulity.

"But we can't even get doctors to work *here*, right in the middle of the city. Why would they want to work in the middle of nowhere? Do you think a young, educated doctor with a family will want to move away from all the amenities of Kolkata and go and live somewhere remote where there's nothing?"

Good point, Nigel thought, but I can't concede!

"Yes, but it's not just city-dwellers who deserve good healthcare, is it?" Nigel replied, warmly and slightly condescendingly.

"Of course everyone deserves good healthcare!" the doctor replied, irritated. "But the answer is to improve the hospitals we already have in the city, attract the best doctors to work in them instead of losing them to the private sector, and then improve transport links to these hospitals so that those living in remote areas can access them quickly and easily! It's common sense, isn't it?"

Good point, Nigel thought, I really should concede but I can't, so I'll just have to say, well, nothing. But Nigel's silence just spurred on the doctor.

"But instead she's spending crores of rupees on massive hospitals which are destined to remain unstaffed and empty. They will be a monument to her lunacy! In a thousand years from now, there will be tours of their ruins, covered in jungle, and tourists will laugh at the profligacy of the great Devi!"

Nigel and the doctor looked at each other, both of them

embarrassed. Too much had been said by the doctor and too little by Nigel.

"I'll have a word with her and see what I can do," Nigel finally said, feeling quite humiliated and also vulnerable as the doctor loomed over his weak body in its flimsy patient gown. Now, he was hoping this was a dream. He'd had many dreams like this before, when he was verbally cut down by one or more assailants who didn't agree with the way Devi was doing things. In these dreams, he would always wake up before he could deliver a brilliant riposte! The doctor just nodded, dropped Nigel's stuff on his bedside chair, and then left.

Within seconds, Nigel bent over and grabbed his mobile phone. He had received no calls whilst he had been in hospital. Why hasn't my wife called, he wondered. Then he remembered that she and their daughter were visiting her parents and wouldn't have realised that he hadn't come home last night. It made sense but then dreams had their internal logic, too. What he needed to do was check the news.

MOTHER OF TRUTH PARTY STRONGMAN SELIM SHAH SAYS SON COMMITTED SUICIDE DUE TO DEVI'S NEGLECT

Nigel rubbed his eyes. He had to be dreaming. Devi was now being blamed for Selim's death! Selim's mother was shouting from the rooftops that her son had been severely depressed because Devi had neglected him ever since his imprisonment. Even after his release, Devi had made no attempt to contact her son, who had been nothing but a loyal party member. Unable to take it anymore, he had ended his life at his parents' home by hanging himself.

And there was already a comment on the news from *anonymous*: maybe Devi persuaded Shah to commit suicide? After all, he did do everything she wanted! And considering that she was vehemently criticised for saying that she was against political violence but then openly having a close relationship with a thug like Shah, perhaps she decided that she was best rid of him, and who best to get rid of him but he himself!

And then Nigel realised he wasn't dreaming. Simply because it wasn't possible to have a dream *this* twisted, *this* preposterous, *this* deranged! I wish I had died from complications due to surgery, he thought, complications would have been simple . . . And no doubt my team are in a tizzy, with no idea how to respond to such absurdity, waiting for me to come and tell them. As for Devi, I don't even want to think about her reaction. Perhaps she has exploded. Perhaps I will walk into her office to find blood and guts and bits of white sari splattered all over the wall. Well, I better find out, I suppose.

The doctor popped his head around the door, looking slightly sheepish.

"Listen, about what I said before," he winced, "if you do manage to say something, I'd appreciate it if you didn't mention my name. My wife says I'm already under enough stress . . ."

"My wife says the same," Nigel smiled, "and I'll be sure to keep your name out of any conversation I have," he promised, knowing that the conversation would never take place. "But before you go . . . stomach ulcers are caused by stress, aren't they?"

"Actually, stomach ulcers are usually caused by the bacteria Helicobacter pylori or else NSAIDs: non-steroidal anti-inflammatory drugs. Although it's *possible* that lifestyle factors like stress can aggravate them. Oh, and smoking might make ulcers worse. You don't smoke, do you?"

Nigel shook his head. But I really should start, he thought.

Sitting on the edge of his bed, hunched over, one foot bobbing, his gaze on the floor, Anil thought: *fuck*, what have I got myself into. That Bhupen isn't a gangster, he's some sort of voodoo witch doctor or something. How on earth did he make it look like suicide? When he told me he'd sort out the situation, I didn't expect *this*. Although, I'm not sure what I expected. Maybe a couple of broken legs or a ruptured spleen or something. Just enough for Selim to leave Tapati alone.

It was too much, too concrete, too real. The news that Selim was actually dead not just beaten-up, that wasn't a jump, it was a pole-vault. It was so too much that it was unthinkable. Like the size of the universe or the number of grains of sand on a beach. The shakiness had gone; he was now scared stiff. What should he do? What was there *to* do? He wasn't Jesus, he couldn't bring back Selim from the dead. But he could leave. Just get the hell out. Anil opened his bedside drawer, pulled out his passport and thumbed through it, seeing which visas were still current. I really wanted to do something, but this wasn't it, he thought. I knew I had to get my hands dirty. And now they're filthy. I've surpassed my expectations in that respect!

What I need to do is call Bhupen. Talk things through with him. There must be some explanation. Maybe Selim tried to fight back and was killed by mistake and then they had to make it look like suicide? Hand tense, Anil picked up his phone, and found Bhupen's contact details, staring at the phone number before he finally pressed the dial symbol. Holding the phone to his ear, he tried to take deep breaths as each ring reverberated through his body. Finally, Bhupen answered, "Ah, Anil, good evening! How are you?"

"Good evening, Bhupen . . . I think you know what I'm calling about . . ." Anil said quietly.

"Is this one of those guessing games?" Bhupen replied, cheerily.

"I'm calling about Selim Shah!" Anil blurted out.

"Selim Shah?" Bhupen repeated thoughtfully. "I'm not sure I've heard of him. Who is he?"

For a moment, Anil was stunned, wondering whether he had heard correctly. But then he realised that he had. His instinct was to shout back: you know who he is! But then he realised that it would be utterly futile. And he was terrified.

Nigel didn't even bother going home to change. He'd taken a shower in the hospital. And he knew that Devi would be in her office. That was where she not so much drowned her sorrows, but pummelled them. She would probably pummel him, too, but he had to accept whatever came his way. He nodded at the security guards and then walked down the silent corridor towards Devi's office. The quietness was ominous. He braced himself, and then knocked. No reply. That's how angry she was. He knocked again.

"My office doesn't need cleaning," she called out, "and I can be emptying my own bin."

"It's not the cleaner, Devi," Nigel said, as he gently pushed open the door, and stuck his head around it. "It's me."

"What are you doing here?" she said gruffly. "You're not well, you should be in hospital."

The tenderness was in the words themselves; there was none in the tone.

"I'm feeling much better," Nigel lied as he walked in and closed the door behind him.

Devi was sitting at her desk with her arms crossed, crossly. She looked him up and down.

"You are looking terrible," she assessed, "far worse than me."

Nigel wasn't sure if that was a joke but she really was looking terrible. Even during the toughest of times, there was always a springy robustness about Devi, like one of those wibble-wobble toys for young children; no matter how hard you shoved it, it never toppled over, it always sprung back up. But now she looked quite deflated and Nigel suddenly felt very sad. Angry, frantic Devi was infinitely preferable to depressed, forlorn Devi. Because at least the former filled him with energy, be it of the nervous, anxious sort, whereas the latter, which he was experiencing for the first time, left him feeling empty and untethered; Devi's rage was like gravity.

"You're looking as fighting fit as ever," Nigel told her.

"If you are really thinking that, then your eyes are having problems as well as your stomach," she replied, deadpan.

Nigel didn't reply. He sensed that Devi didn't want any buttering up about the vivacity or otherwise of her appearance.

"I am supposing you are knowing what is happening and what they are saying about me," she asked, after a moment.

Nigel nodded.

"They should all be put in jail!" he declared. And then he wondered if he had unintentionally come across as sarcastic. He hoped not, he had meant it!

"Even if the scoundrels who are writing these horrible things are all in jail, the people will be thinking the same thing—that Selim's suicide is my doing. And that I failed to honour my moral duty to be taking care of a man who put all his faith in me. Tell me, am I deserving this? Even when everyone said I should be kicking him out of the party, I was sticking to my guns and allowing him to stay. And all of the journalists were criticising me for condoning violence. Now those same journalists are criticising me for using Selim for my own purposes and then forgetting about him and leaving him to rot! But I am never forgetting about Selim!"

Nigel could offer no solution to this quandary except to say, with a mordant shake of his head, "This is the dirty work of those Communists!"

Well, as Devi herself hadn't yet mentioned them, he thought it only right that he should—maybe it would fire her up again! But she seemed to remain morose.

"They have been trying to destroy me from day one, but with loyal supporters like Selim, I have always been prevailing. But if it looks like I can be abandoning my own people when they are needing me the most, then where their loyalty is going to come from?"

Again, Nigel could offer no solution; he tried to avoid looking her in the eye. Devi continued, "You are knowing that I am like a mother to my people. *I might not have given birth but I am a mother!* But if people are thinking I'm a bad mother, then what? I have to be showing everyone that I am a good mother—a mother who is doing what is right for her children!"

Okay, thought Nigel, we're in slightly weird territory here, with the mothering complex, but I guess I'm going to have to work with it.

"We'll show everyone you're a good mother!" he said, feeling rather peculiar as the words came out of his mouth.

"How?"

"You leave that with me," he replied, upbeat, though he had absolutely no idea what he was going to do. "Don't worry, I'll sort this out."

Devi seemed to be mulling this over, and as she did, Nigel thought: what on earth am I doing? I should be recovering in hospital, not promising to unshamble a shambles. I clearly have some sort of mental problem, too. Oh my god, maybe I have a mother-pleasing complex? Hang on, isn't that called an Oedipus Complex? No, wait a minute, that's where you want to have sex with your mother. I don't want to have sex with Devi! . . . Or do

I on some deep, subconscious level? Is that what this is all about? No, no, no, no, *no*. Oh, I feel very queasy now. Maybe I should just go back to the hospital.

"You are a good boy," Devi finally said, and at the word 'boy', Nigel felt even queasier. "I am always thinking to myself, what would I be doing without my good boy!" She seemed to have recovered some of her bounce and Nigel could not help but feel relieved, despite his queasiness. "Yes," Devi continued, with a beatific smile, "I am knowing you will be setting this all straight, because you are the only one who is never letting me down!"

It was only when Nigel was walking back to his office that he thought: I shouldn't have been taken to a hospital, I should have been taken to a lunatic asylum or whatever they're called these days. Does anyone sane discharge themselves from hospital, where they have been treated for a condition aggravated by stress, only to knowingly pile more stress on themselves? I need therapy! Or a brain transplant!

Light was coming from his office. The cleaners must have left it on despite being told numerous times that Devi's green environmental policy started at home and meant that outside of office hours, all the lights should be switched off. Nigel sighed and pushed open the door. To his surprise, Priyanka was still at her desk. Was she waiting for him to tell her what to do? Because he had no idea of what to do!

When Priyanka had agreed to Anil's proposal, she had done so not out of boldness but fear—fear that if she didn't agree, she might in some way be doing her boss a disservice. But after Minister Ray had been exposed in the newspapers as a sexual delinquent, she had felt a different kind of fear—the fear that his downfall was all her fault. I did the wrong thing, she thought, *because* I was trying to do the right thing. It wasn't naivety that was taken advantage of, it was decency!

The anonymous caller that morning had said he was a friend and supporter of Devi, that he had been following the goings-on in Balachuria with interest and that he had some information which he thought might prove useful in furthering Devi's cause. His voice was gentle but instructive. As he told it, Devi was right—Sachin Lohia was trying to pursue his business interests at the expense of the very people he said he was going to uplift, and there would be no upliftment, only exploitation! In his quest, he had brought on board Anima Acharya, the rich daughter of a Bengali zamindar, who was also the owner of a substantial tract of land in Balachuria. This woman, he said, was very clever, very shrewd. Whilst ostensibly being on the side of the locals, indeed, acting as if she was one of them, she was actually planning on selling her land to Lohia in return for being given a very cushy, prestigious job at his new hospital. Together, through duplicity and cunning, they were colluding to rob Balachuria's residents of their right to self-determination and genuine progress. And there was evidence to show exactly what kind of woman Acharya was—a recent party she had thrown for her son at The Grand Hotel had run into hundreds of thousands of rupees. Would a woman who could spend money so recklessly really have the best interests of the impoverished locals in mind? If so, why had she not given any money to *them*? Because she didn't really care about them. Her real interest was in drinking champagne and carousing and hobnobbing with other similarly-inclined folk. She was right at the top of the pile—so far up that she'd get dizzy if she looked down! Compared to Devi, who was the embodiment of simple living and restraint, Acharya was the epitome of high-living and excess. A woman who, unlike Devi, had had everything handed to her, had never had to fight for anything, had never believed in anything! Could a woman like her really be trusted? Could a hypocrite like her be depended on to do the right thing? It was imperative, for the sake of the residents of Balachuria, that Devi exposed this woman for who and what she really was. As for Sachin, well, did anything more need to be said other than he was a Marwari businessman?

Thank you so much for this information, Priyanka had told the caller, you've done the right thing. Now let the demolition job begin!

Feeling powered up—and she was surprised by how much energy being vicious and ruthless gave her, far more than being gentle and considerate had ever done—she had spent the day adding to the case against Anima Acharya. First of all, she had visited Anima's surgery, where Anima's erstwhile personal assistant, who had become quite peeved at Anima's lack of contact, was only too happy to tell Priyanka that Anima had left her job in a hurry, saying that she had health concerns—but that Anima had seemed perfectly healthy to her! And not only that, but Anima had instructed her to tell the patients that she was away on business but had been completely vague about what that business might be. Priyanka took this in, and thanked the assistant for being so helpful. This Anima woman was starting to look devious, that was for sure. It was definitely a good start!

Next, she paid a trip to the new Lohia Hospital, which was mid-construction; the only people around were engineers and builders and none of them had ever heard of Anima. Dead end. But Priyanka, now feeling more aggressive, was loathe to give up. Pretending to be a journalist, she called a few board members to see if there were going to be any new appointments to the hospital's clinical staff and dropped in Anima's name, but none of them seemed to know anything about her. Another dead end.

She went back to Anima's assistant and asked her if Anima had mentioned anything about being offered a position at The Lohia Hospital; another no. And of course she couldn't ask Anil without him cottoning on. Who else? She searched for news on the construction of the new hospital to see if Anima was mentioned in there, but there was nothing, although a Miss Krishna Valiathan—a South Indian studying at Sir J J College of Architecture in Mumbai—was mentioned numerous times for coming up with the winning design. It was worth a shot. Pretending to be a journalist again, she called Miss Valiathan to supposedly talk about the hospital's design. It took quite a while, and a lot of architectural references which Priyanka didn't understand, but finally Miss Valiathan said something useful: the employee of The Lohia Group, Anil Thakur, who had picked her design as the winner, had told her that such a world class design needed a world class medical staff, and to that end, he had lined up a distinguished neurosurgeon from the UK to head up the new neurological unit—an Anima something—and that it was quite a coup! Sorry, what's her name again? Priyanka had asked. Anima, replied Miss Valiathan; she remembered the name because she had an aunt by the name of Anima. Well, that sounds amazing, Priyanka said, perhaps I could do a joint feature on the two of you—the doctor and the architect, two world class women! Miss Valiathan was delighted. And so was Priyanka. Feeling quite upbeat and audacious, she told her colleagues she was going out for lunch at The Grand.

Priyanka never used taxis, she used the metro or bus, but she felt the least that was needed to turn up at The Grand was a taxi if not a car with driver. In the back of the taxi, she looked into her handbag and managed to find a dried out lipstick and kohl pencil which she did her best with, and pulled her hair out of its usual plait. She was now an engaged woman who was in the process of arranging her engagement party!

The hospitality manager at The Grand seemed to be checking her out carefully, and Priyanka was aware that her simple skirt and blouse and workaday handbag didn't peg her as someone who had enough money to have one drink at The Grand let alone throw a party there, but she told herself to keep up the act and not become intimidated. She chatted easily about her fiancé and how she was making a shortlist of venues before he and her mother checked them out. She was surprised at how easily lying came to her. And quite how much fun it was! She said she wanted the party to be lavish but tasteful and that her mother, who was a doctor at one of the city's top hospitals, was keen on a buffet whereas she was leaning towards a sit-down dinner—how many guests could they seat? Ah, said the manager, well, actually, we had a doctor throw her son an engagement party here just the other day. Oh really, nodded Priyanka, that's a coincidence . . . Would you like to see some photos from that event? They're not yet edited, but we're thinking of putting them in our next hospitality brochure. Surely, Priyanka replied.

Wow, she said, as the manager clicked through the photos, it looks amazing. Oh it was a very beautiful event, the manager said proudly, lavish but tasteful. And how much would something like this cost me? Priyanka asked, lightly. About twenty lakhs, the manager replied after a moment's thought. Twenty lakh rupees on a party? Despite her best efforts, Priyanka's couldn't help but show her surprise, which the manager picked up on immediately. Of course, there were a few added extras for this party, he said quickly, for example, the vintage champagne and imported liquor, we could certainly work with you and your budget! Oh, and look, we were actually featured on an international style website—the bride-to-be kindly sent me the link! Priyanka looked at a photo of Paige and Avik against a backdrop of the lit-up pool, with the caption 'Paige MacAllister and Avik Shastry at their engagement drinks, The Grand Hotel, Kolkata'. Paige MacAllister and Avik Shastry, she made a mental note, Paige MacAllister and Avik Shastry. And then she thought: Shastry? Anima's surname was Acharya . . .

Sorry, she said, is this the same party that you said the lady doctor arranged? Yes, yes, the manager confirmed, she was a very charming woman. What was her name? Priyanka asked casually, I'm just wondering whether my mother might know her professionally. Dr. Anima Acharya, the manager replied readily. Anima, repeated Priyanka, I'll ask my mother. And if I could just take the website link, I'll show her the photos, too.

Back in the office, Priyanka got searching. Paige was easy enough, she had a Wikipedia entry. Bottom line, she was descended from a family of mine owners. And she was filthy rich. It couldn't have been better. Avik was easy enough to find, too. He worked at a top private equity fund and one of his most recent deals was buying an American multinational agricultural biotechnology corporation, which not only had a controversial history but was currently conducting trials of genetically modified crops in a few Indian states including West Bengal; there was already fierce opposition from farmers' organisations. It was more difficult to dig up any dirt on Anima herself, there was plenty on her professional career, which was impeccable, but hardly anything on her personal life, though on page fourteen of her search she found an article from a book on the history of zamindars which mentioned Anima in relation to her forefathers—and their land holding in Balachuria. There was also a remark about a brother Pusan who had joined the Naxalites due to what he saw as his family's mistreatment of their tenants. Pure gold. Finally, she looked for Anima's husband to see whether there was any more gold to be panned, but he was an academic type with no interesting background nor any current controversies. A nobody, really. Never mind; she had enough. On their own, each piece of information could be ambiguous, but put all together, the picture was of an unprincipled and amoral family who spent their lives getting rich from ill-gotten gains! She had never thought she was capable of such malice. But she felt quite exhilarated by her ruthlessness. And why not—such a family deserved nothing less than being savaged! And she didn't even need to bother digging up any dirt on Sachin Lohia, he was a Marwari businessman and the dirt was implicit!

"What are you still doing here, Priyanka?" Nigel asked her, as he put his hand against his stomach. He was again wishing that he had stayed in hospital.

"I have very good news for you, Sir."

"What kind of good news?"

"Well . . ." started Priyanka. After half an hour of Priyanka explaining what had happened and going through all her research, Nigel exhaled, utterly flabbergasted. And his stomach no longer hurt.

XXIV

Anima had made up her mind.

"Tipu, I have some news for you," she began, before she had the chance to renege on herself.

"What kind of news, Madam?"

"The good kind."

Tipu looked concerned. Good news was such a rarity that she thought she might have misunderstood, as if Anima had not completed the sentence and what she meant to say was that she would give Tipu the good news first, and then the bad.

"I have a small gift for you," Anima said, "I hope you'll like it."

"What is it?" Tipu asked excitedly. She was very much hoping for a piece of jewellery, even silver would do!

"It's some land," Anima replied.

Land? What was she going to do with land? She wasn't a farmer! She wondered whether it would be rude to ask for a pair of earrings instead. But gracious as ever, she asked, "Land, for growing things?"

"No, not exactly." Anima had forgotten that Tipu would need a detailed explanation of what owning the land would actually mean. "So . . ." Anima started. After her account, during which Tipu, unlike usual, did not interrupt once, Anima asked her, "So are you happy?

Tipu looked dumbfounded. No one had ever done anything for her or given anything to her. Well, her dad had given her plenty of earache but that was about it. "Are you pulling my arm?" she asked Anima, looking a little hurt.

"What are you saying?" Anima replied, astonished. "Of course not!"

"So, this house and all this land, it's mine?"

"Yes," Anima said with a smile, "it's yours to do with as you please. You deserve it. You have been a wonderful and trustworthy housegirl and I want to do something for you in return—see you settled and secure. If you want to sell it to The Lohia Group, you can. If you want to keep it, you can. It's your decision."

"But what about you?"

"I'm going to go back to the city, I have a new job."

Tipu looked downcast at this. She was beginning to see Anima as not just Madam but mother.

"But I'll visit you and you can visit me whenever you like," Anima reassured her. Tipu nodded thoughtfully. "So, are you pleased?" Anima asked again. Tipu nodded her head to one side and then the other. She was still quite keen on a pair of earrings, but a house and land weren't a bad second.

"So, they belong to me now?" she finally asked, brow furrowed.

"Well, I have to have a lawyer change the deeds to your name, and then yes, it's yours."

"Deeds?"

"Just a simple legal document."

Tipu had only one document so far and that was her new CV; Anima seemed very keen on documents!

"Okay," she shrugged, and then asked, perturbed, "why are you giving me this?"

"Because, as I told you, I want to make sure that you're settled and secure. Besides, I'm very fond of you."

That night, lying in bed, with a cool breeze blowing over her, and with Prem and her puppies sleeping in a heap in a corner of the room, Anima gazed at their dark, fuzzy forms, and finally felt like a huge weight had been lifted from her shoulders. The tension in her neck, shoulders, back, legs, feet, *everywhere*, was dissolving. Her brain was no longer crackling and crossing wires, it was resting. The tightness at her temples had eased. She was going to start afresh. She was going to go back to Kolkata and tell The Professor that she knew about the affair, and divorce him. She was going to sell the grand zamindar's house in Kolkata—that had caused so much envy and bitterness, and had been witness to her brother's slow disintegration—or perhaps just give it to the West Bengal tourist board! She was going to lay her family history to rest. She was going to buy a modern flat instead and be a modern woman! She was going to start her job at The Lohia Hospital. She was going to turn her neurological department into the best in the country. She was going to employ a dog walker for Prem and the puppies whilst she was at work. She was going to make new friends. She was going to learn to drive in Kolkata. She was going to be on her own. She was going to be uncluttered, unfettered, unhampered. She was going to be self-sufficient. She was going to be happy and free. She was going to be *her*! She was going to . . . sleep.

Anil sighed. Radesh, the events manager who had arranged the Balachuria roadshow and whom Anil had subsequently decided to employ as his 'man on the ground', had just called him. And the reason for his call? Devi herself was making a trip to Balachuria that weekend and that the townspeople were getting very excited about her visit. Various task forces had immediately proliferated, from preparing the venue to providing snacks to organising a puja. Is there also a task force to kiss her behind? Anil asked. Radesh didn't reply. And despite his position, which would indicate some amount of loyalty to Anil, Radesh himself sounded excited. Anil could tell from his tone and the speed at which he spoke. This is the problem with these places, Anil thought. A billionaire businessman comes to visit them and gives them a real, concrete plan which will result in jobs, and sure, there's some buzz, but when a woman who has done nothing but blow smoke up their arses rocks up, that's when the mass hysteria starts.

"First of all, I must be giving you my sincerest apology for not visiting your wonderful town since you voted me into power, do you forgive me?"

Devi smiled at the eager faces of the huge crowd and they cheered loudly.

"That is a yes?" she asked coyly.

The crowd cheered again, and Devi giggled.

"I hear someone else has been visiting you, also. A certain businessman and a certain . . . *gentle*man!"

Now, the crowd tittered and Devi raised an eyebrow at them, knowingly.

"Look at this lot," Anil shook his head, "these are the people who voted in that woman as an alternative to The Communists. They still want to be taken care of like they're helpless children. Bhupen's supporters—the mine's supporters—are from the new generation, they don't want to sit around receiving hand-outs from the state in perpetuity, they want to get on and make a living for themselves!"

"So now that *Bhupen* is backing your mine, he's OK?" Lalima queried.

"He's just better than *her*," Anil replied stiffly.

"Ah, I see, best of a bad bunch. And of course, self-interest plays no part in your rapprochement towards a Hindu nationalist thug . . ." Lalima replied, rubbing her lips and raising her eyebrows.

"Not now," Anil hushed, "I need to hear what she's saying."

But he knew that she was right. He had always prided himself on the fact that his pragmatism, his do-whatever-needs-to-be-done attitude, had been anchored by a deep and immovable sense of the greater good. Many murky little wrongs could actually lead to a higher, brighter right. But now it had been revealed to him that he could be held hostage by self-interest, like everyone else. He didn't really think Bhupen was better than Devi. In fact, he was worse. Bhupen was a murderer. And murder could never be dismissed as a murky little wrong. Anil should never have had anything to do with the man. But he had. And there was no turning back. In for a penny, in for a pound.

Lalima shook her head, unimpressed, and threw another handful of *jhal muri* into her mouth.

"Now, tell me," Devi was saying, "am I right in thinking those two have been trying to convince you to have a coal mine in this lovely town of yours?"

The crowd nodded in unison.

"And what else have they been promising you? Jobs? Money? A good life? A better future for you and your children?"

The crowd nodded again.

"And what else?" Devi probed.

The crowd didn't know what else.

"Did they promise you asthma and lung disease in your children?"

There was a murmur from the crowd. Anil rolled his eyes and shook his head.

"No?" Devi said, acting surprised. "They didn't promise you that? What about heart disease and strokes?"

The crowd was becoming agitated and Devi put out her hands and patted the air to calm them.

"OK, OK, not those things either . . ." she nodded. "But what about loss of intellectual capacity and reduced IQ in your children from mercury poisoning?"

'Intellectual capacity' and 'reduced IQ' she said in English.

"From what I can see, there's not any intellectual capacity here *to* lose," Anil huffed.

"If you really want to help these people, then you might like to start by not insulting them?" Lalima suggested.

Anil shut up. Lalima was right. The crowd became quiet and looked straight ahead at Devi, waiting for her to reveal what other corporeal calamities awaited them.

". . . Even when they are leaving, the devastation continues," Devi said. "Your local water supplies will be contaminated, and every sip of water will be poison!"

The crowd looked terrified, but Devi was still smiling.

"And on top of all this," she said, "you will be relocated. You will have to be leaving your homes and be living in prison blocks, I mean workers' housing! Now tell me, is this sounding like a good deal to you? Is this sounding like betterment? Is this sounding like progress!"

"You know what," Anil sighed, "I'm actually impressed by

her. It takes real audacity to stand in front of a large crowd and unreservedly spout so much shit."

Devi now took a brochure out of her handbag; it was the Future Balachuria Your Balachuria handout. She pretended to flip through it, nodding to herself.

"Do you think she likes the sketches, she is an artist after all," Lalima said, po-faced.

"Yeah, a bullshit artist," Anil huffed.

"I am knowing what you are thinking though," Devi said, looking up. "You are thinking, but what about all of this?" She waved the brochure around. "The health centre, the park, the shopping mall . . . You are wanting all of this, are you not?"

The crowd murmured, guiltily.

Devi threw the brochure to the ground, as if she was quite disgusted, and the crowd braced itself, waiting to be chastised for their greed. Then she smiled broadly, and revealed, "Well, I am happy to be telling you that you will be having all this! Because I am going to be building a super-speciality hospital right here!"

The crowd started to whoop. Devi lit up and declared, "And unlike others, I am the only one who can be trusted—and trusted to deliver!"

"Let's go," Anil said. "My head's hurting."

"No," Lalima said. "She's not finished, she has that slightly crazed look in her eyes . . ."

Tipu was staring at Avik and Paige, mesmerised and unashamedly awestruck. Forget Devi coming to Balachuria, Avik and Paige had come!

"I wonder what Anil would say about this . . ." Paige whispered to Avik, looking quite smug, as Devi listed the possible catastrophic effects of a coal mine.

"Do you even understand what she's saying?" Avik replied sternly; he understood Bengali, Paige did not.

"Not word for word, but I get the gist. She's very impassioned and spirited!"

Avik let out a derisory sniff and shook his head.

"Well, you're clearly not the first person to mistake bluster as passion."

Paige arched one eyebrow at him and then stretched out her long neck and focused on Devi. Maybe if she narrowed her eyes enough, she would be able to read the brochure in her hand.

"Mum, shall we go?" Avik suggested. "This is all a bit . . ." He rolled his eyes.

"Hmmm?" Anima asked, completely distracted. She had had absolutely no intention whatsoever of coming to the rally. She had no time for politics. It was all so messy. She had always been one for literal and metaphorical surgical precision. And she had even less time for politicians. They were butchers—of principles, of truth. But Tipu, with her relentless eagerness, had insisted on coming. Everyone else was going, why shouldn't Anima? And how to answer that without appearing either arrogant or crabby. And then there was Paige, who seemed to be curiously keen on attending, with her peculiar notions about real life and real people. Well, maybe attending political rallies is what people did on holiday when their actual lives were a holiday, Anima thought.

"Absolutely, let's leave. Is Paige OK to leave, too?"

"Actually, I wouldn't mind staying," Paige replied sweetly. "If that's alright?"

"Oh, yes, that's fine, I'm happy to stay as well," Anima lied. "Whatever you like."

Avik glanced at Paige crossly, but she kept staring ahead at Devi.

"You know," Devi was smiling, "I am enjoying myself so much with you that I am wanting to stay here! Would you be liking me to stay here?"

The crowd roared and Devi giggled coquettishly.

"Yes, you are knowing that I am telling you the truth, because I am, like you, a common person. I am not a fancy one with fancy words and fancy brochures! I am just a simple, truthful woman."

"Where is she going with this fancy thing?" Anil asked Lalima. "We have that angle covered with Sharmila. And Sachin's applying for sainthood so he doesn't fit the bill either."

"You were right," Lalima said grimly, after a moment's thought, "What you said in the car . . ."

"What did I say in the car? When? Today?"

"The night of the party."

"What?"

"Sshhh. Listen."

"I am knowing that there is a certain person who will be trying to tell you otherwise though," Devi was saying, "who will be trying to coerce you to allow The Lohia Group to come here. A respectable person, a person you all trust, a doctor no less! Well, she might be a doctor but do you know what else she is?"

"No!" Anil said, realising to whom she was referring, and shaking his head in disbelief. "Even *she* wouldn't . . . She has to have some boundaries!"

"Like you did when you set up Ray with that prostitute?" Lalima replied, deadpan.

Anil looked at her, shocked.

"I'm not stupid," she said.

Anil's mind raced. Did she know about Tapati Ghatak and Bhupen Mandal and Selim Shah, too? He couldn't ask and incriminate himself but he suddenly felt incredibly vulnerable.

"I'm on your side, Anil," Lalima said, glancing sideward at him, "just don't play the self-righteous card with me, I don't care for hypocrites."

She's right, Anil thought. I wish she weren't. But she is. I have been racing Devi to the bottom not to the top.

Devi was now going into gory detail as she ripped Anima apart from head to toe. She had also switched to speaking in far more vernacular Bengali. Better for really sticking in the knife. No detail was missed. The grand zamindar background: "The kind of family which, as you all know, was in the service of the ruling British and always more than ready to screw ordinary people like us in exchange for being given the title of Raja or Rani!". The land-owning: "The land which, as you all know, rightly belonged to the ordinary people like us who lived and worked on it, but was stolen from us, and, to add insult to injury, which we then had to pay rent and taxes on!". The Naxalite brother: "The kind of scoundrel who said he wanted to help ordinary people like us, but instead made our lives even more of a misery, and brought death and despair in his wake, and then, when he had finished wreaking havoc, ran back to his parents' stately home, where his family connections saved him from being brought to justice.". The obscenely extravagant party at The Grand and the lobster thermidor at over two thousand rupees a portion: "Let me ask you all, what does your weekly grocery shop cost? Less than that I'm thinking! Doesn't that kind of excess really stick in your craw?". The devious son and his devious business deals: "This is a man who has bought a company which is trying to run our own small farmers out of business and load up our plates with food which has been engineered in a laboratory instead of grown in the earth!". His future wife: "This is a woman whose family amassed a huge fortune on the back of other people's hard work, a woman who has never done a day's honest work in her life, a woman who spends her time promoting two lakh handbags. Yes, that's right, handbags which cost two lakhs, is that not an offense against decency? A woman who is so without modesty that she even wore an indecently revealing sari to her own engagement party!". And to tie it all up nicely, the top job at The Lohia Hospital: "Have you ever been inside a hospital like that? Of course not—they're for only rich people. Because this doctor wants only rich patients! Some people are so greedy that they never stop wanting more, and they're only too happy to trample on other people to get what they want! This is the kind of woman you're dealing with!".

"She's really on the rampage," Lalima remarked.

"But it's just bullshit piled on bullshit!"

"Bullshit to you, fertiliser to her."

"But it's just so ludicrous!"

"Stop panicking. What did I tell you that night? We'll put all of this down to the resentment of a woman who promises so much and yet delivers so little. The politics of envy. We have this situation covered."

Anil glanced at Lalima, wanting to be reassured.

"And, in the end," Lalima continued calmly, "the person who wins is the person with the most credibility—but you know that, which is why you've been trying to undermine hers all along . . ."

Anil's stomach dropped. All at once, he had an alarming feeling that Lalima was not who he thought she was. That she was a plant of some sort. Devi's mole! It was not impossible because if what was happening now was happening, anything was possible. Oh my god, he thought, Lalima is a honey trap! What a fool I've been! His mind was racing and before he knew it, he was pushing and shoving his way through the crowd, gasping for air. Behind him, he could hear Lalima calling out, "Anil, where are you going?"

Far, far away from you, Anil thought without turning back.

"Mum," Avik whispered to Anima, "let's go, you don't need to listen to this, it's absolutely outrageous!"

Anima was so bewildered that she couldn't speak. It wasn't like being hit by a truck, it was like personally being hit by a meteorite.

"I'm sorry," she finally managed to say, "I have no idea what's going on . . ."

"Mum, what are *you* saying sorry for!"

"And she dragged you and Paige into it . . . I'm so sorry . . ."

"Mum, you have nothing to be sorry about. Now let's go!"

Paige, who had not understood what had been said, was still smiling beatifically at Devi—impassioned, spirited Devi—but now she twisted her head to hear what Avik and Anima were whispering about.

"What's going on?"

"We're leaving," Avik told her.

"But—"

"I said we're leaving."

Paige had never heard Avik use that tone of voice and any resistance left her immediately.

"Tipu, we're going now . . ." Anima said, referring to herself, Avik, and Paige; she didn't want to assume that Tipu would feel any loyalty towards her considering what was being said. Above all, she was thinking: Tipu will be hurt that I didn't invite her to the party. But Tipu, with an expression which Anima had never seen on her before—of revulsion, as if she had tasted something rotten—simply said, "Yes, let's go, I don't need to listen to any more of this!"

Slowly, the four of them nudged their way through the crowd.

And behind them, Devi's voice boomed, "Are they common people like you? Then why will they be helping you? No, they know only how to help people like themselves. But I am a common person like you—*I am one of you*—and your hardships are my hardships, that is why I, and only I, can be trusted to do what is good for you!"

"She's a very rude woman."

That was Tipu's summary. And it was the worst insult she could think of. She had nothing more to say. Instead, she sat on the floor, playing with Prem and the puppies.

"She was making out that we're The Borgias or something!" This from Paige.

Avik glanced at her, shook his head with a wry smile, and then turned back to Anima.

"Mum, what do you want to do?"

Anima, sitting in an armchair, her limbs heavy, shook her head.

"I have no idea," she shrugged, "I'm utterly stunned. I mean, the locals were pretty suspicious of me to begin with, but now . . ."

"Do you feel safe here or do you want to leave?" Avik asked.

"I don't know . . . If I leave, then it might look like I'm running away—and why would I run away if I haven't done anything wrong?"

Avik considered this but didn't say anything, so Anima went on, "But if the people here think I'm about to sell their land from under their noses, then they might be pretty angry . . ."

She was reluctant to tell Avik that she was going to give the land to Tipu. She had worked on the basis that as he didn't know she had it, he couldn't know if she gave it away. But now that Devi had made the revelation that the land was hers, Avik would want to know what she was going to do with it. And if she told him that she was going to give it to Tipu, it wasn't that he would care as such, but he would certainly wonder why. Because as far as Avik was concerned, she was just the house-girl, and not even a long-serving one at that! Just as Anima thought she had simplified matters, they had become convoluted again.

"Listen, Mum," Avik suggested, "why don't you come to The Andamans with us for the week, get away from it all and think about what you want to do."

But I've only just finished thinking through everything and decided what I was going to do, Anima thought, I don't want to have to think through everything again! My brain is tired. I am tired. So tired. That Devi can't be younger than me but she has so much more energy! I wonder from where she gets it. Maybe it's the years of marriage that have slowly sapped me. Maybe that's why she never married!

"Mum?" Avik repeated.

Finally, Anima replied, "Do you think that's why your friend Anil offered me the job? Because he thought it would be more likely that I would sell the land to his company?" Suddenly, she had become very anxious about the job. She really, really wanted it, and she hadn't really, really wanted anything in a long time. The job was the one thing that was keeping her going. Of course, she knew there were other jobs, but she wanted this one. For she had fallen in love with the hospital as soon as she had seen the spectacular design for it. For her, it was no different from falling in love with a house and thinking: that's where I'm going to live for the rest of my life. My forever home!

"Of course not, Mum. You're probably the best neurosurgeon in the country. That's why Anil offered you the job. He probably didn't even know about you owning the land. I mean, *you* didn't know until recently, did you?"

"No," she answered, "I didn't."

"Well then."

"But do you think the job offer might be retracted?"

"Why would that happen?"

"Because now there's all this," she waved her hands about in the air, "about me. It makes both me and the company look bad. If I were them, I'd cut me loose! That way, they can at least show they weren't trying to buy me off in some way. That the job and the sale of the land are totally unrelated."

"They *are* totally unrelated," Avik stressed.

"Yes, but it doesn't look that way now, does it?"

Avik sighed.

"Mum, we're going around in circles . . ."

Anima looked up at Avik, who was resting against a table with his arms crossed, and then over at Tipu. As the conversation had been held in English, Tipu was oblivious to its contents, and was continuing to play with the dogs. She looked very young. And not just young but naïve. The loyalty which she had shown to Anima before, by leaving the rally, now came across as less the considered loyalty of someone who had weighed up the evidence and then made a deliberate decision, but more the involuntary loyalty of a dog.

I thought that by giving her the land, I'd be doing something good for her. Something that would make her life easier after all the hardships she's endured with her sick mother and brute of a father. I thought I was empowering her! But instead I have pitted her against Devi, a woman who is so ruthless that she would have no compunction in destroying a sweet, teenage girl if it served her purposes. And I don't rate Tipu's chances. She'll either be bullied into doing what that woman wants her to or if she resists, she'll feel the full force of that woman's wrath. I cannot allow that to happen. If anyone should take on that woman, it should be me. But I don't want to! I want to go and work in the beautiful, new hospital! Oh, I don't know. . .

"Yes, Avik," Anima finally said, "I think I'll come to the Andamans with you, I'll have some time to think there—that is if you don't mind, Paige?"

"Of course not!" Paige replied. "You deserve some time away after all of this."

"So you better go and pack?" Avik prompted.

"Yes, yes," Anima said, getting up from her chair, "I'll ask Tipu to help."

On hearing her name, Tipu looked up.

"I'm going to the Andamans for a week," Anima told her, gently. Tipu mulled this over and then asked, very seriously, "Aren't there cannibals there?"

"What's Tipu asking?" Paige said.

"She's asking whether there are cannibals in the Andamans."

"Yes, well I'd rather have lunch with a cannibal than with Paramita Roy," Paige remarked.

As Tipu helped Anima pack, Anima asked her quietly, "Did you actually understand what was being said today?"

Tipu nodded. But Anima wasn't convinced.

"Explain it to me then."

Tipu shrugged but then said, "That woman was saying that you're going to sell the land to that company so they can build their mine here. But you said that the land is mine. That's right, isn't it?"

So, she had understood, but had she understood the *implication*?

"Yes, that is right. But for now, you must not tell anyone that I am giving you the land, OK? *Must not*. Do you understand?"

"Why? Are you not going to give it to me anymore?"

Anima sighed.

"It's all very complicated," she said, "but whatever happens, you'll be looked after."

"So, you *are* giving me the land?" Tipu asked again.

Anima looked at Tipu, carefully. It seemed that *what* she was being given didn't matter so much as whether she was actually going to be given it or not. That was the crux of it for her. Anima could have promised her a new dress or a whole box of shandesh to herself; what Tipu wanted to know was whether she had got her hopes up unnecessarily!

"Yes," she said, "I am. But you're not to tell anyone yet. Do you understand?"

"Yes," Tipu said gravely. "And you don't get eaten by a cannibal. Do you understand?" she added, just as seriously.

XXV

"You think I haven't had insults thrown at me before—a Marwari businessman in Bengal?" Sachin asked Anil, laughing. "It's part and parcel of doing business here. I even went to jail, remember?"

Anil exhaled. Does Sachin not understand the gravity of the situation, he thought. Does he not understand that the proposed coal mine is seriously threatened? The coal mine that is to provide the power supply for The Lohia Group's steel and cement businesses. The coal mine that is to establish The Lohia Group as a serious player in the energy space. The coal mine that will enable The Lohia Group to go some way to establishing West Bengal's energy security and restoring its rightful place in the global economy. This is a big deal, he wanted to shout, which part of that do you fail to understand? And then he thought, or maybe it is I who have failed to understand this situation?

"Well, you might be used to it but I don't think Dr. Acharya is," he replied tetchily.

"I admit, that was unfortunate," Sachin admitted, "but she'll have to get used to it, too."

Is that it? Anil thought. What if she doesn't want to get used to it?

Now Sharmila walked in and looking at Anil's despondent face, she asked Sachin, gruffly, "What's up with that one?"

"He's a bit riled about that woman casting aspersions on an associate of his and trying to bring his proposed coal mine into disrepute," Sachin said, as if Anil was annoyed about a waiter bringing him the wrong order.

"Oh that," Sharmila replied, matter-of-fact. "What did you think she would do?" she queried, turning to Anil. Anil didn't answer because he didn't know.

"Sachin showed me the whole thing on his computer," Sharmila went on. Anil lifted his chin. A video of the rally had been uploaded to YouTube within hours. And it already had too many likes. And various infuriating comments: 'Good on Devi for exposing corruption.' 'One of the only politicians in the world truly willing to take on the rich and powerful.' 'Big business, and as usual, big lies. But the truth always comes out.' 'You would think you could trust a doctor, but apparently not.' Idiots. All of them. And he was an idiot, too, for being on the back foot.

"You should have given her one good slap!" Sharmila continued. "If I were there, I would have. I'm telling you, one good slap from me and she'd be out cold." She guffawed at her own impertinence. That's helpful, Anil thought.

In the car on his way back to the office, Anil took a deep breath and wondered why he was getting so upset. Sachin is right. This is just business as usual. No need to get so emotional. In fact, getting emotional is exactly the wrong thing to do; that's her domain. Emotion is what will lead to mistakes. Composure is what's needed.

Although chivalry had gotten the better of Anil and he had ended up waiting for Lalima to catch him up at his car, he had said nothing to her for the entirety of the journey and had dropped her straight off at home without a word, before making his way to Sachin's. Would she take his call now?

"It was the Bengali in you coming out, getting so fired up over politics!" Lalima said, unperturbed. "Now, I've started to put together two press releases—one to deal with all the stuff about Dr. Acharya's relationship with The Lohia Group being completely above board and without prejudice, including a statement from Onkar. We will *not* address anything whatsoever to do with Dr. Acharya's background or family. We *will* say that all of The Lohia Group's businesses have a comprehensive code of ethical conduct and that we always operate not only lawfully but also conscientiously. As for the histrionics about reduced IQ and so on, I'm waiting for a call back from the head of the West Bengal Directorate of Mines, the head of the West Bengal Power Development Corporation Ltd, Coal India, the Ministry of Industry and Commerce, and basically any governmental body which has anything to do with mining! I've even put in a quotation from a Nobel prize-winning scientist about how clean coal—but coal all the same—is still far more important than renewable energy . . ."

Lalima had it all covered. As she always did. Now, Anil's abrupt hunch that she might be one of Devi's spies seemed completely preposterous. Maybe, Anil told himself, that's what happens when you became devious—you question other people's motives, too. I have sacrificed peace of mind for winning at all costs. But it's a one-way street. No U-turns are possible. And then he also realised that although he might have started the enterprise as a cool-headed, clear-eyed strategist, slowly but surely he had become involved to the point of emotion. What happened now didn't only matter, it mattered to *him*. And not just superficially but on a cellular level. Suddenly, he wondered whether that was why Devi was so emotional all the time—because everything *mattered* to her.

"Now what I don't have covered is the Balachuria locals . . ." Lalima was saying, "I mean, a press release isn't going to have any effect on them—you need people on the ground. Anil?"

"Yes, yes, sorry, Lal, I'm listening. Don't worry, I'll sort out that front. Let's catch up soon. And thank you."

He looked at his phone screen. Then, after a very deep breath, he called Bhupen Mandal. It was becoming an extremely bad habit.

"Did you tell him?" Sharmila asked Sachin.

"No, not yet, I don't think the time is right," Sachin replied. "I don't want to upset him . . ."

"Oh for god's sake, stop being such a wuss. He's a big boy, he can handle it!"

Sachin had made a big decision. He was going to leave his company. The company which he had built up over forty years. The company which was the result, both literally and metaphorically, of his blood, sweat, and tears. The company which he had gone to jail for! And what for? To become a politician.

It was Sharmila's idea. He had gone to her in a rare mood of despondency and resentment. I'm sick of being at the beck and call of all these self-serving Bengali politicians, he told her. I am offended that they think that as long as I'm making money, I should forgive their insults and their contempt. I am sick of them constantly trying to remind me of my place whilst never remembering theirs!

Stop moaning, Sharmila had replied. If anyone has enough gumption to change things, it's you. But if you really want to make a difference, money's not enough, you need power. *Real* power. And real power, whether you like it or not, lies in the hands of the politician. Yet when election time comes, all those Bengalis—so genteel, so respectable—come sniffing around us Marwaris for money and votes. This time, screw them. If we Marwaris had our own political party and stopped supporting those sister-fuckers, they'd soon know who was boss. Our problem is that we've got so used to being treated like suckers, we've become suckers! We're never quite good enough for the high-minded Bengali, no matter what we do! Anything goes wrong in this place—that damn fire at your hospital, that bridge falling down, *any* kind of fuck-up—we're always the scapegoats. So, the question is, are you actually going to do something about it or are you just going to take it like you have all these years? You know, I've always hated politicians—I've never met one who isn't self-serving, self-centred, and self-important. And usually corrupt to boot. But you can be a different sort of politician—a decent one. One who serves. One who cares. One who gives. So, are you up to it? Or are you just going to keep moaning like a child?

So exit the Marwari businessman and enter the Marwari politician. It was going to be a tough sell but Sachin had never been afraid of hard slog. And with Sharmila by his side, he knew that nothing was out of his reach.

Partha, minister of industry and commerce, had been up all night. The first he had known of Devi's Balachuria rally was when a young colleague in his ministry had phoned him and told him to watch the video on YouTube. And what he had watched had made him utterly furious. *Rabid.* And for a man of his gentle disposition, it took a lot to even make him displeased. What on earth had gotten into her? In her quest to bring down Lohia, she had just made a complete mockery of the state's whole coal mining policy. The policy that made it clear that coal mining was a good thing for the state! He had let it go when she had made it her mission to stop the proposed mine in Balachuria. It was just one mine, certainly a good prospect but trying to stop it from going ahead could be deemed specific to Balachuria and its people and environment. Indeed, that was the tack she had initially gone with—trying to find reason for the environmental permit not to be granted. And whilst Partha had not been pleased about that, he had found it just about acceptable; even if the environmental clearance was not given for Balachuria, it didn't mean that clearance wouldn't be given for other blocks. He had even let it go when she had insisted on involving Green Police in the Balachuria matter. Even that, he had managed to convince himself, was a political balancing act—not allowing the state's energy requirements to trample on environmental concerns. But to stand in front of a crowd of people and talk about strokes and heart disease and lung disease and lowered IQ? That wasn't specific to Balachuria. That was general.

Now, the operators of other coal mines in the state were clogging his inbox with demands for an explanation about why Devi had just completely sabotaged their enterprise with her doomsday rhetoric. Already, wrote a few, they had received phone calls from their employees asking about the health and safety of their mines, and threatening not to turn up to work. And on a more philosophical level, if the state believed that coal mining was so deleterious then why had the state allocated coal blocks to be mined in the first place, and why was the state indeed a partner in many of the ventures? State, thought Partha, it's not the bloody state, it's *her*. Except she thinks she is the state! He had also received a long, irate phone call from the Directorate of Mines and Minerals who wanted to know why Devi had just threatened their entire purpose? Had she forgotten that she herself was the directorate's ostensible leader? And had she forgotten how much coal mining contributed to the state's coffers? Partha just listened in silence. And then, of course, the journalists had started to call: what's the score, Partha? Is this a case of friendly fire? Or collateral damage? And he had declined to answer because he didn't yet have one.

He turned off his phone and his computer and went to sit in the dark, thinking: why am I in this mess? It's because I have been weak, I have always caved in to Devi, always ended up going along with whatever she wishes, even when I have known that she is wrong. When she first set out to thwart Lohia, I should have stood up to her. I should have told her that there was no room for personal vendettas in politics and that I wholeheartedly and unreservedly supported the mine. I should have told her that the mine could have been a prime example of a public-private partnership and that it was an enterprise that we would all benefit from. I should have told her that her job was to lead not to meddle. And I should have told her that I would not change my mind and that, if it came to it, I would resign over the matter. But I was too scared to even resign! And now I have been utterly humiliated. Because the woman whom I have spent my political career genuflecting to has repaid me by kneeing me in the balls. She didn't even have the courtesy or decency to tell me what she was going to say. I might not have been able to stop her from saying it, but at least I could have formulated my own response. Instead I have been left choking on her words. And tomorrow morning, things will look worse.

♠

Had a celebration ever been so short, Nigel thought. Straight after the Balachuria rally, Devi had been full of vim. She had socked it to Lohia and his corrupt associates! They had driven back to Kolkata and the whole way, she had jabbered on about exposing the truth and fighting exploitation, and whilst Nigel had been delighted that she seemed to be back in good spirits, he had also begun to have a horrible feeling in his stomach. At first, he had dismissed the feeling as an effect of the surgery, or perhaps just travel sickness, but soon he realised it wasn't that. It was the horrible feeling that something was about to go terribly wrong.

By the morning, after a late night at Devi's house where she had partied, in her way, by singing Rabindra sangeet and reciting poetry and watching the YouTube video of the rally—"Look, I am getting lots of likes!"—it became clear what had gone wrong. Devi had gone wrong, that's what. She had been so thoroughly focused on bringing down Lohia, that she had been blinkered to the extent that she had not seen that she was bringing herself down, too. The newspapers were full of it.

DEVI SHOOTS HERSELF IN FOOT

ROY'S RHETORIC AT BALACHURIA RESULTS
IN COAL MINERS' REBELLION

DEVI'S BLUSTER LEADS TO BLUNDER

ROY RALLY LEADS TO RIDICULE

And then, of course, there was Partha Pratim's public resignation. As for the issue of corruption and underhand dealings, there was nary a mention. A couple of papers had quoted The Lohia Group's own press release about their having a comprehensive code of ethical conduct and always operating not only lawfully but also conscientiously. That was it. It seemed that what Nigel had thought would be a revelation of immense importance was deemed barely of consequence. Where, he thought, was the moral outrage at the workings of the filthy rich? Where was the abhorrence at how the powerful treated the powerless with such calculated contempt? Nowhere! And there was only one conclusion to be drawn—the press clearly had it in for Devi.

Agonisingly, it was actually only in the newspaper of The Communists, that Devi's personal attack on Dr. Anima Acharya and her family was reported fully. And the thrust of their piece was that for all Devi's talk, her own brother had been buying up land at the rate of knots. And her brother's caught-off-guard response, "All that matters is that my purchases are legal". When Nigel had asked Devi whether she knew about this, she had shouted, how shall I be knowing what my brother is doing! But we need to respond, Nigel pressed. I will not be responding to dastardly personal attacks on my family. Nigel took a deep breath. She is not being hypocritical, he told himself, she's just being emotional—and understandably so.

Nigel blamed himself. He should have tried harder to keep Devi aimed at her real targets—The Lohia Group and Dr. Anima Acharya. But once Devi had got going, she hadn't wanted to stop. At her insistence he had found himself searching for the effects of coal pollution at two in the morning. He had very briefly wondered about the implications of laying into the coal mining industry at large, and had even suggested running it past Partha Pratim, but Devi had replied, dismissively, what does he know?

Well, probably quite a lot, Nigel had thought, but he hadn't said this. And there had been no environment minister to run it by because, since Surajit Sinha had resigned, Devi had taken on his remit herself. Still, his instinct, as it had always been, was to advise caution, to step carefully, to keep to what they knew for sure not what they thought they knew, but as far as Devi was concerned, caution was for cowards, and she wasn't scared of anything or anyone! And so she had gone to Balachuria half-cocked at full steam. And now this.

How on earth am I going to formulate a response to this mess, he thought. And Devi herself was of no help at all. She was in one of her violent moods where the only person she wasn't blaming for her current situation was herself. And in the midst of it all, Insaf Khan resigned, too, saying that he could no longer work for an administration where sound judgement had been usurped by foolhardiness. Even Rohini, who could usually be relied on to speak in Devi's defence, was keeping tight-lipped about the whole affair. Now, not only was she minister without portfolio, she was also minister without voice. Devi was on her own this time. In the end, Nigel realised that there was no great rejoinder to be composed, no stunning comeback, he was just going to have to weasel his way out the best he could. He ran his suggested response by Devi and she shrugged. He had assumed that she would, at the very least, hold a press conference herself, but holed up in her office with a forbidding expression on her face, he realised that he would just have to speak to the press himself. And what did he say? Simply that Devi had not meant to imply that the effects of coal pollution were definite but that they were certainly a possibility if the mine operator was inexperienced, as was the case with The Lohia Group, and, additionally, it would be the state which had to pick up the pieces if and when things went wrong. It was a pathetic response and he knew it. And it was yet another black mark against Devi and he knew that, too.

After a night of tossing and turning, Anil woke up to an email from Lalima with that morning's press clippings. He had been expecting umpteen pieces on underhand business practices and dirty-dealing but Devi's personal attacks had made no impression. And her scaremongering about the effects of coal mining had resulted only in her having egg on her face. But it also made him realise that he didn't have as much foresight as he thought he had—and having foresight was half of his game plan. But there was not enough time to take stock and overhaul his whole strategy. Tactics first—contact Dr. Acharya.

Dear Anima, I have been made aware that at a recent political rally, your name, along with that of Avik and Paige, was brought up, in what can be described only as a very unfortunate manner, in connection with the proposed coal mine in Balachuria. As you and I both know, the job offer made to you at The Lohia Hospital is in no way related to, dependent on, or contingent upon any sale of land or indeed any other matter related to the mine. As it is, I certainly hope that you will still join The Lohia Hospital; I believe you will be able to do great things there. On a personal level, I am greatly saddened that politics in this state has been reduced to mean and meaningless personal attacks, but I hope that such repugnant behaviour does not sway your decision. Indeed, it would be a great shame if we allow ourselves to be bullied by people who should know better. I'll look forward to hearing from you whenever you're ready. Yours, Anil

XXVI

Lalima had been right. In Balachuria itself, the reaction to Devi's rally was entirely different. Her tirade had caused a lot of consternation and a lot of talk. People were very confused about whom to trust, whom to back. Indeed, could anyone be relied on when the stakes were so high? Nearly everyone had their own take on the matter, nearly everyone had their own idea on what to do, and not to do. And even those who did not want to get involved and had decided to take a 'what will be, will be' approach, were roundly criticised for either leaving the hard thinking to the others or for their apathy.

Yet, slowly but surely, Devi's supporters began to prevail. Look, they told those who were wavering, Devi's the only person we can trust to look out for us. She doesn't want us to be taken advantage of by a greedy man. Marwari businessmen are known for exploiting people—how else do you think they get so rich? If we let them go ahead, we'll get treated like dogs. And have you seen what coal mines have done to other towns? Everyone's always feeling ill. If they get what they want, we'll all die together coughing and choking! Besides, The Lohia Group is not the only option. Devi has promised to build a hospital here!

Lohia's supporters dwindled to a small but hard core, mainly disaffected young men and a few young women who sensed that the opportunity Lohia was giving them was their only chance to actually stop sitting around and start doing something.

Look what Lohia has done for other towns where he's located his businesses, they said, hoping to triumph through empirical evidence, he *has* brought jobs and money. All that stuff Devi said about poisoning us is scaremongering. Besides, they concluded, throwing in a little hedonism for good measure, we all have to die at some point—better that we enjoy our lives before we do! Let The Lohia Group get on with it, and let's not stand in their way. Because if we do, the only people who'll lose out is us!

But Devi's supporters had no truck with their positivity and gung-ho-ness. The mine's supporters were easily dismissed as just children being childish, with a child's willingness to believe in make-believe.

Exasperated and frustrated, the supporters turned to the negative—the only thing Devi is good for is promises. She promised us plenty before the last election, and what's actually materialised? It's you lot that are gullible! Or maybe you just want to remain at the bottom of the pile for ever?

But Devi's followers dismissed this as yet more childishness from those who didn't have enough experience to know how the world really worked.

As for the moral outrage, which Nigel had been counting on from the press, Devi's followers managed up to make up in spades for the press' impassiveness, soon turning dubiousness into revulsion. Anima might as well have driven into the town's main thoroughfare in a gold-plated, diamond-encrusted car, set alight wads of rupee notes, danced around the bonfire, then snatched a few of the town's children so that she could sell their souls to the devil. That is if the children weren't already on their deathbeds from eating the disturbing, unholy, genetically modified food that her son was going to fill the shops with. Or if they hadn't been sold to her future daughter-in-law as slave labour.

And whilst Lohia's supporters had also been quite stunned by the extent of Anima's family's background and wealth, and her son's business deals and his wife-to-be's tummy-showing, their position could be summed up simply as 'if you can't beat them, join them'. After all, where would resentment and envy get them? And where had taking on the rich and powerful ever got anyone? Indignation and outrage weren't worth the paper they were written on. In fact, the only people who seemed to do well out of discontent were politicians like Devi. But their pragmatism was no match for the others' cynicism. What they were worried about was that Anima would cave under pressure, and *not* sell. But how to make sure she did? She certainly didn't need to. She might just want to avoid the rigmarole and sit tight instead, and they'd all be in the same nowhere-nothing town as nowhere-nothing people.

Heated arguments started to break out. There was the pervading feeling that angry words would soon turn to violence. But there was no going back. The whole town was on edge.

Kalyan was quite smug about how events were unfolding. See, he told anyone who would listen, didn't I tell you from the start that this whole mine business was trouble. And didn't I say Anima Acharya couldn't be trusted. After all, how can you trust someone who won't even drink the local milk? And she smokes and drinks—workmen at her house have spotted cigarettes and alcohol! And she's been trying to brainwash my daughter, too.

Now my daughter doesn't listen to me anymore, she listens to Madam! Yes, she's been teaching Tipu to disrespect me, she even told her to leave home and go to live with her. That's the sort of troublemaker we're dealing with—divide and conquer! We should kick her out of this place.

Adding fuel to the fire was Kalyan's speciality, and it worked a treat. Even Lohia's supporters kept their mouths shut because there was no way to justify that kind of behaviour. Forget the affluent background and the wealth and the privilege, it was the non-milk-drinking and alcohol and cigarettes and causing a girl to disrespect her own father that was beyond the pale.

Tipu heard what her father was going around saying and she was irate. She had never been one for irateness or antagonism or any other kind of anger, usually choosing instead to be hurt or wounded, but this time, she had had enough. It was just too much—the man who had never done anything for her taking a cheap shot at the woman who was doing everything for her. Well, for once, she was going to tell him what was what. Anima might have told her not to, but needs must!

It didn't take long for the news to spread that it was now Tipu who was actually the owner of the land. Some people were incredulous and dismissed the news as nonsense, but in the main, the reaction was surprise followed by acceptance—simply because Tipu was known as an honest girl not given to lying.

Lohia's embattled supporters were delighted, as Tipu had been one of them from the start, indeed she had been the one to gather them together in the first place. What a stroke of luck! They had read stories about loyal servants being rewarded by their masters or mistresses but they had never thought it happened in real life. But it had happened and it meant that they were now on their way to success. All of Kalyan's talk about Anima's dissoluteness? What did he know? He was just one of life's whiners. Nothing he said could be taken too seriously. For, as Anima—milk drinker or not—had shown by her extraordinarily generous gift, she was a thoroughly noble and benevolent person.

Devi's supporters meanwhile were stewing. That Anima woman had outmanoeuvred them before they'd even had time to come up with a strategy to deal with her. Handing the land to a teenage girl, who was, as even her own father said, foolish and easily taken in. Who was, he announced, a silly girl with no mind of her own. *She* was going to decide their fate? Like hell she was. But what could they do in the face of Anima's sneakiness and cunning? How to knock some sense into an impudent, imprudent young girl? What did Devi suggest they do?

After the ridicule piled on her after the rally, Devi was keeping quiet and licking her wounds. But despite Nigel and Rohini suggesting to her that now was the time for her to move on to other matters and leave Balachuria behind, she would not. Could not. She knew everyone thought she was stubborn but she wasn't stubborn, she was committed! But before she carried on with the good fight, she had to be honest with herself. She had been telling herself all along that the reason for her vendetta against Lohia was because of his history with her archenemy, The Communists. Yet the fact was that Lohia was not the only rich Marwari businessman who had been cosy with them. Yet she wasn't going after any of them in the way she was going after Lohia. Why was that? It was because she needed to take him on—and defeat him—before he had the chance to take her on. For from the moment he had stepped out of jail, she had smelled competition. She could sniff out a contender from a mile away. The others had always been after money, but she intuited that Lohia was after something more.

Her job. She could see where all the saintliness and philanthropy and public spirit was heading—right towards her office! And she could also see the people's—*her* people's—reaction to him. They were dazzled by his blinding benevolent light, his humility, and yes, his extreme wealth. It had turned him into something akin to an idol. But a false idol, as far as she was concerned. Yet the pedestal on which they had put him was much higher than the one on which she stood—and she was already slipping, albeit slowly. So it was not fantastical to think that Lohia could well be sitting in her seat if he put his mind to it. And there was another thing on his side. Lohia had an indefatigable will and the hunger to win. Much like her.

But I am not going to let him get his hands on my job, she buttressed herself. I have worked far, far too hard. I have suffered, endured, and withstood. I have taken knock after knock and been kicked to the ground many, many times but still I have got right back up again and kept on going. And I might have to sell my paintings in order to raise campaign funds, but I will not let money dictate who leads this great state. I might not have money, but I have other assets—resourcefulness and grit and purpose! This is why I must not give up on Balachuria, why I cannot. I must show everyone that I am the one true leader. I must show everyone that even the great Sachin Lohia cannot bring me down!

Back at Writers, hoping for some peace and quiet before home-time, she was given the news about Tipu, by Nigel. Stop, she wanted to say, I can't take any more today, I have nothing left to give. But as she had learnt before, problems didn't go away by ignoring them. She mulled over the situation—she was known for taking on the high and mighty, the corrupt, not a lowly, innocent, modest girl, the kind of girl who embodied virtue. Even *she* knew that to set herself up in opposition to this girl would in itself undermine her self-avowed objective of giving power back to the common people. But to not fight would be to hand Lohia the victory. And that outcome was simply unconscionable.

"We will find another way," Nigel told her, "and in the meantime, our legal department is seeing what we can do from that angle."

Devi hated laws and she hated angles, too. She stood for what was right in the soul not in the statutes. As for angles, she liked confronting matters head-on. And as for another way, well, wasn't that what the proposed super-speciality hospital was?

"It *was*," Nigel reminded her, until that open letter was published yesterday in a newspaper, stating that Devi's proposed super-specialty hospitals were a complete waste of resources, that they would be unstaffable, and that there was already a shortage of doctors at the current state hospitals. And in light of the fact that the Medical Council of India was threatening to slash seats at West Bengal's medical schools due to its current hospitals not complying with the required infrastructure for training them, wasn't the only acceptable course of action to scrap the scheme and allocate the resources to where they would actually benefit the patient? Yes, there was now this to deal with, too. It was said that a week was a long time in politics; Nigel felt that a week was a year. Which, by his calculations would make him over two hundred years old. He certainly felt it. He would have expected a bi-centenarian like himself to develop some foresight, but it still seemed to elude him.

Radesh seemed cagey. Anil could tell that his earlier excitement and sense of being chosen to do critical work had now given way to the apprehension that he had unnecessarily put himself in a precarious position. Getting anything useful out of him was arduous. He was vague about there being some amount of trouble in the town, about people being unhappy, about there being a sense of foreboding.

"But no violence?" Anil checked. For if the situation turned violent, it would be a blemish on the project. And Anil was desperate for the mine to go ahead without any brutality or bloodshed. The struggle had to be peaceful, not because he was a pacifist but because bankers didn't like violence, it made them edgy, and it was nearly impossible to get money out of an uptight, risk averse banker.

"No, no violence," Radesh replied.

"OK," Anil went on, "do you think the majority of people are still in favour of the mine, despite Devi's outburst?" This was critical. Because even if Anima agreed to sell the land, the people who lived on it would have to agree to move.

"I don't know," Radesh replied, "you know what it's like, different people are saying different things . . ."

"I know you can't go around canvassing people, but what feeling do you get?"

"No feeling."

"Alright, well why don't you tell me what people are saying."

"Some people are saying that if your company comes here, we'll all get treated like dogs." And then Anil understood. It was not that Radesh was worried about being pegged as an informer; it was that he was afraid that he had chosen the wrong side. He wanted out.

"I see," Anil replied quietly. Right now, he didn't have the energy to try and convince Radesh otherwise. But then, as if Anil's change in tone had aroused some amount of sympathy in Radesh, Radesh threw him a bone.

"There is one thing though. I've heard that the zamindar woman, the doctor, she doesn't own the land, she's given it to a girl called Tipu Nath."

Although he was reluctant to do so, Anil followed up by calling Bhupen Mandal. I thought you were going to send out some of your party members to canvass support for the mine, and try to undo the damage that Devi did, Anil told him, trying to make out as if he was asking a question rather than making an unfavourable judgement. After all, he did not want to get on the wrong side of Bhupen—and he intuited that Bhupen was the kind of man who would be easily offended, even by something as slight as the wrong tone of voice. But, he continued, according to my sources, her supporters are growing and becoming more vociferous. You're worrying unnecessarily, Bhupen told him, just be patient; these kinds of things always have twists and turns. More vagueness. But Anil was uneasy about pushing it. Then, as if he was the one who had to offer assistance, he said, oh, I have heard one thing—apparently, the land has been transferred to a girl called Tipu Nath? Yes, Bhupen said casually, I know . . .

XXVII

After a week with Avik and Paige on Havelock island, Anima was feeling quite refreshed and resolute. Devi's attack on her no longer felt so personal or injurious. It now felt absurd verging on laughable.

Avik had been very upbeat and encouraging. He had dismissed the Balachuria incident as just the kind of preposterous antic which politics was peppered with, and that the only correct response to such asininity was to ignore it entirely. Instead, Anima should concentrate on her next step—the job at The Lohia Hospital, which was very exciting, a great opportunity, a fresh start! And although he hadn't said it outright, he had implied that without The Professor in her life, she was free to do what she wanted. As for the actual matter of the land itself, when Anima had hypothetically suggested that she might just give it away, he had been in complete favour of doing so: free yourself from the wrangling—who needs the hassle, and you certainly don't need the money!

Anima, of course, was not so unsuspecting as to not realise that what her son was trying to do, and not subtly either, was use positive distraction as a method of providing her with a much-needed boost. But she was also not so scornful as to rebuff his efforts without due deliberation. And what he was saying made sense—simplify, shed baggage, put yourself first. Maybe it was the American way—the Indian way was to complicate, burden yourself, put others first (or at least pretend to)—but it certainly had its appeal.

It was back in Kolkata, on the way to Saradindu's office, that Anima read Anil's email, and felt a further boost. She had also been half wondering if The Professor might have emailed her about the incident in Balachuria. She had no doubt that he knew about it. But there was not a word, even of acknowledgement if not sympathy. So that's how it was. I might as well instruct Saradindu to start divorce proceedings whilst I'm at it, she thought, no point in wasting any more time!

"That act of 1894 . . . Replaced by this act of 2013 . . . Which has various provisions for mandating compensation limits and the resettlement and rehabilitation of affected families . . . Though there are different conditions for public-private partnerships . . . And the market price must be paid . . ." Saradindu was going on and on.

Don't you get it, Anima thought, I'm not even vaguely interested in any of this, that's why I want to wash my hands of it!

"Well, that's all extremely interesting," she smiled once Saradindu had come to a stop. "But I assume it doesn't impact my transferring the land to someone else? I mean there was nothing in what you said which means that I am obliged to hold on to it, is there?"

Saradindu looked at her, unimpressed.

"Nothing but a moral obligation," he said snarkily.

"Sorry?" Anima asked, surprised.

"That land has belonged to your family for years, and your forefathers must have made a good amount of money from owning it," Saradindu sniffed. "Perhaps the income has dried up now but there's no doubt that *you* have benefited, however indirectly, from your family owning it."

"Yes, of course, but—"

"Did you know that over a hundred years ago," Saradindu said, in his best didactic way, "much of that land was covered in forest and that your family made a fortune from allowing the British to carry out intensive logging operations."

Anima looked at him, abashed, but did not reply, so Sarandindu went on, "But now you're in a hurry to hand the land over because it's causing you a bit of a headache. I thought you might have had a greater sense of duty than that. As for the person to whom you want to give the land, does it not bother your conscience that you're handing over such a huge responsibility to a young woman who has neither the experience, the wherewithal, or the resources to deal with what will no doubt become a complex and laborious legal and political dispute?"

I can see why your wife is having an affair with The Professor, Anima thought. He might be a pain in the arse but you are definitely a bigger one. And at least he's quite amusing.

"I could appoint *you* as her lawyer," Anima smiled feebly.

Saradindu did not smile back.

Throughout the journey back to Balachuria, Anima wondered how she would tell Tipu that she could no longer give her the land. How to explain to her that not giving her the land was actually in her best interests. And she wondered how she would tell Anil that she could not take the job because she would simply not be able to give it her full attention if she was caught up in the Balachuria affair. She felt thoroughly despondent and down. But she felt like she was doing the right thing.

When they arrived in Balachuria, it was already dark. Anima asked the driver if he wanted to stay the night but he said he would rather drive back to Kolkata, so Anima tipped him well, told him to make sure that he ate dinner on his way back, and waved him off. The lights in the house were on and Anima knew that Tipu would be inside, waiting for her. She braced herself. It's going to be OK, she told herself, Tipu is a sweet girl, she'll understand, and even if she doesn't, she'll forgive me. I know how I'll start, I'll say: look Tipu, I didn't get eaten by a cannibal!

She was walking down the path to the house when she felt her foot touch something soft. She looked down and saw black fur peeping out from under a bush. For a moment, she didn't understand and then she did. They had killed Prem, her dog. Immediately, she remembered when the Naxalites had poisoned her uncle's cat. It had been a warning then and it was a warning now—get out of here. But she was not scared. She was furious. There was something so disgustingly cowardly about killing an innocent animal to make a threat. She took a deep breath and leant down so that she could take Prem's body into the house. She wondered how Prem's puppies would react. They would probably whine and cry. Tipu would probably cry, too. But as she touched Prem's fur with her fingertips, she realised it wasn't fur. It was hair. Tipu's hair. Hands shaking, she slowly pulled out the body and saw the injury. Severe blunt force trauma to the head. A large blood clot was already forming. Trying to compose herself, Anima felt for a pulse. Tipu was still breathing. She looked again at the wound. I can fix this, Anima thought, I can fix this. She ran back down to the road to call her driver but he was already gone. Somebody help me, she screamed, somebody please help me. Her voice pierced the darkness but there was no reply. She ran back to Tipu and lifted Tipu into her arms. In Tipu's hand were her keys—attached to a keyring with the Lohia logo. "Don't worry, Tipu," she said, "I'll mend this." But there was nothing she could do.

Anima didn't know how long she had been sitting with Tipu in her arms, but when she finally came to, she realised that she didn't have a clue what to do. She had no idea what the number was to call the police and no idea where the police station was either, or if there was even a police station nearby. She needed assistance but she felt that she could not leave Tipu's body alone. Finally, she decided to call Anil. She thought he could be trusted to help.

Anil was out at dinner with Lalima when he received the call. "I'll make phone calls," he said, "I'll have the police go around as soon as possible."

It was as he was changing for bed that night and emptying out his jacket pockets that Anil found a folded up piece of paper in his inside breast pocket. It was Tipu's CV. Domestic Affairs Administrator; skills and responsibilities—assessment of key projects, cost-benefit analysis, procurement of tenders, management of direct reports. Suddenly, Anil felt incredibly, incredibly sad. A young girl blotted out just like that. She deserved at least some sort of recognition, if only in death. He called Tapati Ghatak.

"I'm already on my way there," she said.

"OK," Anil said and then he collapsed into bed, exhausted.

Anil woke up with a start the next morning and the first thing he thought was: why had Tapati Ghatak already been on her way to Balachuria? How could she have known what had happened? Quickly, he went to *The United Times* homepage. Tipu's death was the cover story.

DEVI'S SUPPORTERS SUSPECTED IN YOUNG WOMAN'S MURDER

Anil's mind raced. Who would have known to contact Tapati Ghatak apart from the person who had ordered Tipu's death? And then Anil realised that he had been played.

Devi was in shock. Her hands were shaking. Her lips were trembling. And were her eyes watering? Nigel thought they were. And in her wastepaper basket, was that a headless Barbie doll? No matter, the show had to go on. She had to hold a press conference. You must say that you do not condone violence of any sort, he told her. You must say that you did not and would not sanction anyone to carry out what is a despicable crime in the name of politics. You must say that you are deeply distressed by the death of an innocent young woman. You must say that if, indeed, one of your supporters is found to be guilty of her murder, that they will feel the full force of the law and face punishment without mercy. You must say that you believe in peace and democracy! Devi looked up at him.

"Shut up," she said. "Shut up. Shut up, shut up, SHUT UP!"

Bhupen Mandal read the front page of *The United Times.* And as his eyes fell on Devi's name, he allowed himself a little smile.

CODA

The Professor walked slowly out of the committee meeting room and exhaled deeply. Although he had been expecting to feel relief that the whole sorry matter was over, he felt sadness instead. For the committee had decided that the only way to deal with the issue was to ask Polly to leave the university. His only consolation was that the committee had agreed that her record should remain unmarked by the unfortunate episode.

He blamed himself—such a bright and brainy girl, such a mess. If only he had been less interested, less attentive. Maybe then she wouldn't have misinterpreted his behaviour and started to bombard him with inappropriate text messages. He had met with her to explain that, as much as he liked her, their relationship was one of teacher-student, it was nothing more than that, and it would never be any more than that. But still she had persisted. So he felt that he had had no choice but to report the matter to the Student Welfare Committee. Now, though, he wondered whether he had made the wrong choice. He wondered whether if he had told his wife—who always did the right thing—about the situation, she might have come up with a better solution. No matter. What was done was done.

ACKNOWLEDGEMENTS

I would like to thank the following people for their help and support. It is said that it takes a village to raise a child; the same can be said of writing a book.

The Biswases: Allie, Juthika, and Anjan for unwavering support. Alex Bowman—calm and stable when I am raging! My first reader Leon Gore, and his eye for 'infelicities of expression'. Jo Spearing, can anyone read as quickly as you? Preeti Gill, for your reassuring words. James Thorne and Nick Thorne for their kind assistance.

Shashi Tharoor, my sincere gratitude for your generosity in taking the time to read my book.

Matthew d'Ancona, I'm honoured to have your seal of approval.

Garima Shukla, you've made this fun!

Pooja Dadwal and Shikha Sabharwal, for making this happen.

Photo Credit: Jim Gleeson

Tina Biswas read Politics, Philosophy, and Economics at New College, Oxford, and writes whatever she can, whenever she can.

After her highly praised debut, *Dancing With The Two-Headed Tigress*, Tina followed up with *The Red Road*. Her novels have been critically acclaimed in newspapers such as *The Financial Times, The Guardian, The Statesman,* and *The Globe and Mail.*

The Antagonists is her third novel.

She lives in London with her husband and young daughter, and is currently working on her fourth novel.